KT-370-928

sapphire

Also available by Katie Price

Non-Fiction
Being Jordan
Jordan: A Whole New World
Jordan: Pushed to the Limit

Fiction
Angel
Crystal
Angel Uncovered

Children's Non-Fiction
Katie Price's Perfect Ponies: My Pony Care Book

Children's Fiction
Katie Price's Perfect Ponies
Fancy Dress Ponies
Here Comes the Bride
Little Treasures
Ponies to the Rescue
Pony Club Weekend
The New Best Friend
Pony in Disguise
Pony 'n' Pooch
Star Ponies

Katie Price's Mermaids and Pirates
Follow the Fish
Telescope Overboard
Time for a Picnic
Let's Play I Spy
A Sunny Day
Let's Build a Sandcastle

Katie Price
sapphire

Century · London

Published by Century 2009

2 4 6 8 10 9 7 5 3 1

Copyright © Katie Price 2009; Rebecca Farnworth 2009

Katie Price and Rebecca Farnworth have asserted their rights under
the Copyright, Designs and Patents Act 1988 to be identified as the
authors of this work

This book is a work of fiction. Names and characters are the product
of the authors' imagination and any resemblance to actual persons,
living or dead, is entirely coincidental

This book is sold subject to the condition that it shall not,
by way of trade or otherwise, be lent, resold, hired out,
or otherwise circulated without the publisher's prior
consent in any form of binding or cover other than that
in which it is published and without a similar condition,
including this condition, being imposed on the
subsequent purchaser

First published in Great Britain in 2009 by
Century
Random House, 20 Vauxhall Bridge Road,
London SW1V 2SA

www.randomhouse.co.uk

Addresses for companies within The Random House Group Limited can be
found at: www.randomhouse.co.uk

The Random House Group Limited Reg. No. 954009

A CIP catalogue record for this book
is available from the British Library

ISBN 9781846052385 (Hardback)
ISBN 9781846055836 (Trade paperback)

The Random House Group Limited supports The Forest Stewardship
Council (FSC), the leading international forest certification organisation.
All our titles that are printed on Greenpeace approved FSC certified paper
carry the FSC logo. Our paper procurement policy can be found at
www.rbooks.co.uk/environment

Mixed Sources
Product group from well-managed
forests and other controlled sources
www.fsc.org Cert no. TT-COC-2139
© 1996 Forest Stewardship Council
FSC

Typeset by SX Composing DTP, Rayleigh, Essex
Printed and bound in Great Britain by
CPI Mackays, Chatham, ME5 8TD

Chapter 1

Sapphire Jones didn't believe in relationships, not since she had arrived back from work unexpectedly early to discover her husband in bed with another woman. Two years on from the bitter divorce Sapphire remained deeply cynical about men. Of course she still had them in her life – she had no intention of living like a nun – but only on her terms, which was why Jay, her current lover, was four years younger than her, extremely good-looking, didn't place any emotional demands on her (so far, fingers crossed) and was great in bed. What more did a girl want? Sapphire reflected as she parked her cherry red Mini Cooper in the underground garage and headed for the lifts up to her penthouse apartment.

She was looking forward to sipping a large vodka and tonic in the bath, then meeting up with her friends Jazz and Sam for drinks and dinner, and maybe rounding off the night by inviting Jay over for no-strings-attached sex. She loved being one hundred per cent in control and knowing exactly what she was doing, so she was pissed off to discover Jay sprawled out on her sofa (her brand-new, mocha brown Italian leather, *very* expensive sofa) watching the football. What the hell was he doing here?

'Babe!' he called out as soon as he saw her. Sapphire gave him her WTF look. 'You've forgotten haven't you?'

Jay got up. At six foot two he was a fit guy in all senses

of the word. He was a personal trainer, had biceps that Sapphire adored caressing, abs of steel, the cutest bum and long muscular legs. Looks-wise he resembled Wentworth Miller from *Prison Break*, though even better-looking with the same buzz-cut hair, deep brown eyes the colour of molten chocolate, chiselled regular features and a very sexy mouth. Seeing him standing there in his tight white vest and running shorts, Sapphire wondered if a change of plan wasn't such a bad idea after all. She could have sex and then go out for dinner. She smiled as she wound her arms round his neck and pulled him close to her, 'What have I forgotten, babe?'

'You agreed you'd come running with me and then we'd have dinner. You know, so we could spend more time together?' Jay's beautiful eyes had a slightly hurt look.

Fuck! Sapphire had completely forgotten. She hated running. She slid one arm from round his neck and ran her hand caressingly over the steel abs, ending up on the running shorts, the very well-filled running shorts. 'I've got a much better idea,' she whispered. 'And isn't sex supposed to be good for toning up?'

Jay sighed. 'Not as good as running, babe.'

Double fuck! There was no way, just no freaking way that Sapphire was going to forgo her plan of drink, dinner, sex, or sex, drink, dinner for a *run*!

'Trust me: you won't want to miss out on this,' she murmured, falling to her knees. The consolation blow job. Surely Jay would not turn this down?

Another sigh, 'Sometimes, Sapphire, I think you only see me as being good for sex.'

And your problem with that is what? She thought. She stared up at him from underneath her lashes, 'So you don't want me to carry on?' she parted her lips and licked them for good measure, certain that Jay's annoyance wouldn't last once she got down to it. Sure enough he didn't try and stop her as she slowly slid the running shorts off. It was slightly less erotic removing the jockstrap but sometimes a girl's got to do what a girl's got to do.

As she had predicted, Jay didn't tell her to stop. And when she'd rewarded him with a top of the range BJ he reciprocated with some mind-blowing oral work on her. So much better than her last lover who rarely returned the favour. He didn't last long. Sapphire had high standards when it came to her lovers and if they didn't cut it, she wasn't going to hang around. All in all she reflected lying back on the sofa in a dreamy post-orgasmic haze, the evening was going very well. She'd have a quick shower and then dash off to meet Jazz and Sam. She made to get up, but Jay pulled her back next to him, 'Where are you off to?' he murmured sleepily.

'I'm supposed to be meeting Jazz and Sam at half eight.'

'You were supposed to be spending the evening with me.' The BJ glow had worn off a bit bloody quickly. Some men were hard to please!

'I'm really sorry, babe; I'll make it up to you I promise.'

'When?' Jay demanded holding onto her wrist.

'I could probably do tomorrow night.' Hopefully it would rain and surely even Jay wouldn't make her run in bad weather. She could pretend to have a cold coming on or something; she remembered reading that it was very unwise to exercise when you were ill.

'Fine, same arrangement, a run then dinner. Don't worry, I'll cook, I know what a fucking disaster you are in the kitchen.'

Sapphire didn't liked being told that she was a disaster at *anything*. But she decided to be cool. 'Babe, I'm the reason they invented ready meals.'

Jay laughed and let go of her wrist. 'And when am I going to meet your friends?'

Sapphire shrugged and muttered, 'Soon', and dashed to the bathroom before he could think of anything else to say.

It was funny, she reflected, under her power shower; Jay wasn't turning out to be the easy-going boy toy she had hoped for. Please God, don't let him want a relationship!

'Sapphire! You're such a total bitch!' Her best friend Jasmine – known as Jazz to all her close friends – exclaimed once Sapphire had told them her reason for being late. 'I can't believe you were so mean to him.' She paused and frowned, wrinkling her cute nose and flicking back her shoulder-length white-blonde hair. 'Well, actually I can, knowing what you're like.'

'Oh come on, he knew what he was getting into when he got involved with me; I never said anything about having a relationship.' Sapphire sulkily swirled the ice round in her vodka and tonic.

'You're the only woman I know who doesn't want a relationship,' Sam put in. 'Sometimes I don't know whether to believe you.'

Sapphire scowled in mock disgust and drummed her red nails on the table. Maybe she did act all tough where men were concerned but that was because she was never ever going to let herself be hurt by one again.

'Watch the frown lines!' Jazz shot back.

'I'll hit the Botox when I'm thirty,' Sapphire replied.

She'd known Jazz and Sam for years as the three of them had gone to the same secondary school. She couldn't imagine not having them in her life. Jazz was the polar opposite of Sapphire, a pretty, blue-eyed blonde to Sapphire's striking and dramatic beauty: dark blue eyes, full sensuous lips and long jet black hair.

Sam had shoulder-length auburn hair, quite a pretty face, with hazel eyes and a cute dimple on her right cheek. But as far as Sapphire was concerned Sam was hiding her light under a bushel or two. Sam had been dieting on and off for as long as Sapphire had known her, yo-yoing from a size twelve to an eighteen. Now she had a size sixteen. Sapphire supposed it wasn't easy for Sam being friends with her and Jazz – Sapphire was an eight and Jazz a ten, but sometimes she despaired of Sam's lack of self-control and thought if she had to hear about one more diet plan she would scream.

The three girls were as different in personalities as in looks. Sapphire was driven, ambitious and her default position was never to trust anyone. Jazz was slightly dizzy, always saw the good in people and was the most hopeless romantic Sapphire had ever met. She'd been going out with her boyfriend Ben for the last three years and really wanted to do the whole get married, have babies thing, which left Sapphire cold. Sam could be fun and had a wicked sense of humour when she chose. But she was constantly putting herself down and her love life was a disaster area. She always ended up going out with men who treated her like shit, which also drove Sapphire mad: she just didn't get that whole low self esteem mindset that Sam seemed locked into.

The three looked so different that they'd often joked they should form a girl band. There was just one slight problem: none of them could sing. But as Sapphire said, when did that ever stop anyone? Instead, Jazz worked as a beautician in Sapphire's beauty rooms and Sam worked in a small jeweller's and made her own jewellery when she got the chance. She always talked about having a jewellery line of her own. Sapphire didn't like to point out that Sam was nearly thirty and had better bloody get on with it . . .

'So, when are we going to meet sex-machine Jay?' Sam asked.

Sapphire shook her head, in absolutely no hurry to make that arrangement. Since her divorce she found it much easier to compartmentalise her life and tried where possible to keep lovers and friends apart.

'You could always bring him to the school reunion,' Jazz put in.

'God! You're not still on about that are you?' Sapphire had been Facebooked about the reunion a while ago but had no intention of going and had deleted the event from her profile as soon as it came up. She couldn't imagine anything worse than meeting up with some of her class-mates, who were bound to bombard her with questions about Alfie, her ex-husband, who had also gone to the same school.

'It'll be fun,' Jazz insisted perkily, fiddling with the hot-pink hairband that matched perfectly the pink of her immaculately manicured nails. Jazz was into colour-coordinating in a big way and always matched her nails to her accessories.

'Are you having a laugh!' Sapphire snorted. 'That reunion will be as much fun as a colonic irrigation! There's a reason why I'm not in contact with most of the people I was at school with – I have nothing in common with them!' Sapphire did a major eye roll. 'And what if my ex-husband turns up?'

The three girls all quickly made the sign of the cross as if to ward off a vampire.

'Isn't Alfie still in Ibiza running that club? He's not going to come all the way back just for the reunion is he?' Jazz said.

'I suppose not.'

'Anyway, it's final: you're coming. I've got your ticket.' Sam pushed an envelope over to Sapphire. 'You should see it as a networking opportunity – that's what you're always going on about, isn't it?' she added.

'I suppose so,' Sapphire grudgingly admitted and shoved the envelope to the bottom of her bag so she didn't have to think about it.

She might put on a front and pretend not to give a shit about seeing Alfie again, but the truth was she didn't really know how she would cope if she came face to face with him. She wanted to play it cool, make him realise what he had thrown away, walk all over him in her latest Louboutin red-soled shoes metaphorically – and literally, if she could manage it. Ah yes, how satisfying that would be – Alfie always did have a low pain threshold, but what if she crumbled at the sight of him? It didn't bear thinking about. She and Alfie had been childhood sweethearts and married young. She had been devastated when she discovered that he'd been unfaithful. A month later the pain only got sharper when she found out that his lover was pregnant. In the aftermath of the divorce Sapphire was left with a broken heart; Alfie, on the other hand, got a whole new life. While she was sure she no longer loved him, he still exerted a powerful hold over her feelings.

Since the divorce Sapphire had channelled even more of her energies into her work and she loved it. Every time she opened the front door to the pale-pink terraced house she owned in the heart of Brighton's vibrant Lanes where her business was based, she got a thrill. It was all hers! She had started Something For The Weekend five years ago when she'd seen how phenomenally popular Brighton was becoming as a hen-weekend destination. Before that she had managed a lingerie boutique but had always dreamt of running her own business. Now Sapphire offered groups of women luxury weekend packages. Everything was arranged for them – from their hotel booking, to their beauty treatments to securing them tables at some of the city's best restaurants and arranging nightclub entrance. All they needed to do was turn up, L-plates and devil horns optional. She also offered a whole range of other activities from quad biking to lap-dancing lessons and male-model drawing (always a nightmare when the women had too much to drink – she was almost running out of students to employ), make-overs and photography sessions. Downstairs she had a boutique where she sold lingerie and sex toys and upstairs were the beauty rooms where the hens could have treatments – facials, manicures, pedicures and massages – drink champagne, listen to music or watch DVDs.

There was fierce competition now in the hen-weekend market but Sapphire liked to think she offered something a little bit different. She'd designed the house to make it seem like a boudoir of delights, with red velvet sofas, fairy lights, scented candles and black-and-white photos of Daniel Craig, George Clooney, Brad Pitt and Hugh Jackman on the walls. It was just the kind of place women wanted to hang out in. She also gave her clients her personal attention, on call all weekend in case there was anything they needed. And she'd made sure that she'd built up close relationships with the other businesses she worked with.

She often reflected that it was ironic that her work revolved round hen weekends as she was so cynical about marriage. But she kept that cynicism to herself and whenever any of the clients asked if she was married, she generally replied that she hadn't met the right man yet. She didn't want to burst their fantasy that marriage lasts for ever.

The house was busiest Friday through to Sunday, but Sapphire offered beauty treatments throughout the week and had a regular flow of clients. The downstairs boutique did okay as well, as Sapphire had done her research and offered a wide range of lingerie from high-end expensive treats to cheaper everyday items and her customers appreciated the personal service they received there.

Along with Jazz she employed two other people part-time: Vanessa, a statuesque blonde who worked in the boutique, and was also a gym instructor, and Kiki, a tiny redhead, another beauty therapist, who was great but had a bit of a temper sometimes. She could give Perez Hilton a run for his money when it came to getting catty.They'd all been with her from the start and to Sapphire it felt like her real family. Far less dysfunctional than her own . . .

But as well as the business was going, Sapphire was always conscious of the need to be one step ahead, which was why she was so thrilled that Tuesday afternoon when she received a phone call from Georgia Cox, an old schoolfriend of hers who also happened to be a leading actress on a soap.

'Georgia! How are you!'

'I'm engaged! Did you see the story in *heat*?'

Sapphire hadn't but pretended that she had. She had learnt early on in business that massaging her clients' egos was crucial, particularly so if that client happened to be famous. People like Georgia really thought the world revolved around them. Sapphire was not going to be the one to tell them that it didn't.

'Congratulations! That's wonderful news.' Sapphire lied very convincingly, 'Dex is a very lucky man.' The second lucky man, actually, as Georgia had already been married.

'No! I'm not engaged to that bastard! It's Tyler, my co-star!'

Wow, Georgia was a fast worker. As far as Sapphire knew, she and Tyler had only started working together in the last three months. And it was only a few issues ago that she'd seen Georgia draped round another poor bloke in *heat*. Sapphire couldn't keep up.

'He proposed on my birthday, it was so romantic.'

Sapphire made all the right noises as Georgia gave her

blow-by-blow account of the proposal. The romantic dinner at the very exclusive Mandarin Oriental in Knightsbridge; the uber-luxurious Royal Suite, with red rose petals scattered all over the bed where she'd discovered the cutest little white Chihuahua dog sitting in a basket. 'And you know how I adore dogs!' Georgia gushed. 'I was so busy petting the little sweetheart – who I've named Vuitton, by the way.'

What else? thought Sapphire, wondering how much longer she would have to listen to this. Georgia, totally unaware of Sapphire's boredom, went on, hardly stopping for air. 'It took me ages to actually see the ring round his neck, which is insane because the stone is huge! In fact when Tyler went down on one knee I thought he was going to suggest some pervy master and servant game! But you know me, I'm up for anything! Then I saw the ring and I was gobsmacked. I screeched so loudly, that Tyler said I nearly shattered the window! Vuitton didn't like it either and hid under the bed all night but the dog trainer says he will get over it. But I was just so over-whelmed – I mean, the moment I saw Tyler I knew he was the one. We have this really *intense* connection.'

'Really? That's brilliant,' Sapphire replied, hoping she sounded suitably enthusiastic. Georgia had made the exact same comment about the connection between her and her last husband and that connection fizzled out almost as quickly as a sparkler on bonfire night.

'So now I want the best fucking hen weekend ever and I thought who better than you to organise it! Especially since Brighton was my old stomping ground.'

Now Sapphire was perking up. Georgia was a favourite of the tabloids and gossip mags for her colourful private life – her many famous ex-lovers, two boob jobs and frequent trips to rehab to get over her drink and drug addictions – there was bound to be great publicity in it for Something For The Weekend.

'I'll give you the best fucking weekend ever!' Sapphire promised her.

'And I'm going to do a magazine deal – I haven't decided who with yet.'

Even better! Sapphire's mind was already whirring with possibilities.

'There's just one thing – it's in six weeks' time, that won't be a problem will it?'

It certainly would. Sapphire's weekends were booked up months in advance. She was going to have to do some serious juggling.

'That's no problem at all, Georgia. How about I put together some ideas and email them to you?'

'Darling, I trust you completely to arrange it. There will be eight of us. We'd like beauty treatments, dinner, a lovely hotel somewhere, a male stripper – the best you've got – and didn't I read somewhere about a male strip show? I want to go there. I need to see as many different cocks as possible before I restrict myself to the one for the rest of my life! Lucky for me Tyler's got an anaconda!' Georgia laughed raucously.

Sapphire's own laughter was more restrained; she'd forgotten how crude Georgia could be. And my God, a stripper *and* a strip show? Usually she just had to book the one event, not both! Georgia was hardcore in her demands. She pitied any male stripper who had to get his kit off for her. But there was no question that Georgia's hen weekend would be good for business. It was a booking she simply could not afford to turn down.

Georgia continued, 'Oh and I thought I'd drop in on the school reunion – it should be a laugh, are you going?'

Damn. That meant Sapphire would definitely have to go now to keep her client happy and seal the deal. 'Yes, I can't wait.' Sometimes her ability to lie convincingly surprised even her.

After the call, Sapphire sat at her desk for a few

minutes in a daze. Then she logged on to her diary and frantically called up the dates. Fuck! She knew it! She already had a booking. It would be bad business to cancel, but the following week was free: maybe, just maybe, she would be able to shift those hens to there. Sapphire prided herself on treating all her clients equally but she was also a realist and when it came down to it some clients were just more important than others and she couldn't risk loosing the hen that could lay the golden egg or was that a goose? Whatever! She had to accommodate Georgia. She reached for the phone.

Fifteen minutes and some very hard bargaining and promises of a big discount later she had managed to persuade the hen party to move weekends. Now she just had to book the hotel and restaurant and come up with a package to wow Georgia and the magazine.

'Have you had lunch yet?' Jazz had wandered down to the office in her black beautician's uniform. She held up her hands and considered her nails. Today she'd gone for a day-glo orange that made tango look pale and interesting. And she'd coordinated with orange hair slides and orange pumps. Sapphire had tried in vain to get Jazz to go for neutral colours but subtlety was not her forte; besides, lots of the clients loved her look and it certainly cheered the place up.

'Too busy,' Sapphire replied. She'd already tried two hotels and been given the brush-off even with the mention of the publicity. She was getting a knot of tension in her stomach. 'Georgia Cox just called, she wants me to organise her hen weekend.'

'Georgia?' Jazz said sharply. Sapphire knew that her friend had never particularly cared for Georgia ever since she had gone out with one of Jazz's ex-boyfriends while they were at school. Except neither Jazz nor Sapphire was sure if Georgia had waited for him to be an ex. Even back then she always tended to get what or who she wanted with no regard to anyone else.

Sapphire quickly filled her in. 'It's a big deal for us Jazz, we could get some really great publicity.'

Jazz sighed. 'I know, Sapphire, it's just I can't stand the cow. She'd better keep away from my Ben. I'm not having that slapper trying her luck with him.'

Sapphire thought it unlikely that a leading soap star would be interested in someone who was a plasterer and taught Judo in his spare time – cute as Ben undoubtedly was.

'I'll get Kiki to do her treatments; you'll hardly have to see her, I promise.'

'Okay, I'll go along with it and not tell the old witch what I think of her on one condition.' Jazz folded her arms and looked at Sapphire.

'What's that?' Sapphire asked, wondering if Jazz would expect an afternoon off as compensation.

'You let me and Sam meet Jay.'

Sapphire shook her head in disbelief. 'God, you're persistent!'

'Well, what about tonight? We could all go out for a drink to celebrate landing Georgia Cox's hen weekend.'

That sounded like a good idea to Sapphire, then she remembered, 'I can't, I promised Jay I'd go running, I've already blown him off once.'

Jazz sniggered, 'Don't you mean blown him!'

Sapphire rolled her eyes. 'I can't believe I'm saying this but I really have got to go running.'

'Now *that* I have to see, where are you going?'

Sapphire shook her head, 'You'll never get it out of me.'

'I swear to God I'm going to die if you make me run any further!' Sapphire panted as she and Jay ran along Brighton's seafront, past the old ruined Pier, a vast iron skeleton in the sea, and on towards Hove. They'd done about a mile and a half so far. Sapphire hadn't run like this since she was at school and she hadn't liked the experience then; she liked it even less now. Jay was totally unsympathetic as he effortlessly jogged beside her, not remotely out of breath, not even breaking a sweat, whereas Sapphire knew her face had turned scarlet – *so* not a good colour on her – and she had stitch. And people did this for pleasure? They must be masochists!

'We'll just go to Hove, then we'll turn back,' Jay told her. 'And if you make it I'll give you a massage when we get back.' Then he winked at her. Now that was more like it.

Jay's expert massages nearly always turned into something else even more enjoyable. But right now Sapphire did not want a massage or anything else. Great, so not only had Jay put her through hell on this run, but he'd also managed to put her off sex. She'd never thought *that* would be possible! She grunted at him and concentrated on her running. Where was the endorphin rush that Jay had promised her? Suddenly out of the corner of her eye she saw two very familiar figures sitting at a table at one of the seafront cafés and looking expectantly along the promenade. It was Jazz and Sam. There was no way their presence could be a coincidence. They'd come to watch her. Bastards!

They got up out of their seats and began chanting, 'Go Sapphire! Go Sapphire!' and pretended to be cheerleaders – Jazz even performed a mini-routine – waving her hands in the air, high-kicking and then wiggling her bum for good measure. Sapphire could kill them for this! She was all set to ignore them but Jay had slowed down.

'Friends of yours?' he asked, jogging on the spot.

Sapphire nodded and managed to gasp out 'Jazz, Sam' as she pointed out her friends.' She stopped running but

Jay wasn't having that. 'Keep moving, Sapphire, you have to keep your heart rate going.'

He turned to her friends and smiled his cute, sexy, Diet Coke break ad smile. Sapphire could tell her friends were impressed by his good looks – in fact, Jazz's tongue was practically on the floor. It would serve her right if someone trod on it. 'I'm Jay, good to meet you.'

'Lovely to meet you,' Sam replied, Jazz was too busy winding in her tongue. 'We've wanted to meet you for ages,' Sam looked meaningfully at Sapphire, who gave her the finger. 'What are you doing after the run?'

'I'm cooking dinner,' Jay cut his eyes to Sapphire, 'I can cook for your friends as well.'

'Oh, go on then!' Sapphire muttered. She'd agree to anything if it meant she could get home and stop the torture of the run but she didn't like anyone else planning her evening. So what if she was a bit of a control freak? 'I'll see you back at the flat,' she said and sprinted off in burst of energy.

Hah, she'd show them that she could run. Maybe she'd even work up to the half marathon or even the marathon, that would wipe the amused expressions from their faces – even more so when she made them sponsor her for shitloads of money. But the fantasy was short-lived as a hundred metres later she was forced to slow down to a jog, crippled with stitch.

Back at the flat she took a long shower and then felt surprisingly perky, energised by the run, the news about Georgia's hen weekend and the thought of all that money and publicity. She wandered into the kitchen where Jay was already hard at work, chopping up vegetables for a stir-fry. 'How are you feeling?' he asked.

'Good,' she replied, opening the fridge and reaching for a bottle of wine. 'What?' she demanded, seeing the expression on Jay's face. 'Don't I deserve it?'

'Well, you didn't exactly push yourself did you? I reckon you could have gone much faster.'

'Cheeky bastard!' she exclaimed, swiping a punch at his arm.

But he was too quick for her and pulled her into his arms and kissed her. Perhaps those endorphins were finally kicking in but Sapphire now had something other than dinner on her mind. She checked the time, 'Fancy coming into the bedroom, trainer boy?'

'It'll have to be quick. I don't want my Thai sauce to spoil.'

'Nothing wrong with a quickie so long as you push all the right buttons.'

'Don't I always do that?' Jay demanded.

'Every time,' Sapphire replied ten minutes later, after all her buttons had been pushed, very satisfactorily.

She was still in a post-sex/endorphin-rush glow when her friends turned up, which was just as well because it felt strange seeing them sit round her dining table with Jay. Since her divorce Sapphire had avoided situations where her lovers and friends met – frankly because she never chose the men in her life for their conversational skills and she liked things to be on her terms. Jazz and Sam clearly couldn't believe their luck at finally spending time with Jay. Jazz kept catching Sapphire's eye when Jay wasn't looking and mouthing 'He's so fit!' Like, I know that, Jazz! Sapphire felt like replying. Why else would I be with him?

'Jay, that was well good!' Sam exclaimed. 'Too good in fact,' she added ruefully, looking down at her empty plate. She had polished off the king prawn stir-fry very rapidly. 'What about my diet?'

'It's fine to eat like that once a day,' Jay replied, 'and it was all healthy stuff, I promise. If you want to lose weight you should be aiming to eat 1,500 calories a day, and make sure you have a good mix of protein and fresh fruit and vegetables. And make sure you eat fewer carbs the later it gets in the day.'

'Who do you work for, Weight Watchers?' Sapphire put in.

'I'm a personal trainer, remember? And many of my clients want to lose weight, so I advise them about nutrition. It was one of the things I studied at college.'

That put Sapphire in her place, she knew very little about what Jay actually did all day.

'I bet you're very popular with your lady clients aren't you?' Sapphire went on. She didn't know why but suddenly she felt like needling Jay. It had been a great evening, he'd made a fantastic meal for her friends, he was lovely, easy-going, but just too bloody perfect. 'I bet you get some women coming on to you.'

Jazz and Sam frowned at her. Sapphire ignored them.

'Ever shagged one of them?' She had the devil inside her now.

Jay shook his head, 'I'd get sacked if I did. It would be completely unprofessional.'

Sapphire laughed dismissively. 'God, Jay, you sound so up yourself! I bet when some fit bird is thrusting her Lycra-clad arse inches away from your face you think of it. I bet you get a stiffie sometimes.'

Sam came to Jay's rescue, 'Ignore her, Jay. She's got a filthy mind and she's probably only going on because she's jealous.'

Sam's interjection did nothing to improve Sapphire's mood and she could feel hot, irrational anger building up in her.

'Do me a fucking favour! Do I get jealous?' Sapphire exploded.

'Sapphire's got nothing to be jealous of,' Jay replied calmly, 'I'd never cheat.'

'Where have I heard that one before?' Sapphire said bitterly.

Then suddenly she realised why she felt so on edge with Jay: the next day would have been her fifth wedding anniversary. She'd successfully blocked it out of her mind but somehow the date had wormed its way through all her defences. A horribly familiar feeling of hurt and anger coursed through her. She got up abruptly from the table and started clearing the plates away, then stomped into the kitchen and began loading the dishwasher.

'Hey, are you okay?' Jay had followed her in.

She nodded and continued shoving cutlery into the dishwasher.

'I thought you said I pushed all your buttons?'

'I'm fine, Jay, why don't you see if Jazz and Sam want coffee?'

'I've made banoffee pie as well, I'll serve it up and bring in coffee, you go and talk to your friends.'

'Well, aren't you just too perfect to be true?' Sapphire replied sarcastically.

Jay frowned. 'I just want your friends to have a nice evening, Sapphire, what's the problem?'

'Nothing, sorry. Thanks for dinner,' she said abruptly and made to go out of the kitchen.

Jay caught her arm. 'Sapphire, have I done something to piss you off?'

'No, Jay, I told you I'm fine.'

He let go of her, 'If you say so.' But he clearly didn't believe her.

Back at the table her friends weren't going to let her get away with her treatment of Jay. 'Why have you got the hump?' Sam demanded, as Sapphire sat down and poured herself an extra large glass of Pinot Grigio.

'He's lovely, why are you giving him a hard time?' Jazz backed her up.

'He's the nicest guy you've ever been out with.' Sam continued.

18

The two of them were worrying away at her like a pair of terriers. Why couldn't they just drop it?

'Will you both just zip it!' she exclaimed.

Jazz glared back at her. 'I'm not at work now, you know. You can't boss me around. I'm off the fucking clock!'

Sapphire lifted her glass, 'Cheers, here's to what would have been my fifth wedding anniversary tomorrow. How do you think my ex-husband is celebrating?'

Both Jazz and Sam looked appalled, 'Shit Sapphire, I completely forgot,'said Sam.

'So had I, until just back then at dinner.' Sapphire sighed. 'I didn't mean to be such a bitch, it's just whenever I think about Alfie and what he did it makes me feel so angry.'

'Have you ever considered therapy?' Jazz suggested.

Sapphire let out a snort of laughter, 'That is so not me!'

'I know, Sapphire, but it might help. You're good at putting on a front that you're hard and you don't need anyone. But everyone needs someone.' Sam put her hand on Sapphire's arm.

'Oh my God, are we going to have a group hug?' Sapphire joked. She was saved from any more comments from her well-meaning but seriously annoying friends by Jay walking in with dessert and coffee.

While Jazz, Sam and Jay chatted about who they were backing on *The X Factor*, Sapphire was silent, lost in thought. She was remembering just how shocking it had been to discover Alfie had been unfaithful – and not only that – in their marriage bed. It was like he really wanted to rub her nose in it. Alfie had pleaded with Sapphire to forgive him, that it hadn't meant anything, then tried to shift the blame on Brooke, his lover, that it was she who had pursued him, that it would never happen again. For a short time Sapphire had wavered, wondered whether she should try and forgive him, after all lots of other

19

women had in her situation. But then came the bomb-shell: Brooke was pregnant and Sapphire was no longer in a forgiving mood. Once Alfie realised that she wasn't going to forgive and forget he turned nasty, told her it was her fault, that she was emotionally cold, incapable of loving anybody. Cruel, hurtful words that had burned deep into Sapphire's mind.

'So, who do you want to win, Sapphire?' Jay tried to pull her back into the conversation.

'God, no idea,' and then because she knew she had to put on an act she forced herself to joke. 'The young fit one of course.'

That night in bed, Jay went to put his arm round her. 'You know it was true what I said, I'd never cheat on you,' he told her, holding her tight.

Instinctively Sapphire found herself moving away, 'Sorry babe, I'm too hot,' she lied, seeking out the furthest corner of the bed.

Maybe Alfie was right and she was emotionally cold and incapable of loving anyone.

Chapter 2

Sapphire felt on edge the following day and her mood was not improved by knowing she had to go round to her mum's for dinner that night. All she really wanted was to go out with Jazz and Sam and drown her bitter memories in vodka, but she knew her mum would guilt trip her big time if she didn't go. It always felt like something of a duty call as she had never been that close to her mum. Her dad was the one she had always had the connection with but he had died suddenly of a heart attack when Sapphire was fifteen.

Sapphire hadn't only had to cope with her grief but it turned out that her dad was heavily in debt, though he appeared to be successful, providing his family with the big house and pool and two foreign holidays a year. Deep down Sapphire blamed her mum for the debt – even as a child she had seen how her mum always wanted expensive things and had nagged her husband until she got them. After his death the luxurious lifestyle was over, the big house had to be sold and there was just enough money for Sapphire's mum to buy a small terraced house in Hove. There had also been a small amount of money in trust for Sapphire, which she used to start her business. Yet it was a comedown after the lifestyle they had been used to. For years she was furious with her dad for dying and leaving her alone with her mum. But it wasn't really to do with the change in their standard of living, it was to do with how much she missed him.

Sapphire nipped into an off-licence for a bottle of wine, on her way to her mum's; she was definitely going to need something to take the edge off the day. Although her mum's house was small it was in a lovely area, near a park, and it was actually not a bad location, just a bit dull, but her mum had never got over losing the big house and was always moaning.

Sapphire rang the doorbell and looked at her watch. Half six, with any luck she could be out of there by ten.

Christine, her mum, opened the door. She was only fifty, the same age as Madonna as Sapphire was forever telling her, but she behaved like someone far older. She used to be so glamorous and proud of her appearance when Sapphire's dad was alive, but she truly had let it all go. It was as if she'd given up when he died. Sapphire despaired of her mother's dress sense. She hid a perfectly good figure under shapeless jumpers and jeans and rarely wore make-up. She scraped her long black hair, which was now streaked with grey, into an unflattering ponytail. Sapphire thought Gok Wan would probably love to get his hands on Christine and her wangers. She'd certainly lost her va va voom these days. And she could have looked so good! She had the same striking dark blue eyes as Sapphire, but they looked so sad. She also smoked heavily, something else that drove Sapphire mad. But appearance aside, the thing Sapphire really found hard to deal with was the 'poor me', victim quality of her mum.

'I was expecting you half an hour ago.' Her mum's first words to her. Not hi, not how are you?

'I just got held up at work, Mum, you know what it's like.'

Actually, Christine had no idea as she didn't work.

Sapphire trailed after her mum into the living room. Christine had insisted on keeping most of the old furniture from the other house – which was all too big and grand for the terrace – and as a result what could have been a pretty house felt cluttered and claustrophobic to Sapphire; she was strictly into the minimalist look herself. She was enveloped by the familiar feeling of sadness at the state of her mum's life as she sat back on the sofa and stared dispiritedly round the room. She looked at the photographs on the mantelpiece – the one of her mum and dad on their wedding day, and the one of her and her dad taken when she was ten. The pair of them were grinning away at the camera with smiles so wide it almost hurt to look at them. Then her gaze moved to the other side of the room.

'I didn't know you had a lap top,' she exclaimed noticing a computer on the dining table. My God, something different in her mum's life at last.

'I've been doing a course at the college, I told you.' Christine sounded hurt that her daughter hadn't remembered.

Shit, had she? So much of what her mum said passed her by because usually she was moaning about something or other. 'Oh yeah, I remember. It's great you're doing it, mum, about time you caught up.'

'I want you to have a look at it actually, I'm having trouble with my Internet connection – can you try and fix it while I make dinner?'

Sapphire sighed and walked over to the computer. Her dad used to be the one who fixed everything in the house and sorted out all the bills. When he died that role had fallen to Sapphire. Her mum didn't even know what direct debits she had, or how to budget. It had been hard for fifteen-year-old Sapphire coping with her grief over her dad and trying to sort out her mum at the same time. She vividly remembered the feeling of dread she had when she returned from school to find her mum still in her pyjamas, unable even to get dressed.

Sapphire sat down in front of the screen and clicked on the Internet icon. Immediately an error message popped up. This was just what she needed after the day she'd had.

'Have you done it yet?' her mum demanded coming back into the room, 'I have to get back online.' There was a sense of urgency in her voice.

Sapphire shook her head, 'I've no idea how to do it.'

'I thought you were supposed to know all about that kind of thing,' Christine replied, a little tetchily.

'Well, I don't – isn't there someone on your course you could ask?'

Now Christine looked positively agitated, 'I really need to go online tonight, I've got some things I have to do.'

God, what could possibly be this urgent? Sapphire sighed, realising that she would get no peace from her mum until the problem was sorted. She reached for her mobile. There was nothing for it – she would have to call Jay and ask him to help even though that would entirely go against her principle of not introducing her boyfriends to her mum. But she needed her mum off her case.

'Babe! Are you okay?'

He sounded so pleased to hear from her. Too pleased, Sapphire thought.

'I'm fine, I just wondered if you might be able to help me out with something.' Of course, Jay being the sweetie that he was, agreed to come right over. There was just the little problem of introducing him to her mum.

From the moment Jay walked in it was toe-curlingly embarrassing.

'So you're Sapphire's new boyfriend then?' Her mum's first question.

'Not that new, it's been three months.' Both Jay and Christine looked at Sapphire accusingly.

'Well, I'm sorry, Jay,' Christine replied, slightly sulky, 'She never tells me anything.'

'Can we just get on with fixing the computer and cut the guilt trip, Mum?' Sapphire asked.

Christine shrugged and muttered something about checking on dinner. As soon as Sapphire thought she was safely out of earshot she put her arms round Jay and kissed him, 'Sorry, I just like to keep my private life separate from my mum, she always ends up asking so many questions and it does my head in.'

'Whatever,' Jay replied, 'I don't get what your problem is. I told my family about you.'

'We're just more dysfunctional than you,' Sapphire tried to joke.

But Jay still looked pissed off. 'So I am your boyfriend then? And not just your fuck buddy?'

'Of course you're my boyfriend,' Sapphire replied.

God! What was wrong with being a fuck buddy! Why did she seem to have picked the only man in Brighton who seemed to want more!

Jay had Christine back online within ten minutes. Inevitably, as if Sapphire hadn't suffered enough, Christine invited Jay to stay for dinner.

'Prepare for the interrogation,' Sapphire whispered as Christine served up spaghetti bolognese.

As soon as Christine sat down she started the questions. 'So where are you from, Jay?'

Sapphire cringed inside; surely her mum wasn't going to make a comment about Jay being mixed race?

'Brighton born and bred.'

'What about your parents?' Christine ignored the furious looks Sapphire was shooting at her. What had she done to deserve such an annoying parent?

'Mum's from London and Dad's from Luton.'

'Oh.'

25

'My granddad was Jamaican.'

Please let there be no more questions like this, Sapphire prayed. But then her mum surprised her. 'I always think mixed race people are very good-looking. Oh, is it okay to say mixed race? Sorry, it's just that living in Brighton you don't meet that many—'

'Ethnic minorities?' Sapphire quickly put in just in case her mum was going to say something way unPC.

'It's fine to say that. I love Brighton and can't imagine living anywhere else, but it is a bit too white.' He paused. 'I didn't have a great time at school.'

'Didn't you?' Sapphire had never talked to Jay about his schooldays. Well, the truth was she hadn't really talked to Jay about that much of anything.

'I had to move secondary schools because I was racially bullied.'

Sapphire looked at him with concern, 'Were you, babe? I'm sorry.'

Jay shrugged. 'It was a long time ago, but it has left its mark. I think something like that always does.'

Before Sapphire could ask him any further questions, Christine spoke, 'Sapphire was bullied at school. This horrible group of girls picked on her after her dad died, can you believe it? Calling her names, ganging up on her at a time when she was very vulnerable. I was so angry.'

Had her mum been angry? Sapphire couldn't remember her being anything other than completely grief-stricken and powerless to help her daughter.

'Mum! Jay doesn't want to hear about that, it was years ago.'

'I didn't even know you'd lost your dad,' Jay replied.

Cue more accusing looks from Jay and Christine. This was exactly why she didn't like introducing boyfriends to her mum – too many questions, stirring up too many emotions.

26

'Well, it hadn't come up.' Face it; she wasn't with Jay for the sparkling conversation.

This was turning out into the night from hell! Sapphire hated being put on the spot like this. Though at least there was one good thing: Christine clearly hadn't remembered that it would have been Sapphire's fifth wedding anniversary today. Most years she remembered the date only too well and there'd be a rehash of Sapphire's failed marriage and why Alfie had been unfaithful – Christine had always adored him. Sapphire had often suspected that Christine blamed Sapphire for the break-up of the marriage.

Fortunately conversation then turned to other things: how Sapphire's business was going, how her aunt was who lived in America, Jay's own family. But it was a relief when dinner was over. Usually Sapphire would be expected to stay until around ten but tonight her mum actually seemed in a bit of a hurry to get rid of her, saying that she had to get on with her computer work.

'You don't think mum's got an online porn addiction do you?' Sapphire joked as she and Jay walked back along to the seafront to her flat.

Jay ignored the comment. 'Why didn't you tell me your dad had died?'

Immediately Sapphire could feel herself clamming up. 'I just don't like to talk about it, that's all. What is there to say anyway? He died, it was shit, I still really miss him, my mum's life still seems shit but life goes on, doesn't it?'

Jay sighed and put his arm round her. 'Sapphire, you don't have to put on an act for me.'

'I don't put on an act.'

'Whatever. Back to yours?'

Sapphire was all set to say no but actually the thought of being in the flat on her own was not an appealing one right now – she'd only end up thinking about Alfie or her dad or both.

'Yeah, and thanks for helping out with Mum. I appreciate it.'

'No worries, but you now owe me one.'

'Go on then – name the sexual favour of your choice.'

'Yeah, I have that anyway, but I also want you to meet my family.'

Bollocks! Sapphire reluctantly agreed but she was determined to put the meeting off for as long as possible.

'It's my dad's birthday in a few weeks' time, come round for dinner.'

Shit, it wasn't going to be easy getting out of that one. She'd have to pull out all the stops to come up with an excuse.

'Great,' she replied, without making eye contact with Jay. 'I can't wait. Now, about that sexual favour . . .'

Chapter 3

'Can you give me really long lashes?' Sapphire asked Jazz who was making her up for the school reunion. Now there was no getting out of the event, Sapphire was determined to be glammed up to the max.

Jazz tutted, 'God! You're so demanding!'

Sam was already dressed and made up and was looking at herself in the mirror. She turned this way and that, considering herself from every angle. She was wearing a red halter-neck dress with a full skirt, and Sapphire thought she looked pretty good, given that the diet hadn't been going so well. But Sam was in full moan mode, 'I look fat, don't I? I'm wearing magic pants and you can still see my stomach. God, I hate my body!'

Sapphire and Jazz exchanged eye rolls, which Sapphire then regretted as it felt as if her false lashes were going to fall off.

'Don't say that, you look great!' Jazz exclaimed.

'Very sexy,' Sapphire added, 'Perhaps you can spice up the reunion by copping off with someone.'

'Who exactly?' Sam demanded.

'Cal's going.' Jazz replied.

Cal Bailey, the former premiership footballer, had been a couple of years above them at school. He was one of the best-looking men that Sapphire had ever met. As far as Sapphire was concerned there wasn't a chance Cal would fancy Sam. Sam clearly thought so too, as she shook her head.

'What about Dave Greenwich?' Sapphire suggested instead. Not exactly a looker but a nice-enough guy if she remembered.

'Thanks a lot!' Sam exclaimed, sounding offended, 'You mean Dave Fatwich! With the personal hygiene problem?'

Oops, Sapphire hadn't meant to upset Sam. But before she could make it up to her friend Jazz tactfully said, 'Sam is way out of Dave's league. And isn't Cal still hung up on Angel?'

Cal had recently moved back to Brighton after an injury had permanently ended his footballing career and after the break-up of his marriage to the glamour model Angel Summer six months ago. Now he was concentrating on trying to set up a series of football academies. Sapphire had met up with him the previous week for a drink and all Cal had done was talk about his wife.

'Yep, he's gutted.'

'Shouldn't have played away then, should he?' Jazz said, who had been shocked to learn that Cal had been unfaithful. Cal and Angel had been her pin-up couple, their relationship her idea of the perfect marriage. They'd been the nation's golden couple for a while.

'No, he shouldn't,' Sapphire agreed, thinking of her own marriage break-up. Then, because this was not a topic of conversation likely to put her in a good mood, she asked, 'Anyway, shall I go for my Vivienne Westwood corset dress? Or my skinny jeans?'

'Corset dress,' Sam replied. 'I can't be the only one showing cleavage.'

Half an hour and a taxi ride later, the girls arrived at the school hall and immediately felt completely overdressed

30

as nearly everyone else was in jeans. There were groups of people milling around chatting, while a mirrorball spun round, sprinkling the hall with silver circles of light and the DJ played tracks from the nineties. No one was dancing. It was as cringey as Sapphire had feared, God, it even smelt the same – the unmistakeable smell of floor polish mixed in with sweat, smelly socks and Lynx. Definitely not Sapphire's scene.

The girls exchanged rueful looks and immediately headed for the bar, well, the trestle table that was acting as a bar, and grabbed three plastic cups of lukewarm white wine. Sapphire took a sip and pulled a face, 'This is vile!'

'Lucky I brought my own supplies of vodka, isn't it?' Sam replied, pulling a sleek silver flask from her bag and offering it round.

'On to the hard stuff already, ladies?' They all turned round guiltily mid-pour to see Cal looking amused.

'Want some?' Sam asked holding out the flask.

Cal shook his head. 'I'm driving.'

'God, Cal, you're good, drink is probably the only thing that's going to get me through this.' Sapphire replied as they quickly exchanged kisses.

Jazz and Sam got caught up with talking to one of the girls they were at school with while Sapphire remained with Cal. Her friend was as gorgeous as ever, the same male model good looks, olive skin and dark brown eyes, but he looked tired and his eyes had lost their mischievous sparkle. The separation from his wife, who was currently living in LA with a baseball star, was taking its toll.

Despite his looks and success, Sapphire had never really fancied him. That chemistry simply wasn't there between them. Instead, when Sapphire went out with one of Cal's mates they had become good friends and had somehow remained friends after the break-up. It was a friendship that people outside their circle found impossible to understand and they were always convinced that there must be something more.

'So, how's it going?' she continued. The last time they'd met Cal had done nothing but talk about Angel, and his daughter Honey. She sensed that tonight wouldn't be any different.

'Situation normal, all fucked up,' he replied, running a hand over his short black hair, as if to fend off the question. 'But let's not talk about me, I went on enough last time about myself, what about you?'

'I'm good, work's going well.'

'And what about your boyfriend? Are you still seeing him?'

Sapphire nodded. She wasn't used to thinking of Jay as her boyfriend, but she supposed he was.

'Three months. Isn't that your record?'

'I'm not that bad, Cal,' she protested, though it was true. Her flings never usually lasted beyond the three-month mark.

Cal smiled. 'I was just teasing you. But maybe this one's worth holding on to for a change.'

Sapphire shook her head. 'I don't know, Cal, I'm really not into relationships.'

'All I'm saying is if you find a good thing, don't throw it away.' He looked serious again, his eyes full of sadness.

'Cal, you shouldn't be so hard on yourself. You made a mistake. Maybe one day she'll forgive you?'

'Like you forgave your husband?'

Sapphire's face hardened, 'I'm sure you're absolutely nothing like Alfie.'

'And speak of the devil, here he is.'

Sapphire's stomach lurched and a panicky feeling of wanting to escape came over her. Alfie was the last person she wanted to see. But there he was, strolling through the door. She hadn't seen him for nearly two years and even though she hated him for how he'd treated her, she grudgingly had to admit that he was looking good. He had dark-blond hair and stunning, summer-sky eyes, which against his rich Mediterranean tan looked even more lethally blue. At five foot eight he was only slightly taller than Sapphire but he made up for this with an impressively buffed body. By the look of his pecs, which were showcased by his unbuttoned white shirt, he'd been quite the gym bunny in Ibiza.

Alfie always radiated confidence and wide-boy charm and he looked as arrogant as ever as he caught sight of Sapphire and treated her to his cheekiest grin. *Bastard*! He walked straight over as if he had nothing to be ashamed of. He always was a cocky bastard.

'Cal, long time no see, mate.' Alfie spoke with a strong Brighton accent and stuck out his hand, expecting it to be shaken. Cal took it, but didn't seem quite so pleased to see Alfie.

'And Sapphire, looking more beautiful than ever. If that was possible.' Alfie looked her up and down, his eyes sliding over her body as if he was undressing her. Then he leant forward and kissed her deliberately on each cheek, taking his time being close to her.

Sapphire got a blast of his aftershave – he was still wearing Dolce and Gabbana Homme, which she had bought him. She used to adore the scent, now it made her feel slightly sick. 'Alfie, even more full of shit, if that was possible,' Sapphire took a step backwards, almost crashing into the trestle table in her desire to put some distance between herself and her ex.

'Well, I've got some other people to see, I'll catch up with you later, Sapphire.' Cal moved away from them, clearly not wanting to be caught up in a domestic.

'Finally got it together with Cal have you? Funny I never saw you as a WAG.'

Alfie always knew exactly how to wind her up. Their

marriage had been passionate and intense with lots of arguments and lots of making up. Against her will, Sapphire was remembering the making up. Alfie had always been very good at that. He looked at her knowingly.

'I'm not *with* Cal, we're just friends.' Sapphire snapped back. She paused, then asked, 'How's Brooke?'

'She's still in Ibiza, winding up the club. She'll be coming over in a month.'

'What do you mean coming over?' Sapphire could just about handle the thought of Alfie in another country; having him back in Brighton was way too unsettling.

'Didn't you know? I'm taking over PURE. You do business with them, don't you? We'll have to come to some arrangement. I'd like to think that you and I could do business too. We always worked well together in the past didn't we?'

Alfie had helped her get her company off the ground but then he hadn't liked it when Sapphire had become so absorbed in running it.

Alfie continued, 'I've got a new partner – I think you'll like him. Here's my card, we should meet next week, Sapphire.'

Sapphire took the card, not trusting herself to speak. Why hadn't Simon, the manager of PURE, told her about the buy-out? She'd spent the last five years building a good working relationship with the club. And now that was all threatened by Alfie.

Where was Sam? She needed the hip flask right now!

Sam and Jazz had thrown caution to the wind and had hit the dance floor – boogieing on down to Abba's 'Dancing Queen'. They gestured to Sapphire to come and join them, but she was definitely not in the mood. Most of all she wanted to go home. She couldn't risk leaving, though Georgia was supposed to turn up and she would expect to see Sapphire.

As she moved round the hall, chatting to people she vaguely remembered from school, mentioning her business and handing out her card, she was aware of Alfie watching her. It put her on edge. Why had he come back to Brighton? Weren't there any other cities he could go to? And yes, Brighton was a city but it was a small one, and if she kept her business at his club she would be seeing him pretty much on a weekly basis. She didn't know if she could stand it.

To stop herself obsessing she checked her mobile. There was a message from Jay. 'Call me if your reunion doesn't finish too late, I can come over. Are you wearing school uniform? Jx.' In spite of the nightmare evening she was having, she found herself smiling, yes she would call Jay when this was over. She had learnt from her bitter break-up with Alfie not to become a victim and she had no intention of starting now. She made her way over to the bar and grabbed a beaker of cheap wine; she would somehow get through this evening.

'Sapphire!' She spun round to see Georgia, looking every inch the soap star in a cream silk jumpsuit. Georgia did not do understated and whenever she went out it was her mission to show off as much cleavage as possible – her boobs had cost her enough, she was always saying, she may as well get her money's worth. They were certainly on show tonight and it was quite hard not to stare at them as they were practically up to Georgia's neck. Georgia was twenty-seven, the same age as Sapphire, but looked way older because of her habit of plastering her face with make-up like a mask. She was pretty but in serious need of a makeunder.

Sapphire did her best to avert her eyes from the cleavage and look instead into Georgia's violet eyes (fake contact lenses, Sapphire was sure) and spent the next ten minutes chatting with Georgia. It was hardly a two-way conversation, just lots of Sapphire telling Georgia how wonderful she was looking, how slim she was, how well she thought she was doing in the soap blah blah blah. However outrageous the compliments Georgia took them all in her stride, as if they were entirely reasonable. The arse-licking was exhausting, but Georgia didn't seem to tire of hearing how wonderful she was.

'Hey, is that Cal Bailey I can see over there?' Georgia asked, flicking back her long blonde hair extensions and nearly taking out Sapphire's eye. 'It is. God! I haven't seen him since he was going out with Simone Fraser, I have got to say hi. Still hot to trot isn't he?' Georgia winked. 'Come over with me, I'd love it if he could come to my wedding. So would the magazine, they'd probably increase the fee in fact,' she added gleefully.

Sapphire trailed after her. She couldn't imagine that Cal would welcome a conversation with Georgia. By nature he was an intensely private person and although he and Angel had been photographed wherever they went and were a constant feature in the celeb mags, Sapphire knew he didn't enjoy the attention. And she was right about his reaction to seeing Georgia. She watched him endure her flirtatious comments but he looked as if he would rather be somewhere else, very far from Georgia and her fake-tanned cleavage, which seemed to have become even more revealing. Sapphire could have sworn that there wasn't so much on show before Georgia saw Cal – she must have adjusted her zip.

'And Cal,' Georgia reached out and stroked his arm. 'I would so love it if you could come to my wedding. It would mean a great deal to me and Tyler.'

Sapphire couldn't believe how brazen Georgia was being, she hardly knew Cal and Tyler had never even met him.

Cal gave the briefest of smiles which didn't reach his eyes, 'It's very good of you to ask me, Georgia, but it's more than likely I'll be in the States seeing my daughter.'

'Oh yes, Honey, she must be so adorable! How old is the little poppet now?'

Cal's jaw clenched. Any person with an ounce of sensitivity would have seen that he really didn't want to talk about his daughter. Georgia was not one of them.

'Two and a half,' he said abruptly, turning away.

Time to rescue poor Cal. Sapphire turned to Georgia and said brightly, 'So Georgia, where are you going on honeymoon?'

'Tyler's surprising me – all I can say is it better be somewhere bloody amazing like the Maldives or I'll divorce him!' Georgia laughed raucously. She was drunk.

Cal took the opportunity to say his goodbyes. As he gave Georgia the obligatory air kiss, she put her arms round him. 'Lovely to see you, Cal, and I'll send you an invitation to the wedding just in case you can make it.'

She was persistent, Sapphire gave her that; or maybe just desperate for the lucrative deal and all the attention that came with it. Cal just smiled thinly.

'Sapphire, be a darling and get me another drink,' Georgia exclaimed as soon as Cal had gone.

It was on the tip of her tongue to tell Georgia that she wasn't her bloody servant but she couldn't risk jeopardising the hen party booking. By the time she returned with a beaker of wine, Georgia was deep in conversation with Alfie.

'I can't believe you split up with this gorgeous man!' Georgia exclaimed, taking the wine with one hand and running the other down Alfie's arm.

'Really? So you wouldn't mind if you came home to discover your husband shagging another woman?' Sapphire snapped back. She knew she was supposed to be playing arse-licker of the century but she couldn't stop herself. The woman was unbearable!

Georgia burst out laughing, 'Alfie! I'd forgotten about that! You dirty dog.'

'If I could go back in time and change what I'd done, I would,' Alfie replied, looking at Sapphire intently. She used to think his blue eyes were so beautiful and sexy, now she thought they were calculating and lacked depth. She shrugged.

'Ah see, the old spark is still there!' Georgia carried on, noting the gaze, 'And there's nothing more intoxicating than sex with an ex is there? I've had the best, dirtiest sex with nearly all my exes – it's always fantastic because you don't care what the other person thinks of you any more, you're both out for your own pleasure.' She looked significantly at Sapphire, who ignored her. If this was what Georgia was like at a school reunion, what the hell was she going to be like on the hen weekend?

Georgia laughed. 'I had no idea you were this coy, Sapphire. Or it there someone else in your life now?'

Sapphire didn't want to give anything away about her private life in front of Alfie, but felt she had to say something, 'Yeah, I'm seeing someone.'

'Ooh Alfie, competition for you, but I bet you love that don't you, it gets the old testosterone flowing.'

Now Georgia had gone too far. 'Georgia there is absolutely *nothing* between me and Alfie. We're divorced. End of.'

'Oh sweetie, I was just teasing you, sorry. I'm going to the bathroom now.' And she tottered away, swaying slightly as she went.

'Jesus Christ! I can't believe I'm organising her hen weekend!' Sapphire exclaimed when Georgia was out of earshot.

'It'll be a wild one that's for sure,' Alfie agreed, taking the opportunity to move closer to her. 'But she was right about us wasn't she? There is still something between us? Unfinished business? The spark is still there, isn't it?' His voice was low and husky – his seducer voice. Did he really think he had any chance with her? She almost laughed. Why couldn't he just get over it and get over himself while he was at it.

'There is nothing between us, Alfie. Really, I feel nothing for you. Nothing,' she said coldly. 'You destroyed anything I felt for you when you cheated on me. Anyway how's your son?'

Alfie shrugged, 'Don't try and avoid the subject, you always were a terrible liar, Sapphire.'

From across the hall Sapphire saw Jazz and Sam doing the sign of the cross and grimacing. 'I'll call about setting up a meeting – a business meeting, that is,' she replied briskly and headed over to her friends.

By now Georgia had returned from the bathroom. She had taken to the dance floor and was giving Madonna's 'Like a Virgin' her all, flashing ridiculous amounts of cleavage. Sapphire watched one of the lads she remembered from her year, now an estate agent, making his move on her. He began dancing with her, suggestively moving his hips close to her, putting his arms round her and spinning her round. Georgia seemed to relish the attention and in turn wiggled her hips and pressed her body into his.

'Look at the state of her!' Jazz exclaimed. And they all watched in appalled fascination as Georgia put her arms round the lad's neck and began shimmying her body up and down his.

'Looks like she hasn't got on top of her drink problem then,' Sam said.

'She's about to get on top of him though,' Jazz added. 'And wasn't keeping off the booze one of the conditions of her staying on the soap?'

Sapphire put her head in her hands. Georgia was very bad news.

'Do you want me to do something?' Alfie had joined the group. Sam and Jazz visibly winced but managed not to make the sign of the cross in his face. 'Hi,' he said casually to the girls who had once been his friends and the brides-maids at his wedding. He got a nod back in return.

'What can you do?' Sapphire asked. 'Take her back home and shag her? Because that seems to be her mission tonight. Though I guess it would at least distract her from the free bar.'

'I was thinking of getting her a taxi and making sure no press saw her in this state. Otherwise you can kiss goodbye to that hen weekend.'

'Okay, do it,' Sapphire replied, well aware that Alfie was only doing this for himself, whatever he might say. He wouldn't want to lose out on the publicity for his club if the weekend didn't go ahead.

'Don't ever go to a school reunion,' she told Jay sometime later when they were lying in bed together. Sex with Jay had been the only good part of her evening. 'You never know who's going to turn up.'

'You saw your ex-husband right?'

'He's such a creep, I can't believe he's moved back to Brighton.'

She turned over on to her stomach and Jay began massaging her shoulders. 'You feel tense, babe.'

'So would you, if you'd had my night!'

'Just let it go, your ex-husband is the past. Don't give him headspace.'

She knew that Jay was right but that night she couldn't sleep. She endlessly replayed scenes from her marriage. She had been so in love with Alfie, had believed her marriage would last for ever, that he was the one – whatever that meant. Apparently nothing. And now he was back in her city and it was going to take all her strength to keep her barriers up and stay strong.

Chapter 4

Sapphire loved weekends when the hen parties were going well – it gave her such a buzz and it wasn't just about the money: she genuinely wanted the girls to have. a good time, the best time. She may be cynical about marriage, but she was deadly serious about her hen weekends being brilliant.

The weekend following the school reunion she had a lovely group in – just six girls who wanted beauty treatments, a makeover with a make-up artist and photographs followed by dinner. Sapphire enjoyed planning all the hen weekends but every now and then it was a relief not to have to do the whole club/stripper scenario. She went upstairs to check on how the beauty treatments were going.

The girls were having their nails done while a DVD of *When Harry Met Sally* played in the background, and they all sipped champagne. Sapphire was pleased to note that they were just sippling and not guzzling like the last lot of hens who got outrageously drunk even before the night had started. Sapphire liked a night on the tiles herself and could on occasions compete for caner of the year but she had not enjoyed cleaning up the bathroom after one of them threw up all over the floor. This group, thankfully, seemed more sedate.

Lucy was the bride to be, a sweet, fresh-faced geography teacher in her late twenties. Sapphire went over to where she was sitting while Jazz gave her a pretty French manicure.

'How's it going?' Sapphire asked Lucy. 'Are you happy with everything?'

'I'm having a great time, thanks,' Lucy replied. 'This is all going perfectly, I just hope my wedding day is as good.'

'I'm sure your wedding day will be fantastic,' Sapphire said reassuringly. 'What kind of wedding are you having?'

'It's the big white number,' Lucy said.

'She's been saving for it for the last five years,' one of the other hens put in.

'How long have you been with your fiancé?' Sapphire asked. It was always very important to show an interest.

'Six years,' Lucy replied. 'We met at uni, and we've been together ever since.'

Bloody hell, it sounded like a life sentence to Sapphire but she kept that thought to herself, 'Wow, that's wonderful.'

'Are you married?' Lucy asked her.

Bugger, there it was again, the question Sapphire most dreaded being asked, but this time she didn't give her usual spiel about not meeting Mr Right. Seeing Alfie so recently made her go for a different answer. 'I was,' Sapphire paused for effect, 'but my husband died.'

'Oh, I'm so sorry, that's awful,' Lucy looked at her, her sweet face filled with concern, her eyes actually welling up with tears.

Oops, Sapphire hadn't meant to upset her. 'Yes, I really don't like to talk about it.' Sapphire said quickly.

Jazz rolled her eyes at her, but really what was Sapphire supposed to say? Yes, I was married and my husband cheated on me with another woman in my bed and got her pregnant. Now I don't believe in marriage at all and don't trust any man. Sending Alfie to an early grave seemed like a good option.

'She's okay now, though,' Jazz piped up. 'She's got an absolutely lovely boyfriend. Gorgeous, isn't he, Sapphire?'

'I'm so glad,' Lucy replied. 'It's terrible to think of someone being a widow so young. It's wonderful that you found love again.'

It's good that I found a wonderful lover, who knows exactly how to please me in bed, was the answer Sapphire would have preferred to give; instead she went for the safer option, 'I know, I'm very lucky. Anyway, do let me know if there's anything else I can get you.'

'Actually, yes,' one of the other hens spoke up. 'We wanted to buy Lucy some gorgeous underwear, would you be able to get her kitted out?'

After establishing Lucy's size, Sapphire went downstairs and began selecting pieces that she thought Lucy might like. She went for pretty pieces rather than sexy but did pick out one racy black number.

She was just arranging the garments in the changing room when Jay walked in, put his arms round her and kissed her. Sweet as the kiss was, Sapphire hated being surprised. 'What are you doing here?' she exclaimed. 'I'm working.'

'I just felt like seeing you, I was out shopping with Luke.'

Luke was Jay's flatmate, and Jay was always threatening to introduce them. So far, Sapphire had avoided it; she had no real interest in meeting Jay's friends.

'Any chance we can meet up tonight?' Jay asked. He was looking particularly sexy in a black leather biker jacket and jeans.

Sapphire shook her head. 'I'm sorry, babe. I'm having dinner with Cal, remember?'

Jay frowned, 'Yeah, I'd forgotten. Maybe you could come round to mine afterwards?' he added hopefully.

'I've got to work tomorrow. You could come round to mine though.'

'You never come round to my flat,' Jay said, a slightly resentful tone to his voice. 'I don't live in a pig sty you know.' He folded his arms and leant back against the wall.

Sapphire felt ever so slightly guilty but not guilty enough to give in.

'I'm sure you don't, babe, but I'll be knackered and I'll just want to chill. Please come round.'

Jay sighed, 'Okay, but I really do want you to come round mine sometime soon.'

'I will.' Sapphire wrapped her arms round his neck and kissed him, now she had got her own way. And, as the kiss ended and Jay headed out of the shop she looked forward to seeing him that night.

At the doorway, Jay paused and said, 'I shouldn't be worried about Cal should I?'

Sapphire laughed, 'No Jay! We're just friends.'

Jay looked self-conscious and fiddled with the zip of his black leather jacket. 'It's just that he is very good-looking and successful. And rich.'

'He is all of those things,' Sapphire admitted, then did a double take. 'Oh. My. God. You're not jealous are you? Babe, I just don't do the whole jealousy thing.'

Jay scowled. Bad move, at this rate she wouldn't get to shag him tonight. Focus. Trying not to show how annoyed she was at Jay being possessive she smiled and walked over to him, and put her arms round him again. 'But I don't fancy him – never have done – and he doesn't fancy me either. I promise we're just friends.'

Jay looked relieved. 'See you later, babe.' He kissed her one last time and was out the door.

'Wow! Is that your boyfriend? He *is* absolutely gorgeous!' exclaimed Lucy, walking into the boutique.

Sapphire smiled, 'I know. Now come into the dressing room and I'll show you what I've picked out.'

She had expected that Lucy would go for the pretty

numbers first, but she went straight for the sexy black number. 'I love this!' she exclaimed.

Sapphire left Lucy to try on the garments; she pulled the red velvet curtain across the changing room and walked round the boutique, making sure everything was in place.

'What do you think?' Lucy called out a few minutes later, poking her head round the curtain. Sapphire walked over and considered Lucy in the skimpy lingerie.

'You look great,' she told her. 'And the fit seems perfect.'

Lucy looked at herself anxiously in the mirror. 'It's a bit revealing isn't it?'

Sapphire smiled, 'I think that's the idea.'

'It's just I'm not used to wearing underwear like this. I bet you wear sexy stuff like this all the time for your boyfriend.'

Sapphire shook her head, 'I do like wearing expensive lingerie not just for him but for myself.'

Lucy considered her reflection again. 'Oh, what the hell, I'll take it. I'm sick of wearing sensible underwear!'

'Good move, and why don't you try one of the other sets? Your friends have given you enough for you to get both.'

Lucy looked embarrassed, 'Well, actually I was thinking about getting something else. I'm not sure though.' She paused, 'I'll get dressed and come out.'

Sapphire put on her best sympathetic you-can-tell-me-anything expression. She'd put money on Lucy wanting to buy a vibrator.

A few minutes later Lucy emerged from the cubicle, clutching the lingerie and looking hesitant.

Sapphire reached out for the garments, 'Here, let me take that for you.' She put it on the counter ready to be wrapped. 'So shall I show you what else we have in the store?'

Lucy nodded and Sapphire decided to take it slowly.

45

'We're got a range of massage oils. They smell gorgeous and you can use them with condoms.' She pulled off the lid from one of the bottles and held it up for Lucy to smell. 'Might be nice to have this for your honeymoon, not your wedding night, you'll probably both be knackered, but the next day.'

They moved on to the edible body paint. Sapphire thought that might be a step too far for Lucy but showed it to her anyway. She was just preparing to move on the sex toys when Lucy blurted out, 'I've never had an orgasm.'

'Well, it's good that you came here then,' Sapphire concentrated on seeming totally unfazed but on the inside wondered what on earth Lucy and her fiancé had been doing for the last six years. 'I tell you what, why don't you have another glass of champagne and I can talk you through the range of toys we have in my office.'

The boutique had three other customers browsing. She steered Lucy towards her office then gathered a selection of vibrators. So she'd been right! Lucy was sitting down the sofa, looking embarrassed, her cheeks had turned bright pink.

'I'm sorry, I can't believe I said that to you!'

Sapphire handed her a glass of champagne, 'Don't worry about it.'

'I suppose you think I must be completely frigid.'

Sapphire shook her head. 'No, but I think your fiancé has probably got a lot to answer for.'

'It's just he seems to think I will be satisfied with penetration and it doesn't do it for me. I think there's something wrong with me.' Lucy leant forward and whispered. 'I have to keep faking it.'

'So maybe he doesn't know he's doing anything wrong?' Sapphire said kindly, 'Haven't you tried showing him what he needs to do?'

Lucy shook her head, now scarlet with embarrassment.

Something was beginning to dawn on Sapphire, 'Have you not ever had an orgasm with a bit of you know, DIY?'

Another head shake from Lucy. Sapphire spent the next few minutes pointing out the different features of the vibrators. 'Buy this one,' she held up one of her best-sellers, 'and take it straight back to your hotel room and give it a test drive. I'll tell the others you've just gone for a quick walk.'

Sapphire had the feeling that Lucy was not the kind of girl who shared her most intimate secrets with her best friends. 'And take this as well.' She handed her a half bottle of champagne.'

Lucy hesitated.

'Go! I promise you won't be disappointed.'

Sapphire smiled as Lucy stashed the champagne and sex toy into her bag and walked hurriedly out of the shop, looking guiltily back over her shoulder as if fearing one of her friends would catch her. Such innocence, Sapphire thought, continuing to check the displays in the boutique. At least that was one thing she couldn't accuse Alfie of in their marriage, whatever his many failings. He had always been a really good lover. But not, she reflected, as good as Jay.

An hour later a radiant-looking Lucy returned and gave Sapphire the thumbs up. 'Thank you,' she mouthed to Sapphire, as she headed back to her friends in the beauty room. She definitely had a new spring in her step.

Sapphire smiled. 'You're welcome.'

'So how was your day?' Cal asked her as they met up for dinner at a cosy Italian restaurant in the Lanes later that night.

'It was good.' She paused and then grinned, 'I helped a woman have her first orgasm.'

She knew Cal prided himself usually on being uber-cool about everything. But he almost choked on his wine,

47

then tried to collect himself by saying, 'That's great, Sapphire. I had no idea you were interested in women.'

Sapphire burst out laughing. 'I'm not!' and she went on to tell him what had really happened.

Cal looked bemused, 'I can't believe that a woman could have sex for so long and not have an orgasm.'

Sapphire smiled again, 'Oh my God, Cal, you're not going to say that no one has ever faked it with you, are you? I'll be forced to re-enact the scene in the deli from *When Harry Met Sally*. I saw it again this afternoon, so I'll be pretty good at it.' She flicked back her long black hair in preparation and speared an olive and popped it in her mouth. Cal looked slightly worried. He didn't like anything that drew attention to him in public.

'Okay, okay point taken. So do you fake it, Sapphire?'

She shook her head, and muttered, 'Never with Jay.'

'Sounds like he's definitely worth keeping,' Cal repeated his words from the school reunion.

Sapphire shrugged, 'You know me; I just like to enjoy the moment. I don't make long-term plans with men any more.'

Cal raised his eyebrow. Sapphire stuck her tongue out. 'I am what I am, and what I am needs no excuses.' Now she reached for a piece of ciabatta and dipped it in olive oil, she was starving.

Cal smiled. 'You put on this tough front, but underneath you're like the rest of us, Sapphire: you want to be loved. Seriously, don't be afraid of letting your barriers down if you like him. Love really is what it's all about. You could have the greatest career in the world but if you don't have love, then it's just not enough. I know that now.'

Oh God, he sounded like Sam, and much as she liked Cal, Sapphire hated being analysed by anyone. A change of subject was in order; she muttered 'Um' – she liked Cal

48

too much to say 'whatever', but that's really what she felt like saying. Then she asked Cal if he'd chosen what he wanted to eat.

Over main courses of seafood risotto, conversation turned to Angel. Six months after she left him, Cal's sense of hurt and pain was just as raw as if it had happened yesterday. 'I just can't bear to think of her with that' – Cal's jaw clenched – 'that *man*. I can't even say his name. I fucked up so badly. She was, she *is* the love of my life! I never should have betrayed her.'

Sapphire tried to reason with him, 'You told me how strained things had become between you because of her depression,' she added hastily. 'Not that you knew about the depression.'

Cal sighed and pushed his plate away, even though he had barely touched the risotto. 'I should have realised something was wrong with her, but I was so self-obsessed, worrying about my football career, putting that above everything else. I didn't see it and even when she tried to tell me how she was feeling, I pushed her away, I didn't listen. No wonder she left me.'

It was so painful listening to Cal torturing himself like this. She very much doubted that Alfie had given her a second's thought after they broke up, whatever he claimed. But then Cal always had been a bit of a one-off. Just a little too perfect for her to fancy . . .

'So, have you got any new pictures of Honey?' She was desperate to stop Cal beating himself up.

Cal immediately brightened, 'Are you sure you want to see them?'

'I'd love to,' Sapphire insisted, though she wasn't particularly interested in children.

He got out his phone and selected images from the menu. Sapphire clicked through the series of adorable pictures of the two-and-a-half-year-old. Honey had Cal's dark colouring, black curls and olive skin and Angel's stunning green eyes.

'She's beautiful, Cal,' Sapphire told him, handing back the phone.

'She is, isn't she?' Another sigh. 'I just hate to think that she might end up calling that man Daddy.'

Sapphire regretted asking him to show her the pictures as Cal went on another downward spiral about missing his daughter. Sapphire suddenly felt grateful for one thing – at least she hadn't had children with Alfie. It would have opened up a whole new dimension of pain. She ordered them both a brandy – neither of them wanted a dessert, even though Cal looked like he needed one.

'I'm sorry, Sapphire, I've been terrible company haven't I?' Cal said swirling the amber liquid round in the glass.

'Not at all, Cal – it's always good to see you and you know you can always talk to me.'

Cal smiled. 'Thanks, Sapphire, you're a true friend. So what have you got coming up?'

Sapphire grimaced, 'Georgia Cox's hen weekend. Though after seeing what she was like at the school reunion I'm seriously worried about it.'

'She certainly looked like a force to be reckoned with,' Cal sympathised, 'I still can't believe that she asked me to her wedding. I didn't really know her from school.'

Sapphire gave a mirthless laugh, 'She's just thinking about the magazine deal and how good it will look to have you in the pictures.'

'Well, she can dream on.' Cal replied. 'No way would I turn up to her tacky wedding. Besides I've no intention of running into Simone.'

'Oh my God! I'd almost forgotten about her. She turned out to be a right nutter didn't she?' Simone Fraser was a former soap actress and ex-WAG who Cal had gone out with before Angel. Simone had been devastated when Cal left her for Angel. Sapphire remembered Cal describing how she had stalked him, damaged his car and bombarded him with text messages until Cal threatened to go the police.

'Thank you for reminding me,' Cal said drily.

'I bet she'll be coming to the hen weekend.' Sapphire now had even more reason to dread the event.

'Just don't rub her up the wrong way,' Cal said. Then noticing the anxiety in Sapphire's eyes added, 'It'll be fine – she was only ever a bunny boiler where I was concerned. To everyone else she's lovely. She's far too worried about what people think of her.'

She could only hope that Cal was right. Simone Fraser was not the sort of woman she wanted to make an enemy of. She suddenly felt tired out and longed to be in bed with Jay. Much as she loved them, the hen weekends did take it out of her – constantly being on hand to keep everyone happy, always on call to sort out any problems, putting on a smiling face at all times. Then, unexpectedly, this dinner with Cal had been quite emotionally draining.

'Hey are you okay?' Cal asked, putting his arm round her as they left the restaurant. Sapphire was about to reply when a photographer stepped in front of them, thrust his camera in their face and took a picture.

'Oh for fuck's sake!' Cal said with feeling. 'Don't you people ever let up?'

He marched angrily past the photographer and opened the taxi door for Sapphire. The photographer continued snapping away at them. Sapphire resisted the temptation to give him the finger, knowing that would be the picture they'd use and it wouldn't do her business any good.

'What a wanker!' Sapphire exclaimed as taxi pulled away.

'Yeah, but now that wanker is going to make it look as if there is something going on between us. Jesus Christ!' Cal put his head in his hands. 'The last thing I need is for Angel to see the pictures and jump to the wrong conclusion.'

'Oh Cal! I'm sorry, I didn't think of it like that,' Sapphire replied.

'And it's not just Angel, what about Jay? He'll probably be wound up by the pictures.'

'Jay'll be cool,' Sapphire replied. 'He knows he can trust me.'

'Well, if you need me to call him now and explain what happened, I will. I don't want to cause any trouble for you, Sapphire.'

'Thanks Cal, but it'll be all right.'

To Sapphire's relief Jay was already at the flat. She walked straight into his arms and stayed there without saying anything while Jay stroked her hair. 'Long day?' he finally murmured. 'How about I run you a bath?'

She nodded gratefully. Jay was so sweet. She'd never gone out with a man who looked after her like he did. For the hundredth time she compared him to Alfie. Even on those occasions when she'd been ill with flu or whatever, Alfie hadn't gone out of his way to look after her. Instead he had been more concerned that he would get ill. What had she ever seen in him?

While she had her bath, Jay sat on the floor and chatted to her. She told him all about her evening with Cal and about the photographer. 'So if you see pictures that make out there is something between us, I swear there's not. I wonder if I should get a message to Angel? Jazz knows her best friend.'

'You could but maybe that looks as if you've got something to feel guilty about. Best to ignore it, babe.'

'How did you get to be so wise for such a young boy?'

she demanded, leaning over the edge of the bath and kissing him.

'Maybe I've learnt from all the older women I've been out with,' Jay replied, kissing her back.

'Cheeky bastard!' Sapphire exclaimed and reaching in the bath water for a sponge threw it at Jay, soaking his T-shirt.

He stood up. 'Seeing as how you got me all wet, I'm going to join you in the bath, Miss Jones.'

And to Sapphire's delight he peeled off his wet T-shirt and shucked off his jeans and boxers and got in the bath with her. And at the sight of his gorgeously toned body she no longer felt tired . . .

That night in bed Jay held her closer than ever. She felt completely blissed out and happier than she had been for a very long time, until Jay whispered 'Love you, Sapphire,' so quietly that she thought she must have imagined it. She immediately tensed, the blissed out feeling vanished. The L-word complicated everything, it was just not somewhere she wanted to go with Jay; she wanted things to stay exactly the way they were . . .

Chapter 5

In the days that followed, Sapphire was so busy planning for Georgia's hen weekend that she barely had time to think about anything else. Jay's *love you* hung in her head somewhere like an unanswered question but she tried not to think about it. And ever since her father's death Sapphire was very skilled at burying things she didn't want to deal with. Right now it was her business she needed to focus on one hundred per cent.

Although Georgia had said that she was going to leave all the arrangements to Sapphire, she then changed her mind and asked Simone Fraser to oversee the weekend. Bad news. Simone Fraser couldn't miss an opportunity to stick her nose in and make diva-like demands. She wanted to know what was to happen practically minute by minute. Sapphire had visions of herself running around on the day with a headset and clipboard timing every event and taking her orders from Simone.

Simone wasn't particularly friendly to Sapphire and Sapphire thought she knew why. The photographs of her and Cal did indeed make it into the tabloids and celeb mags. It was no great surprise, Cal was still such a star. For a week or so Sapphire was besieged by press outside her business and apartment building; they also bombarded her with phone calls. 'No there's nothing going on between us, we're just friends,' Sapphire exclaimed.

Even Jay found himself stopped by the press wanting to know what he thought about his girlfriend cheating on him with Cal Bailey. Sapphire was pretty pissed off by the whole thing – she'd been reluctant to refer to Jay as her boyfriend and now it was plastered all over the papers. Jay was chilled about the press intrusion and laughed it off and Sapphire tried to do the same. It was Cal she felt sorry for, knowing that he would be torturing himself with worrying if Angel believed the rumours. All in all it was a completely mad time and Sapphire was so up against it she almost forgot about her upcoming birthday. But Jazz hadn't and was on her case.

'Just let us know what you want and we'll plan it for you,' Jazz said to her, reapplying her lipgloss as Sapphire locked up for the day.

'Can't we just go out for dinner? I'm really not bothered.'

Jazz looked shocked, she absolutely loved her own birthdays and spent weeks planning them. Sapphire used to love them herself; her dad had always made such a big deal, arranging fantastic parties for her and all her friends, buying her wonderful presents. After he died she had never felt the same way about them.

And in any case Sapphire had other things on her mind. She was stressing because there was one part of Georgia's hen weekend that she hadn't sewn up – the trip to the male strip club – which meant she would have to see Alfie. It was something she had kept putting off, but she had finally made the appointment to see him. His club had been closed for a complete refit and the truth was Sapphire had missed it as a venue. It was the best club in Brighton for her hen parties and the only club to offer a private cabaret room where they could hold a male strip show. She had to face facts: she was going to have to see Alfie pretty much on a weekly basis.

'Anyway, you look hot to trot – are you meeting Jay?' Jazz asked as the two girls strolled through the Lanes.

'Nope, I'm meeting Alfie. This is my kick-ass, I don't give a shit what you think of me outfit.'

Jazz whistled, 'It's well sexy. You look fierce. Are you sure you're not going to send out the signal that you're still interested?'

Sapphire paused and considered herself in one of the shop windows. She was wearing a tight black pencil skirt, black leather biker jacket, and her treasured black Louboutin pumps with the wickedly high heel. She'd gone for smoky eyes, with black eyeliner and tons of mascara, a dash of lipgloss, and she'd tied her long hair back into a slick ponytail.

Sapphire shook her head, 'No way would he ever get that idea again. We are O.V.E.R. big time. This is just business.'

'Okay, scary lady, do you want me to come with you?'

'Thanks Jazz, but I'll be fine.'

'Well, Sam and I are going to be meeting in the Star Bar if you would like to join us later. She wants to talk to me about her latest diet.'

'Sure, I'll probably need a drink after seeing that skanky bastard.' She waved goodbye to Jazz and continued on to the seafront, where Alfie's club occupied a prime position under one of the arches of the promenade. She was just about to ring the buzzer when her phone beeped with a text message. It was from her mum, saying that she needed to speak to her urgently. Sapphire sighed in exasperation, no doubt something had stopped working in the house, the computer had gone offline again or the washing machine had gone on the blink. And it would be up to Sapphire to fix it. The joys of being an only child. She'd phone her mum later; right now she had to concentrate on her meeting with Alfie.

*

56

In spite of her best efforts to be kick-ass, Sapphire still felt nervous as she rang the buzzer and Alfie let her in. She wondered if he had been watching her on the CCTV screens in his office. It would be just like him, getting a little power kick out of it. She made her way through the club, where a team of cleaners were hard at work, clearing up after the night before. The dance floor dominated the club, surrounded by three bars and then there were a number of rooms that led off from the main area. The last time Sapphire had been in PURE it was mainly decorated in tired and trashy purple, and looked frankly in need of a restyle; Alfie had gone for stylish black and white. It looked good, not that she was in any rush to admit it to him.

She went up the flight of stairs behind one of the bars. Alfie was sitting in his office, which he had also refurbished, behind a mahogany desk, with his feet propped up on it, while he sprawled back in his chair and chatted on the phone. His whole attitude said 'Look at me! I'm the boss.'

Sapphire looked round the room. There was a large black leather sofa – no doubt for all those times when Brooke was at home and he couldn't take his latest conquest back; Sapphire was convinced that Alfie would still be up to his old tricks. He gestured for Sapphire to sit down. She made sure she chose the leopard-print armchair rather than the sofa – she didn't like to imagine what Alfie got up to on it. He seemed in no hurry to finish his call. Typical, trying to assert his authority in some macho, game-playing way. He laughed and joked away while his gaze lingered on Sapphire. But she had no intention of sitting there hanging on his every word. Looking sublimely indifferent to Alfie she pulled her iPhone out of her bag and began texting Sam. That seemed to work and he quickly wound up his call.

'Sapphire, thanks for coming in. D'you fancy a drink?'

'A vodka and tonic would be good.' Sapphire carried on writing her text and only when she'd pressed send did she look over at him. Two could play power games.

Alfie rang down to the bar and ordered the drinks. 'Ryan said he'd be here in a minute. So did you get back okay after the reunion?'

'Did you?' she countered.

He smiled. 'You mean did I shag Georgia? As a rule I like my women to be conscious.'

She grimaced. Was she really going to be able to do business with him?

He caught the look and said, 'Do you have that low an opinion of me, Sapphire? Of course I didn't shag Georgia Cox. I got her back to her hotel room and tried to get some coffee down her. She would have been up for it though, she was all over me. I pity the poor bastard she's marrying.'

There was a pause. Was he expecting her to congratulate him on his self-restraint? Tosser. She simply arched one of her eyebrows. Alfie, realising she wasn't going to say anything, carried on, 'So, on to business.'

'That's why I'm here,' Sapphire couldn't resist saying sarcastically. Did he seriously think there could be any other reason?

Alfie registered her tone with a wry smile. 'I know you're not my number-one fan, Sapphire, but I hope we can at least be friends.'

Sapphire wanted to say that her friends didn't usually betray her but decided that would only extend the line of conversation and really she just wanted to hear Alfie's business proposition and get the hell out of there. She nodded slightly and Alfie took that as encouragement to carry on, 'So, I've been working on some figures and here's the deal we can offer you, if you agree to continue to use the club on a regular basis.'

He reached across the desk and handed her a sheet of

paper. Sapphire scanned the figures. She wouldn't have to pay an entry fee for any of her parties, they'd get to see the strip show for twenty pounds per person, with two free drinks thrown in. It was a better deal than before.

'Why such good terms?' she demanded, instantly distrustful.

'Because I want a guarantee that you'll always use the club. It's worth giving you this deal to secure that.'

At that moment there was a knock at the door and one of the bar staff walked in holding a tray of drinks. She set them down on the desk. 'Anything else, Alfie?' she asked in a thick East European accent. She was pretty, but she looked ever so thin and her dyed auburn hair badly needed the roots redoing.

'No thanks, Larisa, we're cool.'

Larisa left the office.

'Where's she from?' Sapphire asked, just making conversation.

Alfie rolled his eyes. 'The Ukraine, I think, somewhere like that. Ryan, my business partner, has got this thing going with Eastern European workers, an endless supply it seems.'

Alfie appeared ill at ease talking about it and Sapphire was about to press him when there was another knock at the door.

'Come in,' Alfie called out and in walked one of the most drop-dead gorgeous men Sapphire had ever seen. He was just under six foot, with a powerful, muscular body, jet black hair, wickedly sexy green eyes, and a sensuous mouth. Hello! Instinctively Sapphire smoothed back her hair and sat up straighter.

'Sapphire, this is Ryan.'

'Hi,' she said, looking at him from under her lashes as they shook hands.

'Hi, I've heard so much about you from Alfie but he really didn't do you justice.'

Sapphire liked the flirtatious comment – very much, and not just because Alfie obviously didn't. Ryan had the most gorgeous Southern Irish accent – Sapphire was a sucker for a lovely accent.

'So, shall we get down to the matter in hand?' Alfie put in, a little abruptly.

Ha! Sapphire thought, this should make business meetings more interesting.

As they talked about what bookings Sapphire had coming up, and in particular, Georgia's hen weekend which absolutely had to go well, Sapphire found herself sneaking glances at Ryan when she thought he wasn't looking. But every now and then their eyes locked. It seemed Ryan was as interested in her as she was in him. The feeling of apprehension she had about having to work with Alfie was now being replaced by one of excitement. As long as Ryan was in the picture, it even made dealing with her ex-husband bearable.

At the end of the meeting Ryan offered to show her round the refitted club. Sapphire had no great interest in what Alfie had done but she was perfectly happy to spend more time with the gorgeous Ryan.

In fact, although she hated to admit it, Alfie had transformed the club, which had been looking decidedly seedy, into a sophisticated, cool space. He'd made the most impact in the private strip club, which had been a homage to the eighties and not in an ironic good way. Now it was an altogether more intimate space with dark red walls, ornate gold mirrors, a mix of private red leather booths and gold tables and chairs, and a large mirrorball that threw out circles of light.

'I love this,' Sapphire exclaimed walking in. 'It's a massive improvement.'

'Glad you think so,' Ryan said, sitting on one of the tables. He seemed the kind of man who was at ease in any situation. Sapphire found his confidence very sexy. 'I designed it. In fact I came up with the design for the whole club.'

Typical Alfie, trying to take the credit to impress her, she thought.

'It reminds me of my own place,' Sapphire continued, walking round the room, intensely conscious of Ryan's gaze on her.

'It should do – you inspired me. I took a look at your place a couple of months ago to get some ideas. You've created a fantastic business.'

Sapphire glowed with the compliment; she liked nothing better than to be praised for her work. They stood looking at each other for a second longer than you would if you were only business associates. Sapphire was the first to speak, 'I've really got to go now; I'm meeting some friends.'

'I'll see you out,' Ryan said, walking her through the club. He paused at the door, 'I still don't feel I know Brighton very well as I only moved down a month ago. Any chance you could show me around sometime?' He gazed at her with his green eyes, challenging her, daring her.

'Sure, no problem,' she said casually, while inside she performed a little victory dance. *Sapphire Jones, you have not lost your touch!* 'I'm tied up for the rest of the week but I could do something next week.' She didn't want to sound too available. 'We could go for lunch and take a walk round the city.' Lunch, businesslike, safe. She wasn't doing anything wrong, he was a work contact that was all.

'I'd like that. Here's my number.'

He handed her his card and their fingers brushed against each other. Sapphire tried to ignore the chain reaction that this triggered inside her, but she couldn't deny the jolt of attraction. Ah well, she reasoned walking along the seafront and towards the bar, there was nothing wrong with a little flirtation. That never hurt anyone did it?

She was still smiling she walked into the Star Bar, an intimate, trendy bar, just off one of the roads by the sea which the girls had adopted as their local. Jazz and Sam were sitting at their regular spot, on the brown leather sofa by the window. 'So, it wasn't that bad seeing the evil one then?' Sam said as she and Jazz noted the smile. 'We were expecting you to have the right hump.'

'Not so bad at all. The deal he's offering me is a good one and,' Sapphire's smile broadened, 'he has got the most gorgeous business partner!'

She looked at Jazz and Sam expecting them to share her enthusiasm but they both frowned. 'You've got a gorgeous boyfriend – remember?' Sam put in.

'I know! I was just window shopping, keep your hair on!' Sapphire shot back, hating her friends' judgemental attitude. She hadn't done anything wrong. 'Shall I get the drinks in? Or do you want to carry on having a go at me just because I happened to say that another man is good-looking?'

'Vodka and coke, please,' Jazz replied.

'Mineral water for me,' came Sam's request.

Sapphire raised her eyebrows, 'Not like you, Sam.'

'Yeah, well, I'm on this diet and for once I'm going to stick to it and that means no alcohol. I know myself too well. I'll have one drink and then I'll have another then another and then I'll be starving and it won't be the steamed fish and veg I reach for but a bloody great bucket of KFC, but not this time!' Sam's hazel eyes took on a determined gleam. 'This is the year I become a size 12 and meet the man of my dreams!'

'Go, girlfriend!' Sapphire replied. Please let this diet work, she didn't know how many more times she could listen to Sam going on about her weight.

Sam rolled her eyes, and Sapphire added, 'I wasn't being sarcastic. Honestly, I think it's great. I tell you what, why don't I ask Jay if he could give you some one-to-one training sessions. I could pay; it could be my early birthday present to you.'

She was fully expecting Sam to make a list of excuses as she hated going to the gym, and was pleasantly surprised when she replied, 'I'd love that Sapphire, do you really think you could?'

'Course, I'll speak to him tonight.'

Sapphire headed off to the bar, feeling very pleased with herself, convinced that Jay could work wonders with Sam. It was while she was waiting to be served that she remembered her mum's text. Shit! She reached for her phone and discovered she had two missed calls from her mum and when she accessed her voicemail the messages her mum had left sounded desperate. She didn't usually sound so upset when she called Sapphire; something really must be wrong. Quickly Sapphire selected her mum's number. Christine answered on the first ring and was decidedly shaky.

'Mum, are you okay?' Sapphire asked, feeling suddenly anxious.

'No, I'm not, Sapphire. Can you come over? I can't talk about it on the phone.'

Wondering what on earth could be that urgent Sapphire made a quick goodbye to her friends and grabbed a taxi to her mum's house.

Her mum never exactly looked like the life and soul of the party but even so Sapphire was shocked at her appearance when she opened the door. She seemed to have aged ten years, her skin looked sallow and she had dark circles under her eyes. As soon as she saw Sapphire her face crumpled and she broke down in tears. Sapphire hugged her. 'Hey Mum, what's the matter?'

63

'I'm so sorry, Sapphire,' was all she could say as Sapphire led her through into the kitchen. Sapphire hadn't seen her mum in this state since her dad died; she couldn't imagine what had caused it.

'Okay, Mum, sit down and tell me what's wrong, you're freaking me out.'

Her mum slumped at the kitchen table and picked at a thread in her jumper.

'Sorry,' she said again.

'*Mum* – please, tell me what's up!' Sapphire repeated, growing more and apprehensive.

Without saying anything her mum reached across to the pile of mail on the kitchen table and handed Sapphire three letters. Sapphire read the first one with a feeling of complete disbelief. Her mum's overdraft stood at five thousand pounds and the bank wanted to know when she was going to pay it off. They were threatening to take her to court. Sapphire didn't even realise her mum had an overdraft. She knew her mum wasn't exactly rolling in it but she thought that she had enough to live fairly comfortably. The other two letters were from credit card companies – she owed a further five grand on her cards. What the hell had she been spending her money on?

'I don't understand, Mum, how on earth did you get into this much debt?'

There was a pause where her mum seemed to slump still further into her seat. 'I've been playing poker,' she said quietly.

'What? At the casino?' Sapphire said incredulously; her mum rarely went out and if she did it was with one of her friends to see a film or go for dinner. She simply couldn't imagine her mum in a casino.

Christine shook her head and in a barely audible voice said, 'I've been playing online.'

'Jesus Christ, Mum!' Sapphire slammed her hand on

64

the table, causing Christine to wince. 'What the fuck possessed you!'

Christine winced again at the language but Sapphire was having none of it.

'You've just burnt ten grand, I'm allowed to say fuck!'

She couldn't believe that her mum had got into this situation. How could she have been so foolish? Tears continued to slide down her mum's cheeks. Sapphire suddenly felt sorry about her outburst, her mum looked so upset. However shocked she was by this bombshell, she was going to have to pull herself together and take control.

'Okay, I'm sorry, I really wasn't expecting this. Why don't I make us a cup of tea and we can talk this through.'

Christine nodded. Sapphire tried to collect her thoughts together as she went to put the kettle on and reached for the mugs. She suddenly had a splitting headache. For the millionth time she wished she had a sibling to share the responsibility that pressed down on her so relentlessly. She set the mugs of tea on the table and added a generous teaspoon of sugar to each, 'But I don't take sugar!' Christine protested.

'It's good for shock,' Sapphire said grimly, 'Now I want you to tell me from the beginning what happened.'

Christine reached out for her cigarettes, lit one with a trembling hand and then began to speak. The gambling had all been a bit of fun to begin with, she was lonely on her own, didn't Sapphire realise that? At first she won, three thousand pounds in fact. She was going to suggest that she and Sapphire went on holiday somewhere really nice. But then she thought she could make more money if she gambled with the three grand. And then she started losing heavily. And the more she lost the more she bet, convinced like so many gamblers before her that she just needed one win to make everything right. Christine concluded the sorry story by saying, 'I'm really worried that I'm going to lose the house, Sapphire, and it's all I've got.'

Sapphire was tempted to reply that her mum should have thought of that before she started gambling. Instead she said, 'We'll have to come up with a way of paying the bank and credit card companies back in instalments. I can cash in my ISA and pay off half the debts but I think you're really going to have to get some kind of job. I don't want to take any money out of the business if I can avoid it; things aren't that great at the moment.'

She wanted to say we're in the middle of a credit crunch, do you know what that is? But her mum seemed so defeated, she didn't have the heart.

Christine nodded, 'Thanks so much, Sapphire, I knew I could rely on you.'

'Just promise me, Mum, that you're going to stop gambling right now.'

'I promise, I won't go near those sites again. I'm going to get a job and I'll pay you back.

They sat in silence for a few minutes, Christine continuing to chain smoke, before Sapphire said more gently, 'Do you think you need to get help with the gambling, Mum? There are helplines you could ring.'

Christine shook her head dismissively, 'I'm not an addict, Sapphire, I just had a blip. I swear it will never happen again.'

Sapphire just prayed she could trust her.

Chapter 6

Sapphire couldn't bear to confide in anyone about her mum; it was almost as though if she didn't tell anyone then she could pretend it hadn't happened. Jay and her friends noticed she was down and kept asking her what was wrong. She shrugged it off saying she was worried about Georgia's hen weekend, and they seemed to believe her. Inside she was a mass of anxiety about her mum. She called her every day and went round to see her as much as she could, terrified that her mum might start gambling again. Christine swore that she wasn't. If only her dad were still alive, then none of this would have happened. But it was pointless to wish for that; as usual Sapphire just had to stay strong – strong enough for both her and her mum.

'So what do you want for your birthday?' Jay asked her as they lay in bed. He hadn't said the L-word again and Sapphire was almost beginning to think she must have imagined it; or that if he had said it, he had regretted it and hadn't really meant it. 'I want to get you something really special.'

Sapphire put her head on his chest, 'Well I have seen these Louboutin shoe boots on Net-a-Porter. They're wicked, very, very sexy. I'd love a pair.'

She spoke without thinking. In spite of Alfie's many,

many shortcomings he'd always been very generous at birthdays and Christmas and had lavished expensive gifts on her and she had become used to asking for lovely things. Realising her mistake she looked up at Jay.

He frowned as he said quietly, 'I'm not sure I could afford to get you those, Sapphire.'

Sapphire felt awful. 'I'm sorry, Jay, I wasn't thinking. I'll get the boots for myself if Georgia's hen weekend goes well. You could get me some perfume – I'm nearly out of Coco Chanel.'

'Okay,' Jay replied, but Sapphire sensed she had made him self-conscious. She sighed. 'To be honest, I'm really not into birthdays; you don't have to get me anything at all.'

'Of course I want to get you something!' Jay said, outraged at the suggestion, 'You're my girlfriend!'

'Okay, babe, whatever you get me I'm sure it will be lovely.' Sapphire felt too emotionally drained because of the recent events with her mum to continue the conversation and turned over.

But Jay hadn't finished. 'I bet you wish you were with someone who could buy you expensive things.'

'No, Jay, I really don't, believe me. Now please can I go to sleep, I'm knackered.'

The days before her birthday continued to be so busy that Sapphire barely gave it a second thought. She had Simone on the phone at least three times a day asking yet more questions: what beauty products did Sapphire's salon use? Would the hens be given any free samples? What thread count were the hotel's Egyptian cotton sheets? And on top of the daft questions were the outrageous demands. 'Georgia really wanted to give all her hens goodie bags with gifts, would you put those together, Sapphire? And as well as beauty products, what about some jewellery?' Each time, before she had the chance to object, she'd think about the publicity everyone would get and that stopped her from complaining. 'Good for publicity'; it had better be bloody good for publicity after all the favours Sapphire was pulling in from other businesses.

'Anyone would think Georgia was some massive Hollywood star with all these requests, instead of a C-list soap bunny,' Sapphire grumbled to Jazz after she finally managed to get Simone off the phone. 'And I wouldn't mind but she hasn't paid me a penny yet. I've sent two invoices already.'

'You know what these types are like – complete tight-wads, expecting something for nothing,' Jazz replied.

'Maybe she's waiting until she gets the money from the magazine shoot,' Sapphire wondered. 'God, and as for dealing with Simone every day, it's doing my head in! I can't believe that Cal ever went out with her! She's so demanding! I can't wait for this weekend to be over!'

'At least there's your birthday to look forward to,' Jazz pointed out.

Sapphire frowned at her friend, 'Just promise me you're not going to surprise me with anything. You know I hate surprises.'

Jazz sighed, 'That's only because you're such a control freak. Sometimes you just have to let things go. You can't be in control of everything.'

'Hmm.' Sapphire wasn't at all sure. Jazz didn't have a business to run or a mum with a gambling addiction, everything was so easy for her. To stop herself snapping at Jazz she went over to the window where Vanessa had recently finished setting up a new display of exquisite black lace La Perla lingerie. Something didn't look quite right to her and she began making changes.

'I rest my case,' Jazz called out, going back upstairs to the beauty rooms.

'I can't help it!' Sapphire shouted back. 'It's just the way I'm made!'

She knew her control freakery wasn't her most loveable quality. The trouble was she'd had to rely on herself for so long she didn't know how to behave in any other way.

On the morning of her birthday Jay brought her breakfast in bed – fresh croissants, orange juice and a glass of champagne.

'Happy birthday, babe,' he said, setting the tray on the bedside table

'This is so sweet of you!' she exclaimed, leaning over and kissing him.

'And here's one of your presents,' he said, handing her a package which she was sure was perfume. 'You'll get the other one later,' he added as Sapphire ripped off the paper to reveal the bottle of Coco Chanel.

'Thanks Jay.'

He'd just had a shower and looked gorgeous. A black towel was wrapped round his waist, showcasing his sexy chest. Sapphire took a sip of champagne and decided that she would unwrap a far more exciting present than scent as she reached out and whipped off Jay's towel. 'Now that's what I call a present,' she said, admiring what was now on view. 'Tell me it's all for me.'

'It's all for you,' Jay murmured taking her in his arms and kissing her.

Afterwards Sapphire stretched out in bed. She felt very mellow, maybe her birthday wasn't going to be so bad after all. 'So what have the girls got planned for me tonight? They just told me to dress up.'

Jay shook his head, 'No idea, they wouldn't tell me.'

'Oh come on! I bet you know,' Sapphire protested, running her hands down his body and ending up on the part which had just had a spectacular workout.

'They knew you'd try and get it out of me, so they said it was better if I didn't know,' Jay replied.

'That's because I have ways of making you talk,' Sapphire murmured, now moving down the bed and kissing Jay's chest, abs and going further still.

Just at that moment the doorbell rang. Sapphire was all set to ignore it. 'Babe, get the door,' Jay told her, 'I need a rest!'

Sapphire grabbed her black silk robe and padded to the door. She looked on the video monitor and saw a woman in the lobby holding an enormous bouquet. She buzzed the woman up and took delivery of the exquisite arrangement made up of some of her favourite flowers – white roses, yellow roses and lilies. Jay was such a sweetheart! She put the flowers on the dining table and went back into the bedroom to thank him.

'You really didn't have to, you know,' she said, walking in as he sat up in bed.

'Didn't have to what?' he asked.

'Get me those beautiful flowers, they must have cost loads.'

Jay shook his head, 'They didn't.'

Sapphire laughed at the lie. 'Well, anyway, they are beautiful and it was so clever of you to get all my favourites.'

Now Jay looked blank, 'I got you roses, babe.'

The doorbell went again. Another delivery of flowers for her. This time a sweet bouquet of twelve white roses, with a note saying, '*To my beautiful Sapphire, love Jay x.*' So who were the other flowers from?

Jay followed her into the living room and saw the first arrangement lying on the table. 'Oh, I see what you mean now,' he said, sounding slightly put out. 'So who are those from?'

Sapphire shrugged. 'No idea.' She ripped off the small white card attached to the bouquet and read it. As she took in the words, suddenly her heart felt as if it was beating that little bit faster. 'Happy Birthday Sapphire, looking forward to working with you and getting to know you better. Ryan x'

'Who are they from?' Jay repeated.

'Just Alfie's new business partner,' Sapphire said, trying her best to sound casual but aware that her cheeks were flushing. She slipped the card into her robe pocket.

'Very generous of him,' Jay said suspiciously.

'Oh you know what these businessmen are like. He just wants to make sure that I carry on using the club for the hen nights.'

'Hmm,' was all Jay said. He didn't sound convinced. Sapphire was about to reassure him when the doorbell rang again.

'More flowers?' he said with a slight edge to his voice. Sapphire tried to see it from his point of view, but really, he didn't have to be such a baby.

It wasn't more flowers but a package addressed to Sapphire. She opened it to discover the iconic blue of a Tiffany jewellery case. Inside was a beautiful diamond pendant. Who the hell could have bought her this? It was hardly likely to be her mother, and generous as Sam and Jazz usually were, she couldn't see them stretching to this. It must have cost several thousand pounds. Jay stood next to her looking at the jewel. 'Very nice. Who's it from?'

'I've no idea, babe.'

'Well, aren't you going to find out?' He sounded seriously pissed off as he handed her the small envelope that accompanied the gift.

'No way!' she said as she read the message. 'To Sapphire, Happy Birthday. I hope you can believe me when I say that I'm sorry for all the hurt I caused you. I miss us. Love Alfie x.'

'I'll have to give it back to him, there's no way I can keep it.'

It was so typical of Alfie to unsettle her like this. He'd

72

always tried to buy himself out of trouble when they were married – Sapphire had a whole drawer full of 'I'm sorry' jewellery from Alfie.

'It makes my perfume look a bit cheap, doesn't it?' Jay said, handing her back the card. He walked towards the bedroom.

'Jay! I love your present and your roses. And my breakfast in bed.' Sapphire went after him and took his arm. 'I don't want expensive presents, least of all from my ex-husband.'

Jay stood there looking so disconsolate, Sapphire couldn't bear it. She put both her arms round his neck, 'Please don't be funny about this.'

Jay remained with his arms by his side for a few seconds before he softened and put his arms round her and hugged her. 'Anyway,' he whispered, 'I still have another present for you tonight.'

'Oh good,' Sapphire murmured back, 'you know I'm more than a one-shag-a-day girl.'

'I didn't mean that,' Jay shot back.

'What then?'

'You'll have to wait and see.'

After Jay went to work, Sapphire had several text messages to send. She thanked Ryan for the flowers and told him that she was looking forward to working with him. She was tempted to add that she was looking forward to getting to know him better too, but stopped herself. To Alfie she texted: 'Thank you, but I can't accept the necklace. I'll give it back to you next time I see you.' He instantly texted back, 'It's yours. Please keep it.' He was so frustrating!

Sapphire had thought about having the day off – she hadn't taken any holiday in ages, one of the drawbacks of running your own business. She took a long shower and toyed with the idea of going shopping, but in the end she realised that she had so much on, she had better get to work. But Jazz was having none of it. As soon as Sapphire walked through the door she whisked her upstairs for some treatments.

'My birthday treat – I'm giving you a facial and a manicure. You've been working too hard lately.'

Sapphire tried to protest but Jazz continued, 'And it's the wicked witch's hen night in less than a week's time; you've got to look your best for that.'

Jazz had a determined glint in her eye and Sapphire reasoned that just this once she would give in to her demands. It had been ages since she'd had any pampering treatments and she knew she could really do with them. She was relaxed for the rest of the day after that, but as the afternoon wore on, she felt uneasy as she started to wonder what her friends had got in store for her. Frankly, she wouldn't put anything past them – one year she'd ended up in Amsterdam, another in Paris and she really didn't have time for anything like that right now.

'Happy Birthday, Sapphire!'

Sam, Cal, Jazz and her boyfriend Ben raised their glasses as Sapphire walked into the tapas bar with Jay later that night. Sapphire was relieved; she could cope with champagne and tapas. 'I can only stay for the first part of the evening, if that's okay,' Cal said as he kissed her and handed her a present. 'I'm catching an early flight to LA.'

'I'm just glad that you're here at all,' Sapphire replied. She knew how rarely Cal went out these days and appreciated that he had made the effort for her.

'So what did you think of Jay's present?' Sam asked expectantly as she gave Sapphire her gift.

'It was lovely, it's my favourite perfume,' Sapphire replied, wondering why Sam thought perfume was such a big deal.

'Oh,' Sam sounded surprised.

Sapphire saw her look enquiringly at Jay, who shrugged and said quietly, 'I haven't given it to her yet, there were too many other distractions, like diamond necklaces from her ex and flowers from someone called Ryan.'

Clearly Jay was still feeling pissed off. 'Don't be like that babe,' Sapphire implored him, 'I'm giving Alfie the necklace back the next time I see him.'

'Ryan sent you flowers?' Sam asked in a way that showed her disapproval.

Sapphire rolled her eyes, 'It was just to say that he was looking forward to working with me. It's no big deal!'

Suddenly Sapphire's birthday spirit was ebbing away.

'So aren't you going to open your presents?' Jazz asked as Sapphire looked down at the little pile in front of her.

Sapphire unwrapped the presents and she was delighted with a bejewelled cuff from Cal – he always did have fantastic taste – Moulton Brown bath oils from Jazz and a cute necklace with a collection of charms on it from Sam's own jewellery collection. Sapphire was actually impressed. She had always thought Sam's jewellery creations were just a hobby but looking at the necklace, she could see her friend had real talent.

'Not as grand as the Tiffany necklace, I'm afraid,' Sam said as Sapphire picked up the necklace and looked at the tiny silver love heart, the starfish and a pearl.

'But much nicer because it's not from a fuckwit, but from my friend,' Sapphire paused. 'Maybe I could sell some of your necklaces in the boutique.' Even on her birthday she still had her business head on.

'Really?' Sam said excitedly.

'Yeah, let's talk about it tomorrow.'

'Okay, birthday girl.' She picked up the bottle of champagne. 'Another?'

'Fill it up!' Sapphire replied holding up her glass.

After that the conversation flowed more easily between the friends and there was no further mention of Alfie or Ryan. Several times Sapphire noticed Sam exchanging looks with Jay as if the two shared a secret and she wondered what the pair had hatched up, but mostly Sapphire was enjoying herself.

In fact, all in all Sapphire was thinking that this counted as one of her best birthdays ever when Sam came out with her bombshell. 'Right, get your coats, we've got a salsa lesson in twenty minutes.'

'But you know I'm crap at doing that kind of dancing!' Sapphire wailed.

'That's why you're having lessons, sweetie!' Sam replied. 'We're having the lessons and then staying on for salsa night, it'll be fun.'

'And one two three four five six, move those hips, Sapphire, I just know you've got the Latin spirit in you!' declared the salsa teacher, a stunning woman with the petite figure of a ballerina and waist-length black hair.

'And Jay! Lovely Jay, let me see your hips!'

The group had been working on the dance moves for the last forty minutes, and in spite of her earlier reservations Sapphire was loving it. Jay was fantastic, as was Sam. In fact, Sam's dancing was a revelation – she moved with fluidity and grace. It was Jazz and Sapphire who were slower to pick up the moves, but still, Sam was right it was fun. *Strictly Come Dancing* eat your heart out . . .

They didn't end up leaving the club until half two. Back at the apartment Sapphire collapsed on the sofa, 'That was just the best night ever!' she declared, slipping off her shoes and wincing because her feet were killing her.

'So you'll come dancing with me again?' Jay asked, sitting next to her. He began massaging her toes. He's so lovely! Sapphire thought as he eased away the tension.

'Definitely, babe! Even though you're a way better mover than me and you know how competitive I am,' she leant in for a kiss.

'So, he murmured, 'are you ready for your next present?'

'Oh yeah, baby!' Sapphire exclaimed, slipping her hands inside his shirt and caressing his smooth skin.

'You can have that one later; I've got something else for you first. Close your eyes.'

'Jay, you really didn't have to get me anything else!' Sapphire protested.

'I did, now close your eyes and hold out your hand.'

Sapphire did as she was told, hoping that Jay hadn't spent too much money. She still felt guilty about her request for the Louboutin boots. Jay placed a small object in the palm of her hand. Sapphire was relieved: at least he hadn't maxed out his credit card getting the boots.

'Okay, you can open them now.'

The relief vanished when she discovered a red velvet jewellery box. When she opened it she felt as if her heart had stopped beating from shock because there was a ring. And not just any old ring, it was unmistakeably a diamond engagement ring. She looked over to Jay who now had moved off the sofa and was on one knee. This was so wrong, off the scale wrong, in fact! Sapphire's mind scrambled to make sense of what was happening.

'Sapphire, I know we haven't been together long but I love you and I know with all my heart that you are the one for me; you're the woman I want to spend the rest of my life with.' Jay gazed at Sapphire, his beautiful brown eyes, warm and passionate. 'So will you?' There was such hope and longing in his voice.

Sapphire had a sick feeling in the pit of her stomach and her mouth suddenly felt as dry as sandpaper. There was no way, just no way that she could possibly say yes. She hesitated for a just a second before saying, 'Jay, I'm really sorry but no. I can't marry you. I don't want to marry anyone. I thought you knew that.'

Jay looked as if he had been struck. 'Won't you at least think about what I've asked? I love you, Sapphire.'

If you had to dream up the perfect man Jay would tick every box – he had stunning good looks, a lovely personality, a strong character and was fantastic in bed. There were so many other women who would have jumped at his proposal. But right now all Sapphire felt was completely suffocated and she wanted to pretend the proposal had never happened.

'Jay, I love what I have with you, but I'm just not ready for anything more right now.'

Jay stood up now, 'And what exactly do you have with me, Sapphire? I'm just your fuck buddy, aren't I? You see me when you want, on your terms, and you never quite let me in, do you?' The warmth and passion in his eyes had now been replaced with wounded pride.

'That's not true, Jay, I do let you in. You're the first man I've had a proper relationship with since my marriage broke up. And I'm sorry if I don't want to marry you and I've hurt your feelings but that's just the way it is.' Sapphire felt a steely determination inside her; she was not going to be made to feel bad just because she wanted different things to Jay. It wasn't her fault that he had proposed. God knows she had never asked for that!

'Well, I'm tired of it being a casual thing!' Jay exclaimed angrily. 'And I'm sick of you never taking me seriously. I'm not just your boy toy, Sapphire.'

'I know you're not! But as for the rest, come on Jay, you don't exactly live in the fast lane do you? Are you going to be a personal trainer for the rest of your life?'

Jay glared at her, 'D'you know what? Fuck you, Sapphire.'

And with that he grabbed his jacket and stormed out of the flat, slamming the door behind him.

What the fuck! Sapphire was furious – firstly at the whole proposal and then at Jay for leaving like that. And it was her birthday! She was too wired to sleep, instead she curled up on one of the armchairs with a glass of brandy.

She stared out of the window and into the darkness; the lights strung along the seafront, the inky black sea in the distance. Why did Jay have to complicate things like this? She had been perfectly happy with the way things were. She hated feeling under pressure. She looked back into the living room and the bouquet of flowers Ryan had sent her caught her eye. All she had ever wanted from a man since Alfie was fun, flirtation and very good sex. Why wasn't that enough for Jay?

Because of her late night she didn't get into work until midday. But if she was hoping to forget about the events of the night before she was in for a shock as both Jazz and Sam looked at her expectantly when she walked in.

'Well?' Sam asked, 'How did it go?'

She was beaming at Sapphire. Clearly Sam must have known all along that Jay planned to propose. Jay had obviously bought the ring at her store, probably with Sam's advice. It was irrational but Sapphire suddenly felt furious with Sam. She, of all people, knew how Sapphire felt about marriage; why hadn't she made Jay see sense?

Sapphire ignored the question, 'I don't know what you mean, why aren't you at work?' She couldn't stop herself sounding cold and offhand.

'I've brought my jewellery range round, remember? You said you might be able to stock it in the boutique?' Sam replied, frowning at Sapphire's tone. 'What's your problem? I thought last night was great.'

'Yeah, Sapphire, why've you got the hump?' Jazz put in.

Whoa! Her friends were skating on thin ice! Sapphire again ignored the question, walked over to one of the lingerie displays and began checking that the bras were in the right size order. She efficiently clicked through the hangers, the model store owner, but all the while she could feel anger building up inside her.

'What is your problem, Sapphire? You've got the most gorgeous boyfriend who adores you! Sometimes you really can be the most ungrateful bitch!' Sam exclaimed, sounding as if she had seriously lost her cool. She never usually spoke to Sapphire like this, it was a shock.

Sapphire swung round. 'What? Because I didn't want to get engaged to Jay! You knew he was going to propose didn't you? Why the fuck didn't you try and persuade him not to? You know I absolutely never want to get married again!' Sapphire had lost her cool as well.

'Why?' Sam advanced towards Sapphire, hands on hips. 'Maybe I think that Jay is the best thing that ever happened to you,' she was shouting now, 'and that it's wonderful that he's in love with you, and that you could have a fantastic relationship with him. I can't believe you can be so dismissive of him!'

'Fuck off, Sam! I don't care what you think!' Sapphire let rip. Sam took a step backwards, stunned at Sapphire's vicious tone. 'Yes, Jay's a nice guy, a lovely guy, but all I'm looking for is fun. I never want to be tied down to one person ever again. *Ever!*'

Jazz moved towards them, 'Come on, guys, take a chill pill.'

Sapphire shook her head. 'I'm sorry, I feel really wound up. I'm going for a walk. Leave your necklaces on the counter, I'll sort them out later.'

And without giving Sam and Jazz a second glance she stormed out of the boutique, slamming the door behind her. She was oblivious to her surroundings as she practically ran through the Lanes and towards the seafront. She needed to get away from everyone, needed space right now.

It was a glorious October day, the sky a wonderful bright blue, the air fresh when she breathed it in; the sea was millpond flat, the cries of the gulls harsh but familiar to her and somehow comforting. It was still warm enough to sit outside and people were sipping lattes, chatting and laughing, while Sapphire stormed past them. Fuck fuck fuck! Why did this have to happen? She was so lost in her thoughts that she failed to notice Ryan running towards her along the promenade.

'Hey, Sapphire!' Ryan called out. She looked up to see a vision of male gorgeousness standing in front of her. Ryan was wearing a tight black vest and sweatpants. The vest showcased some pretty impressive pecs. Suddenly some of Sapphire's spectacularly bad mood started to lift.

'Hi,' she smiled back warmly. 'Thank you so much for the flowers, they were stunning.'

'It was my pleasure,' Ryan replied, then lifted his vest to wipe his face, showing off some even more impressive abs and gorgeous golden-brown skin. A shot of pure lust replaced the anger pulsing round her body. Sapphire had to stop herself from staring. The man was hot, hottie hot!

'So what are you doing?' he continued, while Sapphire hoped that her face wasn't betraying just how attractive she found him.

'Just needed a walk to clear my head. I've got a lot on at the moment.'

'Too much to let me take you for lunch?'

Sapphire considered the invitation. A day out with Ryan might be just what she needed after last night and would surely help put everything in perspective.

You want to flirt with him, her conscience pricked her, while the bad-girl side tried to make out the day was just about business. Bad girl won.

'I'd love to.'

'Fantastic. I'll meet you in Hotel du Vin, at say, half one. I should take a shower first.'

'Fine, see you then,' Sapphire replied, businesslike and professional. Little did he know she was having a deliciously dirty thought about him in the shower . . .

Sapphire phoned Vanessa and told her she wouldn't be coming in for the rest of the day. She was still too annoyed with Jazz to speak to her. And as for Sam, well Sapphire was going to take her time apologising to her. In fact she felt it should be Sam doing the apologising. She couldn't believe the way her friend was treating her. She also expected to hear from Jay but nothing from him either. She did not take kindly to being told to fuck off. He would have some serious grovelling to do.

She headed back to her apartment and took ages deciding what to wear. The ring box was still lying on the coffee table. Sapphire could almost feel it looking at her accusingly as she padded around getting ready. She picked it up and opened the box. A pretty, three-diamond, white-gold engagement ring sparkled back at her. Somehow the sight of it aggravated her even more. If she ever did get engaged again, and this was speaking hypothetically because she was *never* going to get engaged again, she wanted a bloody whopper of a ring! She stuffed the box at the back of her dressing table drawer and carried on getting ready.

Just then her mobile rang. It was Jay.

'Hi,' Sapphire said curtly.

Jay sighed. 'Look, I'm sorry I said fuck you, but you really pushed me last night. I don't even think I should be phoning you after everything that happened. But I knew you wouldn't call me. And I don't like playing games, Sapphire.'

'Nor do I,' Sapphire shot back.

'Can't we just go back to how we were?' Jay replied. 'Forget last night ever happened, it was a mistake, okay? I'll never mention it again.'

This was more like it.

'*Okay*, the way we were, then,' her mood had softened towards him.

'And by the way it's my dad's birthday meal tonight, you said you'd come, remember?'

Not such good news. 'Sure, I'll be there.'

'And don't mention what happened last night, I don't want anyone to know.'

'Fine by me, see you later, babe.'

With the reconciliation complete Sapphire could focus on getting ready. She was glad they had made up, she didn't like things to be unresolved. As she didn't want Ryan to think that she'd made too much effort, she decided to wear her skinny jeans, black knee-high boots with killer heels, a sheer black shirt and a black leather jacket. As she made one final check in the mirror before setting out she was starting to feel in a much better mood. She knew she looked good. And the expression on Ryan's face when she walked into the bar of Hotel du Vin told her that he thought so too. Sapphire felt herself glowing under his gaze.

As they sipped champagne and talked Ryan made no secret of the fact that he found Sapphire very attractive, giving her appraising looks, making her feel that he only had eyes for her. He seemed interested in everything she had to say and wanted to know all about how she started her own business. She in turn was very interested in him. He intrigued her and was definitely more than just a pretty face. He was thirty-three and for the last five years had been running clubs in Ibiza, and before that he was a model.

'I'll have to Google you when I get back,' she joked.

'Ah, my glory days of defined abs,' he replied.

Sapphire thought back to the morning when she'd caught a glimpse of his abs and golden-brown skin. He still looked bloody good! But he didn't seem like he needed the compliment so she kept it to herself. Before the modelling he'd played in a band, taught scuba diving and travelled round the world. Now he wanted to make a success of the club and maybe start others around the country. It was refreshing talking to someone about business and who'd had such a varied career. There was only so much interest she could show in Jay's work as a personal trainer.

The subtle flirting continued over lunch. Sapphire felt as if all her senses were on high alert. She was hyper-conscious of her body and of his. When her hand brushed against his as she reached for her glass she felt as if she'd had an electric shock.

'So, how come you got the name Sapphire?' Ryan asked.

Sapphire smiled, 'My mum wanted to call me Sara but my dad said that wasn't nearly exciting enough for his daughter and that he wanted me to be called Sapphire, to match my blue eyes. Dad didn't realise that all babies are born with blue eyes – luckily for him, and me, my eyes stayed blue.'

Ryan did another of his direct gazes into her eyes, 'They're an incredible colour.' He paused. 'But then you're an incredibly beautiful woman.'

Sapphire, who always tried to come across as uber-cool in her dealings with men, felt herself blush. She mumbled, 'I'm not, but thank you,' doing a mental head slap for sounding so unsure of herself.

Ryan was having none of it, 'Oh, I think you know the effect you have on men.' Another pause, then he said softly, 'You're having quite an effect on me. I've hardly stopped thinking about you since we met.'

Sapphire's stomach flipped dangerously. Fortunately or unfortunately, Sapphire was feeling too flustered to decide which, the waiter arrived with their main courses – sea bass for her, duck for Ryan – and she was saved from having to reply. Instead she steered the conversation in a completely different direction asking Ryan how he met Alfie and what plans they had for the club.

Ryan answered all her questions as if they amused him before leaning over the table and saying, 'You can't distract me that easily. I told you, I've hardly stopped thinking about you.'

'I've got a boyfriend,' Sapphire replied, flicking her hair back, still trying to play it cool.

'Lucky him . . . what does he do?'

'He's a personal trainer.'

Ryan's lips twitched, 'Impressive body I imagine.'

'Very,' Sapphire replied, trying to channel thoughts of Jay and how lovely he was to stop the lustful thoughts of Ryan that were taking over her mind.

'But—' Ryan hesitated.

'But what?'

'I can't imagine he's your equal. I would have thought it wouldn't take much for a woman like you to get bored.'

Sapphire shook her head, 'Actually, you're wrong. Jay is a lovely guy. I'm lucky to have him.'

She suddenly felt horribly disloyal sitting flirting with Ryan. She was sure Jay would never behave like this with another woman. It's just business, she tried to tell herself. But she knew it wasn't just business. For the remainder of the meal she did her best to pull herself together, to stop all the eye contact, but still she was aware of Ryan's gaze, of his long legs just inches away from hers. And Ryan was on a mission to know more about her. 'I'm sure Alfie would be jealous if he knew we were having lunch together.'

'Why do you say that?'

'I think he realises he made a mistake when he let you go.'

'He didn't let me go! I divorced him for cheating on me!'

Ryan leant closer. 'For what it's worth, I think he was a fool.'

'Yeah, well, he's ancient history now, believe me.'

'So you don't have any feelings for him any more?' Ryan continued.

Sapphire shook her head. 'I can just about face seeing him about business but that's it.'

Ryan smiled, as if satisfied with her answer.

After the meal, which he insisted on paying for, despite Sapphire's protestations – usually she always paid or went half – he asked if she had time for a coffee in the bar. They'd spent so long over lunch it was already five. She was due at Jay's family in an hour and a half. She should probably make a move, but somehow she wasn't ready to leave just yet. She was enjoying his company far too much.

While Ryan ordered coffee, Sapphire nipped to the bathroom and checked herself in the mirror. Her cheeks were flushed and there was a glint in her eye. It's nothing, she tried to tell herself, I'm just window shopping, no more than that, but she took her time touching up her make-up all the same.

When she returned she discovered that Ryan had chosen a sofa in the darkest, most intimate part of the bar. There were no other chairs, she would have to sit next to him. 'I thought we were just having coffee!' she exclaimed as Ryan handed her a rather large brandy.

He smiled and held up his glass, 'Cheers, thanks for coming out for lunch with me, Sapphire.'

'Thank you,' she clinked her glass against his. Ryan stretched out his arms, so one was draped near her shoulder. She could feel to the warmth of his arm through her flimsy shirt. He was so sure of himself, it was very sexy. She'd missed that with Jay. She was always the one paying for dinner when they went out, even though he always offered, but he couldn't possibly afford to take her to the places she wanted to go. She couldn't deny that it was nice being treated for a change.

'So, do you have a girlfriend?' she asked, trying to ignore the delicious rush she was getting from being so close to him.

He shook his head, 'Just split up with someone. I'm entirely single.'

Suddenly a treacherous thought snaked its way into Sapphire's head that right now she wished that she was as well. Then she'd be free to flirt with Ryan and not just flirt . . .

He took another sip of his champagne. 'So, how long have you been seeing your boyfriend?'

'Nearly five months.'

'As long as that? Time for the five-month itch, isn't it?' He grinned wickedly.

Sapphire shrugged. She could have defended what she had with Jay, which after all, for the most part was very good, but the devil inside her made her say, 'Yeah, it probably is.' She sipped her brandy and looked at Ryan. 'Actually he just asked me to marry him.'

As soon as she said it she felt another stab of disloyalty. Why was she doing this? She just couldn't help herself.

'He's keen. I admire his style. But,' another pause, another considering look, 'you're not the marrying kind any more are you?'

'Why d'you say that?'

'Just a feeling I get. You're like me, you don't want to be tied down to one person, you want to experience everything life has to offer. I see a lot of myself in you.'

'How much exactly?' Sapphire asked naughtily, wondering how many inches, then giggled. 'Sorry I didn't mean that.'

'Bet you'd like to know, wouldn't you?' Ryan leant closer to her. Sapphire was aware she was now in extremely dangerous territory. It was time to pull back. She shook her head, 'No, no. That's one thing I have plenty of, believe me.'

'There's always room for an upgrade though, isn't there?' Ryan said softly.

If it had been any other man bragging about his sexual prowess Sapphire would have been quick off the mark with a put-down. Somehow Ryan left her lost for words.

Suddenly she remembered the time. She checked her watch. Shit! It was nearly seven. She was horribly late for Jay's. 'Look, I've really got to go, thanks so much for lunch.'

'Next time we'll do dinner,' Ryan told her, standing up and helping her on with her jacket. Again she felt a rush of lust at his touch. Bad girl. 'It was good to spend time with you Sapphire, I hope I'll see you again soon,' he said, then ducked down and kissed her cheek.

Sapphire practically ran out of the bar, not easy as she was in her high boots, and raced into an off-licence to buy a bottle of champagne, then dashed to the taxi rank. She checked her phone, there was already a text from Jay asking where she was – 'am on my way, sorry', she texted back.

During the taxi journey Sapphire tried to compose herself. She felt light-headed, not just from drinking at lunch time but also from all the flirting with Ryan. At the time it had been so intoxicating and exciting, knowing how much he wanted her. Now guilt was creeping in. She never should have behaved like that, what had she been thinking of? It was all very well blaming Jay for his proposal, which had derailed her; she knew she had crossed a line. But the fact was she really did find Ryan very attractive. She just about managed to pull herself together by the time the taxi drew up outside a small terraced house. Clearly Jay's family were not afraid of colour as the house was painted purple with sky blue doors and window frames. Jay's mum, Vicky, opened the door to her. She was a very pretty blonde in her mid-forties, dressed in skinny jeans and a cute red T-shirt with a cherry motif that Sapphire had her eye on in Topshop.

'You must be Sapphire. Come on in!' Sapphire stretched out her hand but instead Vicky gave her a warm hug and kiss on the cheek and led Sapphire downstairs to the large basement kitchen–dining room where the family were well into their first course.

Immediately Jay leapt from his chair and hugged her. 'Where were you babe? I was worried.'

'Sorry, I got held up in a business meeting.' God, she hated herself for lying.

'Come on, Jay, let Sapphire sit down and pour her a drink, she's probably had a really long day.' Vicky declared, making Sapphire feel even more guilty.

Sapphire sat opposite Jay's twin sisters, Estelle and Marissa, two stunning fifteen-year-old girls.

'You're well too good-looking to be going out with Jay!' Marissa exclaimed.

'Just ignore them,' Jay said, 'They're total air heads.' He introduced her to his dad Clayton next, a tall, handsome man in his late forties.

'Happy birthday,' she said, getting the champagne out of her bag.

'The good stuff,' Clayton replied. 'Thank you Sapphire.' He looked over at his son and said, 'Keep this one Jay!'

'If she plays her card right,' Jay said cheekily.

Marissa piped up, 'You're older than Jay aren't you?'

'Yep, Jay's her boy toy,' Estelle put in, causing both girls to giggle.

'Nothing wrong with that!' Vicky protested, 'I wish I'd had one instead of an older man like you, Clayton! But he cradle-snatched me when I was eighteen.'

'And how old was I? All of twenty? You were the one who had her eye on me if I remember.' He turned to

Sapphire. 'I had no chance when we met at the Honey Club in Brighton.'

'Cheek! You were the one who went after me!' Vicky exclaimed.

Jay rolled his eyes at Sapphire. 'Sorry, babe, you see what I have to put up with.'

As Jay opened the bottle and poured out champagne, Sapphire was struck by the warmth and energy of his family and by the easy chatter flowing between them all. It was so different from her strained conversations with her own mum, where neither of them ever really said what they felt. 'You're lucky,' Sapphire told him, 'it's no fun being an only child.'

Vicky overheard and asked Sapphire about her family. Usually Sapphire hated talking about her mum and about her dad dying, but Vicky was so easy to talk to, so sympathetic, that she found herself opening up, telling them how worried she was that her mum hardly seemed to do anything or have any kind of life. She didn't mention the gambling.

'She's only fifty and yet she acts as if her life is over, it's so depressing.'

'Why don't you get your mum to come over here? I'm a hairdresser and I work from home, I'd love to give her a new look. I always want my clients to make the best of themselves.' Vicky's face lit up – she obviously really enjoyed her work.

'Well, Mum's certainly not doing that at the moment,' Sapphire said drily, recalling that the last time she saw Christine she was wearing a baggy velour purple track-suit that had seen better days.

'Interrogation over!' Clayton ruled. 'Let the poor girl eat.'

Sapphire looked down at the food piled on her plate. She wasn't in the least bit hungry. She managed a few mouthfuls of chicken and glanced round the room. The kitchen–dining room was a riot of colour – the walls were burnt orange and covered in photographs of the family and in the children's drawings from when they were little; there was a fire blazing away in the fireplace, a fat ginger cat asleep in front of it, a green velvet sofa covered in brightly coloured cushions. The whole feel of the place was warm and vibrant. Sapphire thought of her mum's house – the sterile, white kitchen that was always spotless, the living room cluttered with furniture and memories from another time. Now on top of feeling guilty about Jay, she was feeling guilty about her mum.

'That was delicious,' she said, putting her knife and fork down.

'Jay cooked, he's good isn't he?' Vicky replied.

Sapphire looked at Jay and suffered another pang of guilt about Ryan. It must not happen again. She might not believe in relationships but one thing she did believe in was staying faithful to the person she was with at the time.

At the end of the meal she offered to clear up with Jay.

'I bet you two just want to cop off together,' Marissa said cheekily.

'If you want to do the washing up,' Jay replied, 'be my guest.'

Marissa made a hasty exit upstairs to the living room.

'So,' he said, putting his arms round Sapphire once they were alone in the kitchen,'it wasn't so bad meeting my family was it?'

She stood up on tiptoes and lightly kissed him. 'Not bad at all,' she replied, then kissed him again, this time deeper.

If she could just take Jay back home with her and make love she'd be able to erase all memories of sexy Ryan. She wrapped her arms round him tightly, 'You know I love being with you, Jay.' She pressed her body into his and closed her eyes. Lovely Jay with his lovely body, more than a match for Ryan any day. 'Come back to mine, I still haven't had my extra birthday present, babe.'

She was so used to Jay doing exactly what she asked that it was a shock when he shook his head and said, 'No, I need some headspace after last night.'

'But I thought we were back to the way we were?' Sapphire said petulantly.

'We are, I just need some time.'

Sapphire felt irrationally angry. 'Okay, I'll call a taxi now then, and you can get your fucking headspace.'

'I'll call the cab, we can share it.'

They did the washing up in silence. Sapphire snapped out of her bad mood to say goodbye to Jay's family. She really had liked them. But she returned to giving Jay the silent treatment in the taxi, not even sitting close to him. She was furious that he wasn't coming back with her. When the taxi pulled up outside her apartment she was all set to get out with a curt goodbye, but Jay took her arm.

'Babe,' he whispered, and for a second Sapphire thought he might have changed his mind, 'it does you good to not always get your own way.'

Bastard! Sapphire muttered 'Bye' and got out of the taxi, slamming the door behind her. She stomped into the lobby and jabbed the button for the lift. She momentarily cheered up when she discovered she had a text from Ryan, 'Still thinking of you Sapphire, Rx.' She spent the next ten minutes wondering what to text back. She didn't want to seem too flirtatious in her reply, but neither was she able to simply ignore the message. In the end she went for 'Thanks for a lovely lunch, my treat next time, Sx'. She ignored the voice in her head which told her she was playing with fire. And she couldn't help thinking that Ryan would have jumped at the chance to come back with her . . .

Chapter 7

Sapphire took her time saying sorry to Sam for the row. It was three days before she finally picked up the phone. Sam seemed fine about it, but Sapphire could tell that she had upset her.

'Look, I'm sorry Sam; I shouldn't have spoken to you like that, I was out of order. It's just that you know what I feel about marriage.'

'I don't want you to be blind to what you've got. Jay is a really special guy.'

There Sam went again, telling Sapphire what to think, it was infuriating. And Sam never usually had such strong opinions about things. Sapphire would have liked to tell her to back off but didn't want another argument so she sighed and said, 'I know he is and I will make it up to him.' She paused, 'I just don't want to marry him. Anyway I've got to go, Georgia's hen party's tomorrow; I'm up to my eyes in it.'

Sam wished her luck as they said goodbye, but there was still a coolness between the two friends. Sapphire didn't have time to worry about it right now. She hadn't been lying to Sam – she was desperate to make sure that everything went smoothly for Georgia's big weekend.

The eight hens arrived at the boutique at two the next day for their beauty treatments. It was an invasion of soap stars and C-list celebs. The beauty salon was quite spacious but the hens packed it out with their massive designer bags and the air was sickly sweet with eight different designer perfumes competing with each other. Clearly more was more where these hens were concerned. And God they were noisy – if they weren't screeching at each other and cackling, they were screaming down their mobiles. Sapphire didn't think she had ever seen so many fake boobs and hair extensions in one room at the same time. And she nearly got the giggles when one of the hens – a glamour model called Erin, who was beyond orange – wanted a spray tan. Sapphire couldn't imagine what colour she was aiming to be, certainly no colour seen on a human before.

At first everything seemed to be going smoothly, apart from Danielle, a singer who had had one hit record after coming second on a reality show, getting the hump when she was told she couldn't smoke in the salon. Georgia adored the house and was full of compliments. But within half an hour Simone Fraser came and found Sapphire in the boutique to complain that the hot water in her hotel bathroom was not hot enough.

'Well did you take it up with them?' Sapphire asked 'There's nothing I can do.' What was she, a freaking plumber?

'You could at least give them a ring, isn't that all part of the service?' Simone replied.

God, she was high maintenance! Sapphire just didn't get how Cal could ever have gone out with her, but maybe he just made a massive error of judgement, though in fairness Simone was undeniably pretty. She had long glossy brunette hair, a heart-shaped face, large brown eyes, and a slender figure. But she ruined her looks by having a permanent sulky expression on her face. And she'd had something done to her lips, which protruded weirdly – it was not quite a trout pout but it was close. Lady, Sapphire wanted to say, you need to step away from the Botox/collagen/Restylane whatever else you've had pumped into you. And being so slim was definitely more ageing. She was only thirty but looked much older.

'Okay, okay, I'll phone them,' Sapphire promised, anything to get the woman off her back. 'Is there anything else?'

Simone looked at her intently. 'Are you seeing Cal Bailey?'

Sapphire had been expecting another whinge so the question caught her off guard. 'What do you mean, seeing? He's one of my oldest friends.'

'I saw the pictures of the two of you together last month. It all seemed very cosy. But I thought you should know that Cal's a real player.' She was now looking absolute daggers.

Sapphire decided to play it cool. Simone was a client; it simply wouldn't do to tell her to fuck off, which is what she itched to do. She smiled. 'Like I said, we're just friends.'

Simone looked sceptical. 'You can tell me the truth, I won't tell anyone. And I could give you some good advice on how to handle Cal.'

Yeah! Like your relationship with Cal worked out so well! Sapphire thought. She wouldn't confide in Simone if she was the last person on this earth.

'Really, we're just friends,' Sapphire said calmly.

Simone gave a false little laugh,'You know that's exactly what Angel told me about her relationship with Cal. And look at what happened to them.'

Sapphire was about to reply when there was an ear-piercing shriek from the beauty salon upstairs, followed by, 'How dare you say that! Of course I haven't got a fucking verruca!'

Shit! It sounded like all hell was breaking loose up

there. Sapphire quickly raced upstairs. There she was confronted with the sight of Kiki holding her face and shouting, 'You can't bloody hit me you old cow!' as Georgia stood over her, barefoot and furious. She had a white face mask on which was cracking as her features contorted in rage. 'Well don't fucking say I've got a verruca then!'

'Actually, you haven't just got one! I saw at least three,' Kiki shouted back.

Georgia lurched forward. Sapphire quickly stepped in front of her to stop another assault. 'Now, why don't we all calm down. Kiki, can you go downstairs and work in the boutique for me, and I'll finish off Georgia's pedicure? I'm sure it's all been a misunderstanding. In the meantime, who wants another glass of champagne?'

All the hens shouted back 'yes!' There were already four empty bottles. Jesus, these women could put it away. She managed to get Georgia to sit down and steered Kiki out of the room.

'I could do her for assault you know,' Kiki told Sapphire when they were safely downstairs. 'Look.' She moved her hand to show off an angry red mark on her face.

That was not the kind of publicity Sapphire wanted! 'Please don't, Kiki! I'm begging you. I know she was bang out of order, but I'll make it up to you, I swear.'

'You'd better,' Kiki muttered then added, 'By the way she does have verrucas – watch out for her right foot,' as Sapphire turned to go back upstairs. 'Just don't touch any part of your body with your hands and wash them straight after and you should be okay.'

Great! She was going to end up covered with verrucas, just how much better could the day get? She had finally managed to calm Georgia down, with more champagne and finish painting her nails a hot pink (and yes, she did have several verrucas, yuk) when Owen, the photographer from the celeb magazine, a tall intense-looking thirty-something man with steel-rimmed glasses, arrived.

'My brief is to be a fly on the wall and capture the day,' he told Georgia and was all set to start taking pictures of her straight away, face mask and all.

'Hold your fucking horses, mate!' Georgia exclaimed. 'I'm not going to be photographed looking like a minger! I want full make-up and my hair done.'

'But that wasn't what I was asked to do: the magazine specifically said fly on the wall,' Owen protested, but really it was futile. Having necked practically a bottle of champagne, Georgia was a force to be reckoned with. 'You can snap away all you like once I've been made up – until then keep that lens right away from me.'

Owen looked thoroughly fed up. Sapphire took him to one side, 'Look, why don't you grab a coffee downstairs. You'll get better pictures if she's happy. We won't be long, I promise.'

Famous last words. It took another hour and a half and all Jazz's skill and patience to get Georgia ready. She hated the first make-up Jazz applied, saying it was too natural-looking. 'But you're supposed to be relaxing, do you really want the full works?' Jazz asked.

'Of course I want the full fucking works and then I'm going to be fucking air brushed!' Georgia held up her empty champagne glass, 'Sapphire, be a darling and fill me up. Tyler won't let me drink any more, this is my last fling then I'm on the wagon.'

Sapphire took the glass. It was only four in the after-noon. Georgia was going to be completely hammered by tonight. It did not bode well. She gave Georgia a refill – like she needed it – and went back downstairs to the boutique. In her office she checked her messages and groaned. Andy, the stripogram she had booked to surprise Georgia, had flu and there was no way he could come out. She phoned him straight away and begged him to do the booking, but he refused. He'd catch his death and was sweating like a pig and had a temperature of over a hundred.

Fuck! What was she going to do? She tried all her other contacts but they were booked solid. 'Darling,' one of them told her in a voice heavy with sarcasm, when she pleaded with him to help her out, 'if I could clone myself I would, but I can't be in two places at once and the first booking has to take priority.'

It was on the tip of Sapphire's tongue to tell him to get a penis enlargement while he was at it, as from what she could recall he didn't have that much to flaunt, but there was no point. One day she might need his sharp tongue and tiny dick. She put her head in her hands. God, how she wanted this weekend to be over. Just then there was a knock at the door and Simone sauntered in.

'I just wondered what time you've booked the stripper for tonight.' She held up her hands and looked at her immaculate French manicure.

'Bad news I'm afraid, the guy I normally use has just cancelled, he's got flu.'

'It's probably only man flu, surely he'll still do it.'

'No, it's flu. He wouldn't let me down unless he absolutely had to.'

'But Georgia is expecting a stripper,' Simone exclaimed, looking sternly at Sapphire and folding her arms across her chest like she meant business. 'What are you going to do about it? She'll be really pissed off if there isn't one. And I mean *really* pissed off. You saw what she was like about the verruca slur.'

'Okay, okay I'm taking care of it.'

Simone arched one of her perfectly shaped eyebrows. 'I advise you to do just that. You want her to talk up your business don't you?'

Fuck! What was Sapphire going to do? Go out and pick

up some fit lad off the street and ask him to do it? She'd get arrested for sexual harassment! She paced round the office, willing inspiration to come, and suddenly she realised she had a fit lad of her very own: Jay. He would be absolutely perfect.

'No way, Sapphire! You can't ask him,' was Jazz's predictable reaction.

'I can't risk pissing Georgia off again. You saw what she's like, the woman's a fucking Rottweiler!'

'Think about it the other way round – how would you feel if Jay asked you to strip for a stag night?'

Sapphire shrugged, 'It's not the same thing at all and anyway, this is about business. *My* business.'

Jazz sighed. 'I just hope you know what you're doing.'

Sapphire picked up her phone, trying to push the doubts out of her mind. 'It's got to be done.'

However, it was no easy task persuading Jay. At first he refused point blank. Sapphire begged some more, saying that the success of the hen weekend depended on him doing this one little thing for her and didn't he want her to do well? She laid it on thick. Without Jay, the weekend would be ruined; Sapphire's reputation would be in tatters. It was appalling emotional blackmail but she was desperate. Finally Jay threw her a lifeline, 'I'm not taking everything off. I'll strip to my boxers and that's it.'

Thank God, Jay was giving in. 'Babe, I will so make this up to you, I swear.'

'You *so* will,' Jay replied grimly. 'And I don't want any of the women touching me.'

'No touching, I promise. Jay you've saved me, you're a complete star.'

It would have been the perfect moment to tell him that she loved him but Sapphire just couldn't. She really liked Jay, but love?

They ended the call by agreeing that Jay would turn up at the bar in black tie and Sapphire would arrange to have the Bond theme playing. Perfect, what could go wrong?

Three hours later she met up with the hen party in one of the flash new bars by the seafront. They'd switched from champagne and were now drinking tequila shots. They were all pissed – except Simone.

'Sapphire! Come and sit down with us!' Georgia called out when she saw her.

'We were just talking about our favourite sex position. Mine's on top, obviously, so I can check out my very expensive boobs, Erin's is from behind, and Danielle's is a cheeky 69 – what about you?'

Georgia's hair and make-up still looked immaculate, and only the glassy glaze in her violet eyes gave her away. Sapphire laughed, 'I never kiss and tell.'

'I bet you're a really dirty one aren't you?' Georgia persisted. 'I could just imagine you dressed up in black leather and whipping some fit bloke.'

'No, I've never been into bondage.'

She exchanged a look with Owen, the photographer, who was looking distinctly uncomfortable. As she went over to the bar to check that Lee, the manager, was happy with the music, Owen followed her over. 'They're completely caned. Lucky I've got most of the shots. I'll just stay on for the restaurant and then head off. Are all hen parties like this?' He looked scared. 'Usually I just cover the celeb weddings and I'm going to stick to them in future.'

Sapphire laughed, 'No, this lot are especially extreme.'

'Georgia just asked me to get my cock out because she had a bet about how big it was! They're like bloody beasts! I pity the stripper you've lined up.'

Suddenly Sapphire started to get a very bad feeling. She looked back towards the group. Georgia was inviting men sitting at the next table to guess which of the hens had boob jobs and was getting very cosy with one of the lads. So cosy that when he said he'd never felt a fake boob before, she took his hand and put it firmly on her right breast. 'What do you reckon? Feels good doesn't it?'

'Very,' the lad agreed, leering and having a good old grope.

'One for the magazine spread?' Sapphire whispered to Owen.

'I tell you, wild beasts,' he replied darkly.

At that moment Jay walked into the bar. He looked absolutely male-model gorgeous in a black tuxedo. Immediately Sapphire gave Lee the signal and he switched from pulsing house music to the Bond theme. Sapphire pointed out the table to Jay and he strode over, looking mean and moody and very very sexy. He took his position next to Georgia, who had brushed away the groper and was staring transfixed at Jay. 'I really hope you are what I think you are!' she exclaimed.

Without saying a word Jay pulled off the black bow tie. The hens wolf-whistled in appreciation as he shrugged off his black jacket and began unbuttoning his white shirt. Sapphire edged closer to the group, praying things would go as planned.

'You are one fit boy!' Georgia exclaimed. 'The best-looking stripper I've ever had! Not that I've had you yet.' She gave one of her raucous cackles which instantly set Sapphire's teeth on edge.

Jay continued to say nothing. By now he was stripped to the waist, allowing everyone to see his abs of steel, his gorgeous smooth skin and toned chest. He turned round to show off the black tattoo of the jaguar rippling across his shoulders, then faced the hens again.

'Oh, I have got to touch those abs!' Georgia exclaimed, reaching out and nearly falling off her chair as Jay took a step backwards.

'Me too! exclaimed the other hens all getting off their

seats, surrounding Jay and running their hands over his abs.

Jay looked over at Sapphire his eyes pleading her to stop but she just gave a false little smile and did the thumbs up. Surely Jay wouldn't object to a little feel? It was harmless fun. But that wasn't what the women had in mind and suddenly Georgia was attempting to unbuckle Jay's belt. Now Sapphire was forced to act; she quickly walked over to the group. 'All in good time, Georgia,' she smiled. 'Take your seats ladies and the act will continue.'

Reluctantly the women prised themselves away from Jay and returned to their table. Georgia looked especially petulant, 'This better be worth waiting for.'

Jay turned away from the women and Sapphire took the opportunity to whisper, 'It's nearly over, babe.'

Jay didn't look at her. She was going to have some serious making up to do after this. He turned round and unbuckled his belt, then in one fluid moment he slid his trousers down revealing his very well-filled Armanis.

'Wow!' Georgia exclaimed. 'You could give Beckham a run for his money couldn't you?'

Jay stood there for a few seconds flexing his muscles and looking gorgeous. Then clearly he thought that was it as he blew Georgia a kiss and turned to go. But the hens were having none of it. 'Get them off!' they all shouted. 'You've got to get them off!'

'Off off off!' chanted the lads at the adjoining table, a chorus picked up by the other drinkers. 'Off, off, off!' Jay simply smiled and bent down to pick up his clothes. But he had reckoned without the persistence of the hens, who got up from their chairs and surrounded him once again like a pack of animals, each one of them reaching out and attempting to pull down his boxers. Sapphire tried in vain to move in front of Jay to protect him, but they roughly knocked her to the ground. Meanwhile Georgia was advancing on Jay with a tube of squirty cream in her hand and a leer on her face. Jesus Christ, what the fuck was she doing?

Sapphire got up on her hands and knees and tried to stand up but someone kicked her in the stomach and for a moment she was bent double in agony and couldn't see what was happening. She managed to get up and saw Jay struggling to get away from the women, who had nearly managed to pull down his boxers. Then somehow he managed to make a break for it and was heading for the door. Thank God for that! But Sapphire's relief was short-lived as just before he got there the guys from the table circled round him and blocked his exit. Jay tried to push his way through but it was five against one, he didn't stand a chance. They roughly pinned his arms behind his back and dragged him back over to the hens. 'I think the ladies want a bit more from you, mate, and you don't want to let them down, do you?' said the vile groper.

Sapphire was desperately trying to push her way through the crowd that had gathered round Jay and the hens but a mob mentality had taken over and she couldn't get near him. She caught a glimpse of Jay still struggling to get away. Then one of the lads punched him in the stomach and face. Georgia was in front of him now and to Sapphire's absolute horror she reached out and pulled down Jay's boxers to roars from the crowd. 'Leave him alone!' Sapphire shouted trying to get to Jay but one of the women in the crowd elbowed her sharply in the face. Through the tears of pain Sapphire saw Georgia spray the cream onto Jay, 'I'm going to have a good lick of that now! It's the last cock I'll be sucking before my husband's and I intend to make the most of it.'

But just before she could get down to it Lee, the barman, pushed his way through the crowd, flanked by three massive bouncers and stopped her. 'Sorry love, but I'm not going to lose my licence because of this. Lads, you need to sling your hook.'

The bouncers hussled the lads out of the bar, while the hens rallied around Georgia and supported her to their table. Finally people began to go back to their seats, some of them looking quite shamefaced. They realised they had gone too far. It was suddenly very quiet. Sapphire ran over to Jay. He had managed to get his boxers back on but he had a split lip and bruised eye from the assault.

'Jay, I'm so sorry,' Sapphire said, reaching out to wipe the blood away from his face.

'Don't touch me,' he spat back at her. 'Just get my fucking clothes.' But Owen had them already. 'There you go, mate,' he said, handing them over. Barely acknowledging him, Jay put on the jacket and trousers and walked out of the bar without saying another word. She wanted to run after him but she had the hens to deal with and God knows what they'd do next if she left them alone. And she had the feeling that she was the very last person Jay would want to see right now. Why had she ever thought it would be a good idea to involve him?

'Well, that was a fucking let-down!' Georgia snapped when Sapphire went over.

'I don't know what his problem was! It can't be every day that a star like me offers him a blowie!'

'Actually, he's my boyfriend and was being the stripper to help me out as my regular guy's got flu. And my regular wouldn't have let you suck his cock either.'

Sapphire was way past being charming with Georgia; all she wanted was for the night to end so that she never had to set eyes on the woman again.

She was expecting a right ear bashing; instead Georgia burst out laughing. 'Well you're one lucky girl, Sapphire. Tell him no harm intended; I was only going to give it a little lick anyway, what do you think I am! Is it time for us to go to dinner yet? I'm starving!'

*

On the way to the restaurant, which was in a boutique hotel, Sapphire texted Jay, desperate to let him know how truly sorry she was for what had happened. She was absolutely appalled when she thought of it and dreaded to think what might have happened next if Lee hadn't intervened. It had an uncanny resemblance to that scene from *Lord of the Flies*, which she'd studied for GCSE when Piggy, the fat boy with glasses, gets hounded to death by the other boys. But although Piggy had died at least his trousers hadn't been pulled down. She wondered if Jay would ever want to see her again. She remembered Jazz's question – how would she have felt if it had been her having to strip for a group of men? If she'd been subjected to the same treatment as Jay she would have felt as if she'd been assaulted. Well, the fact was he *had* been assaulted! She knew Jazz was out having a drink with her boyfriend but suddenly she felt as if she needed the support of her friend. The night was still young; God knows what else Georgia was going to get up to.

Thankfully Jazz agreed to meet her at the hotel bar, which adjoined the restaurant, so she could keep an eye on the hens. Fortunately for the other diners the hens had their own private dining room. But even then they seemed intent on causing chaos. Georgia sent back every single dish, complaining that there was something wrong with it, another hen smoked in the loos and set off the alarm system, they sexually harassed the young male waiter, pinching his bum and they were so raucous, singing 'I Will Survive' at the top of their lungs, that they caused a chorus of complaints from the diners in the main restaurant. Pascal, the French maître d', came and sought Sapphire out at the bar where she was sitting, drinking coffee with Jazz and willing the night to be over. Fortunately she had a good relationship with him but she

105

could tell that the hens had pushed him to the limit. 'I never, ever want another group like this again, Sapphire.'

'Nor do I, Pascal, I'm really sorry. But the restaurant will be mentioned in the magazine, it will be good publicity.'

Pascal raised his eyebrows and looked sceptical. 'Not if it attracts clientele like them.'

They both turned to watch Erin and Danielle tottering unsteadily to the bathroom, clinging on to each other for support. One of Erin's hair extensions fell out on the floor but she didn't notice. 'Pure class, n'est-ce pas?' Pascal said sarcastically, adding, 'I'm going to give them the bill and try and get them out of here.' He walked briskly away.

Sapphire just hoped he wouldn't let it affect her booking the restaurant again. It was one of *the* places to eat in Brighton. She checked her phone, anxious to see if there was a message from Jay. But there was nothing.

'Leave it, Sapphire,' Jazz advised her. 'You're best off going to see him tomorrow in person. Maybe he'll see the funny side of it then.'

Sapphire shook her head, and shuddered. 'There really wasn't a funny side to it, Jazz – it was horrible.' She knew she'd made a mistake asking Jay to strip.

Pascal returned with a face like thunder. 'I need you, Sapphire. Georgia is refusing to pay the bill; she's saying the meal should be free because of the publicity. I'm prepared to let them have the food for free but they've just drunk five hundred pounds' worth of champagne and wine. I can't write that off.'

Knowing that it would be pointless to try and argue it out with Georgia, Sapphire reached inside her bag and handed Pascal her credit card. 'I'll pay for the drink, and take an extra hundred and fifty for the staff.'

She just hoped that was enough of a sweetener to take

106

away the nasty taste that the hens had left behind in everyone's mouths.

Eventually it was time to bundle the women into the limo and drive them to their final destination of the night: PURE, Alfie's club. The one good thing about the evening so far was that it had been so much worse than she had expected that she'd had no time to get uptight about seeing Alfie. As the club was basically his scene, it was down to him to give the hens a good time now.

'What happened to you? Got yourself a bitch slap scar?' Alfie asked as soon as he saw her, taking in the red mark on the cheek. He reached out to touch her and instinctively she flinched away. He laughed at her, 'Don't worry, Sapphire, I won't bite. Well, only if you want me to.'

She ignored him. 'So, is everything set up for the cabaret?' she asked brusquely.

He nodded, 'Yep, I've told the lads to make it as raunchy as possible. Should be good, are you going to watch?'

Sapphire shrugged. 'From a distance.'

The hens had a quick spin on the dance floor to pumping house music – spin being the accurate word for four of them who were almost too drunk to stand up. Simone was still sober and Sapphire was aware of her eyes burning into her. Her link with Cal was clearly disturbing her. Sapphire remembered Cal telling her how devastated she had been by the break-up, and that she had stalked him. Sapphire could well imagine it; Simone looked as if she was capable of anything.

Sapphire kept checking her watch, willing the night to be over. At midnight it was showtime. Sapphire and Jazz rounded up the women and led them upstairs to Alfie's intimate cabaret room. Three other hen parties were already installed at the tables, while topless waiters in tiny silver shorts took their orders.

Georgia took a good look at them and then turned to Sapphire, 'Not a patch on your fella and I bet they're all gay aren't they?'

'Probably.'

Alfie strolled over to the table, 'Can I get you ladies anything else? Champagne? Cocktails?'

'Vodka and Red Bulls all round, I think, Alfie my darling,' Georgia replied. Her eyes slid over him appreciatively. 'I really don't know why Sapphire was in such a hurry to get rid of a dish like you. We all make mistakes, don't we darling? You'll have to come to my wedding, I need more gorgeous men there – it will look better in the magazine shots.'

'Thank you, Georgia, I'd love to come,' Alfie replied, while Sapphire gritted her teeth. Bastard! He must know how much that would wind her up.

She looked away from the pair of them and noticed Ryan walking through the door. He looked very good in a black suit and black shirt, sophisticated and slick. Suddenly the night didn't seem quite so bad as he walked over and lightly kissed Sapphire on the cheek before introducing himself to Georgia. 'You'll have to come to my wedding too!' Georgia exclaimed. 'I had no idea there were so many good-looking men still on the market, otherwise I might have taken my time getting hitched again.'

Ryan smiled, 'Thanks but I'm not the marrying kind.' He was looking straight at Sapphire who felt herself blush again.

Georgia might have been off her head but she was still quick to pick up on the vibe, 'Now, now Sapphire, don't be greedy, you've already got that gorgeous boyfriend. Don't you think you ought to leave Ryan for someone else? Simone's single at the moment.'

Sapphire was mortified; she couldn't bring herself to look at Ryan.

108

Georgia gave a dirty laugh. 'Now, have I got time to go to the bathroom before the boys come on? I don't want to miss anything.'

'Plenty of time, Georgia.' Alfie assured her.

Georgia got unsteadily to her feet, accompanied by Erin. They were both so drunk that they had to hold each other upright. Alfie shook his head at Sapphire then went over to help them.

Sapphire was left standing next to Ryan. 'Sorry about that, she's very drunk. She's already sexually assaulted my boyfriend.'

'Poor bastard,' Ryan replied. 'But she's right isn't she? Pissed as she is, even she could pick up on what's going on between us.' He stared at her.

Sapphire's stomach did the dangerous delicious flip thing but she managed to shake her head and say coolly, 'I don't know what you're talking about.'

Ryan moved closer to her, and whispered, 'You're lying to yourself if you believe that, Sapphire.'

Sapphire was saved from having to reply by Simone marching over and saying accusingly, 'Where's Georgia? The cabaret's about to start and she won't want to miss it.'

Reluctantly Sapphire made her way to the ladies'. Jazz intercepted her at the door. 'So is that Ryan?' she demanded.

Great. Now she was going to get the third degree from Jazz. 'Yeah,' Sapphire mumbled.

'He's way too smooth. Jay's much more handsome.'

Sapphire turned to her friend in exasperation, 'I know! Look Jazz, I don't fancy Ryan. He's just a business contact.' It was such a lie Sapphire almost expected her nose to suddenly grow three inches. 'Let's just get that silly cow out of the loos. She's bound to be puking up in there.'

There was a queue of women waiting for the cubicles and Sapphire and Jazz had to push their way through, ignoring the tuts. 'I don't want to go, I'm just looking for someone,' she said, not wanting another punch in the face.

'Georgia,' she called out, 'are you in here? The cabaret's about to start.'

No response, where the hell was she? She tried calling her name again.

Then a voice came from the cubicle at the end: 'She's in here, I don't think she's very well.'

Great, so she was puking up, typical! Sapphire marched down to the cubicle and braced herself. She knocked at the door and Erin opened it, looking scared. Georgia was lying down, unconscious.

'Shit! How long as she been like this?'

'I dunno,' she whined, 'I've been trying to get her to wake up.'

'Has she taken anything?' Sapphire asked, bending down, suddenly fearful that Georgia had stopped breathing.

'I dunno.'

God the woman was infuriating! Meanwhile Georgia barely seemed to have a pulse. Jazz knew some first aid and quickly put Georgia in the recovery position on her side. Georgia still didn't open her eyes. Jazz looked at Sapphire. 'She might just be pissed or it might be something else. If I were you I'd phone an ambulance.'

Sapphire scrambled for her mobile in her bag and then called 999, all the while looking anxiously at the unconscious Georgia as she explained the situation to the operator.

'Erin, can you go and find Alfie and tell him what's happened?' Sapphire asked after she'd made the call. Erin looked at her blankly, still too out of it.

'Oh for God's sake! Jazz will you be okay if I get Alfie?'

'Yeah, but don't be long,' Jazz said as she knelt down beside Georgia. Sapphire pushed her way back through the women queuing for the loo and raced back to the cabaret room to find Alfie.

'Shit! You could have asked me first,' he exclaimed when she told him she had called an ambulance.

'I was worried that it might be serious.' Sapphire shot back.

'It's not the kind of publicity we need,' Alfie was looking anxiously at Ryan.

How typical for Alfie to be thinking of himself at a time like this.

Ryan just said, 'Chill, Alfie, it's probably just the drink.' He turned to Sapphire, 'You haven't seen Georgia take anything have you?'

'Nope. Just drink bucket loads. I'd better get back to her. Is there a chance that you could get the other hens back to the hotel? I really don't think I could stand for anything else to go wrong.'

Ryan reached out and touched her shoulder, 'Don't worry, Sapphire, everything will be fine, I promise.'

'What the fuck's going on?' By now Simone had joined them.

'Nothing that Sapphire can't handle,' Ryan said soothingly. 'You must be Simone Fraser, I recognise you. But you look even better in the flesh than you do on TV.'

Ordinarily such outrageous flattery would have Sapphire reaching for the sick bag. But right now flattery was the only thing standing between them and a whole lot of trouble.

Simone smirked and looked coy, 'Thank you, but that doesn't answer my question.' Underneath that simpering exterior was a will of steel.

'Georgia has passed out. I've just called an ambulance,' Sapphire said quickly.

'I knew you shouldn't have plied her with so much alcohol,' Simone said accusingly. 'I did warn you.'

She had done no such thing. In fact Simone had been

111

the one ordering more drinks for everyone all the time, even though she herself seemed barely to have touched a drop.

'Why don't we take Simone to Georgia?' Ryan suggested. 'I'm sure you'd like to be with your friend wouldn't you?'

'You should work for the United Nations,' Sapphire whispered under her breath as Ryan led Simone out of the cabaret room.

'All part of the service,' he replied, winking at her.

The next hour was a frenzy of activity. The paramedics arrived and checked Georgia over. She still hadn't regained consciousness. 'She'll be okay, won't she?' Sapphire asked them anxiously.

'Let's just get her to hospital shall we?' One of the men said calmly and Sapphire could only watch helplessly as they attached an oxygen mask to Georgia's face and lifted her onto a stretcher. Simone went with her in the ambulance while Sapphire and Jazz took a taxi to casualty.

'Don't worry, Sapphire, I'm sure she'll be fine,' Jazz did her best to reassure her friend. Sapphire only hoped she was right.

Walking into the casualty waiting area on a Saturday night was like entering a war zone. It was packed with the walking wounded, a high proportion of them pissed. Sapphire noticed Simone sitting on one of the blue plastic chairs at the far side of the room and walked over, with Jazz following behind. 'How is she?' Sapphire asked taking a seat next to her.

'I don't know, they're still trying to work out what's happened.'

Under the harsh overhead lighting Simone no longer looked so immaculate. There were deep lines around her eyes, the sign of too much sun worship and her forehead looked unnaturally shiny, a consequence of Botox. Mind you, Sapphire was sure she didn't look too good either. The three of them then watched a very drunk man weave his way past them, pausing to throw up over his shoes and narrowly missing Sapphire's Louboutins. Really, it was enough to put anyone off alcohol for life.

'Gross!' Jazz exclaimed, as the smell of vomit hit them, 'Let's go and sit somewhere else.'

'I hope the press don't get wind of this, it could really damage Georgia's career,' Simone said darkly as they relocated to the opposite corner of the room.

'Well, I'm not going to tell them,' Sapphire replied, 'but an awful lot of people saw Georgia at the club.'

'I suppose we can say its food poisoning or something,' Simone continued.

'We can't – that will reflect badly on the restaurant!' Sapphire protested.

'All you think about is your precious business! My best friend is lying in there unconscious.' Simone must really be summoning up what precious little acting ability she had now. Melodramatic is the word Sapphire would have used to describe her performance; that or hammy.

'She's unconscious because she fucking caned it!' Sapphire was on the verge of losing it.

Jazz shot her a warning glance and luckily before Sapphire could say anything else, the nurse called them over. As Sapphire had suspected, Georgia had simply drunk too much. She'd had her stomach pumped and they were going to keep her in overnight. Sapphire wanted to see her, but Simone insisted that Georgia wouldn't want to see anyone but her. Jazz called for a taxi and the two girls went outside to wait for it – both of them had had enough of being stuck in A&E.

Sapphire felt completely shattered. She reached for her phone again. Still nothing from Jay. 'This has been one of the worst nights of my life! And all because of that silly cow,' Sapphire told Jazz.

'It'll be all right,' Jazz replied, linking arms with her to keep warm while they waited. 'Hopefully the press won't find out.'

Famous last words. Sapphire had only been asleep for two hours when her mobile rang, shrill and piercing. It was a journalist wanting all the dirt on the hen weekend and promising her a hefty fee if she dished it.

'No comment!' Sapphire shouted and angrily hung up, throwing her phone across the room. She tried to go back to sleep but it was no good. Guilt about Jay and stress about what the press were going to make of the hen weekend put sleep out of the question. She looked at her bedside clock – it was only eight o'clock. She got up, showered and put on her jeans and leather jacket. She had to see Jay to apologise for what had happened. Outside it was a stormy November morning.

The sea was a forbidding slate grey, matching the sky. Sapphire couldn't face walking and drove the mile and a half to Jay's flat. Jay lived in the Kemptown area of Brighton, which had a studenty, bohemian vibe, in a two-bedroom flat, just off the main high street. It took her ages to find anywhere to park, and when she rang the doorbell there was no reply. She tried shouting through the letter box. She called his mobile again but nothing.

She couldn't face going home after that and headed instead to the boutique. The treatment rooms looked as if a bomb had hit them. It took her nearly an hour to clear up. Georgia and her gang had got through ten bottles of champagne before they'd even made it out. And there were empty glasses and bottles everywhere, plus plates of half-eaten sandwiches.

Sapphire had a feeling that she wasn't going to see any money for the weekend. The magazine was hardly likely to run an article where the bride to be gets hospitalised at the end of her hen weekend. She sat down in her office and with a sinking heart tried to calculate the exact cost of the weekend to her business. Never mind the impact on the rest of her life, she thought bitterly, her relationship with Jay and the damage it had done to her professional relationships. By her reckoning she was going to be out of pocket to the tune of at least five and a half grand. It was the last thing she needed after the five grand she had shelled out to cover her mum's gambling debts. She checked both her business account and personal bank account online and felt distinctly uneasy. She had some money in reserve, but not much. She had been pinning her hopes on Georgia's weekend giving the business a boost. She'd noticed that bookings had been down lately because of the recession but had been too busy focusing on Georgia to worry. Now, she was worried.

She sat at her desk drinking coffee, trying to work out what she could do. Several times her business line went with still more journalists wanting the inside story. Bad news travelled fast, it seemed. She wondered who had tipped them off, then realised it was a pointless question – there were so many people who could have done it.

She sent another text to Jay asking him to call her. Then she texted Georgia asking her how she was; and if there was anything she could do. She felt horribly vulnerable, as if suddenly everything was outside her control and she was powerless to do anything. And there was no one she felt she could turn to. It would be no good telling her mum, she would only worry. Jazz and Sam would tell her she'd be fine. She needed to speak to someone who understood about business. She found herself reaching for her phone again and this time she selected Ryan from her contacts list.

'Hi,' he said sleepily. Clearly he was still in bed.

'I'm sorry, I didn't mean to wake you.'

'No, no it's fine, I was going to call you. How are you, Sapphire?'

'Stressed, to be honest,' Sapphire could actually feel tears pricking her eyes. 'I'm really worried about the impact this weekend is going to have on the business.'

'Hey, don't worry. It'll be okay. This has just been a blip, in a week, it will be forgotten. You're a great businesswoman, Sapphire. Soon you'll probably look back at this weekend and laugh.'

Ryan sounded so sympathetic and warm, Sapphire could feel some of the anxiety leaving her. Then he continued and she immediately tensed up again, 'I'm seeing Simone for lunch today; I'll make sure I sing your praises.'

'You're seeing Simone?' Sapphire couldn't hide the surprise in her voice.

Ryan laughed. 'I'd much rather be seeing you, believe me, but I thought it would probably be useful to all of us if I took her out for lunch, made her feel good about the weekend. She does know an awful lot of people with connections and we don't want her badmouthing your business or mine. Georgia's fine, by the way. Tyler came to pick her up first thing and he's taken her straight to the Priory. I think she's going to fess up about what happened and say it was a cry for help and that she's going to get herself cleaned up.'

'Hasn't she been saying that for the last three years?' Sapphire replied sarcastically.

She couldn't help feeling jealous that Ryan was seeing Simone. Was lunch all he had on his agenda? Just how far would he go to keep her sweet? And more to the point, why was she concerning herself? She ended the call feeling in an even worse mood. God, Cal had been right, Simone was a complete bitch.

*

116

She spent the rest of the day spring cleaning the boutique, sorting out all the stock. They were in the run-up to Christmas now and she had a large order of La Perla and Calvin Klein lingerie coming in on Monday. She wanted everything to be in place. By five, when she had still heard nothing from Jay, she plucked up courage to phone his mum. She just prayed that Jay hadn't told his family what had happened – she had a feeling that Vicky would be like a tigress as far as her children were concerned and wouldn't take at all kindly to Sapphire if she knew what she had asked Jay to do. Vicky answered the phone. She hadn't heard from Jay but that wasn't unusual. She thought he had gone up to London for the day with Luke, and she promised to get him to call Sapphire as soon as he got back.

'Jay's not the type to stay angry for long,' she said kindly, probably thinking they'd just had a lovers' tiff. She added, 'And he really likes you Sapphire. I mean *really* likes you.' The guilt was almost unbearable.

The next week was hideous. Jay continued to ignore her calls. Georgia's exploits were all over the tabloids, sparking debates on their pages and on TV and radio that women were getting out of control and whether hen parties now had as bad a reputation as stag nights. Sapphire staunchly resisted all requests for interviews, fearing that she would be misquoted, but then *Morning Edition*, one of the TV breakfast shows, was having a discussion and she was invited in as a guest speaker.

It seemed like her chance to set the record straight and both Jazz and Sam urged her to do it. 'Just go on, look fabulous and say your piece. Not all hen weekends end up like Georgia's, we know that. Why shouldn't girls have fun?' Jazz told her.

'Can't you do it?' Sapphire moaned.

She was not feeling especially fabulous right now. To

117

her surprise she really missed Jay and felt very down. To distract herself she flicked through *heat* magazine and ended up on the 'Spotted' page. A sudden irrational flash of jealousy went through her when she caught sight of a picture of Simone looking loved-up with Ryan out and about in Brighton. Clearly something more than lunch had been on the agenda, judging by the expression on her face . . . She shut the magazine in disgust, furious with herself for being jealous and furious with Ryan and Simone.

'Come on, Sapphire, you've got to do it,' Sam said. 'Repeat after me, "I'm a kick-ass businesswoman."'

Sapphire shook her head, 'I really don't feel very kick-ass right now.'

'Pathetic! Jazz and me are going to make you do that programme because you'll so regret it if you don't.'

Sapphire moaned some more and then gave in – she knew her friends were right.

But that didn't stop her being incredibly nervous on the morning of the programme. Luckily Jazz had come with her to do her make-up and give her moral support and she did her best to keep her calm by chatting away to her as they sat in the dressing room with some of the other guests. The young female researcher had told Sapphire on the phone that it would just be a light-hearted discussion about hen weekends, nothing too heavy.

'God, Jazz, I need to go to the loo again!' Sapphire exclaimed as it got closer to her slot. 'I've already been three times in the last hour! I'm going to be crap!'

'You're going to be great,' Jazz told her. 'Come on, it's a brilliant chance to mention the business. Stop being a wimp!'

Finally after two more trips to the loo it was time for Sapphire to be shown onto the set. It felt very strange sitting on the familiar red sofa which she had seen on TV and staring out at the cameras and production team milling around. She felt extremely hot and self-conscious under the lights. Tina, the bubbly presenter, was as down to earth in real life as she was on TV, but Sapphire was shocked when Olivia Smithson, a right-wing columnist who had extremely strong views on women and drink was shown on set and took her place next to Sapphire. Olivia Smithson did not do light-hearted discussions, what she did do was to stick the knife in and take no prisoners. Sapphire was about to ask Tina what was going on when the ad-break finished and they were on air. From the moment the discussion kicked off, Olivia was like a Rottweiler, attacking Sapphire for everything she said. Tina, was powerless to stop her.

'It's people like you who are responsible for the binge drinking culture in this country, which is wrecking lives and costing the NHS millions of pounds as yet again it has to pick up the pieces after one of your depraved hen parties.'

'Of course I'm not responsible for binge drinking! I provide a service that women want. It is extremely rare that someone attending one of my parties becomes ill through drinking excessively.'

Suddenly Sapphire's nerves had deserted her and she felt confident about her own argument. How dare this stuck-up journalist criticise her, and not just her – all women who wanted to have a good time.

'You provide a service so that women can get drunk and behave disgracefully! You should be paying an extra tax to cover the cost of sorting out those drunken women.'

'You're being so extreme – I've just explained that it has never happened before that a woman has ended up in hospital following a hen party with my business and that's all I can say in order to respect my clients' privacy. In general the women who come on my weekends want to relax, have fun, and yes, maybe have a few drinks, but there's no law against women being able to have a good time is there? Would you like us to go back to the days when women couldn't drink in public? Or is it that you don't like to see women of a certain *class* out there enjoying themselves?'

Yeah, that was it, stuck-up snob.

The studio audience burst into spontaneous applause as Olivia tried to bluster on in her plummy voice that of course class wasn't an issue. But clearly it was.

'Sapphire, you were great!' Jazz exclaimed when Sapphire returned to the dressing room, 'I was well impressed!'

And Jazz wasn't the only one. Emily, the show's producer sought her out and told her she was exactly the kind of contributor they wanted to have on the programme – a strong, articulate, opinionated young woman – and asked if she would be interested in coming on again. Sapphire considered for a few moments and then agreed that she would.

All the way back to Brighton she was bombarded with texts from her friends telling her how good she'd been, even her mum told her she'd been brilliant, and it was rare that she praised Sapphire. Vicky texted her too to say well done. But there was still nothing from Jay. She should have been glad that she had done something to salvage her reputation after Georgia-gate; instead he was all she could think about.

Usually Sapphire was completely cool about her affairs ending, and usually she was the one doing the ending. But now she felt differently about Jay. It didn't seem as if whatever she had with him had run its course yet. She hated to think that it would end over the stripogram incident nor did she like the feeling of guilt that had hung over her all week. She had to do something. If he didn't want to see her any more she had to know – she couldn't carry on in this limbo.

Chapter 8

It was half six by the time she arrived back in Brighton and she was desperate to know either way whether Jay still wanted to see her. It was a Friday night and they'd fallen into the habit of chilling out at Sapphire's place – Jay would cook or they'd get a takeaway and watch a DVD. Sapphire had come to enjoy those nights. Jay was such easy company and she felt she could completely relax with him; there weren't many people who could make her feel like that. The truth was she had missed him this week.

'Just go round to his flat!' Jazz had urged her throughout the journey.

'I'm sure he doesn't want to see me – if he did, he'd have called. He obviously thinks it's over.'

'He was most likely really pissed off and angry and needed a bit of space. He's had that now.'

Sapphire wasn't so sure but she couldn't wait any longer, she had to go and find out for herself.

A twenty-something man with a gym-fit body, short blond hair and a little too much fake tan opened the door to her. She reckoned it must be Luke, Jay's flatmate. Sapphire gave him her most dazzling smile, but the look Luke gave her in return was decidedly unfriendly. 'Hi, I'm Sapphire, is Jay in?'

'I know who you are.' Luke replied tersely. 'Wait there, please,' and he shut the door in her face.

Sapphire tried to tell herself that it didn't matter if Jay didn't want to see her any more – they'd had fun and it was probably time to move on, but deep down she knew that wasn't true.

Luke took his time coming back to her, so long that Sapphire was about to give up and leave. 'He's in the living room. He'll see you.'

Jay was sitting in the armchair by the fire drinking a beer. He made no move to get up when Sapphire walked in and barely acknowledged her. She wanted to go over to him and put her arms round him, tell him how sorry she was but she didn't think he'd respond to that very well. She stood in the middle of the room, clutching her bag to her chest, as if it was a security blanket.

'Hi,' she said, 'I've left messages all week. I wanted to say sorry, Jay. I'm really really sorry about what happened.'

'Yeah, I expect you are. It probably wasn't good for business.' There was an edge to his voice she hadn't heard before.

'It's nothing to do with my business!' she protested, 'I'm sorry I put you through that. I had no idea those women would behave so badly.' She took a step towards him. 'Please, Jay, I really am sorry. If it's over between us, tell me and I'll go, I just wanted you to know how sorry I am.'

'Oh yeah, I forgot – three months is usually your limit with a guy isn't it? I guess I should be grateful I lasted five. Is that what you want, for us to be over?'

Sapphire surprised herself by saying, 'No, Jay, that's not what I want.'

Usually it was one of her rules never to let her guard down. They stared at each other for a few seconds, not saying anything. Then Jay spoke, and his voice was warmer, 'Well you don't get rid of me that easily. Come here.'

Sapphire walked over to him and he took her hand and pulled her onto his knee. She buried her face in his neck, breathing in the scent that was twenty per cent Dior Homme and eighty per cent Jay, while he stroked her hair.

For a while they said nothing and just held each other; then Jay spoke. 'When those fuckers held me down and everyone was crowding round me I had a flashback to being bullied at school. It took me to a really dark place. I've only just been able to deal with going to work and that's it.'

Sapphire felt even worse knowing the pain she'd caused Jay. 'Sorry,' she whispered. 'I'm so sorry.'

'I know you are, babe.' He reached up and lightly touched the bruise on her face, 'But let's forget about it now.'

Sapphire felt an unexpected wave of happiness roll through her. She really was glad that Jay wasn't dumping her. He kissed her softly on the lips. Sapphire waited for the kiss to become more passionate. It didn't. Maybe Jay hadn't quite forgiven her. But then he said, 'Will you stay with me tonight?'

Sapphire nodded. She was breaking a lot of her dating rules tonight. 'Hungry?'

'Yeah, but I don't expect you to cook, why don't we get a takeaway?'

'No, I've been eating crap all week, I'll cook. Come on, you can help.'

As Sapphire stood up she said, 'Will Luke be in the kitchen? He's not exactly my number-one fan is he? I thought he was going to punch my lights out when he opened the door to me.'

Jay laughed. 'He's resistant to your charms anyway, babe, as he's gay.'

'I expect last week probably turned you that way.'

'Never,' Jay ducked down and kissed her neck. And Sapphire wished they could skip dinner and go straight to bed.

Luke was sitting at the kitchen table flicking through *Grazia* when Jay and Sapphire went in to prepare dinner. He stayed put while Sapphire chopped onions, peppers and mushrooms for the pasta sauce Jay was making. Sapphire wished he would just go. Then he started in on her.

'So does that kind of thing happen often at your hen weekends?'

She didn't need to ask what kind of thing he was referring to. She took a deep breath, steeling herself for the confrontation. If she could handle Olivia Smithson on live TV, she could certainly handle this.

'Never – I mean, we often have strippers but none of my clients have ever behaved like that.'

'If Jay had been a woman how would you have felt about it then?' Luke fiddled with the silver earring in his ear. Elaborate and brightly coloured tattoos of flowers covered both his arms. If it had been anyone else Sapphire would have commented on the tats.

'I wouldn't know as I wouldn't have been going out with her,' Sapphire tried to keep it light.

Luke pursed his lips, 'You know what I mean. If a woman had been treated like that it would have been classed as a sexual assault, but Jay was fair game wasn't he?'

Sapphire concentrated on chopping up the onions and tried not to get wound up. It was clearly Luke's intention to provoke her. 'Those women were bang out of order. And I've apologised to him.'

Jay walked over to Sapphire and put his arm round her. 'Luke, you don't have to give Sapphire a hard time. She didn't mean it to happen. I know she's sorry and that's all that matters.' He dipped his head down and kissed Sapphire. 'Good chopping, babe.'

Luke wasn't finished. 'You should have seen the state of Jay this week. He suffered from panic attacks, which he said he hadn't had since school, he was really down.'

Jay shot him a warning glance, 'That's enough Luke; you don't need to go on about it.'

Luke got up abruptly from the table. 'I just think some people need to think about the consequences of their actions.' And he marched out of the room.

'Dinner won't be long,' Jay called after him.

'I'm not hungry, I'm going out,' came the reply. And a few minutes later the front door slammed.

'Whoa, he's touchy!' she said. She had clearly had got off on the wrong foot with Luke.

'Oh, he'll be okay. He's just split up with his boyfriend which doesn't help.'

Jay's attention turned to dinner. Sapphire wandered off to the bathroom, which was impressively clean and stylish for a boys' flat. She decided to have a nosy at Jay's bedroom. She opened the door to one room which was tastefully decorated in black and white – a black four-poster bed, white rug, white muslin curtains at the window. There were a few black-and-white photos on the wall but occupying pride of place directly opposite the bed was a poster-sized picture of Jay in colour sitting on Brighton beach, with his shirt off, the ruined West Pier in the background. He looked gorgeous.

'Isn't it vain of you to have a picture of yourself on the wall?' she demanded walking back into the kitchen.

'That's Luke's room.'

Sapphire frowned, 'Well then, isn't it a bit strange for him to have a picture of you on his wall?'

Jay shrugged, 'He took it for his photography port-folio, so not really. He's got other pictures in his room.'

'Okay now I need to check out your room,' Sapphire replied.

'No! I haven't tidied it!' Jay protested.

'I have to see it!' Sapphire exclaimed and made a run for it before Jay could stop her. His bedroom was at the end of the corridor. It was a complete mess – clothes, copies of *Men's Health* and *FHM* and his iPod were strewn across the floor, the bed unmade, and about five mugs on the bedside table.

'I told you not to look!' Jay ran in after her.

'Jay you are a total scumbag! I thought your room would be tidy!'

Jay laughed and pulled her onto the bed with him, 'I can't be tidy, a good cook and good in bed.'

Sapphire enjoyed the feel of his body lying on top of hers. She wriggled into him suggestively. She had really missed him.

'Are you good in bed?' she asked coyly. 'I think I've forgotten; it's been *so* long.'

'It might be time to jog your memory, then,' Jay replied and this time when he kissed her it was deep and hard and there was no going back.

After a very satisfying reminder of exactly how good Jay was in bed, the acrid smell of burning coming from the kitchen reminded them too late about dinner. 'Shit! It'll be ruined!' Jay leapt out of bed and, quickly wrapping a towel round his waist, sped into the kitchen. He came back a few minutes later holding his phone. 'What kind of pizza do you want?'

Sapphire had no hen party booked in for the weekend and fully expected to chill out with Jay on Saturday. They both slept late, then stayed in bed until lunch time, catching up. Sapphire had *really* missed Jay. 'So how about I take you for lunch?' Sapphire said afterwards, snuggling up to him.

'Well, I did promise Luke I'd do something with him.

I know he feels gutted about his ex. So why don't we all go for lunch and then I'll hang out with him. Then you can come round tonight and we can all watch a DVD together.'

Three was not the magic number, especially where Luke was concerned. But Sapphire felt she had some serious making up to do and simply replied, 'Great, shall we go to Browns then?'

Lunch was a disaster. Luke continued picking at her from the moment they sat down together, 'So do you think it's acceptable treating men like pieces of meat to satisfy drunk women?'

Jay rolled his eyes while Sapphire shrugged and said, 'Luke, I've already told you it never should have happened, what more do you want me to say?'

'But you'd employ a stripper again wouldn't you?'

Sapphire sighed. Luke was giving her a headache. 'I don't force men to become strippers, Luke! I pay them good money, they do their act and that's it. What happened with Jay was a one-off, it will never happen again.' She picked up the menu and put her hand over Jay's. 'What do you fancy, babe?'

As she did so she was aware of Luke giving her another of his filthy looks. Was he jealous of her because he had feelings for Jay? Whatever, there was a tension between them that could have been sliced, diced and served on a plate. Sapphire did her best to ignore the looks and continual barbed comments about drunk women and how unattractive they were. 'Drunk men aren't exactly a thing of beauty!' Sapphire shot back, heartily sick of his jibes.

She looked around the restaurant and her heart sank when she saw Simone walk in hanging on to Ryan's arm. Oh God, of all the people, why did it have to be them! Sapphire pretended not to have seen them but Ryan had spotted her and was walking over. As he kissed her cheek Sapphire regretted not making more of an effort that morning. She'd gone for the casual look, which Jay loved – skinny jeans, Uggs and a big grey cashmere jumper – and was wearing hardly any make-up. Not so Simone, who was glammed up to her eyeballs in a brown silk leopard-print dress, killer heels and full make-up. And Ryan looked particularly handsome in a charcoal grey suit.

Sapphire quickly made the introductions, all the while aware of Ryan's gaze lingering on her, and Simone giving her the once-over. She felt Jay tense up when he recognised Simone from the hen party and she squeezed his hand reassuringly.

'Oh Jay! I hardly recognised you with your clothes on!' Simone exclaimed. 'Not that I had anything to do with what happened, I can assure you.'

Jay simply nodded. What was he supposed to say? Sapphire thought bitterly. Clearly picking up on the tension Ryan changed the subject, 'I saw you on *Morning Edition* – very impressive performance, Sapphire; you could make a career of it.'

Sapphire could feel herself blushing – God, why did he have this effect on her! She was like a giddy teenager around him.

'I just wanted to set the record straight. We had so much flak about what happened with Georgia.'

'So the unfortunate incident might turn out to be to your advantage after all?' Simone put in, a sly smile on her face. 'All publicity is good publicity – isn't that what they say?'

God, she really was unbearable!

'Believe me, I'd rather have no publicity than that,' Sapphire said grimly.

Before Simone could goad Sapphire anymore the waiter signalled that their table was ready and the pair sauntered off. Simone hung on to Ryan's arm as if she owned him. Sapphire couldn't imagine that little fling lasting very long.

'Is that your ex-husband's business partner then?' Jay asked as soon as the couple were out of earshot. Sapphire nodded. 'Bit flash isn't he?' Jay continued.

Sapphire shrugged. She just wanted to change the subject. 'He's okay,' she managed, pouring water into her glass to avoid meeting Jay's searching gaze. 'Put it this way, he's better than dealing with my ex-husband.'

Luke had been silent for a while, but all the time Sapphire was aware of him either looking at her or at Jay. After lunch Jay and Luke hit the shops while Sapphire went to the boutique. It was completely empty. Vanessa was leaning against the counter filing her nails and looking bored.

'Shit!' Sapphire exclaimed, 'Has it been like this all day?'

Vanessa shrugged, 'I've seen about ten customers, I guess. It's been quiet.'

This was not good news. On a Saturday, just a few weeks away from Christmas, Sapphire would expect the boutique to be buzzing. She went upstairs; at least Jazz and Kiki were busy doing manicures. But that wasn't exactly going to keep the wolf from the door. She'd been so busy planning Georgia's hen weekend that she felt as if she'd let the rest of the business slide.

She spent the rest of the afternoon sitting in her office and working out various promotional ideas to entice customers into the boutique. She'd hold a champagne night where all the red lingerie was discounted and free beauty treatments were on offer and she'd try a men-only night too where they could buy lingerie – expensive lingerie – as Christmas presents. She figured she'd get Vanessa and Kiki to model the lingerie, but Kiki was having none of it, 'No fucking way, Sapphire! I want the

129

business to do well and everything, but I'm not getting my kit off for a bunch of dirty old men.'

'I take it that's a no then,' Sapphire replied drily.

'Well, would you do it?' Kiki demanded.

'Looks like I'm going to have to. I can't expect Vanessa to do it on her own.'

Jazz waited until Kiki was out of the room then asked, 'We've never done anything like this before. Are you worried about business, Sapphire?'

'A little bit I guess,' Sapphire downplayed her fears; she didn't want her anxiety rubbing off on the staff. 'But I'm sure it will be fine.'

'I'm sure it will,' Jazz echoed. 'Those promo ideas of yours are great and if there's anything I can do to help, bar taking my kit off, let me know.'

Sapphire smiled gratefully at her friend, then returned to her office to write up the copy for the promotional leaflets she was going to have printed off, and updated her website to flag up the promotions there. It was after seven by the time she'd finished and the last thing she felt like doing was spending her Saturday night with the poisonous Luke. She called Jay, hoping to persuade him to come over to her place.

'Babe, I'm sorry but I promised Luke.'

Sometimes Jay was just too damn nice! Sapphire was all set to say that she would leave them to it but then Jay murmured, 'Please come over, I really want to see you. I'll do whatever you want in bed.'

That did it, lust won the day.

The moment Sapphire saw Jay that night, all she wanted to do was get him on his own. She snogged him passionately when she arrived, then suggested sneaking into the bedroom, but Jay resisted. 'Come into the living room, I've made fish pie and we're going to watch *Black Hawk Down*.'

'Isn't that a war film?' Sapphire asked, her spirits sinking.

'Yeah, Luke chose it. He doesn't want to watch anything romantic right now.'

Sapphire followed Jay into the living room, sulky as a teenager. Luke was sitting on the sofa. Jay sat next to him. There wasn't enough room to sit beside him, so Sapphire went to sit on his lap.

'Babe, sorry, my knee's playing up and I've got football tomorrow. Can you sit on the chair?'

Sapphire was sorely tempted to give him the finger and say, 'Can you sit on this', but no doubt that would give bitter little Luke far too much satisfaction. So she simply smiled sweetly, then leant down and whispered, 'Your loss – I'm not wearing any underwear.'

'I heard that,' said Luke. 'Don't you think it's really unhygienic?'

'I've had a shower,' Sapphire snapped back, stalking across the room to the armchair. God this was going to be a long night. The film was so disturbing that Sapphire's spirits plummeted still further and not even the lovely Josh Hartnett could cheer her up. She sipped her wine moodily and flashed her best sultry, come-and-get-it looks at Jay, but he was totally engrossed in the film. Over two and a half hours later as the credits rolled Sapphire made a big show of yawning. It was after midnight, surely Jay could leave Luke on his own now.

'Babe, I'm knackered,' Sapphire told Jay. 'I'm going to bed.' She walked over to him, expecting him to come with her.

'I'll be with you in a minute, just let me tidy up.'

God, it was like being with Aggie and Kim! 'I'll help you,' she replied, not wanting to one little bit but desperate to get him alone.

'No, it's okay, you get to bed.'

131

Sapphire wanted to say something suggestive, but Luke was giving her the evil eye, so she simply sauntered out of the room. By now the heating had gone off and Jay's bedroom was freezing. Instead of lying seductively spread out on the bed Sapphire was forced to wrap up in Jay's black hoodie, put on a pair of his football socks and dive under the duvet. Ten minutes went by. Just how long did it take to clear up a few plates? Another ten. Sapphire could feel herself getting more and more wound up, but she'd only just got warm, she didn't want to get cold again by seeing what Jay was up to. She'd give him a few more minutes, then she would seek him out. And that was the last thought she had before falling fast asleep. She woke up to sunlight streaming through the curtains and Jay pulling on his football shirt.

'Hey, sleepyhead,' he said, leaning over and kissing her.

Fearing her early morning breath might be minging rather than minty she pushed him away, and leapt out of bed, 'I have to clean my teeth!' She raced to the bathroom and raced back. Jay looked ready to go. This would not do! She had needs. She pulled him back onto the bed with her and wrapped her arms tightly around him, 'What happened to you last night?'

Jay sighed. 'I was all set to come to bed and Luke broke down. I couldn't leave him.'

Cunning bastard! No doubt if he wasn't having any fun, he didn't want anyone else to either.

'Poor bloke,' she managed. 'But at least you're here now.' She wiggled into him.

Jay groaned, 'I'm going to be late!'

Sapphire inched down his shorts, 'I'm telling you, Jay, if you don't fuck me now, that's it. I was burning for you last night.'

'How do you think I felt knowing you were sitting there with no underwear on? You're such a tease. So this

132

will be all the sweeter then.' He lifted the sweatshirt and kissed, then sucked her nipples while his hand caressed her smooth stomach, then went further, caressing her with tantalising circles that drove her wild, then he moved down her body and caressed her with his tongue. He was so good. It was so good, Sapphire felt the delicious flicker of orgasm begin to pulse through her.

Suddenly Luke called out, 'Jay, where are you?'

Jay froze, and Sapphire murmured, 'I swear I will kill you if you stop.'

He carried on and took her all the way. And then he slid inside her – the perfect, sweetest fuck. Afterwards, they lay in each other's arms, 'I'll be rubbish at football now,' Jay murmured.

'Their loss is my gain,' Sapphire whispered. 'Anyway you could always come back to mine and we could spend the rest of the day in bed.'

'So you have missed me then?' Jay said looking at her.

'Very much,' Sapphire replied truthfully.

'Good – I'll call you later.'

After he left Sapphire got dressed as quickly as possible. She would have a shower at home before going round to her mum's. She was just opening the front door when Luke came up behind her. 'Oh hi, Luke,' she said, aware that she sounded falsely bright, 'I'm just off, see you sometime.'

'He'll wise up soon to the way you treat him,' Luke said.

'What do you mean?' she demanded. God, Luke was loathsome.

'Jay's very smitten right now, but he won't put up with being treated like shit for long.'

'I don't treat him like shit!' Sapphire said hotly. 'And anyway it's none of your business.'

'He's my friend, I look out for him, and I saw the way

133

you acted when that Ryan bloke came into the restaurant yesterday – all flirty and coy.'

There was no way Sapphire wanted to get into a slanging match with Luke, there was too great a risk that she'd tell him what she really thought of him. Using all her reserves of self-control, she turned to Luke and said, 'I really don't know what you're talking about.' And she quickly opened the door and stepped outside before Luke could say anything else.

She spent the rest of the day with her mum, and the familiar feeling of depression about her mum's life settled on her. She tried to ask her mum about the gambling but she clammed up and said that everything was fine and that she didn't want to talk about it. But she looked worried and Sapphire couldn't help feeling anxious that she might have gambled again. Just as she was steeling herself for spending the evening with her mum, watching *Midsomer Murders*, Jay called and asked her and her mum round for dinner. Sapphire was all set to refuse, but her mum overheard and told her she'd love to.

'Promise you won't say anything embarrassing,' Sapphire said she drove them over.

'Of course I won't! Jay's a lovely lad, I'm sure his family are lovely too.'

'They are,' Sapphire admitted.

Everyone was incredibly welcoming to Christine – Vicky and Clayton chatted away to her, as if they'd known her for years. Sapphire still felt on edge for the first hour, dreading that her mum might make some comment about Clayton being black but her mum was surprisingly chilled. 'I love your style,' Sapphire heard her mum exclaim to Vicky. 'It's so bright and warm. And you look fantastic. I can't believe you've had three children.'

It was most unlike her mum to be this open. But Vicky

seemed to have a knack for making people feel relaxed. Sapphire envied Jay, she wished her mum was more like Vicky.

Vicky looked at Christine, considering her, 'Have you ever thought about a change of hairstyle?'

Christine's hair was shoulder-length and pulled back into an unflattering Croydon facelift.

Christine sighed, 'I used to love my hair, it was just like Sapphire's. Now I just can't be bothered. It's easier to tie it back.'

'I have to be honest, Christine, it's doing absolutely nothing for you like that.'

Jay and Sapphire had been listening, '*Mum!*' Jay exclaimed. 'Don't be so personal.'

Sapphire was relieved to see that it wasn't just her mum who was capable of causing embarrassment.

'You know me, Jay, I speak as I find. Christine, you're a good-looking woman but I must be straight with you, you've let yourself go.'

Jay rolled his eyes at Sapphire, 'What are they like?'

There was a pause where Sapphire prayed that her mum didn't snap at Vicky to mind her own business as she had every single time Sapphire had tried to point out that she was stuck in a style rut. To her relief Christine smiled and said, 'You're so right, I have. I never used to look like this. I used to care about clothes and my appearance. I just wouldn't know where to begin to get back on track.'

Vicky's face took an expression of sheer happiness, 'Look no further than me! I love doing makeovers! I can cut and restyle your hair and then I'll take you shopping.'

'Bloody hell!' Jay muttered. 'I hope your mum doesn't mind being bossed around.'

But apparently not, as Christine was looking at Vicky with her eyes shining with gratitude.

Clayton went off to work – he ran his own minicab and van-hire company. Vicky spent the rest of the evening holed up in her bedroom with Christine, putting make-up on her and suggesting new styles, while Sapphire and Jay sprawled out on the sofa together.

'So, it's official, your flatmate hates me,' Sapphire told Jay.

'No, he doesn't, babe. He's just very protective of me is all – he's great when you get to know him, honestly.'

'Yeah, like that's going to happen! He can't stand me, Jay, surely you can see that!'

Jay shrugged, 'Chill, babe. I get on okay with your friends, I'm sure you and Luke will get on eventually. Maybe you need to make more of an effort with him. You can be quite offhand with people sometimes – even with your own friends, I've noticed.'

Sapphire sat bolt upright and pulled away from Jay's embrace. 'Well, thanks for that. Perhaps that's because I've got a business to run!'

'I know you've got a business to run and you're very good at it. All I'm saying is that sometimes you need to make a little bit more effort with people. The world doesn't just revolve around work, you know. Other things, other people are more important.'

'Yeah, like all we need is love,' Sapphire replied, her voice spiked with sarcasm.

She really resented that, she was trying to make something of herself. She was ready to bite back at Jay but he sighed, and put his arm round her. 'Come on babe, let's not argue. I'm away for the next week on a course, let's make the most of tonight.'

'I didn't know you were away,' Sapphire snapped.

'I told you the other week,' Jay replied, sounding slightly resentful. 'I expect you were busy sorting out the hen weekend and forgot.'

Suddenly Sapphire felt a pang of guilt. Maybe Luke

136

was right and she didn't deserve Jay. She turned and kissed him, 'Sorry. I know I have been preoccupied lately.'

At that moment Christine and Vicky walked into the living room. Sapphire's mouth fell open in astonishment. Her mum looked fantastic, wearing make-up for the first time in ages and dressed in a cobalt-blue wrap dress that revealed a great figure.

'Mum, you look stunning!'

Christine seemed thrilled at the compliment. 'And Vicky asked us to spend Christmas with them, isn't that wonderful! I know how you hate spending Christmas just with me.'

Great, so now her mum was making her sound like a total bitch. 'I don't hate it, Mum,' Sapphire said quietly. 'It just makes me feel sad that there's only two of us is all.'

Vicky caught her eye and smiled, 'Well, there's going to be eight of us, so it should be a right laugh.'

Sapphire fully expected Jay to come back to her place that night – she felt she'd done her bit by spending two nights at his. Instead Jay replied that he had to get ready for his course, and wanted her to come back with him. 'Will Luke be there?' she asked.

Jay sighed, 'Of course.'

'Well, I think I'll go back to mine. I'm pretty knackered.' Sapphire wasn't at all tired but she couldn't bear having more snide comments directed at her.

'Okay, Sapphire, it's up to you. I'll miss you though.'

Then come back to mine! Sapphire wanted to say. Instead she kissed him. 'I'll miss you too.'

Chapter 9

But in the week that followed, Sapphire was so stressed about work she hardly had time to think about anything else. She had two hen parties cancel on her, both citing the credit crunch, which sent her into a tail spin – though she was relieved it was nothing to do with the bad publicity from Georgia's disastrous weekend. She just had to find ways of generating more income with the boutique. She went ahead and booked her Christmas promotions. She didn't get to bed until after midnight every night because she was working and she barely remembered to text Jay.

On Friday morning she was busily decorating the boutique with Christmas decorations when Ryan walked in.

'Very festive,' he commented as Sapphire hung glass stars from the lights. 'But tasteful, just how I like it,' he continued.

He waited until Sapphire had finished what she was doing then kissed her cheek. Don't blush, she told herself sternly.

'So how are you?' she asked casually. But her heart raced that little bit faster.

'Good,' he replied, walking round the boutique and pausing every now and then to pick up a set of lingerie and consider it. No doubt he was a connoisseur of expensive underwear.

Sapphire decided to go for the direct approach, 'I imagine Simone is probably a 32D but if it's the wrong size, you can always change it.'

Ryan smiled, 'I'm not buying anything for her; I'm just looking.' He picked up a lingerie set in midnight blue and held it against Sapphire. 'Now that would look fantastic with your skin.' It was an electric moment and Sapphire felt sure he must have known the effect he was having on her.

'Perhaps I'll ask Jay to get it for me for Christmas,' Sapphire said lightly.

Ryan looked at the price tag and whistled. 'I doubt he could afford this.'

Sapphire frowned. Even though she found Ryan undeniably attractive, she didn't want to be disloyal to Jay. Ryan caught the look. 'Anyway, I came to ask if you fancied coming to a club opening tomorrow night in London. Thought we might both be able to pick up some ideas.'

'Is Simone going?'

Ryan smiled, 'No, she's filming something or other.' He paused and gave a rueful smile. 'It was only supposed to be a fling, but she's kind of hard to shake off. I think she wants a relationship.' He shrugged.

Sapphire considered the offer. It would be great to have a night out in London and it would be useful to research other clubs. But deep down she knew that wasn't the reason. The lure was having time with Ryan, alone – picking up their flirtation where they left off . . .

As far as Sapphire was concerned no one else needed to know about her little jaunt to London, but the following morning Jazz asked her and Sam round for a girls' night in. Sapphire was incapable of lying to her friend, and Jazz gave her the real third degree, asking her why she was going, was Ryan's girlfriend going, was she going to tell Jay?

139

'It's just a work thing,' Sapphire said airily as Jazz glared at her. 'There might be some useful people.'

'And how would you feel if Jay went out to some club with another woman?' Jazz put to her. 'On his *own,*' she added.

Sapphire shrugged. 'I'd be fine about it. Look Jazz, there's nothing going on between me and Ryan, I swear.' But she couldn't look Jazz in the eye and she was trying to convince herself as much as her friend.

'Just be careful, Sapphire. He's a player and he's obviously after you, otherwise he would have asked Simone.'

Bollocks! why did Jazz have to be so bloody perceptive!

'So what are you going to wear?' Thankfully Jazz changed the subject.

'Oh, I don't know,' Sapphire lied.

As soon as Ryan had asked her she had been planning her outfit. She was going to wear her high-street copy of a strapless black, Hervé Léger dress, the most figure-hugging, curve-enhancing dress she possessed, with her Louboutins – in other words, her full seduction outfit.

But Sapphire felt guilty throughout the train journey to London and was almost tempted to get the train straight back home to Brighton after she received a sweet text from Jay saying how much he missed her and how he couldn't wait to see her the next day. However, her devilish side won and she took a taxi to the Sanderson where she was to meet Ryan before going on to the club.

As the doorman held the glass door open for her and she walked into the airy minimalist lobby and got her bearings, the nerves kicked in. It suddenly seemed like a big deal to be meeting Ryan like this. But she shook back her hair determinedly and walked into the bar. It was packed and it took her several minutes to find Ryan. She felt the tell-tale sign of her heart racing a little bit faster when she saw him sitting at the ultra-stylish, glowing onyx

Long Bar, a whisky in front of him. He looked sexy and sophisticated – a very tasty combination, she thought.

'You look gorgeous, Sapphire,' he told her, kissing her lightly on the cheek.

Sapphire shook her head as she arranged herself on the chair next to him – body con dresses were all very well when you were standing up, not so great sitting down. She inched her skirt down, trying to cover up the expanse of thigh she'd just revealed. But Ryan was having none of it. 'Don't be falsely modest, it's really boring, you know how good you look.'

Sapphire gave in, 'Thank you. So how did your meetings go today?'

Ryan had told her he had lined up several business meetings as he and Alfie wanted more investors in the club.

Ryan pulled a face. 'Not great. No one seems to want to loan us any money and we need to expand. It's tough at the moment.' He paused and looked serious. 'Well, there is one person who I might see later.' He shrugged. 'Let's not talk about it, I'd much rather talk about you.' He gave Sapphire the full benefit of his green eyes.

God, he was fit, especially with that accent! She could feel her self-control wavering. They stayed in the bar for a couple of Mojitos, which went straight to Sapphire's head as she hadn't been able to eat all day. It was good being somewhere anonymous – not like Brighton where there was a strong chance that someone they knew would see them together and jump to the wrong conclusion. But was it the wrong conclusion? Sapphire was feeling more and more attracted to Ryan. She loved the rush that being with him gave her – the delicious, flirtatious, giddy feeling. Yes, she found Jay very attractive but there was something extra about being with Ryan – something dangerous, exciting, and unpredictable – something that appealed to Sapphire's thrill-seeking side.

Just after midnight they hit the club. It was already packed – Sapphire spotted at least eight ex-reality show contestants desperately clinging on to the last nano-second of their fifteen minutes of fame. They seemed a pretty pathetic bunch to her – the girls in the most revealing outfits possible, short of actually being naked, the blokes pumped and fak-tanned up to the eyeballs. Sapphire had always wanted to succeed in business and been driven by her ambition and desire to make something of herself. She didn't get the appeal of being famous just for appearing on a reality show. Especially now it seemed that people had to behave in more and more extreme ways to get themselves noticed. She smiled to herself as one of the girls shimmied past her in a minuscule pair of hot pants. She seemed so desperate for attention you could almost smell it in the air.

Ryan was on the guest list and he led Sapphire through to the VIP area. Sapphire was secretly hoping they could just carry on with their flirting but Ryan spotted someone he knew. 'That's the club owner over there; I might have to talk business with him for a while.'

Sapphire followed him over to where a thickly built man in an expensive-looking suit was sitting. Ryan introduced her to Markov, a Ukrainian in his mid-forties. Sapphire didn't warm to Markov one little bit, he had the coldest pale grey eyes she had ever seen and she didn't like the predatory way he looked at her. His hair was dyed white-blond, which looked strange against his dark skin and eyebrows. He made a big show of taking Sapphire's hand and kissing it, plus he was wearing so much aftershave, a strong, sickly sweet smell that got right up Sapphire's nose.

'Sapphire!' he exclaimed in strongly accented English. 'What a beautiful name, but it is perfect for a beautiful woman like you. Would you like champagne? I have vintage Cristal or Laurent Perrier. Whatever you want, I will get for you.'

'Cristal would be lovely,' Sapphire tried to be polite but she felt Markov was a right creep.

'I just need to borrow Ryan to talk business for a few minutes, Sapphire. You don't mind do you? I promise we won't be long. You can talk to Alina,' he gestured at a stunning blonde with sculpted cheekbones and green eyes who had been sitting next to him and then turned away and started talking quietly to Ryan.

Sapphire felt as if she was being treated like some bimbo trophy girlfriend. She didn't like it at all. She tried to make conversation with Alina then gave up as she seemed strung out, from drink or drugs Sapphire couldn't tell. She sat back on the gold leather sofa and tapped her foot on the floor in irritation, while the beautiful blonde texted on a crystal-encrusted phone. She was a fool to have come here with Ryan – she could have been chilling with her best friends and having a laugh. Ten minutes went by, Markov and Ryan continuing to whisper conspiratorially. Then Markov turned to Sapphire. 'So Ryan tells me you are quite the businesswoman. I am impressed. Only twenty-seven and already you have a successful business. Beauty and brains – what a combination, eh Ryan?'

He put his arm round Ryan as if they were best buddies. Ryan appeared as if he was forcing a smile. Sapphire was about to reply when Alina knocked over her glass, spilling champagne all over Sapphire's dress.

Instantly a change came over Markov – gone was the smile and buddy act. He looked absolutely furious and fired off something in Ukrainian that had Alina cowering back on the sofa. Then Markov stood up and gestured at the men sitting at the neighbouring table. Two men built like wrestlers, their heads shaved and wearing identical black suits came over. One of them reached out and took Alina's arm, forcing her to stand up and before Sapphire could say anything he led her away while the other one handed Sapphire a napkin. Then he picked up Alina's bag and phone and left.

'There is nothing worse than a drunk woman,' Markov said in disgust. Sapphire shot Ryan a WTF look, but he just shrugged.

Markov then smiled at Sapphire. 'I'm so sorry for your dress. You will let me know how much it was and I will replace it.'

'There is no need,' Sapphire said. 'Please. I didn't want Alina to have to leave. It was just an accident.'

'She needs to go home – she will be fine.'

Sapphire suddenly felt as if she needed to get away – Markov made her feel claustrophobic, and muttering something about wanting to find the bathroom she stood up and walked quickly away from the table.

She paused at the bar on her way back and ordered herself a vodka. She was in no hurry to return to the men. What had happened to Alina? God, she hoped she was okay.

She looked round the club. Markov clearly had a thing about gold – there were gold pillars, gold walls and gold chandeliers. The black-and-gold wallpaper behind the bar caught her eye, and she realised the pattern was of couples shagging in different positions – classy.

Ryan appeared at her side, 'I'm so sorry, Sapphire, we had some business to discuss, I couldn't get out of it. Markov's a hard man to pin down; I had to take my chance when I could.'

'So I noticed,' Sapphire said feeling more than a little put out. She hadn't come to the club to feel like she was just something pretty for Ryan to show off or to meet a creep like Markov.

It was crowded by the bar; Ryan frowned as someone

knocked into him. 'Come back to the VIP area, we can't talk here.'

Sapphire remained standing where she was – she didn't want to go anywhere near Markov again. She folded her arms. 'How well do you know Markov? I really didn't like how he treated Alina.'

Ryan sighed, 'I need him for business. And don't worry about Alina, I've just seen her, she's going home. She had a bit too much Cristal is all. I know Markov seemed harsh but he's been trying to help her.'

'Really?' Markov didn't seem to want to help Alina; punish her, more like.

'Really,' Ryan replied. He moved closer to Sapphire and gave her the full benefit of his stunning green eyes as he lowered his voice. 'Please come back, I want to make it up to you.'

'Promise I don't have to see that Markov again?'

'I promise,' Ryan replied, putting his arm lightly round her and steering her back to the VIP area.

As they sat on the sofa together Ryan kept his arm round her. 'Friends again?' he murmured.

'Possibly,' Sapphire replied, arching one of her eyebrows flirtatiously.

Now Markov had gone, her mood improved dramatically.

Ryan moved closer still, and whispered in her ear, 'But I think we both know we'd like to be more than just friends.' His voice sounded husky with longing. 'I still can't stop thinking about you, Sapphire. You don't know what you do to me.'

He was so close, Sapphire could feel the warmth of his body, could feel his breath against her skin, could smell his musky aftershave. Her mind said no but her treacherous body longed for his touch. She was finding the look of desire in his eyes such a turn-on. Rational thought went out of the window. He moved closer still and now his lips were on hers and they were kissing. His lips were soft and firm, different to Jay's, not better, just different. She liked the novelty. Now he was sliding one of his hands along her thigh, a knowing hand, that tantalised her skin, made her long for his caress to go higher.

He pulled away from the kiss to gaze at her. 'Beautiful Sapphire, we could be so good together. We belong together.'

Sapphire stared back at him, her body fizzing with lust, but she could not do this to Jay. No way. This was wrong. She had to go. She got up abruptly but Ryan seized her hand, 'You're not going anywhere.' She was about to reply that oh yes she was when Ryan caught sight of someone behind her and instantly his face clouded over. 'Shit,' he muttered, abruptly letting go of her hand. Sapphire turned round and came face to face with Simone. She was smiling at the couple but it was a smile that didn't reach her hazel eyes.

'Simone!' Ryan exclaimed, standing up, while Sapphire stepped away from him. Please let Simone not have seen the kiss!

'How did the filming go?' Ryan went on. He had quickly regained his composure and Sapphire was slightly put off by the way he slipped so effortlessly into the role of Simone's boyfriend, kissing her and, stroking her arm. Sapphire just prayed she couldn't detect her perfume on Ryan.

'We finished early so I thought I'd surprise you, babe,' Simone said smoothly, but there was a definite edge to her voice.

She must have seen the kiss, Sapphire thought. Now she felt even worse. Much as she disliked Simone, she didn't want to do the dirty on her; she really wasn't that kind of person. And she knew how dangerous Simone would be when she was hurt. She reached for her bag and tried to appear casual, even though she was sure she was sending out guilty signals like a distress beacon. 'Well I'm off, thanks for inviting me, Ryan,' she couldn't bring herself to look at him.

'Stay for another drink,' he replied, seemingly guilt free.

'No thanks, I really have to go.'

Sapphire walked briskly through the club but just as she was about to reach the exit she walked straight into Markov. 'Going already, beautiful? But the night is so young.' God, could he only talk in clichés? 'Come drink some more champagne with me.'

He put a proprietorial hand on her arm and his sleeve fell back revealing a completely hairless arm, which freaked Sapphire out. His hand felt moist and fleshy against her bare skin. Sapphire shook her head and suppressed a shudder. 'Thanks but I've really got to go.'

Mercifully Markov let go of her. 'We should talk. I'm very interested in expanding in Brighton.' He reached into his pocket and pulled out his card and handed it to her. She noticed a huge diamond ring on his finger, which looked like the real deal. Markov clearly was loaded, but that didn't mean she wanted anything to do with him. Reluctantly Sapphire took the card.

'And can I have yours?' It was more an order than a request.

She scrambled in her clutch bag for her business card and handed it over, eager to get away. Markov looked at it intently, ' "Something For The Weekend", I like it. I'll be in touch, Sapphire Jones. I really think we could do business together to both our advantage. I imagine you are always on the look-out for new investors and in these times it must be worrying to be a small business – you never know when the banks are going to, how do you say it – plug the pull.' He smiled at her, showing off brilliantly white teeth.

'Pull the plug,' Sapphire muttered her correction, but

she had a feeling Markov knew perfectly well what he should have said. 'I really must go,' she repeated and practically ran out of the club, not wanting to spend another second in his company.

It was freezing outside and she shivered in her black leather jacket and thin dress as she waited to hail a taxi. In her desperation to get away she hadn't even thought about how she was going to get home. By the time she reached Victoria station it was after three in the morning – she had nearly an hour to kill before the next train. All the cafés and bars were closed and Sapphire had to keep walking around to keep warm, even though her feet were killing her in her heels. She felt very conspicuous in her revealing dress and bitterly regretted the night.

She was just going through the ticket barrier when a familiar and not at all welcome voice said, 'Hi, Sapphire, had a big night out?'

Shit! It was Luke, travelling back on the same train as her. His eyes skimmed over her, taking in the short dress. 'You must be cold.'

'I'm fine,' Sapphire replied, trying desperately to stop her teeth from chattering. 'I went to the opening of a new club. It was useful for business.'

Luke walked beside her to the train. He looked amused as he replied, 'Do you always dress like that for business events? Isn't it hard to be taken seriously?'

He was clearly determined to needle her yet again, but no way was Sapphire going to have him in her face all the way back to Brighton.

'I'm just going to find the loo,' she lied and walked ahead of him. When she thought she'd lost him she found a carriage with other people in it and curled up on one of the seats, hoping that Luke wouldn't find her.

She checked her mobile; there was another message from Jay saying he would be back in the morning and what time should they meet up. Great, now she'd have to tell him about the trip to London. The question was, could she get away with not telling him about Ryan?

Jay was so loving when she met up with him again that she felt even more guilty. He wanted to take her straight to bed but Sapphire insisted that she had something to tell him. She couldn't believe that Luke would have missed an opportunity to let Jay know what she'd been up to and put some nasty little spin on it but apparently he hadn't as Jay looked surprised when Sapphire said she'd seen him. 'Alfie's business partner invited me to this club launch, and I thought I may as well go.'

Jay frowned, 'What, that flash one who fancies himself, the one we saw in the restaurant?'

'Yep, he was there with his girlfriend Simone.' Sapphire busied herself pouring them each a glass of wine, and turned away from him as she continued, 'Yeah, I hardly saw them, but it was useful, I guess, to see the new club and I met a few people.'

Even as she lied so convincingly the memory of the kiss with Ryan flared up inside her mind. It had been so good. Sapphire couldn't help loving those early flirtatious encounters with a man, they were so addictive, the surge of adrenalin and lust so compelling. It made her feel so alive. Jay was a fantastic lover, but their time together was sometimes just a little bit safe.

Jay walked over to her and put his arms round her waist and kissed her neck. 'Glad you had a good night, babe; you deserve it after working so hard.'

Oops, his being nice levered up her sense of guilt. Sapphire leant against him. Sweet Jay, why couldn't she just accept how lucky she was and forget all about Ryan and his sexy knowing eyes?

'What's this?' he asked, his gaze falling on the wedding invitation Sapphire had just received from Georgia.

Frankly, she thought Georgia had a nerve, after everything that had happened but equally she supposed it could be useful if she went. 'You're not going are you? After what she did?' Jay sounded shocked.

Sapphire shrugged, 'Babe, I know she behaved atrociously and I can't stand the woman, but there might be some useful contacts and the way business is at the moment, I can't afford to be that choosy. Things are really, really tough.'

Jay abruptly let go of her. 'I'd feel really insulted if you went, Sapphire. It would be like saying what they did to me didn't matter, that *I* didn't matter to you. I really don't want you to go.'

Sapphire stared at him in disbelief. He looked seriously pissed off. He was usually so easy-going, so pliable. What the fuck was this about? 'Of course it wouldn't be saying that, Jay! You're completely overreacting!'

Sapphire had actually been in two minds about going, but now she was convinced that she should – she hated being told what to do.

'So you're going to go? And arse-lick the woman who humiliated me in public and treated me like shit? Jesus Christ, Sapphire, I had no idea you were so unfeeling! You're so single-minded, aren't you?'

He was shouting now and Sapphire had lost her cool as well. 'No, I'm not unfeeling!' she shouted back, 'I'm just being realistic! And not letting my feelings get in the way of good business! Just because you've got no idea how hard it is running a business right now – you're all safe and cosy in your little world, where everyone is nice to each other. Well, wake up and smell the fucking coffee! The real world isn't like that! I don't like Georgia either, in fact I hate her for what she did to you, but it really could help my business if I went. I just don't get why you can't see that.'

They glared at each other. Sapphire had never felt so

angry with Jay before and it was clear he was just as furious as she was. 'So that's your final word on it is it? Jay shouted. 'You're going to the wedding, even though I've just told you how much it will piss me off?'

Sapphire nodded. She expected another tongue lashing from Jay but he just shrugged. 'Okay, at least I know where I stand.' And he started walking towards the door.

'Hey!' Sapphire called after him, 'I thought we were supposed to be spending the night together!'

Jay turned round briefly and said, 'I hope the wedding's worth it for you.'

Jazz and Sam completely failed to see Sapphire's point of view when she caught up with them later that night in their usual bar, full of outrage about Jay's behaviour.

'Come on, Sapphire, can't you understand why he's so pissed off?' Jazz put in reasonably after Sapphire had ranted for at least ten minutes about how naive Jay was being.

'No I can't, I think he's being totally precious,' she snapped back.

Sam had been largely silent but now she spoke. 'Sapphire, if you go to that wedding you will lose Jay. I don't think he will ever forgive you and if I was him, I wouldn't either. He's the best thing that's happened to you in such a long while, but if you want to throw him away, go to that wedding and it will be a done deal.' Sam looked so serious and so disapproving that it just hardened Sapphire's resolve.

'Whatever. I got on perfectly fine before I met Jay and I'll get on perfectly fine without him. I don't need him in my life. I don't need any man in my life.'

Somewhere a small voice said that she did want Jay, that she would miss him, but the arrogant side of her that

151

hated to be told what to do silenced it. 'In fact,' she continued, 'fuck him!'

At this Sam abruptly stood up and grabbed her bag. 'I'm going. I've got an early start tomorrow. See you, Jazz.' She paused and with some effort added, 'See you, Sapphire.'

Sapphire waited until she was out of earshot then exclaimed, 'What's her problem, Jazz?'

'She just cares about you,' Jazz replied. 'We both do.'

Sapphire gave a false little laugh, 'I'm a big girl, Jazz, I can look after myself.'

They were brave words and she wasn't feeling so confident two days later when she still hadn't heard anything from Jay, despite texting him several times.

She threw herself into her work but it felt strange not talking to Jay. The truth was she missed him. Ryan was on her case though and called her several times. Although she got a jolt of excitement when she saw his name come up on her phone, Sapphire did not feel like speaking to him. She hadn't liked the way he had so easily handled Simone appearing at the club. He seemed too smooth an operator. She also received a very unwelcome text from Markov asking if she could meet up with him. She thought about his cold shark eyes, no way! She simply texted back that she was too busy. However, a day later a package arrived for her containing a black Hervé Léger strapless dress that Sapphire knew cost over a thousand pounds. There was no note and when she texted Ryan to ask if it was from him he told her it wasn't. That could only leave Markov. It seemed an extravagant gesture and one which made Sapphire feel uncomfortable. Beautiful as the dress was, Sapphire left it in her office and did not try it on. She promised herself she would send it back.

Right now she was too preoccupied with Jay. By Friday

she'd still heard nothing from him. The wedding was the following day. There was no question in Sapphire's mind: she had to go. Something good had to come of the disastrous hen weekend – who knows, she might make some useful contacts. Her business head knew that she was doing the right thing – that the company had to come first – but she woke up on Saturday morning with a feeling of apprehension. She tried to shrug it off and quickly got ready. She just wanted the day to be over and done with.

Georgia's wedding was the full works in a large country house just outside the M25. She had managed to hold on to her magazine deal, probably after drastically slashing her demands, but security was still tight and Sapphire and all the other guests had to leave their mobiles behind. She sent one last text to Jay asking if they could meet up on Sunday but by the time she left her hotel room, there was still no word. Hopefully by Sunday he would have it out of his system and Sapphire could talk him round again. Hopefully.

The marquee had been given a winter wonderland makeover, with ice sculptures all around of polar bears and swans, and occupying pride of place in the middle of the room was an ice sculpture of the couple embracing naked. Fortunately their bodies were pressed together so the guests didn't get the full works. There were trees sprayed silver and decorated in twinkling fairy lights, crystals had been encrusted on just about everything, from the bar to the vases filled with white roses. Every now and then fake snow would fall down from the ceiling in a flurry.

Sapphire looked around. At the far side of the marquee she recognised six of the hens from Georgia's hen night, who had all gone for revealing silver or white dresses. Shit, she didn't want to have to make small talk to those mingers. She quickly turned the other way. She took a glass of champagne from one of the waiters dressed as a naughty angel in a pair of tight white shorts and a set of white fluffy angel wings and nothing else, and walked around feeling self-conscious. If the whole wedding was going to be like this then she may as well not have come. Then she caught sight of Alfie. Oh God, she had very much hoped that Alfie wouldn't turn up. Maybe he hadn't noticed her and she could somehow avoid him. But he waved at her. She hesitated for a second then reluctantly made her way over to where he was standing. Somehow in this situation it seemed to be better to be with the devil you knew.

'Looking gorgeous, babe, better not stand too close to the bride or you'll upstage her,' Alfie told her, his eyes doing their usual survey of her body in the shoulder-revealing, black silk halter-neck.

Sapphire laughed dismissively. 'You don't need to waste your compliments on me. I'm immune remember – why don't you find someone else?'

Alfie shrugged. 'You've got the hots for Ryan, haven't you?'

Sapphire curled her lip. 'We get on well, but isn't that good for business? Besides, he's seeing Simone.'

'Just be careful, Sapphire. I wouldn't want to see you get hurt,' Alfie said seriously. 'There are things about him I don't think you would like.'

Sapphire burst out laughing. 'Alfie, I had no idea you could be this jealous.'

'Just be careful,' Alfie repeated.

God! Why was it that everyone was so determined to tell her what to do? 'Your concern is touching,' she said. 'What a pity that feeling wasn't in your mind two years ago when you were shagging Brooke. I guess that's why you can warn me about Ryan because you know he's just like you. Well, I'm not the same person that I was back then. And I know exactly how to handle Ryan.'

'Don't think I don't regret what I did, Sapphire,' Alfie said, staring into her eyes. 'There isn't a day that goes past where I don't regret it.'

A declaration of love from her ex-husband! That was all she needed. She was about to tell him not to be so stupid when Ryan and Simone sauntered over. Simone looked stunning in a silver sequinned dress and Sapphire was going to tell her how good she looked when Simone shot her a glacial stare – if the ice sculptures started to melt she could be stationed next to them and they'd freeze in seconds.

Ryan's look was altogether warmer. Sapphire forgot her reservations about his behaviour in the club as he looked at her with his stunning green eyes. In fact certain regions were definitely getting warmer. Things were certainly starting to look up. Sapphire felt herself relax, everything would be okay – she'd get through today and then make things up with Jay – she'd use her infatuation with Ryan to give their lovemaking an extra edge. She did love make-up sex, it was always hotter. She smiled to herself as she sipped her champagne.

Simone caught the smile. 'So where's your boyfriend? Georgia did ask him didn't she? I know she wanted to apologise for the night of the hen party.'

'He had to work, I'm afraid, otherwise of course he'd have come,' Sapphire replied.

Simone laughed, 'Of course, he's your boy toy isn't he? I expect he does everything you say.' She turned and ran her hand possessively along Ryan's arm. 'I'm more into men myself.'

Sapphire noticed that Ryan looked uneasy.

The four stayed chatting throughout the champagne and canapés – not that Simone ate anything. Sapphire could see Georgia and her husband-to-be circulating round their guests. Georgia certainly hadn't gone for a virginal bride look in a slashed-to-the-navel slinky white silk number that looked like it was staying on by sheer willpower alone. Her make-up would not have been out of place on a drag queen. She had a huge diamond tiara on her head, and a white fur wrap draped round her shoulders, that Sapphire hoped was fake. Eventually she made her way over and introduced her groom, Tyler. He was boyishly good-looking with a slightly hunted look in his eye. Sapphire couldn't help feeling sorry for him; he surely couldn't know what he was letting himself in for. But then again, maybe he was really stupid and deserved Georgia.

'Darling Sapphire! I'm so glad you could make it. I really did want to apologise for what happened.' She looked around. 'That gorgeous boy not with you? I expect he was worried that I might ask for an encore.' She burst into her trademark raucous cackle, then whispered in Sapphire's ear, 'Fabulous cock. I'd hang on to him if I were you.'

Sapphire backed away and gave a stiff little smile. 'You look amazing, Georgia.' That was a safe comment and it was always essential to compliment the bride, even if she did look like a hooker.

When it was time for the ceremony the guests were directed into the house and into a large hall. Here the theme was still white but it was a little more tasteful than the marquee – maybe the owners had put their foot down about having nude ice sculptures and fake snow. Sapphire sat next to Alfie, and Ryan and Simone sat on the chairs the other side of the aisle, which was lined with storm lanterns, each filled with white rose petals and a large scented candle, and which led up to a huge fireplace decorated with hundreds of white flowers.

Sapphire did her very best not to look across at Ryan but every now and then she glanced over at him and their

156

eyes would meet. Sapphire would always look away first. A string ensemble were playing something that Sapphire was pretty sure was Vivaldi, then they switched to playing the Hot Chocolate number 'You Sexy Thing' as first Tyler walked up the aisle and then Georgia sashayed behind him, clearly relishing the attention.

'You couldn't make it up,' Alfie whispered to Sapphire and she had to agree.

The ceremony was mercifully brief, though during the vows Georgia did an outrageous stage wink when she promised to be faithful which had many of the guests barely able to contain their laughter.

'I give it six months,' Alfie whispered again to Sapphire.

She shook her head and held up three fingers.

Sapphire found herself sharing a table with Alfie, Ryan and Simone for the wedding breakfast. In spite of her earlier tough-girl act she couldn't deny how unsettling it was to be at a wedding with her ex-husband. She kept remembering their own. Neither had much money and so their wedding had been a small registry office job at Brighton Town Hall with a meal for close family and friends at Sapphire's favourite Italian restaurant afterwards. It had been a glorious late September day, the sunshine gave everything a golden glow and after the meal they'd all gone down to the beach and drunk champagne until the sun set. Sapphire had thought it was the happiest day of her life.

Alfie must have been thinking about their wedding day too because at one point during the meal he put his hand over hers and said quietly, 'This must have cost a thousand times more than our wedding and yet it's nowhere near as stylish is it?'

He was right but Sapphire still wasn't in a place where she could even begin to forgive Alfie so instead she replied, 'Yes, our wedding was more stylish but turned out to be a sham because of what you did. Maybe, whatever we think, Georgia's will better stand the test of time.'

She quickly moved her hand away from Alfie's and unfortunately caught Simone's eye. She gave a knowing smile. 'Must be weird for you two being at a wedding together.'

Sapphire shrugged; no way was she going to give the slightest hint that she felt anything. She would not allow Simone that satisfaction. 'Not really. So have you ever been married, Simone?'

Simone's face clouded over. Ha! Sapphire had touched a nerve, then. No doubt Simone would have given anything to marry Cal Bailey. Ryan spoke up, 'I think Simone's like me, she's a free spirit, doesn't want to be tied down, do you?'

Simone managed a smile but Sapphire reckoned Simone would have liked nothing better to be married to someone wealthy. She was over thirty now and looked it. Clearly she put a lot of effort into her appearance but there were all those twenty-somethings snapping at her Louboutins, landing the sexy roles in soaps and all the tastiest premiership footballers. Simone had been a WAG for a while but now she was on the WAG scrap heap, too old to catch a top player. Sapphire might even have felt a tiny bit of sympathy for Simone, if she hadn't despised her for trading off her looks and being such a bitch.

Suddenly Sapphire wished she hadn't come to the wedding. She hadn't made any useful contacts and she'd upset Jay for nothing. She looked at her watch – another three hours to go before she could realistically slip away to her hotel room and watch TV. The speeches were next. Georgia's dad was so drunk he could barely speak – it must run in the family then – the best man's speech was crude and full of references to Tyler's past sexual exploits, which might have had most brides blushing but Georgia laughed uproariously. Then it was the dancing. Georgia and Tyler took to the floor first. They were both the worse for wear and could hardly stand up as they shuffled round the dance floor to 'Three Times a Lady', an ironic choice as Tyler groped Georgia's bum.

'Now that's what I call classy,' Ryan whispered sarcastically to Sapphire. He was temporarily free of Simone who was caught up with chatting to some friends.

Sapphire smiled.

'That's practically the first time I've seen you smile all day,' Ryan went on. 'Sorry about the other night by the way, I had absolutely no idea she was going to turn up.' He gazed at her with those dangerously gorgeous green eyes, 'I've finished with her you know, I'm only here because she practically begged me to come with her, and because I wanted to see you.' Ryan stepped closer; Sapphire's stomach lurched treacherously.

'You're the sexiest woman I've ever met, Sapphire. After that kiss I know we could be so good together.'

They were such corny lines and if anyone else had said them Sapphire would have laughed in disbelief. But she really didn't feel like laughing. She was flattered, intrigued and she wanted Ryan to find her sexy, wanted it very much. Ryan shifted his gaze away from Sapphire to take in the crowded marquee. 'Look, it's so busy in here, why don't we go outside and look at the stars.'

Without even waiting for her answer he lifted two glasses and a bottle of champagne from the table and began weaving his way through the guests. Sapphire looked behind her cautiously, and when she'd satisfied herself that neither Alfie or Simone had seen her, she followed Ryan. The temperature was hovering just above freezing outside and Sapphire's breath formed clouds in front of her face. Stars glittered and the half moon looked dramatic in the clear night sky. Heaters had been erected around the marquee and Ryan sought out the one furthest away, which was half in shadow. But even with the benefit of the heater Sapphire was shivering in her silk dress. Ryan took off his dinner jacket and slipped it round her shoulders. It was warm from contact with his body, and the warmth caressed her skin. It felt very intimate. Sapphire got goosebumps again but that wasn't down to the cold.

'Alone at last,' Ryan said softly, running his hand lightly along Sapphire's cheek, another corny line yet still she wasn't complaining. 'I thought I'd never be able to prize Alfie away from you. He still wants you bad doesn't he?'

Sapphire shrugged. 'He can want all he likes; he's never going to have me.'

'Poor Alfie, I almost feel sorry for him.' Ryan smiled showing off his perfect, even white teeth.

'Don't feel that sorry for him, he put me through hell,' Sapphire said darkly.

'I don't. Anyway I don't want to talk about him.' He moved closer towards her. 'I don't want to talk at all.'

Closer still, his lips were on hers. And this time it was a hungry, searching, passionate kiss that left Sapphire in no doubt what he wanted. She closed her eyes and lost herself in the kiss, forgot about Jay, forgot about Alfie, just enjoyed the delicious moment. And then Ryan's hands were caressing her body, her breasts, turning her on almost unbearably. She loved his sexual confidence, loved the feeling of someone else taking charge for a change. She pressed her body against his. But suddenly Ryan was pulling away. 'Shit, that woman has a habit of turning up when she's not wanted,' he muttered and Sapphire saw Simone marching towards them, or rather attempting to march but her high heels kept getting stuck in the grass. It would have been comical but for the look of sheer venom on Simone's face. 'I might have guessed I'd find you two together. Thanks a lot for the humiliation, you bastard. I won't forget it.'

Ryan was about to speak but Simone threw the contents of the glass she was carrying in his face. While Ryan attempted to wipe his eyes, Simone turned her furious gaze to Sapphire. 'So, does your boy toy know what you get up to behind his back? I tell you one thing, you and Ryan are made for each other, neither of you seems to give a shit about anyone else. Well, fuck you both.'

Her voice caught with a sob and she turned to go. But as she attempted to storm away, her shoe came off. Ryan went to try and help her as she flailed around trying to put it back on her foot. 'Leave me alone, you fucker! I was so stupid, I thought you liked me, but you were just using me weren't you, until you'd lined up the next one.'

Tears were streaming down her face but Simone seemed oblivious to the havoc being wrought to her make-up – mascara streaked her cheeks and one set of false eyelashes were coming off. Sapphire was in the uneasy situation of actually feeling sorry for Simone, the display of hurt and humiliation was so raw. She and Ryan watched in silence as Simone stomped back into the marquee. Then Ryan put his arm round Sapphire but she moved away and handed back his jacket. For her the spell had been broken, guilt washed through her.

'I'm going to head back to the hotel,' she said quietly, feeling thoroughly ashamed of her behaviour.

'I suppose it would be pointless for me to ask if I could come with you?' Ryan asked.

Sapphire nodded and looked away.

'Okay, I understand.' He ducked down and gave her final kiss on the lips. 'You're definitely worth waiting for,' he said softly, sending shivers of longing running down her spine, even as she reflected that he thought a lot of himself.

As soon as she got back to her hotel room she reached for her mobile. At last a text from Jay. It took a few seconds for the message to sink in. Oh my God! She was being dumped. 'I can't see you any more, Sapphire. We want such different things. I can't be with someone who won't commit to a relationship. Take care. Jx.' Jay had finished with her! Sapphire couldn't believe it! If ever anyone was going to finish this relationship she thought it would be her. She was seriously pissed off. How fucking dare he! She angrily paced round her hotel room, raided the mini-bar and drained two miniatures of vodka before she calmed down. Then she reached for her phone. Ryan was going to get lucky after all.

He wasted no time in coming over and then it was all about sex, hot, raw sex, no tenderness, just two people out to get what they wanted. Ryan was a very practised lover, skilful, attentive, but Sapphire didn't feel treasured, or adored like she did with Jay. Instead she felt like she was something being ticked off a list – Ryan wanted her, now he'd got her. She was a trophy. Another notch to his bed post. And as he thrust inside her all she could think for a moment was that she wished she was with Jay . . .

'That was even better than I imagined,' Ryan panted as he flopped down next to her on the bed. 'You're fucking gorgeous, Sapphire.'
    'You're not bad yourself,' Sapphire resorted to banter to hide her feelings. All she wanted to do now was to have a shower then go to sleep, to shut out the images of Jay that were crowding into her mind.

Chapter 10

In the morning Sapphire woke up with an evil hangover and a sense of loss. For a second she couldn't remember why, then realisation hit her like a punch in the guts. Jay had finished with her. Well, fuck him! She didn't need a boy like that in her life, who didn't understand the realities of business.

She turned over and looked at Ryan who was lying on his stomach, one arm dangling over the side of the bed, out for the count and snoring quietly. He had thrown off the covers in his sleep and stank of booze. Sapphire supposed she must do as well. She didn't feel remotely turned on as she took in his naked form – his richly tanned skin, powerful muscular body and cute bum – though they'd certainly gone for it last night. She felt totally disconnected from him and everything else. It must be the hangover making her so depressed, she thought, as she hauled herself out of bed and headed for the bathroom.

When she returned Ryan was sitting up in bed, just ending a phone call. He grinned broadly when he saw Sapphire and whipped off the sheet to reveal his early morning erection. 'Come here baby, your services are needed urgently.'

Sapphire was really not in the mood, but she didn't see how she would get out of it. She walked towards the bed and shrugged off her robe. This was what she'd always wanted wasn't it? No-strings-attached sex?

'And now I've got something for you which is almost as good as what I've just given you,' Ryan murmured afterwards. Clearly Ryan did not do modesty.

'Oh yeah, what's that?' Sapphire asked, propping herself up on her elbows and looking at him.

'Vegas, baby.'

She shrugged, 'What about it?'

'You and me are going tonight, I've just booked the tickets. Five days staying at The Palms hotel – the one with the kinky suite. I can't wait to watch myself fucking you in the ceiling mirror.'

Sapphire abruptly sat up. 'There's no way I can go away so close to Christmas! It's such short notice.' And, she wanted to add, how dare he assume that she would want to go away with him?

'Shush babe – I knew you'd have all these objections, but really, you need a break. And we can discuss business when we're out there. Plus you've got your iPhone, you can still work. You're a great businesswoman but sometimes I think you need to chill more. Life isn't a rehearsal you know.'

Suddenly the fight went out of her. Why not go to Vegas? Why not do something impulsive for once? She'd been working like a dog lately, wouldn't it be good to have some downtime for a change? And a small voice said, wouldn't it be good to have something to take her mind off losing Jay?

There followed a week of complete hedonism. Practically all the staff seemed to know Ryan and welcomed him back like an old friend. Sapphire hoped that she wasn't one in a long line of girls getting the same treatment but in the end decided not to stress about it – she hardly wanted Ryan to declare his undying love for her. So every day the couple would get up late, lie in the jacuzzi drinking champagne, make love all afternoon or rather, have sex, and hit the casinos and clubs all night. Sapphire checked in regularly with work and Jazz assured her that everything was fine – though she couldn't hide the surprise from her voice when Sapphire revealed that Jay had finished with her or that Sapphire had plunged headlong into an affair with Ryan.

'Don't give me a hard time, Jazz,' Sapphire said after she'd told her friend the news. 'Jay finished with me, don't forget that.'

'I won't, Sapphire, I just hope you know what you're doing.'

'I'm just having fun, Jazz, that's all.'

But in spite of Ryan telling Sapphire that she needed to chill, in fact he was the one who was on edge. He hardly slept and spent a lot of time making calls back home which seemed to agitate him. After such calls, he would insist that he and Sapphire head to the casino, where he would inevitably end up losing. Sapphire didn't really feel that she was getting to know him. There was plenty of banter, flirtation and sex but nothing beyond that. Whenever she asked Ryan any personal questions he deflected them. 'I'm an open book, baby, what you see is what you get,' he would tell her.

The day before they were due to fly home Ryan said he had some work calls to make and Sapphire decided to take advantage of the hotel spa. She was halfway to the lift when she realised she'd forgotten her purse. She made her way back to their suite where she discovered Ryan in the middle of a furious phone call. So far she had only ever seen Ryan as a flirtatious, sexy, smooth operator. The Ryan on the phone seriously freaked her out – he was shouting, out of control, 'No I can't get you any more

165

fucking money, Markov! I told you it's tied up in the business! You're destroying me, man!'

Sapphire knew that she should just grab her purse and go but she was irresistibly drawn to hearing more. She hovered outside the living-room door.

'No more girls, either! I can't deal with any more right now, and you need to tell your heavies to lay off them. That last girl you brought me had a broken jaw, what the fuck are they doing to them? This isn't what I signed up for.'

Sapphire's mind was racing – what murky deals was Ryan tied up with? Suddenly she didn't want to hear any more. She tiptoed out of the suite although any thoughts she had about relaxing in the spa had been blown out of her mind. She needed a stiff drink but first she had a phone call of her own to make.

Alfie answered his phone on the first ring, 'Trouble in lovers' paradise, Sapphire?' he said drily.

'What's Ryan's connection to that Ukrainian?'

There was a sharp intake of breath on the other end of the line and then Alfie said, 'I think I know the man you mean.' He sighed, 'Do yourself a favour Sapphire, just don't go there.'

'Please Alfie, if you know something, tell me.'

'I can't over the phone.'

Sapphire laughed in disbelief. 'Why, do you think your phone is tapped?'

She expected a wisecrack reply from Alfie, but instead he said seriously, 'Enjoy the rest of your stay and I'll see you when you get back.'

What kind of bullshit answer was that? Sapphire stormed over to one of the many bars in the hotel and ordered herself a double vodka and tonic. And then she ordered another. It wasn't going to solve anything, but it took the edge off.

Halfway through her drink Ryan found her. 'I thought you were going to the spa, babe.' He was back to being the smooth operator again. She shrugged. 'I didn't feel like it after all.'

He sat on the stool next to her and ordered himself a large whisky and surveyed the scene. 'God, I love it here. It's like a pleasure dome where you can forget about the real world and just enjoy yourself. I wish we were staying another week. In fact I reckon I could stay here forever and never get tired of it. Who needs Paris when you can see the Eiffel Tower here?'

Any longer and it would be Sapphire's idea of hell. It was becoming clear that she and Ryan really had very little in common.

'Is there something on your mind, Ryan?' Sapphire asked, hoping that he might take the opportunity to open up about what was troubling him. She didn't want to admit to eavesdropping on his phone call.

'Nothing on my mind, babe, but plenty in other areas.'

He took her hand and guided it onto his jeans where she could feel his erection straining against the denim. 'How about we finish our drinks and go back upstairs? We've only one more day of the mirror experience and I want to make the most of it.'

It wasn't exactly the answer Sapphire had hoped for.

She felt unsettled for the remainder of their trip – there were no more phone calls but Ryan continued to seem on edge. As for Sapphire, she felt a tightness in her chest every time she thought of Jay. When she was on her own she found herself looking at the pictures of him she had on her phone, wondering if he was thinking about her. Probably not – she had blown that one big time.

Back in Brighton Ryan seemed no closer to confiding his troubles, whatever they were, to Sapphire. When she went to see Alfie he was evasive and a little on edge himself. For a start he wouldn't even talk to her in the club but insisted they went for a walk on the seafront. It was mid December and bitingly cold. They grabbed a coffee from one of the cafés and clutched the cups for warmth.

'So what is it about Ryan and this Markov? Is there something dodgy?'

Alfie shrugged, 'I don't ask, Sapphire, and if I were you, I wouldn't either.'

Sapphire wasn't about to give up. 'But Ryan said something about girls and about one girl having been hurt, do you know what he was talking about?'

At this Alfie's face clouded, 'I mean it, Sapphire, just don't go there, you don't want to know.'

Sapphire suddenly felt even colder and that wasn't just due to the icy wind whipping off the sea. 'I met him with Ryan and he insisted on me giving him my card, said how he was looking to expand in Brighton. Said it would be good for my business to have his investment. He texted me suggesting we meet up. And I'm pretty sure he sent me a designer dress.'

Why had Ryan introduced her to him? He hadn't exactly been thinking of her best interests, only his own.

Alfie put his arm round her in a gesture of reassurance and Sapphire was feeling so anxious that she didn't even try to push him away. 'Just keep your distance, it was probably a power kick he was on. I'm sure it will be okay.'

But even Alfie didn't look as if he believed his words.

Sapphire couldn't get rid of the anxiety in the days that followed but she did what she always did when she was stressed and buried herself in her work, and there was plenty to do in the run-up to Christmas, including the lingerie night, and pre-Christmas pampering parties they were laying on where women could get beauty treatments and chill out after Christmas shopping. Everywhere the talk was of the recession and the credit crunch, of businesses folding and people losing their jobs. Sapphire almost stopped wanting to listen to the news, or read a newspaper; to her it felt like the country was willing itself to disaster. And on top of all that was the dull ache she felt inside every time she thought of Jay, no matter how many extravagant dates she went on with Ryan.

'So is it serious between you and Ryan?' Jazz asked Sapphire as the two prepared the boutique for the men-only shopping night. Sapphire was arranging champagne flutes in rows and was hoping she could restrict the guests to one glass.

Sapphire's heart sank, she didn't welcome personal questions right now. She put on her breezy, I'm fine voice. 'Not especially, but that's good right now. I think we're quite similar, neither of us wants a long-term relationship – we just want to have fun.'

But had she been having fun? Sapphire wondered. There'd been the Vegas trip, plenty of expensive meals out, and nights out clubbing, Ryan seemed incapable of ever staying in and chilling. But she wasn't sure if it had been *fun*. Underlying everything was her worry about what Ryan might be tied up with and of course there were the women – Ryan flirted with practically every woman he came into contact with and his good looks meant he received a great deal of female attention. Was he faithful? Sapphire didn't know, but she knew she couldn't trust him. When she asked him if he believed in fidelity, he just laughed and said how could he have the energy to shag anyone else after her? It wasn't exactly what she'd been hoping to hear.

'Well, I guess you've got your no-strings-attached fling that you wanted,' Jazz continued and by the tone of her

169

voice Sapphire knew she disapproved. Both she and Sam had met Ryan several times now and she could tell they didn't exactly warm to him. And while Ryan was his typical charming flirtatious self with Jazz he was slightly less charming to Sam, and Sapphire couldn't help wondering if that was because he didn't fancy her because he thought she was fat. By comparison, Jay was friendly and easy-going with everyone, so kind and loyal, so many things that Ryan wasn't. Jay would never judge anyone on their appearance, but he wanted more than Sapphire could give. Ryan was shallow and egotistical, but he didn't place any demands on her. And that was what she wanted, wasn't it?

'Yeah, it's great,' Sapphire decided to be economical with the truth. 'I mean, I really liked Jay, but he was a bit of a boy, and now I'm going out with a man.'

Jazz frowned. 'Jay is a man, don't be so dismissive of him, Sapphire, just because he was nice to you and didn't flash cash around.'

Sapphire felt the familiar tightness in her chest at the mention of Jay's name. She tried to keep her feelings about the break-up locked away and she wouldn't, just wouldn't, think about Jay, wouldn't think about all the very good things about him, wouldn't allow herself to admit just how much she missed him.

'I know, I didn't mean it to sound like that, let's not talk about it, okay? I've got to focus on tonight. I need you to help me to decide what lingerie set to wear. Vanessa is going for the red, I thought maybe the cream? And we'll both wear silk robes.'

'Rather you than me,' Jazz said grimly.

Sapphire sighed. 'Well it's not exactly my idea of fun, but I need to get those punters in and spending money. And if baring some flesh is what it takes to do it, then I'm just going to have to grin and bear it – pun intended.'

*

170

Two hours later everything was ready in the boutique and Sapphire was kitted out in the cream silk lingerie. She'd had to down two glasses of champagne very quickly in order to give her confidence. She felt horribly exposed in the lingerie and stockings, even with the robe. This had better work, or she was going to feel like a hooker. It was getting the men through the door that worried her most. Once they were in, she was pretty sure of her sales techniques. For the first twenty minutes her worst fears were realised as no one turned up.

'Any minute now tumbleweed is going to start rolling through the store,' she tried to joke to Jazz, but she was on the verge of tears.

Then Ryan walked in, accompanied by four Eastern European-looking men. 'Brought you some customers, babe,' he said, taking her in his arms and kissing her, then he pulled back and whistled. 'You look fantastic.'

'Just make them spend,' Sapphire whispered.

'Will do,' Ryan replied and winked. He was a little worse for wear; she could smell whisky on his breath.

'So come on, gentlemen, pick out an outfit for your girlfriends and wives and my lovely girlfriend and Vanessa here will model it for you.'

Sapphire exchanged a slightly anxious glance with Vanessa. But Vanessa shrugged; she had no problem with showing off her gym-toned body, her view was if you had it, you may as well flaunt it.

Immediately the men made a bee-line for some of the more revealing outfits. Hopefully the end would justify the means so long as the men dug deep into their wallets, Sapphire thought grimly as she wriggled into a tiny black lace thong and matching bra that one of Ryan's friends selected for her. She had at least put out her most expensive underwear. The customers had no chance to be cheapskates in her boutique. By now more men had come into the boutique, swelling the numbers to around

171

twenty, and Jazz was busy handing out glasses of champagne and bottles of beer and generally being chatty.

Vanessa got everyone's attention by emerging from the dressing room in a hot-pink number. She looked fabulous; the men stopped talking and stared at her as if they couldn't believe their luck, as Vanessa turned and faced them, hands on hips, looking like a gorgeous supermodel. 'Gentlemen, welcome to Something For The Weekend, where we hope you will pick up something lovely for the lady in your life. To help you make your selection Sapphire and myself will be modelling a range of lingerie, so if you want to see something on, please let our sales representatives know.'

'Can't we see it off as well?' one lad shouted out to a chorus of laughs.

Without batting an eyelid Vanessa shot back, 'Spearmint Rhino is round the corner, but that'll cost you way more than getting something sexy for your girlfriend – which really, boys, as I'll think you'll agree, is the gift that keeps on giving.'

She then nodded to Jazz who turned up the music while Vanessa strutted her stuff across the room to Kylie's 'Can't Get You Out of My Head', pausing at one end to strike a pose, then sashaying back. She definitely had the moves, Sapphire thought enviously and from the captivated expressions on the customers' faces, they thought so too.

Then it was Sapphire's turn. She felt horribly self-conscious as she came out of the dressing room. It's for the greater good, she chanted to herself as she paraded across the boutique as if on a catwalk, pausing at the end to strike a pose, though she was sure her pose was more wooden than Vanessa's. Ryan caught her eye and winked and she managed to smile back. However uncertain she was of her performance, the modelling seemed to have broken the ice and many of the men began looking through the lingerie on display – clearly the prospect of seeing it on Vanessa and Sapphire was tempting.

Jazz and Kiki were rushed off their feet getting the right sizes for the girls and writing down which man wanted what so they could close the sale with them afterwards.

By the fifth outfit Sapphire was starting to feel more blasé; she was pleased to see that they had already sold several of the more expensive lingerie sets so she had an added spring to her step when she strided out from the dressing room in a sexy leopard-print number. But something in the crowd – a flash of white-blond hair – caught her eye. She froze for a few seconds as the two muscle-bound bodyguards she recognised from the club moved to one side revealing their boss, a dressed-down Markov in designer jeans and a pale cream leather jacket who smiled at her. Yuk – he looked like mutton dressed as ram and what the hell was he doing here? She felt a shiver of repulsion run down her spine at the memory of his meaty hand on her bare skin and as she recalled Ryan's phone call to him with his comments about girls being hurt.

Hating his gaze on her she swiftly made her way back to the cubicle. She and Vanessa had decided to take a short break to allow the customers to make their purchases, so Sapphire slipped on her robe and began circulating, chatting to the guests, making sure they had bought something, all the while avoiding Markov.

'Can't I have you for Christmas?' one cheeky bloke asked.

Sapphire was about to reply that there was no way that he could afford her, just as Ryan came up behind her and put his arms round her possessively. 'Mate, I've got exclusive rights on this bird.' And to Sapphire's annoyance he slapped her playfully on the bum. She might be having to parade half-naked but that didn't mean Sapphire wanted to be treated like a bimbo.

She managed a smile and then moved away. Ryan followed and when she was sure no one could hear them she hissed, 'Don't do that again.'

'Don't do what?' Ryan slurred. He'd been hitting the champagne and seemed pissed.

'Slap me on the bum.'

Ryan just laughed and reached out and groped her bum, 'Why not? It's such a lovely arse and anyway it gives me a proper thrill knowing how much these men want you but only I get to have you.'

Sapphire didn't want to make a scene but she was perilously close to telling Ryan to fuck off. She didn't like being mauled like this. Who did Ryan think he was?

'Babe, I've got to work, I'll catch up with you later,' she said disentangling herself from his embrace and she moved swiftly away before he could lurch for her again.

But then she found herself walking slap bang into another unwelcome situation as Markov stepped in front of her, 'Ah, the beautiful Sapphire.'

'What are you doing here?' she said through gritted teeth, almost gagging on his overpowering aftershave.

'Ryan invited me. You enjoyed Vegas, I hear. I'm always happy to treat my friends. Maybe next time you will come with me.'

'What d'you mean?' A horrible realisation was dawning on Sapphire.

'As I said, it was my treat.'

Sapphire felt sick – it was as if she'd been bought by Markov.

'And did you like the dress?' So it *had* been from him.

'I meant to return it, Markov, in fact I'll go and get it now.'

Sapphire made to go but Markov put his hand on her arm to stop her. She flinched at his touch as his eyes roved round the room, before resting on Sapphire for longer than was comfortable. 'No need, it's yours. Nice place you've got here. Very intimate. I congratulate you, Sapphire. I like everything I see very much.'

Now his eyes skimmed over her appraisingly and instinctively Sapphire pulled her robe together more tightly, a futile gesture really as he'd just seen her half-naked but it made her feel better and she managed to shake off his hand. Sapphire had always prided herself on her confidence, and on her ability to stand up to anyone, but she felt so intimidated by Markov. There was something deeply unpleasant about him and, if she was honest, menacing. He really was the kind of man you would cross the road to avoid, the kind of man whose eye you did not want to catch. She felt almost violated by his presence in her boutique. Why the hell had Ryan asked him?

'So have you seen anything you would like to buy?' she asked, trying to be the perky saleswoman.

'Plenty of things,' he replied. 'I am wondering what would suit you best. Would it be black?' He held up a black lacy number against Sapphire, the lingerie brushing against her skin – she felt a flush of humiliation and loathing spreading up from her neck at the gesture. 'Or would it be the cream?' He held up another set. Sapphire stood rooted to the spot. She suddenly felt like an object, powerless to move, which was no doubt exactly what Markov intended. He tilted his head to one side to consider her, 'Both look good, but of course,' he lowered his voice and continued, 'you would look best naked, say with a diamond round your neck.' At this he trailed one stubby finger round Sapphire's neck. Sapphire couldn't stop herself from flinching. He smiled then asked, 'How is business going, Sapphire?'

None of *your* business, she wanted to say, instead she muttered, 'It's tough for everyone isn't it?'

'You should think about starting something up in my country for your hen weekends – it's so much cheaper there than here and anything goes. I could help you,' Markov said. 'At times like this, we all need to be a little more creative.'

'Thanks, but I'm not looking to expand at the moment,' Sapphire replied diplomatically, inwardly shuddering at the thought of any involvement with Markov.

'And why do you waste your time with Ryan? You should really be with someone like me – a man who can give you whatever you want.'

Sapphire laughed nervously. 'But I am with Ryan. I'm very happy with Ryan,' she insisted, wondering where he was when she needed him.

Markov shrugged and muttered something in what she thought was Ukrainian; then he gestured at one of his massive bodyguards. When the man obediently came over Markov handed him both sets of lingerie. 'Pay for these and have them gift-wrapped.'

'A good choice,' Sapphire commented, trying to return the conversation to somewhere near normality. 'I'm sure they will suit your girlfriend.'

'I am glad you like them, they are for you. I will enjoy thinking of you wearing them.'

Now Markov had totally creeped her out. She wanted to tell him to fuck right off. But Markov wasn't the kind of man you said those things to. So instead she said quietly, 'I'm perfectly happy with Ryan.' She had to get rid of him. 'Thank you for coming tonight, enjoy the rest of your evening.'

'I will,' Markov replied, those cold eyes boring into hers, 'even though I would have enjoyed it so much more with you. But I'm a patient man, I can wait.'

Markov blew her a kiss and then headed over to the men Ryan had brought with him. As soon as he was out of earshot Sapphire sought out Ryan, who was still

176

knocking back the champagne. 'Why did you ask Markov here?' she demanded. 'You should have heard the way he was talking to me. Ugh! He totally creeped me out.'

Ryan's green eyes struggled to focus as he said defensively, 'He saw the invitation in my office, I couldn't exactly say you're not welcome. And I can't afford to piss him off right now. So sorry, babe, but you're a big girl, you can easily handle someone like him.'

He seemed unconcerned about Sapphire's feelings. He was beyond selfish. She saw red, 'So you don't mind some man groping me and making suggestive comments?'

Ryan shrugged, 'He's like that with all women, Sapphire, it's a power thing. My advice to you is just don't take it personally. Smile and look pretty. And be nice to him or he will take it out on me, and you wouldn't want that, babe, would you?'

He might just as well have said smile at a shark, Sapphire thought in fury as she headed once more for the cubicles. She clenched her fists and tried to calm down. She would not let Markov ruin her night. This was her business and he was not going to take it away from her. She hurriedly put on her next outfit – a turquoise blue silk number which she knew looked stunning against her hair and skin.

Jazz popped her head round the curtain, 'Are you okay? I saw you talking to that blond geezer and you didn't look very happy, was he hassling you?'

'Sort of,' Sapphire replied, not wanting to let on how disturbed she had been by Markov and his comments.

Jazz frowned. 'Well, why didn't you get Ryan to chuck him out?' Sweet Jazz, everything was always black and white to her.

'He's one of Ryan's business contacts, I couldn't do that. I'm sure it will be fine, Jazz, it's just that he's got a bit of a thing about me. But I can handle him, so don't worry.'

Jazz looked doubtful. 'Well, he's gone – him and those two fat baldies.'

Sapphire didn't let on quite how relieved she was. 'Good so go out there and get me some more orders!'

'Will do, boss,' Jazz replied.

After she'd gone, Sapphire looked at her reflection, trying to compose herself. Everything is *fine,* she tried repeating to herself, Markov is just on a power trip. But involuntarily she found herself rubbing at her neck, where Markov had touched her, until she had pulled herself together enough to face her customers again. There was a great buzz now in the boutique with some forty customers. They were buying underwear and also going for some of the other items, like the massage oils and cheeky sex toys. At least three of Sam's necklaces had sold as well. As Sapphire paraded across the room this time, she allowed herself to feel satisfied that at least the night had gone well and Markov had gone, which was an added bonus. But that satisfaction evaporated when she happened to glance out of the window and caught sight of Jay walking by with an exceptionally pretty blonde, who looked at least five years younger than Sapphire. She felt as if she'd been hit right in the solar plexus. He turned and looked inside the store and for a second their eyes locked, then he gave a brief nod of recognition and carried on walking. Sapphire just stood frozen to the spot, staring after him. A toxic, sickening feeling of jealousy wormed its way through her. The rational side of her ordered her to pull herself together and somehow she managed to shake her hair back confidently and carry on but inside she felt crushed. Who was the girl? Was she his girlfriend? Her mood wasn't improved by seeing Ryan necking back yet more champagne. She marched over to him. 'Babe, go easy on the champagne, I'm running out,' she whispered.

'Chill, babe,' he slurred back, 'I've brought you all those customers, you can afford to be generous.'

Sapphire caught sight of Jazz coming out of the office holding up a bottle of bubbly, 'Last one,' she mouthed to Sapphire. Sapphire turned back to Ryan and steered him away from the drinks table. She decided to change tactics with Ryan and turn on the charm, she really didn't want to fall out with him, even though he was being a major pain. 'So have you seen anything you fancy buying?'

'I like what you're wearing, I'm going to get that for you, how about you wear it later and I'll shag your brains out in it.'

'You say the nicest things,' she said. 'Come on, then, I'll put it through now.'

She just wanted Ryan to buy the lingerie and go. There was a dangerous glint in his eyes, an air of devil may care that she could do without. She hadn't seen him like this before and she didn't like it. But when Ryan went to pay, his credit card was declined. Ryan tried to shrug it off and handed Jazz another card but that too was declined.

'Bollocks! I must have forgotten to pick up my new cards.' He swayed unsteadily on his feet. 'D'you want to get it for me babe and I'll pay you back?'

Sapphire definitely did not want to spend two hundred quid on a present for herself but she didn't let on, 'Sure I'll get it when everyone else has gone. Do you want me to order you a taxi?'

'No, I'm going back to the club with the boys. Come and join us after.'

'I'll let you know, I'll have to see what time we finish here.' It was half ten and Sapphire was knackered. She wanted to curl up in her PJs and chill, no way did she want to go a club. But an even more compelling reason was that she feared Markov might be there. One encounter with that man was quite enough for one night.

She saw Ryan and his friends out then turned her

attention to getting the five remaining customers to buy something. The evening had definitely been a success, she was relieved about that, but she couldn't help feeling uneasy about Markov and Ryan, and as for seeing Jay – she wouldn't even let herself go there. He was history and she had to let him go.

But why then as she lay in bed later that night couldn't she sleep? And why was it Jay's face she kept seeing? He had looked so happy with that girl, so carefree. So different from how Sapphire felt lately: the pressure of business weighing down her, her mixed feelings about Ryan, her fear – and that wasn't putting too strong a word on it – about Markov.

'Somebody loves you,' Jazz commented, seeing Sapphire taking delivery of an impressive bouquet of oriental lilies and pink roses the following morning. 'Is that Ryan's "sorry I was such a drunken fuckwit" gesture?'

Trust her friend to get it spot on! Sapphire thought, as she nodded. 'Well at least he realised what a knob he was last night,' Sapphire replied. 'Everyone makes a fool of themselves every now and then.'

'Hmm,' Jazz replied.

Sapphire really wasn't up for a discussion about Ryan. She pointedly looked at her watch. 'Shouldn't you be getting the salon room ready? Mandy is due for her Brazilian in ten minutes and you know she goes mental if the room isn't warm enough.'

Jazz grimaced: intimate waxings were not her favourite activity but Sapphire had insisted they offer them on their list of salon treatments. Sapphire took pity on her. 'I'll buy you lunch, what do you want?'

Jazz snorted with disgust, 'Like I'm going to have an appetite after doing that!' Then as she flounced upstairs she called out, 'The most expensive thing I can think of.'

*

Two hours later Sapphire found herself paying for sushi, which was the most expensive meal Jazz could find in Pret as the two took a break together. Sapphire felt exhausted and on edge. Even with the success of the lingerie night her profits were down on last year. Sapphire's business had been enjoying a boom, and it had been easy to believe that it would continue, but now she was genuinely fearful about the future. She had put so much into her business, sacrificed other things in her life for it, she couldn't bear to lose it.

'You look knackered,' Jazz said, squirting soy sauce neatly on to the sushi and carefully arranging slices of ginger on each piece.

Sapphire sighed and put her hands round her mug of latte as if to draw comfort from its warmth. 'I am. I'm worried about the business and,' she hesitated, 'last night I saw Jay. He was with someone – a girl.'

She felt the tightness in her chest and for an awful moment thought she was going to cry. This was so not her! She made a big effort to pull herself together before continuing, 'So he's moved on.'

Jazz frowned, 'I don't think he's got a girlfriend. Sam bumped into him at the gym and he didn't mention one.'

'Sam's still going to the gym!' Sapphire exclaimed incredulously.

'Don't sound so surprised!' Jazz shot back. 'She's been going for months now. She's really determined.'

Sapphire felt bad for sounding so down on her friend. 'I meant to say the other day how fantastic she looked.'

'Yeah,' Jazz continued, 'she's lost seven pounds, isn't it great? She says she might even run the London Marathon. I think she wants to do it in memory of her aunt.' Sam's aunt had died the year before from breast cancer and Sam had been very close to her.

'Wow!' Sapphire was impressed. 'So did Sam say how Jay is?'

181

Even though she was with Ryan, deep down Sapphire wanted to hear that Jay missed her, that he still had feelings for her.

Jazz's breezy, 'Good I think,' was something of a slap in the face.

Sapphire was grateful for the distraction caused by her mobile ringing. It was Ryan on full charm offensive. 'Sapphire, I'm so sorry I was pissed last night. Come out for dinner with me tonight, I want to make it up to you.'

Sapphire was all set to say no. She really felt like she needed some distance after his behaviour but somehow hearing about Sam doing so well with her fitness regime and about Jay being okay made her feel as if she had to prove that she was perfectly happy with Ryan to herself as much as to anyone else. She agreed and arranged to meet him at an expensive French restaurant, which was one of his favourites.

She looked back at Jazz, who said, 'All okay?'

'Great, he's taking me out for dinner. That's one thing I definitely missed out on with Jay, he could never afford to take me anywhere special.' Sapphire's plan to make out she was happy backfired as she realised her last comment made her sound bitter and snide. She frowned. 'Sorry, Jazz, I'm sounding like such a witch! I've never expected to be taken out for dinner. I think everything's getting a bit much.'

'Or maybe,' Jazz replied, her blue eyes looking searchingly at her friend, 'you still have feelings for Jay.'

'No way!' Sapphire blustered, shaking her head. But she couldn't meet Jazz's eye. She felt unsettled for the rest of the day. It's just that he broke up with you, she tried to tell herself, you don't really want him back. But she didn't sound convincing even to herself.

Chapter 11

Sapphire had hardly seen her mum in the run up to before Christmas. She was grateful that the boutique and beauty rooms were frantically busy – finally – but it didn't give her time to think about much else. Nor had she seen much of Ryan, which didn't seem such a great loss right now. He was spending Christmas with his family in Dublin. He had suggested that she fly out on Boxing Day but without much enthusiasm and nor was she bothered. She realised that she had got what she thought she wanted with Ryan, only to find that actually she wanted more – just not with him. God! Sometimes life seemed so complicated! And on top of that, Sapphire hadn't liked Christmas since her dad died. She would spend Christmas Eve with Jazz and Sam, then go round to her mum's on Christmas day for a traditional Christmas lunch, which would only serve to remind them that there were only two of them in the family. Christmas Day often felt to Sapphire like one of the loneliest days of the year and she was secretly jealous of her friends with their large extended families, even as they moaned about having to buy presents for their various aunts, uncles, nieces etc.

Sapphire had completely forgotten about Jay's mum inviting them over for Christmas, so it was something of a bolt from the blue when Christine announced that they were still going when Sapphire called to ask what her mum fancied for Christmas.

'Don't forget the presents for Jay's family as well,' Christine replied.

'*Mum!*' Sapphire protested. 'We've split up, remember! There's no way I can still go!'

'Honestly, Sapphire, he is so lovely, I don't know what possessed you.'

'Whatever. Look, I really don't want to talk about it but please, Mum, get this into your head: I can't spend Christmas at Jay's.'

There was a sharp intake of breath from Christine. 'That is just like you, Sapphire – only ever thinking of yourself. Vicky has insisted the invitation is still open. I've been seeing quite a lot of her, we've become good friends. And,' she hesitated, then blurted out, 'Clayton's brother Jason, is going to be there, and we've been seeing each other. But if you don't go to Vicky's I won't be able to go either.'

Sapphire struggled to take in her mum's news and deal with the heavy emotional blackmail. 'You mean you've got a boyfriend?'

'There's no need to sound so shocked,' Christine shot back. 'I'm fifty, not a hundred and fifty. The same age as Madonna, that's what you're always saying, isn't it? And at least Jason *is* my age, not young enough to be my son.'

'I'm not shocked,' Sapphire replied, though she was, 'I'm really pleased for you, Mum, really. So what's he like?'

As Christine chatted happily away, sounding completely infatuated, Sapphire reflected that it was great for her mum to have someone else in her life. There was just the matter of Christmas. When Christine paused, Sapphire said, 'He sounds lovely. I'm just still not sure that I can go to Jay's family. Maybe I could go to Jazz's. It might be awkward.'

184

Awkward didn't even cover the conflicting emotions the prospect of seeing Jay aroused in her.

'Please come Sapphire – don't you think I deserve to have a decent Christmas after all these years on my own? I really couldn't go without you.'

God, her mum could turn on the pressure! Sapphire reluctantly agreed and the Academy award for emotional blackmail went straight to Christine Jones.

'Happy Christmas!' Jay's family chorused when they met Sapphire and Christine on Brighton seafront on the morning Sapphire had been nervously anticipating for the last week. While she wondered where Jay was, Christine embraced a tall black man, who bore a striking resemblance to Clayton.

'Sapphire, this is Jason.'

Jason smiled warmly as he reached out and shook Sapphire's hand. 'Good to finally meet you Sapphire, I gather you're quite the entrepreneur and always working. But Christine, are you sure she's your daughter? Surely you two are sisters!'

'Flattery will get you everywhere!' Christine exclaimed, looking adoringly at Jason. Sapphire smiled and tried not to be too disconcerted by the sight of her mum arm in arm with another man. But Jason clearly had a positive effect on Christine. She looked at least ten years younger. Vicky had cut her hair into a sleek bob, and coloured it a rich chestnut to disguise the grey, making her deep blue eyes appear bluer, and she was finally wearing make-up. She looked great. It clearly wasn't about surgery, chemical peels and hours at the dentist, Sapphire reflected, more about falling in love . . .

'She fab doesn't she?' Vicky noticed Sapphire taking her mum in.

'Yeah,' Sapphire agreed, shoving her hands deep into her coat pockets. The wind was bitingly cold.

'Jay's off on a run at the moment. He's training for the marathon. He'll join us at the house,' Vicky continued as if reading Sapphire's mind. 'So how are you, Sapphire? You look great.'

And so she bloody should Sapphire reflected as she'd spent the best part of two hours getting ready, straightening her hair, putting on fake lashes, taking ages to decide what to wear – in the end a purple pencil skirt, a tight black cashmere sweater, shoe boots, and a huge black fake fur coat.

'Thanks Vicky, so do you,' Sapphire said, feeling self-conscious. God knows what Vicky must think of her.

'I'm so glad you and Christine could come, and I really don't want there to be any awkwardness. Christine and me have become good friends and what happened between you and Jay is your business. You're very welcome to join us for Christmas.' Vicky smiled warmly at Sapphire.

Sapphire so appreciated Vicky's words that she could feel tears prick her eyes. 'Thanks,' she replied and rewound her scarf round her neck so Vicky wouldn't see her crying.

After a brisk walk along the promenade – it really was freezing – the group gathered at one of the cafés on the seafront for hot chocolates laced with brandy. Sapphire sipped her drink while families and friends strolled by – children riding brand-new bikes or tentatively skating on roller blades – everyone smiling and looking happy. It was an idyllic scene but Sapphire just felt so lonely.

Back at Vicky's everyone was enlisted to help with some part of the meal. Sapphire found herself peeling a huge pile of spuds and carrots and then laying the table. There was still no sign of Jay but her heart beat faster every time someone clattered down the stairs into the basement kitchen. But in spite of her feelings about Jay

186

Sapphire couldn't help but be caught up in the atmosphere – everyone was laughing and chatting and she hadn't seen her mum look so happy in such a long time.

'So who are you going out with now?' Estelle, one of the gorgeous twins asked, picking up a carrot that Sapphire had just peeled and crunching it.

'Just some guy,' Sapphire replied, suddenly remembering that she hadn't even called Ryan to wish him happy Christmas, 'I must phone him actually.'

She grabbed her phone and nipped into the garden, wanting a bit of privacy, but Ryan didn't pick up and she could only leave a voicemail message. Compared to the warmth and laughter that was surrounding her at the house her relationship, or whatever it was, seemed hollow and brittle. She and Ryan looked like the perfect couple on the outside but really there was nothing there. Her phone beeped with a message as she was about to go back inside. At least Ryan had replied. But it wasn't a message from Ryan. 'Happy Christmas, Sapphire, I look forward to seeing a lot more of you in the New Year, Markov x.' God, of all the people contacting her, why did it have to be him? She quickly deleted the message, wishing she could delete Markov as easily away from her life.

She was coming back into the kitchen when finally Jay came downstairs. He'd just showered and he was wearing jeans and a tight black T-shirt. He looked gorgeous. In spite of feeling rattled by Markov contacting her, a shot of pure lust went through Sapphire, while at the same time she felt consumed with nerves, exactly like a shy teenager who finally gets to spend time with the boy she really fancies. She could even feel herself blushing. Pathetic! You are a successful businesswoman with a sexy boyfriend, get a grip, she told herself. But the pep talk was all for nothing, as when Jay came over to wish her happy Christmas she could only mumble back and barely

187

look him in the eye. In contrast to the impact he had on her, he seemed completely unaffected by her presence. He was polite and friendly, and if he had once been in love with her, no one would ever have known. He and his mum got on with cooking, and refused all offers of help so Sapphire and the others sat by the fire drinking champagne.

'We should hand out our presents, Sapphire,' Christine said.

'Oh no!' Vicky groaned. 'I hope you haven't spent too much, I meant to say only spend a couple of quid – credit crunch and all that.'

Sapphire began pulling presents out of a large carrier bag, eagerly watched by Estelle and Marissa. She had felt so anxious about Christmas Day that she had in fact spent quite a bit on presents for the family – she'd given each of the twins make-up sets from MAC; Clayton a very expensive bottle of whisky; Vicky, some lovely lingerie from the boutique and an iPod for Jay. For the first time that day he looked slightly awkward as he unwrapped it. 'Thanks Sapphire, that's wicked, mine has just broken and it's been a nightmare running without it. But you shouldn't have.'

'Your mum mentioned you'd broken it.'

'But I haven't got you anything.' Jay seemed embarrassed.

Sapphire smiled, 'I've got a present from your family and you've been generous to ask me and Mum, you don't need to get me anything.'

For a second they looked at each other, but it didn't last; Jay looked away.

After a delicious Christmas dinner everyone collapsed on the sofas, too stuffed to move. The twins clamoured to watch the *Doctor Who* special but Vicky insisted that they play a game of charades. And when they were done with that they played cards. In spite of the awkwardness of being around Jay, Sapphire hadn't enjoyed Christmas so much since her dad died. For a day at least it seemed that all her other worries were put on hold. By nine she thought it probably was time to make a move but when she hinted to her mum that they should go, Vicky was having none of it. 'I'm not having you go back to an empty flat Sapphire! And Christine and Jason are staying here, I've made up the spare room. You can have the sofa bed, Sapphire, I insist.'

Sapphire looked at her mum in appeal for support; surely she would see how awkward it would be for Sapphire to stay the night. But her mum was snuggling up with Jason, oblivious to her daughter's concerns.

Sapphire tried again, 'But I haven't got any overnight things.'

'I can lend you some PJs and I've got a new toothbrush you can have, I always carry extras for guests. You're staying, Sapphire, that's final. Now who wants to watch a film?'

'Finally we can have the TV on!' the twins exclaimed.

They piled onto the sofa next to Jay, leaving just a small space. Sapphire went to sit down on the floor, but Vicky stopped her. 'Sit next to Jay, for goodness' sake, or you'll ruin your skirt. Everyone budge up!' But even with everyone shifting along there really wasn't much room and Sapphire found herself sitting so close to Jay that their bodies were touching, so close that she could smell his aftershave. All her senses were on alert by being in right next to him. She watched *Mamma Mia*, which she'd seen before anyway, in a complete daze. Every fibre of her being was transfixed by being next to Jay. She kept sneaking glances at him, but he never once looked at her.

Around midnight everyone else trooped off to bed and Vicky ordered Jay to make up Sapphire's bed. Sapphire felt awkward again as Jay put up the sofa bed in the living room and fetched her a duvet and pillow. As he smoothed out the sheet on the sofa Sapphire had such a pang of longing for him that she thought she might actually cry.

'Are you sure you'll be okay down here?' Jay asked.

The flirty, I can do what I like Sapphire would have replied, 'Why don't you test out the bed with me?' But that Sapphire seemed to be on holiday, right now she was incapable of flirting.

'Fine,' she mumbled. 'Thanks for being so cool about me being here.'

'Well, my mum wanted to ask you and as you see she always gets her own way, no matter what anyone else thinks.'

Wow, that didn't seem so friendly. Perhaps the cool, I'm-not-bothered attitude had been a front all along.

'Well, thank you anyway,' Sapphire replied, trying not to show how hurt she was by his comment.

'So didn't you want to spend Christmas with what's his name?' Now he sounded seriously pissed off. 'I thought he was your ideal man: rich, flash, not interested in commitment.'

Sapphire was stung by Jay's snide tone of voice. She'd spent the day thinking they could at least be friends but Jay didn't seem to want that. He actually seemed to dislike her.

'We get on fine – we just don't want to spend all our time together is all. We had a week in Vegas recently. I like my space, he likes his.'

'Vegas,' Jay seemed to sneer. 'So you didn't end up getting married in some Elvis chapel? No, of course you didn't, Sapphire Jones doesn't believe in marriage does she?'

He glared at her from across the sofa bed. Sapphire longed to say please let's be friends, but the proud side of her vetoed that and she found herself glaring back at him, arms folded defensively across her chest, a 'come and have a go if you think you're hard enough' look on her face.

'No, I don't believe in marriage. Ryan knows that and yeah you're right, we're pretty well suited. He understands about business, doesn't put too many demands on me. It's pretty much a perfect arrangement.' My God! How easily the lies could pour out of her.

Jay scowled, 'Well, I'll just say goodnight then, leave you to dream about Mr Perfect.'

Yeah, thought Sapphire bitterly as she tried to get comfortable on the sofa bed after Jay had marched out of the room, Mr Perfect indeed; Ryan hadn't even bothered to call, he'd just texted her. And when she did fall asleep and dream of Mr Perfect, it wasn't Ryan . . .

In the morning Sapphire managed to get out of spending another day with Jay's family by saying that she had to get the boutique ready for the sale that was starting the following day. Really it was only a couple of hours' work but she couldn't bear to be around Jay any longer, feeling his disapproval and fearing that he actually disliked her. Ever since Alfie's massive betrayal Sapphire had thought that nothing a man could do would ever actually hurt her again, but she was beginning to find out it could. She hated the thought that Jay didn't even like her any more. She felt blue as she opened up the boutique and stepped inside.

She'd had a delivery, which seemed odd as it was Boxing Day. She bent down and picked up the small package addressed to her. She'd seen that handwriting before she was sure, and she ripped open the package to find a jewellery box and a card. She opened the card first, 'Diamonds are a girl's best friend, I hope we can be friends very soon, Happy Christmas love Mx'.

191

Markov! Why couldn't he let it drop! She opened the box and a stunning pair of diamond earrings confronted her. This had to stop! She marched into the office and threw the box down on the sofa, alongside the dress and gift-wrapped lingerie that she had yet to put back on the shop floor. Then she reached for her phone – she would get Markov's address from Ryan and stop this right now. She got straight to the point when Ryan answered but his reply was infuriating, 'I don't have his address, babe, and Markov will be well offended if you return them. It's just his way. Chill. And I'll see you on New Year's Eve.'

'Aren't you free until then?' Sapphire asked, in surprise.

''Fraid not, babe.'

He didn't exactly make her feel wanted.

Sapphire had never especially enjoyed the days between Christmas and New Year. It always seemed like a bit a of limbo time – she just wanted the new year to begin, for there to be a fresh start. But this year the economic forecasts continued to be gloomy – in Brighton there were already shops closing down.

'People are still going to get married,' Jazz reassured her when she caught Sapphire looking through the books the day before New Year's Eve. Despite the massive reductions on the lingerie she hadn't sold as much as usual and the treatment rooms had been quiet. 'Perhaps it's karma,' Sapphire replied. 'You know, because I've always been so negative about marriage.'

'Yeah right, let's blame the recession on you having a cynical attitude to relationships! God, Sapphire, you're supposed to be the logical, clear-headed one. What's happening to you?'

Sapphire wrapped her black cashmere cardigan more tightly round her body before replying, 'I think it was seeing Jay and realising that he doesn't even like me. I guess I thought it wouldn't bother me, but it really did, Jazz. It was awful when he was having a go at me. I thought whatever happened at least we'd be friends but he obviously thinks I'm a really bad person.' She paused. '*Am* I a really bad person?'

'Well, you're a terrible control freak and you need to accept help from other people, but no of course you're not a bad person! You're a brilliant person, a great friend to have, loyal, funny, generous.' She paused and in the gap Sapphire filled in, 'Just a rubbish girlfriend.'

But frankly she didn't have such a great boyfriend right now. She'd hardly spoken to him since Boxing Day, and he'd just called to make sure she was coming to the New Year's Eve party at the club. 'Who will be there?' she asked cautiously; she didn't want to run into Markov again if she could help it.

'Only Alfie and his girlfriend, some of our mates, and about two hundred other people. Bring Jazz and Ben if you like and the other one, I can never remember her name.'

'You mean Sam, I suppose.'

Sapphire hadn't seen Sam for two weeks and she was absolutely stunned when they met up on New Year's Eve at Sapphire's for cocktails before going on to the club. Sam must have lost nearly two stone over the past couple of months and dropped from a size sixteen to a twelve and this was the first time Sapphire had seen her in such body-conscious clothes – normally she went for leggings and tunics, but not tonight. Sam looked incredibly sexy in a vivid green vintage silk dress, her body looked toned and curvaceous. She'd had her auburn hair cut into a sleek long bob with a fringe framing her heart-shaped face. Sapphire, dressed in a black silk shift dress and black tights, felt completely drab by comparison.

'You look amazing!' Sapphire exclaimed, hugging her friend.

'So I bloody well should! I have been running ten miles twice a week and starting next week my running group is upping it to fifteen miles. It's bloody tough!' But she had a big smile on her face when she said it.

Sapphire held up the cocktail shaker and asking everyone what they fancied. She felt the need to take the edge off the night. She'd asked Ryan to come over but he said he was too busy getting ready for the party. But drinking just intensified her feeling of loneliness – Jazz and Ben were so loved-up, Sam seemed extremely happy in her skin. Sapphire suddenly felt as if she had nothing to look forward to in the new year. She'd been working so hard and it just looked as if she had more of the same ahead of her, with precious little reward.

'You must be looking forward to seeing Ryan tonight,' Sam said, following Sapphire into her bedroom so they could both add final touches to their make-up.

'I guess,' Sapphire shrugged, applying another layer of lipgloss, 'but I expect I'll hardly see him, he'll be busy with the club.'

Sam lightly brushed powder over her flawless make-up, then adjusted her gold necklace which had a several pretty gold butterflies hanging from it.

'That's nice – is it one of yours?'

'Yep – d'you want some for the boutique?'

'Sure,' Sapphire replied, a little dismissive.

'I'll need to know soon, as I've got some other orders.' So Sam not only looked good, but her jewellery designs were taking off. Sapphire suddenly felt slightly jealous, as if she was being left behind.

Her mood was not improved when they arrived at the club. Ryan barely spent any time with her. He just kissed her and patted her on the bum, he didn't seem to care how much it infuriated her. 'Good to see you, babe, I've missed you,' he murmured.

'Really? I'd never know,' Sapphire replied slightly bitterly.

Ryan laughed, 'I thought you liked keeping things light. I thought that was what we both wanted. Oh, don't look like that!'

Sapphire was aware that she had a sulky expression, but she couldn't help it – Ryan seemed to have so little regard for her.

'Babe, I'm working – it's a big night, but I promise I'll make it up to you. Got to go now,' and with that Ryan wove his way through the partygoers.

'Isn't Ryan going to join us?' Jazz asked as the group settled round the table Ryan had reserved for them, and cracked open the complimentary bottle of champagne – Sapphire was surprised he hadn't charged them for it.

She shrugged. 'He's working, I'll catch up with him later.'

She tried to throw herself into chatting with her friends, even dancing wildly – the club was playing dance anthems from the last ten years. But she couldn't help feeling slightly depressed. A feeling which was not improved when she saw Alfie and his girlfriend Brooke. In spite of Alfie claiming that he had made a mistake when he was unfaithful, he looked like a man who was very happy with his lot as he stood with his arm round Brooke, as they talked to another good-looking couple. It seemed everyone was happy except her. She was hoping to sneak past them unnoticed, but Alfie saw her and waved her over.

'Sapphire! Good to see you – has your party got the champagne I sent over?'

'I thought it was from Ryan,' Sapphire replied.

'Oh yeah – it's from both of us.' There was an awkward moment when Sapphire and Brooke stood looking at each other.

195

'So, you remember Brooke?' Alfie said, not at all sounding like his usual confident self. Brooke gave a tight little smile, clearly not enjoying the encounter one little bit.

'Hard to forget,' Sapphire said drily, an extremely unwelcome image flashing into her head of Brooke and Alfie fucking on her bed. She so did not want to go there again. 'And you're wearing the same perfume,' she added as she got a waft of Poison, a fragrance which she had loathed ever since.

'Anyway, Happy New Year,' she said, knowing that she sounded falsely bright and then continued on her way to the ladies'. There was the usual massive queue for the loos and as Sapphire waited her turn she couldn't help overhearing the conversation of a couple of girls touching up their make-up at the mirror.

'She says tonight's the night!' a redhead said, giggling. 'She reckons she's going to have him in the club.'

'I suppose it's a step up from the back of a car,' giggled the brunette, putting another layer of mascara on already thickly coated lashes.

'He's well fit though, I'd have him anywhere!' the redhead again. 'Whereas she's supposed to be rank down below!'

Sapphire did a mental eye roll, did the girls realise how slaggy they sounded?

'Well, he's loaded,' the redhead continued. 'Owns this club.'

Sapphire froze, her feeling of superiority vanished. Were they taking about Alfie? But he hadn't seemed like a man about to do the dirty? They must mean Ryan? She had to find out.

She left her place in the queue and stormed through the club, trying to find him. Is this why he had hardly seen her lately? He was seeing someone else? What a complete bastard!

There was no sign of him around any of the bars or in the VIP area. She stood by one of the pillars and surveyed the club. By now it was four minutes to midnight – the DJ was winding the crowd up, getting ready to welcome in the new year, playing 'Hot in Herre'. Where was Ryan? And suddenly she realised where he must be.

She pushed her way back through the crowds to the opposite side of the club, to the door to the office upstairs. She pushed it open and raced up the stairs. At the top she hesitated, in two minds about whether to go any further. Did she really want to put herself through this? She could just finish with Ryan, things had hardly been great lately anyway. If she was honest with herself, they never had been. She could go back to her friends, see in the new year and leave with her dignity intact. But she had to know. She marched forward and opened the door to the office. Ryan and a blonde were on the leather sofa. Ryan's jeans were round his ankles as he pumped away at the blonde, her legs wrapped round him, still wearing her shoes. 'Come on, baby, you can do it! Hold on for the big one!' They were both so lost in the moment that neither was aware of Sapphire.

She had seen more than enough. She turned and swiftly ran back along the corridor. Of all the ways to see in the new year, that surely counted as the worst. Downstairs the clubbers were embracing each other, letting off streamers, and thousands of silver sequins were released from the ceiling. Sapphire couldn't bear it. She felt sick, hurt, disgusted – not just with Ryan, but with herself for ever having let such an unscrupulous, unfeeling, bastard into her life. How could she ever have found him attractive? He was a sleazeball. She just wanted to get out of the club, away from all the revellers. She was just weaving her way through, trying to avoid getting kissed by various random men, when she ran into Alfie.

'Happy New Year Sapphire!' he exclaimed and went to kiss her. Then he registered the expression on her face and stopped in his tracks. 'Are you okay?'

'I've just seen Ryan.' She couldn't bring herself to say what he'd been doing, but the look on her face said it all, 'Why didn't you tell me what he was up to?'

Alfie looked awkward, 'I did try to, if you remember.'

'Well, I've just seen him screwing another woman. I mean, is there something about me that says all men have to treat me like complete shit!' Her eyes were welling up with tears now at the sheer humiliation.

'No, Sapphire, you just picked the wrong man, it's nothing to do with you. Let me take you over to your friends and I'll get you a brandy.'

Sapphire vehemently shook her head. 'I have to get out of here.' And before Alfie could stop her she ran out of the club. It was bitterly cold, icy rain was sheeting down, which seemed appropriate under the circumstances. But Sapphire was oblivious to it soaking through her clothes as she ran along the seafront back to her apartment. How had she let herself get into this situation? She had thrown away Jay for a man who treated her like dirt. She was a fool, a complete and utter fool.

Chapter 12

'So not the best New Year's Eve?' Cal said sympathetically. He had asked Sapphire to the press launch of one of his football academies in Brighton, three weeks into January. She had vowed not to mention anything about what had happened, the memory was still too raw, but Cal had a way of knowing something was up and she had ended up confiding in him.

Sapphire took a sip of champagne then shook her head. It had been hard to bounce back from Ryan's spectacular infidelity. When she had found out about Alfie she had been powered by sheer anger, which had somehow got her through, but Ryan had left her feeling so low, had made her question herself and her judgement. Of course he'd tried to win her back, saying it was just a one off – where had she heard that before? Did all men only ever have a certain number of excuses that they used in such situations? Did they Google I'vefuckedup.com and get a ready-made list? But Sapphire was having absolutely none of it. She wouldn't take his calls, wouldn't reply to his texts, except to say 'It's over.' She had told Alfie that she could only do business with him from now on. Ryan persisted for a week, sent flowers and champagne, but after that gave up. Now, all Sapphire could hope was that she never set eyes on him again or Markov.

Cal carried on, 'Don't let it make you put your barriers up, Sapphire, not all men are like Ryan.'

'Or like Alfie,' Sapphire added. 'Maybe it's not them, it's me,' she tried to sound as if she was joking, but she wasn't. She felt at an all-time low.

'Bollocks, you're a beautiful, generous, clever, sexy woman. Any man would be lucky to have you,' Cal retorted.

'Thank you, Cal, I'll be ringing you at regular intervals to hear that again.' Sapphire tried to pull herself together, this was after all, Cal's night. At that moment the PR woman came over and claimed Cal's attention. Sapphire moved away and observed her friend as he shook hands with various guests. He was so passionate about his football academies and so determined to give kids from disadvantaged homes a chance. It was admirable and inspiring. Why weren't there more men like Cal? If only she could fancy him! she thought jokingly, besides he was a one-man woman, still longing for his Angel.

Earlier he had told her what a nightmare Christmas had been. Angel and Honey had come back to the UK to spend it with her family and to give Cal the chance to see his daughter. But then Angel's new partner, Ethan, had insisted on coming too. Cal said it had been torture seeing the couple together and he had only got through it by focusing all his attention on his daughter. 'How did Angel seem?' Sapphire had asked, wondering if Angel still had feelings for Cal.

'Blissfully happy,' Cal said abruptly. And Sapphire, seeing the pain in his eyes, had changed the subject.

'He's good at talking the talk isn't he?' Sapphire turned to discover an attractive dark-haired man next to her.

'Gavin Wright,' he stuck out his hand and Sapphire shook it, introducing herself in return. She recognised him as a former teammate of Cal's from Chelsea. Now he was one of the pundits on *Match of the Day*. Sapphire found herself talking to him for the rest of the night. He was very charming – not flash like Ryan, but old school, a gentleman. He was good-looking with warm brown eyes and handsome, rugged features but Sapphire felt as if her mojo had been switched off. Ryan had sapped it from her. Still, at the end of the night she gave Gavin her number when he asked for it and agreed to go out for dinner sometime with him in London. And as she said goodnight to Cal he whispered, 'Gavin is very taken with you. He's one of the good ones, Sapphire. I promise.'

'Cal, I'm really not interested in any kind of relationship at the moment.'

'Just don't shut yourself away, Sapphire, you don't want to end up like me.'

The night out with Cal had been a distraction from her biggest concern at the moment, which was the state of the business. Usually she would have expected a full diary of hen weekends, but in January she only had two bookings which almost went down to one when one bride to be called her to pull out. Sapphire practically begged her not to cancel, offering her all kinds of discounts.

'It's not just the cost when we're in Brighton,' Lisa, the bride to be told her, 'It's getting down there from Birmingham by train; it's going to cost us loads. I just don't want to give my mates that expense. We're having the hen weekend in Birmingham instead.'

In desperation Sapphire tried to think of something, anything, to entice them to come. She was desperate to hold on to the booking and then, thank God, inspiration struck, 'What if I arranged for you all to be picked up, so you didn't have to pay any travel? I could hire a minibus.'

'And we wouldn't have to pay anything for it?' Lisa said cautiously.

'No, I would cover the cost.' There was a pause, during

which Sapphire crossed her fingers, please, please let Lisa take up the offer!

'Yeah, we'd be up for that.'

Sapphire put the phone down with a feeling of relief. Now, there was just the matter of a minibus and paying for a driver. When she went round to her mum's later that day, for once she found herself being more open about her worries. Now her mum had Jason, she didn't seem quite so self-obsessed and so doom and gloomy about everything.

'You should ask Clayton – he'd probably be glad of the business.'

Sapphire had already thought of him and rejected the idea – the memory of Jay laying into her on Christmas night was still too fresh in her mind.

She muttered that she probably shouldn't but Christine wasn't having any of it and insisted on phoning him herself. 'There you go,' she said to Sapphire a few minutes later, 'all sorted, he'll pick you up at midday on Friday.'

'Thanks, Mum,' Sapphire said gratefully.

'And, the offer is still there if you need me to help out in the boutique – you know I would do it for nothing.'

Vanessa had recently handed in her notice as she was going to go travelling for a year and Sapphire was thinking of not replacing her as a cost saving. She would never have considered having her mum work for her in the past but lately they had been getting on so much better and Sapphire was starting to realise that she needed all the help she could get.

'Thanks, Mum, I'll see how it goes,' she replied.

Christine looked at her daughter, a serious expression on her face, 'Just don't feel that you always have to do everything on your own. I can help you.' She paused. 'I know I haven't always been a great mum.' Sapphire was about to protest, but Christine wouldn't let her, 'No, I was too busy thinking about myself for far too long. But I want you to know that I am here for you now.'

It was quite possibly the nicest thing Christine had ever said to her and Sapphire was about to tell her so when her phone rang.

She frowned as a number she didn't recognise flashed across her screen. Oh God, it was probably another hen party cancelling. With a feeling of trepidation she answered. But it was Gavin, the sexy ex-footballer asking if she would be free to go for dinner the following night. Sapphire was all set to say no, and then she thought, why not? Her confidence had been so bruised by Ryan she could do with feeling better about herself. Also she was still obsessing about Jay. Dinner would be a distraction from all that.

'So is he nice?' Jazz asked later, when Sapphire revealed her plans. 'I'm not sure if I know which one you mean, all those footballers look the same to me – unless they're Ron – that Spanish one, in which case phoarr big time!'

'Yeah, he's very good-looking, and he seemed nice, but then, so did Ryan.'

Jazz rolled her eyes. 'No, Ryan never seemed nice, babe, he always had flash bastard written all over him. We did try and tell you.'

'We did,' Sam seconded, from where she was lying stretched out on Sapphire's sofa. She'd just finished a fifteen-mile run and claimed to be knackered, but to Sapphire she looked amazing. She had lost even more weight and now must easily be a size ten.

Sapphire flipped open her lap top, 'I'll just Google Gavin and you can give me your verdict.' A few seconds later Gavin's picture filled the screen. 'What do you reckon, girls?'

Jazz and Sam wandered over. 'Very tasty,' Jazz. 'Hot' from Sam, who then added, 'You lucked out there, babe.'

Sapphire rolled her eyes. 'It's just a dinner date and I'm only going because I could do with a night away from Brighton – every time I go out I keep worrying that I'm going to run into Ryan and the temptation to kick him in the nuts is still very strong.'

'Ugh, don't do that, you'll have to have physical contact!' Jazz shuddered.

Both she and Sam had been appalled to hear what Ryan had done. Sapphire almost felt bad telling Jazz, she had such a sweet nature, but Sam hadn't seemed that surprised and that made Sapphire feel even worse about ever going out with him in the first place.

Gavin had booked a table at Gordan Ramsay's restaurant at Claridge's – a restaurant Sapphire had always wanted to go to. Inside the luxurious space with its Art Deco style she felt temporarily cut off from her worries, in a bubble of wealth, protected from the harsh realities of everyday life. She had dressed to impress in a sexy asymmetric mini-dress in midnight blue and Gavin had as well in a sharply cut suit. He looked good and was as easy company as he was on the eye.

The first half of the evening was actually fun, Gavin was quite flirtatious, and kept giving her the old eye contact. Sapphire waited in vain for some response to kick off inside her, but nothing happened. She was forcing herself to flirt. Good-looking as he was, she might just as well have been having dinner with a wrinkly old man. When his leg brushed against hers there wasn't even a flicker; when their hands touched as they clinked glasses, nothing. I really have lost my mojo, she thought miserably. Then later the conversation became more serious. 'I think we have something in common,' he told her over brandy. 'I got divorced last year and Cal tells me you did two years ago.'

'Yeah, it's not exactly a club I thought I would be

joining when I got married,' Sapphire replied drily.

'Me neither,' Gavin replied. 'And what makes it more ironic is that my ex-wife insisted that we get a magazine to cover the wedding. I feel like ringing them up and asking them why they don't do divorces too – they could do photospreads of the ex-wife and her new lover, living it up in style in my old house.' His jaw clenched. It seemed to Sapphire that Gavin still had plenty of baggage when it came to his failed marriage. He seemed to collect himself. 'Sorry, I didn't mean to go off on one.'

But the comment cast a shadow over the night and Sapphire felt sad both for Gavin, who was obviously haunted by his failed marriage, and for herself and for her longing for Jay. Both of them drank quite a bit, and at the end of the meal Gavin suggested going back to his hotel for a nightcap. Why not? Sapphire thought.

The offer of a drink was naturally code for another activity. And in the taxi Gavin put his arm round her and gently kissed her. It developed into a passionate kiss. Sapphire kissed him back, willing herself to feel something. But there was no absolutely no spark; instead she felt as if she was partaking in a master class in how to kiss, thinking about what she was doing and not once losing herself in the moment. She probably should have left then and there but somehow it seemed like too much effort and she ended up going up to his luxurious penthouse suite. Gavin poured them both a large brandy while Sapphire sat on the sofa. She was starting to get the spinny head feeling, but what the hell.

More kissing followed. Gavin unzipped her dress, caressed her exposed skin, expertly, she thought. He kissed her breasts, nothing wrong with his technique but as he moved over her body, Sapphire felt completely detached, as if she was staring down at herself from above. And suddenly she thought, do I really want to do this? It wasn't about lust or desire or longing, it was partly because she could and partly because she felt she had got herself in a situation where it seemed inevitable. But it really wasn't what she wanted. Gavin's caresses became more urgent with his desire, he lay on top of her and his body felt heavy and insistent on hers and suddenly she felt suffocated. There was only one man she wanted to make love with and it wasn't Gavin.

He inched up her skirt. Sapphire reached out for his hand and stopped him, 'I'm sorry I just can't. It's not you, it's me.'

No doubt someone like Ryan would have tried to persuade her, would have been offended, but Gavin was a complete gentleman about the whole incident, giving her time to get herself together, and calling her a taxi. It seemed that Cal was right: Gavin was one of the good ones, the trouble was he did absolutely nothing for Sapphire.

But while she and Gavin knew nothing had really happened between them, it wasn't the spin the tabloids put on their night out. Gavin was a big name and the couple had been papped leaving the restaurant and going into the hotel. Sapphire was mortified to see the pictures the following day, especially the one of them in the taxi where they were photographed kissing and her dress had ridden up, revealing an expanse of thigh. She hated to think that she might be seen as a wannabe WAG, desperate to bag herself a footballer.

'You dirty girl!' Jazz exclaimed, adding, 'I hope Ryan saw that and realises what he's missing.'

Jazz flopped down on the sofa in the office where Sapphire was going through her books, clearly up for a good gossip about what her friend had got up to the night before. Sapphire sighed and pushed her hair behind her ears. 'He's not missing anything, because nothing happened beyond that kiss in the taxi and a bit of a fumble in his hotel room. I just couldn't do it, Jazz. I think I may be turning frigid.'

'Don't be daft, you just didn't fancy him. Or maybe you're turning into a lesbian?' she added cheekily. 'I could line you up with a lovely lady.'

Sapphire did a major eye roll. 'I do not want a lovely lady, nor do I want a lovely man. Thanks for the offer. I didn't realise you had added pimp to your list of qualifications.'

'Hmm I wonder if there are any female pimps?' Jazz mused, checking her perfectly manicured nails. Today they were cobalt blue, accessorised with matching suede pumps and huge hoop earrings that a small bird could happily have perched on.

'Haven't you got any work to do?' Sapphire asked. 'I'm sure there are lots of other beauticians out there who would bite your leg off for such a great job, with such a great boss.'

'Yes, I suppose so. I'm psyching myself up for Mandy's nail appointment. She's getting a divorce and she's pretty bitter about it. She gives me a blow-by-blow account of every thing she hates about her husband, including some very intimate details. Did I need to know about the wart on his balls? Or how much he used to sweat when they had sex, I mean *perlease!*' Jazz pulled a disgusted expression and flicked her white-blond hair back. 'I really should get paid extra for all the therapy I have to do.'

'Just smile and be nice to her,' Sapphire warned her, 'She might be annoying but she's one of our most loyal customers.'

Jazz gave her the finger, showing off one of the impressive cobalt nails, and sauntered out of the room.

Sapphire quickly finished what she was doing, the books made for such depressing reading. She was going to have

207

to seriously consider her mum's offer of help and she wouldn't be able to pay her. She was struggling to pay the wages as it was and had taken a pay cut herself in order to give Jazz and Kiki the pay rises she had promised them in better times. She rifled through her bag, checking she had all the details for picking up the hens. Clayton was due at the boutique any minute with the minibus and she wanted to leave straight away.

But it wasn't Clayton who came through the door a few minutes later. A shot of pure lust ignited in her, blowing away any idea of her being frigid as Jay knocked on the office door. He muttered 'Hi,' and went on with very little enthusiasm, 'Dad's got flu, so I'm going to drive.' He shoved his hands into the pockets of his leather jacket, looking moody and heartbreakingly gorgeous.

But his lack of enthusiasm was like an icy bucket of water over her happiness at seeing him. 'I really appreciate your offer Jay, but you should have cancelled, I'm sure I could have got someone else,' Sapphire replied, put out by Jay's tone.

'My family always honour their commitments,' Jay muttered. 'Besides, you wouldn't have been able to get someone at such short notice. Do you know where we're going?'

'Yes, I've got the details. Shall we go?' Her businesslike, matter-of-fact tone disguised how shaken up she was by seeing him.

For the first thirty minutes of the three-hour journey he was monosyllabic, resisting all her attempts to make conversation. Yes, he was fine, yes, training for the marathon was going well, yes, work was okay, yes, his family were okay. God! This was going to be the longest car journey ever! It was such a contrast to how they used to chat so freely and Jay was so relentlessly offhand, that finally Sapphire exclaimed, 'Jay, can't we at least be civilised? It's going to seem like a really long journey if we can't even be nice to each other.'

He shrugged, 'I'm cool.' A pause and then he added, 'Actually, 'I'm surprised to see you out and about, I thought you'd still be holed up in some flash hotel with Gavin Wright. Still, he's a major trade up from that wanker, isn't he?'

Sapphire took a sharp intake of breath. Maybe the silent treatment was best if this was what she was going to be on the receiving end of this sort of talk. 'Not that it's any of your business what I was up to, but nothing happened between Gavin and me.'

'What? So they Photoshopped those pictures of you snogging his face off in the taxi? You should sue,' Jay retorted, in a voice laced with sarcasm.

'No, I did kiss him, but that's all. The truth is there was no chemistry between us and he's still getting over a divorce. It was really embarrassing, if you must know, I'd rather not talk about it.'

She got her wish as another hour and a half of silence followed. Sapphire stared out of the window at the motorway, Radio One pumped out of the stereo. Then Jay, 'Sorry.'

He had spoken so quietly that Sapphire wasn't sure if he'd actually said it. She turned to look at him. 'Sorry,' he repeated, 'I didn't mean to give you such a hard time. You're right, it's none of my business who you get involved with.' The passion had gone out of his voice but somehow the politeness was worse than him being angry; at least when he was angry it seemed as though he had some feelings for her still.

They had an hour to kill in Birmingham before picking up the girls. They ended up in Caffè Nero eating panini, and drinking lattes, neither speaking to the other. Jay read the paper and texted and Sapphire pretended to be riveted by *Marie Claire*. Her heart ached for what they had once had – the warmth, the banter, the easy conversation. She remembered how Jay could always calm her down if she was feeling stressed. For the hundredth time she thought about what a fool she had been to push him away.

At least the hens were a distraction on the journey back, singing along to the soundtracks of *Dirty Dancing* and *Mamma Mia* and flirting outrageously with Jay. They were so excited about their weekend away and so grateful to Sapphire for picking them up. 'It's brilliant that you've done this,' Lisa exclaimed. 'There's just no way we could have afforded the weekend otherwise.'

Sapphire smiled, at least someone seemed to appreciate her.

Sapphire pulled out all the stops to give the party a good time – word of mouth about a business, she knew, was worth a thousand ads. And she was relieved to see that the girls didn't stint on the weekend. The hens spent over two hundred pounds in the boutique on presents for the bride to be and had extra beauty treatments. By Sunday afternoon though she was exhausted after the full-on weekend and all she wanted to do was collapse on the sofa at home in her PJs. But there was the drive back. She had assumed that Clayton would be better, yet it was Jay who turned up. At least he seemed slightly more relaxed around Sapphire and she didn't feel quite so on edge.

The hens were partied out and mercifully didn't sing. Sapphire wasn't at all sure she was up to another rendition of 'Time of My Life'. instead they chatted quietly or listened to their iPods. Meanwhile Sapphire was struggling to stay awake and kept yawning.

'I would have been happy to drive the party back on my own,' Jay commented as Sapphire yawned for about the tenth time in a row. 'Thanks, but I felt I ought to come. In fact, I might need to learn how to drive a minibus as I've got another party to bring down from Leicester in a couple of weeks' time.'

'Just get Dad or me to do it, you've got enough on haven't you? Dad could do with the business as well, things aren't great for him at the moment.'

It was practically the nicest thing Jay had said to her since they split.

By the time they had dropped the hens off and were halfway down the M6 it had started snowing. At first there were flurries of tiny flakes that spun in the headlights and it didn't seem as if they were going to settle. 'Wow, it hasn't snowed in ages,' Sapphire exclaimed, getting a childlike rush of excitement at seeing the snow. 'Bet it won't settle. Mum's always going on about the snow she remembers as a child and how she went sledging.'

But Sapphire was wrong and the snow began falling more heavily, driving into the windscreen. Jay leant forward and gripped the wheel in concentration. 'Oh my God! This is like a blizzard,' Sapphire exclaimed again.

'It's not like a blizzard,' Jay corrected her, 'it *is* a blizzard.'

The traffic in front slowed down dramatically. They crawled along at twenty miles an hour until they reached a service station with a hotel. 'I think we'd better sit this one out,' Jay said turning down the slip road. Sapphire had expected that he meant have a cup of coffee and wait until conditions improved; instead Jay booked them into the hotel. Many other drivers had the same idea and there was only one double room left.

'Are you cool with that?' Jay asked.

'Not a problem,' Sapphire lied.

They trooped over to the service station area for burgers and fries and hot chocolates. The snow seemed to have relaxed something in Jay and instead of the monosyllabic exchanges, conversation was freer between them as they chatted about Christine's relationship with Jason, what his twin sisters were up to, and how his work was going. There was nothing more personal than that and Sapphire was frustratingly no nearer to finding out whether he had a girlfriend. At one point as she returned from getting refills of hot chocolate Jay was busy texting someone and when he received a reply he had a warm smile on his face which didn't seem like a response to something his mum would have sent him. She could just ask if he had a girlfriend, she supposed, but she worried that she would give too much away if the answer came back as yes. And maybe she didn't want to know.

They spent a good couple of hours in the restaurant area, but by half ten they couldn't put off going to the hotel room any longer. Sapphire had bought shower gel and toothpaste but there hadn't been anywhere to buy any pyjamas – she was going to have to sleep in her clothes. And by the chilly feel of the room when they let themselves in, in her coat as well. The tiny radiator was giving off hardly any heat. There was just a thin duvet and blanket on the bed. Jay touched it and frowned, 'I was going to offer to sleep on the floor but I reckon I'll end up with hypothermia if I do.' He paused. 'Would it be okay with you if slept on the bed?'

'Course,' Sapphire replied and then to break the awkward moment said she was going to have a shower. Or more a dribble, she found out as she stood under the tiny shower which was barely giving out any water. She had the quickest wash, got dried with a towel which was so hard it was like being exfoliated, and put her clothes back on. This was definitely not the kind of hotel where you got those lovely soft white robes. When she went back into the bedroom Jay was stretched out on the bed watching *Friends* and eating popcorn. 'And look,' he held out a beer, 'I went and got us these as well, I figured we might need some alcohol to get us through tonight. I've got my jacket on and I'm still freezing.' There was a definite draught coming from the windows. Sapphire went over and pulled back the curtains. Outside had been transformed into a winter wonderland, with trees powdered with snow, their branches looking elegant and ethereal against the night, the patchy grass covered by a perfect white blanket of snow. It was like the scene from the snow globe her dad had once given her. 'Everything looks so beautiful in the snow,' she said, 'Even really ugly things look better don't they?'

'Yeah. Even that Georgia Cox would look better covered in it.'

Sapphire steeled herself for another comment, maybe this was the moment they were going to talk about their relationship, but Jay was looking at the TV. 'Maybe not her,' Sapphire replied, returning to the bed. She sat so close to the edge she was in danger of falling off, but the bed had other ideas, the mattress had lost its spring and she found herself sliding towards the middle. 'Sorry,' she said as she brushed against Jay for the third time and then tried to inch away.

'It's the bed, just forget it,' he said.

The room seemed to be getting colder. Sapphire got up and put her fake fur leopard-print coat round her, now regretting she hadn't worn more clothes.

'Easy, tiger,' Jay joked, noticing the coat.

'Oh, I'm a pussy cat really.'

For a second they held each other's gaze. Jay was the first to look away. They carried on watching TV but the atmosphere seemed to have shifted between them again and Sapphire was sure she wasn't imagining it – there was a definite undercurrent of attraction. As she sat on the bed, sipping beer, she was aware of Jay looking at her every now and then. Oh God, please let him still like her! At half twelve Jay suggested they turn off the TV and try and get some sleep. Sapphire made another dash to the bathroom and when she got back Jay was already lying down in bed. It almost broke her heart seeing him there. In the past she'd have curled up next to him. She switched off the light, took off her coat and slipped out of her jeans, and then crawled under the thin duvet. She tried to stay at the far edge but the treacherous bed tipped her back into the middle. 'Goodnight,' she said quietly as Jay turned and faced the other way,

''Night,' he replied.

But sleep eluded Sapphire. She was so aware of Jay beside her, his warm body, just inches away from her. She turned away but slid back so they were lying back to back. It was like some kind of exquisite torture. Sapphire hardly dared breathe. But it seemed to her that there must be a great big speech bubble coming out of her head, saying 'I want you!' that seemed so noisy to her, she was amazed Jay couldn't hear it. She longed to slide her arms around him, feel his smooth skin and gorgeous hard muscles and that wasn't the only hard thing she longed to feel – she was horny as hell! And bloody freezing – even next to Jay, Sapphire had to clamp her teeth together to stop them from chattering.

After twenty minutes of shivering, when Sapphire was seriously thinking of putting her coat on, Jay turned round. 'Can't you sleep either?'

'I'm so cold,' Sapphire replied. 'Do you think I'm going to get hypothermia?' she tried to joke as goose-bumps erupted on her skin.

'Here, does this feel better?' Jay put his arm round her and pressed his body against hers so she got a blast of warmth from him.

'Hmm,' Sapphire replied as her nipples hardened at his touch. She was never going to get to sleep at this rate, but right now she didn't care. She slightly shifted position and found herself made very aware that she wasn't the only one who was feeling aroused. How to play this? It was uncharted territory. Sapphire decided that direct action was needed. She wriggled her bum further into Jay and into the unmistakeable erection. For a few minutes they both lay still, but the stillness of their bodies belied the battle of lust and desire that was raging inside Sapphire and apparently Jay as well as he gently ran his hand along her thigh, slipping it beneath her top and resting it on her stomach, igniting a powerful chain reaction just below his hand. 'Feeling warmer now,' he murmured. As if she was about to burst into flames, Sapphire thought!

This was more than a friendly gesture, it was crossing a line, and Sapphire wanted to go further. She took his hand and moved it on to her breast where her erect nipple had way more to do with Jay than with the cold. There was an intake of breath from Jay, but he didn't move his hand, instead he lightly stroked her nipple. Then she turned to face him and lightly kissed him. 'I'm getting there,' she murmured back, 'but aren't you supposed to have skin-to-skin contact when its really cold, and that's the only way of staying warm?'

With that she slipped her hands under Jay's T-shirt and ran them over his abs, then lower still as she caressed him through his Armanis. And then they were kissing and scrambling to remove each other's clothes – Jay pulling off his T-shirt, Sapphire inching down his boxers. Both caught up in irresistible desire, Sapphire literally didn't care about anything else, right now all she wanted to do was fuck Jay, feel him inside her, she was consumed with an intense, overwhelming urge for him, that was beyond reason. And he seemed to feel the same by the way he was passionately kissing her, sliding his hand into her briefs and caressing her . . . Sapphire thought she would orgasm right then and he'd barely touched her. 'God, I want you,' he murmured, kissing her neck, her breasts, as she put her arms round him and pulled him on top of her, his cock pressing against her,

'Fuck me,' she murmured back, putting her hand on him to guide him into her. This was what she had been waiting for, for so long.

But suddenly Jay was pulling away from her, was fumbling to get his clothes back on.

'What's the matter?' Sapphire exclaimed. Talk about anticlimax.

Jay sat on the edge of the bed, his head in his hands. 'This should never have happened.'

Sapphire moved to touch him, but he flinched as she put her arm round him, 'Jay, we still want each other, I don't see the problem.'

'I'm seeing someone,' Jay's reply was barely audible; for a second Sapphire wasn't sure if she'd heard him.

Sapphire clutched the duvet to her. 'You've got a girl-friend?' she asked.

He nodded, and said again, 'This should never have happened, I'm sorry.'

He got up and slipped on his jeans and jacket and, still not looking at her, said, 'I'm going to get a coffee, clear my head.'

And with that, he left the room, leaving Sapphire reeling. She wanted to run after him and say, 'Forget your girlfriend, it's obvious we're meant to be together.' Instead she curled under the duvet, a ball of misery in the pit of her stomach. Jay was out of reach for her more than ever now. And suddenly she realised that there was more than a physical attraction at stake here: she was in love with Jay.

Chapter 13

'So what do you think?' Christine asked as Sapphire dragged herself into the boutique two days later. It was her mum's first day working for her. She had finally accepted her offer to work for free. Sapphire looked round the boutique. Her mum had clearly been busy – the stock had all been neatly arranged and she had put up a Valentine's Day window display. It actually looked really good. Christine had gone for a naughty-and-nice theme, with one model arranged in pretty pink lingerie and the other in a saucy black lace number complete with a whip in her hand. She had also hung up several of Sam's gold butterfly necklaces. Sapphire had no idea her mum had such a good eye for design.

'It looks great, Mum, but maybe lose the whip.' Sapphire replied.

'Oh I don't know – there's a lot of money in bondage, I gather. But if you like I can swap it for a dildo.'

God her mum really was getting into the swing of things. 'Or maybe a rose? I don't want to attract the wrong kind of customers,' Sapphire replied.

Christine nodded and as she removed the offending item, Sapphire wandered aimlessly round the boutique. Valentine's Day was just a couple of weeks away and usually she loved the run-up – the boutique always did well. But right now she was having a hard time caring.

The realisation that she was in love with Jay and the revelation that he had a girlfriend had floored her. She felt like bursting into tears one minute and then at others she would be filled with such intense longing. She had spent the night she returned from Birmingham going through all the text messages Jay had ever sent her, torturing herself by reading them, and then she had taken the engagement ring from the back of her dressing table. She had opened the red velvet box and gazed at the ring. It was beautiful, elegant and classic. How had she ever thought otherwise? She had slipped it on to her finger where it fitted perfectly. And that made her burst into tears – Jay must have found out the exact size of her ring finger. She thought of how brutal her rejection would have seemed to him. She gently kissed the ring, and murmured, 'Sorry Jay,' and then put it back in the box. But later she found herself opening the box again and this time she put the ring on a long gold chain which she then fastened round her neck – the ring cool against her skin at first and then warming up. Since then she hadn't taken it off, she was wearing it now, and from time to time instinctively she put her hand up to her neck to check it was still there, though the ring was tucked out of sight below her jumper. She sighed. Valentine's Day was another cruel reminder of the fact that she didn't have Jay. Who was his girlfriend? She wondered as she went into her office to check her emails. Probably that pretty blonde she'd seen him with just before Christmas.

'I meant to say, someone called in for you this morning,' her mum said, popping her head round the doorway. She handed Sapphire a card, adding, 'He was foreign, Eastern European, I think.'

'What did he want?' Sapphire asked, sounding sharp in her nervousness.

'He just said he had some business to discuss with you.

He looked very wealthy. Maybe he's useful. He was very charming, full of compliments about the boutique.'

Okay, so it was great having her mum help her out in the boutique but no way did Sapphire want her interfering with the rest of her business and absolutely no way did she want her to have anything to do with Markov. But she didn't want to alarm her mum so she simply said, 'He's in business with Ryan, so I'm not exactly keen to see him.'

She hoped that would be enough for her mum to leave the matter; instead Christine said perkily, 'Well, you never know. Sometimes you have to be open to new things. Look at me and the rut I was in and now here I am working, I've got a boyfriend and we're going to go to Venice which is somewhere I've always wanted to go.'

Her mum was not to know that being open to Markov was probably like inviting the Devil into your house.

Sapphire sat looking at Markov's card. What the hell did he want? She had hoped that now she was no longer with Ryan she would have nothing more to do with him. She turned it over and read 'Call me x'. She suppressed a shudder. What was the best response – to text him saying don't bother me again or ignore it in the hope that he would get the message that she absolutely wasn't interested? There was no knowing with someone like Markov – he didn't seem to follow the rules of conventional behaviour. Ignoring seemed like the best idea. She ripped the card into tiny pieces and threw it in the bin. Then whilst supposedly checking her emails she went back to daydreaming about Jay.

Jazz then wandered in to the office. As it was coming up to Valentine's Day she was channelling red and pink and plenty of love hearts – red nails, pink love heart hair slides and necklace and pink pumps. 'What are you wearing tomorrow night?'

Sapphire stared at her blankly.

219

'Don't tell me you've forgotten!' Jazz exclaimed. 'It's Sam's birthday!'

'Shit, shit, shit! What am I going to get her?' Sapphire wailed. 'She always buys me such great presents!'

'Just go to Topshop and get her some clothes – she's now a size ten, can you believe it! I know that's what she wants. All her clothes are way too big now, she says she's living in skinny jeans.'

'God I haven't seen Sam for ages,' Sapphire suddenly realised. 'Over three weeks. Is she okay? I meant to tell her that I've sold five of her necklaces.'

'It's okay,' Jazz said breezily, 'I told her when we went out the other night.'

'Oh,' Sapphire replied, slightly put out that she hadn't been invited.

Jazz looked slightly awkward and fiddled with her pink plastic love heart necklace. 'She just wanted a chat about stuff like her diet. And she knows how boring you find that.'

She does? Sapphire thought she had always hid her frustration at having the blow-by-blow calorie countdown.

'So, what's the plan for tomorrow night – is it just the three of us?' She tried to pull herself together. She really hoped so; she wanted to confide in Jazz and Sam about her feelings for Jay. She needed their advice.

Jazz rolled her eyes, 'No, mate, it's a big night out. Ben's coming along with loads of Sam's friends from work. We're meeting for cocktails and then going for dinner at Zilli's.'

Sapphire's confession to her friends would have to wait.

She bought Sam a great new outfit – a red-and-white candy-striped strapless dress – something Sam would never have wanted to wear when she was bigger but which was now going to look so cool on her. Sapphire would have loved to buy something new to wear to Sam's birthday. She hadn't bought any clothes for herself in such a long time in her anxiety about money. In the end, after staring vacantly at the clothes in her wardrobe, she went for her silver mini-dress. It didn't look great, she'd lost so much weight lately that it practically hung off her. Her usually perfect skin looked sallow, however much make-up she put on, and her eyes seemed to have lost their sparkle. Somehow being in the party dress accentuated how rough she looked, so in despair she took it off and instead went for her skinny jeans, Uggs, long black jumper and her favourite Louis Vuitton animal print scarf round her neck. I may as well get some more wear out of it before I sell it on eBay, she thought bitterly. She tucked the long gold chain with Jay's ring underneath the jumper. But as soon as she walked into the Star Bar she realised she was wildly underdressed. Sam looked gorgeous in a bright turquoise halter-neck dress; she resembled a luscious brunette Scarlett Johansson with her extravagant black eyeliner and perfectly red lips. By comparison Sapphire felt like Dorothy in *The Wizard of Oz* stuck in dreary old Kansas before everything went Technicolor.

'Happy birthday,' Sapphire exclaimed, hugging Sam and handing over her gift. 'You look beautiful!'

'Thanks!' Sam beamed back happily. 'I feel fantastic. How are you, Sapphire?'

'Good, thanks,' Sapphire lied.

'I thought you were going to wear your silver dress,' Jazz said to her as she also joined the two women. Jazz had pulled out all the stops in a bright orange mini-dress and matching accessories.

Sapphire shrugged, 'I know I look really shit.'

'You don't,' Sam reassured her. 'You always look good.'

'It's nice of you to say so,' Sapphire replied. 'But I can't

221

believe how amazing you look, Sam! You are so going to get lucky tonight!'

Sam looked slightly awkward, 'Actually, Sapphire, I've already got a boyfriend. We've been going out a month now.'

While Sapphire was thrilled for her friend – Sam's single spell had gone on way too long – she couldn't help feeling hurt that this was the first she knew of it. Something seemed to have happened to her friendship with Sam lately. They used to be so close. It was her work, she supposed. But as usual she put a brave face on. 'That's fantastic.' Then she added cheekily, 'I hope he's a gorgeous fuck machine!'

Sam and Jazz seemed to freeze, expressions of appalled horror on their faces. Come on! Sapphire felt like saying, I've said way worse things before. And then she realised the reason for the looks as she turned to see Jay standing just behind her. For a mad second she thought he must have come to see her but then he moved next to Sam and put his arm round her and said wryly, 'You always used to think so, Sapphire.'

Oh. My. God! Sam was going out with Jay! If someone had set out to deliberately torture Sapphire they could not have devised a more effective method than this. She felt her heart would break as she took in the sight of Jay looking more gorgeous and sexy than ever, just a few feet away from her, but out of reach.

Sapphire looked down at the floor and mumbled, 'I'm sorry, I had no idea you were seeing each other.'

'No, I'm sorry Sapphire; I've been meaning to tell you for a while.'

Somehow Sapphire managed to lift up her head. Sam looked as mortified as she felt. Sapphire could not bring herself to look at Jay, though she was intensely aware of him and made an excuse about wanting to say hi to one of their friends.

Somehow she made it to the ladies' without breaking down but as soon as she slammed the cubicle door behind her she leant against it and gave in to the tears. It seemed too cruel that just as she had realised that she was in love with Jay, one of her best friends turned out to be in love with him too. And why had Sam waited to tell her like this! The pain was turning into anger – at Jay, and at Sam. After a few minutes she became aware of a gentle knocking at the door,

'Sapphire, are you okay? It's me, Jazz.'

Sapphire sniffed and grabbing at some tissue began wiping her face. 'I'm fine,' she muttered, though it must have been obvious that she'd been crying.

'Is anyone else out there?' she asked; she couldn't bear to be seen in such a state.

'No, it's clear.'

Sapphire opened the door and stepped out of the cubicle.

'Why the fuck didn't you tell me!' she exclaimed, suddenly angry at Jazz as well. 'D'you have any idea how it felt finding out like that!'

Jazz bit her lip. 'I'm sorry, babe, I so wanted to tell you but Sam made me promise not to.'

'But I'm supposed to be your friend! How could you all do this to me! God, isn't it enough that I lose the man I love, but I also lose my friends as well!'

'You love him?' Jazz asked, sounding surprised.

'Yes! And I don't need a lecture from you about how I managed to fuck it all up completely.' Sapphire caught sight of her dishevelled reflection in the mirror – mascara streaked both her cheeks and her eyes looked puffed up and red.

'Sam and me didn't know you felt like that about Jay. And Sam would never have got involved with him if she knew that,' Jazz said quietly. 'D'you want me to fix your make-up?'

'What, so I can go and make polite conversation with my ex and my supposed friend? I'm not fucking staying.'

And with that Sapphire swung her bag over her shoulder and, not caring how shit she looked, marched out of the bathroom. She stormed through the bar, ignoring Sam who called out her name, and pushed open the door and stepped into the bleak February night. Then, she started running towards the sea, desperate to get home.

'Sapphire!' It was Jay calling her name. Sapphire carried on running. But it didn't take long for Jay to catch up with her. He ran alongside her and put his hand on her arm to stop her.

Sapphire shook it off. 'Leave me alone!' she shouted, out of breath, furious, hurt, humiliated. But she stopped running.

'Look, Sam wanted to know that you were okay.'

'Oh yes, Sam, your girlfriend – the girlfriend you forgot all about the other week when we ended up in bed together. What was that about? Trying to humiliate me?'

Whoa! She was sounding far too emotional, but she couldn't stop herself. Jay hung his head and seemed to have a problem with eye contact. 'Sam wanted to tell you herself.' He hesitated and seemed extremely uncomfortable. 'And I'm sorry about what happened the other week. It was just circumstances. Please promise that you won't say anything to Sam, I would hate to hurt her.'

What about me! Sapphire wanted to shout back; instead, she said passionately, 'I would never ever do anything to hurt Sam. As for that night – it's forgotten.'

Though even as she said it a memory of him kissing her burnt brightly in her mind. How could she ever forget?

She stared back at Jay, trying to hide her intense hurt.

'Anyway, I was always open with you, Sapphire. You were the one who was economical with the truth. Like when was it exactly that you decided to cheat on me with

Ryan?' Jay was sounding pretty emotional now.

'I didn't ever cheat on you with Ryan,' Sapphire protested. She so wanted to say that she had made a mistake, that she was in love with Jay but knew she had to stay silent.

Jay glared at her in disbelief. 'Okay, I admit I flirted with him and,' she hesitated, knowing how bad this made her sound, 'and I kissed him, but that was it until you and I had split and I'm not proud of it.'

And she wanted to add that he didn't exactly deserve to have the moral high ground after their night together.

'Whatever,' Jay said as if nothing Sapphire could say about the past could possibly interest him any more.

Sapphire felt stung. 'I'm telling the truth Jay, why the fuck would I want to lie about it now?'

'Because you always want to come out of a situation looking good, don't you?'

'No, I don't, Jay,' Sapphire could feel her eyes filling with tears at the accusation. 'Didn't you stop to think what it would be like for me seeing you and Sam together? Awkward doesn't even cover it. And to find out like this!' She turned to go before Jay could level any more criticism at her, then swung back round and added, 'Was there no one else you could have gone out with? Did it have to be one of my best friends?' She was shouting again.

Jay looked seriously pissed off now. 'Sapphire, it's not about you, it's about me and Sam. I couldn't help falling for her. If it was up to me I'd be happy if I never saw you again, but for Sam's sake I think we need to try and be friends.'

Sapphire felt an icy cold blast of rejection. She only had herself to blame, she had pushed Jay into saying this, but that didn't make it any easier. 'I'll make sure I keep out of your way,' she replied in a hard, brittle voice. Then she turned and walked swiftly along the pavement. She had to get away; the tears were falling now, turning the scene around her into a blur.

'Look, Sapphire, I didn't mean that,' Jay called after her.

Sapphire ignored him, just keep on walking, she told herself, keep on walking. When she finally got home, she took off the necklace and shoved it into the back of her jewellery box. That dream was over.

She poured herself a very large vodka, and sipped it neat; somehow the burning sensation seemed appropriate. She felt so betrayed by everyone. She had always thought that whatever happened in her dealings with men that she would always have Sam and Jazz to rely on, but it seemed she didn't. She was entirely alone.

Her phone rang but she let it go to answerphone. It was Jazz. 'Sapphire, please pick up, I just want to know that you're okay. Please, Sapphire, I'm so so sorry. Pick up.' Jazz sounded on the verge of tears but Sapphire remained where she was. She didn't want to speak to anyone right now. The phone went again, this time it was Sam leaving a message. 'I'm sorry, Sapphire. I know I should have told you before, but there never seemed to be a right time. Don't blame Jazz, I made her promise not to tell you. I didn't think you were bothered about Jay. Can we talk tomorrow?'

Sapphire buried her face in her hands. What a fuck-up she had made! She'd been blind to what she had with Jay; she was obviously a crap friend – why else would Sam and Jazz have found it so easy to lie to her? At the thought of Sam a fresh wave of humiliation rose up in her – did everyone know about her and Jay? In spite of not wanting to speak to anyone she found herself reaching for her mobile and calling her mum. She got straight to the point 'Did you know Jay was seeing Sam?'

'What?' Christine sounded genuinely surprised. 'Sapphire are you okay?'

226

'Did you know?' Sapphire insisted.

'Of course not, love! I'd have told you if I did! Vicky did mention that Jay had a girlfriend, but I had no idea it was Sam. I'm so sorry, love. You sound really upset, shall I come over?'

'No,' Sapphire said quietly, trying to hold back the tears, 'I expect you're with Jason.'

'No, I'm not, but even if I was, I'd come over. You sound really low.'

'I'm fine, Mum, it was just the shock. I've made such a mess of everything.'

'Sapphire! Don't say that! You have made such a success of everything – think of your business. You're so strong, everyone admires you. Please let me come over.'

'No, thanks Mum,' Sapphire repeated. 'You know I always need my own space. I'll call you in the morning.'

Chapter 14

'Hi, can I help you with something?' Sapphire asked the young blonde-haired woman who had just walked into the boutique.

Two days after Sam's birthday Sapphire was back into saleswoman mode, trying desperately hard to carry on as normal, but inside hurting so badly. The young woman shook her head and said quietly, in what Sapphire thought was an Eastern European accent, 'Actually I wanted to talk to you.'

Sapphire stared at her, puzzled – she looked vaguely familiar but as she was wearing huge dark glasses it was hard to tell. 'Do I know you?' she asked, wondering what the young woman wanted. The woman took off her glasses and instantly Sapphire recognised her. She was Alina, the woman she had seen with Markov at his London club several months ago.

'Please, can we talk somewhere private?' Alina said urgently, looking anxiously around her. She looked exhausted, her face was drawn and there were dark shadows under her eyes. She was no longer the stunning beauty Sapphire remembered. Sapphire was surprised at the request but nonetheless she got Jazz to watch the boutique while she showed Alina into her office.

'So, what can I help you with? I'm afraid if it's about work, I don't have any vacancies right now.'

Alina shook her head. 'It's not that.' She hesitated and picked at the red nail polish on her fingers.

Sapphire felt like saying, well what is it? She didn't exactly have time for guessing games.

'I came to say there's someone you need to be careful of.'

'Who's that then?' Sapphire tried to sound confident but her heart sank: there was only one person Alina could be referring to.

'Markov – I know he likes you. Well, more than that, I think he is becoming obsessed with you. I just wanted to tell you – please don't have anything to do with him.'

'Trust me, I don't want to have anything to do with him!' Sapphire exclaimed with feeling. 'But why are you telling me this? I'm sure you wouldn't want it getting back to Markov?'

Alina pulled an expression of disgust. 'That bastard! I was his girlfriend for six months. He is all smiles on the outside but he is vicious when he's crossed. I put up with it because he gave me plenty of money to send back to my mother to care for my son.' At this she pulled out her wallet and showed Sapphire a picture of a cute toddler with chubby cheeks and brown curly hair. 'He's five now so he looks different. I haven't seen him for three years.'

'Can't you go back?' Sapphire asked.

Alina shook her head, in resignation. 'I couldn't support my son if I did that, and anyway Markov has contacts everywhere.'

'And are you still with Markov?' Sapphire was appalled at Alina's plight. She remembered watching a TV documentary about Eastern European girls imprisoned in brothels. Surely that wasn't Alina's fate?

Alina grimaced. 'He told me I had stopped pleasing him. I'm with one of his friends now.' She shook her head. 'But I don't want to talk about it. He's down in Brighton with Markov and I managed to I slip away.' She checked her watch. 'I'd better go, they'll wonder where I am. I just wanted to tell you to be careful.'

Sapphire would have liked to say that she could look after herself but she remembered only too clearly how powerless she had felt in Markov's presence, the feel of his hand on her bare skin. 'How do you know he is interested in me?'

'I heard him talking to one of his boys, boasting about how he was going to get connected to a local business and how the owner was very beautiful. He's just bought an apartment in Brighton, I think he's planning to spend half his time down here now.'

'Oh shit,' Sapphire said with feeling.

'Just don't be alone with him. He has a way of getting at people and controlling them. You have friends and family and you are from this country. It is different for you. I'm an illegal. But I hope one day to go home and see my son.'

Sapphire felt desperately sorry for Alina and wanted to help her but when she voiced this, Alina said sadly, 'There's nothing you can do, I just wanted to warn you is all. I couldn't live with myself if didn't at least do that. Markov has ruined enough lives.'

After Alina left, Sapphire remained haunted by her story. Every time the door opened she jumped, thinking it might be Markov. She felt as if there was no end to her troubles at the moment. She called Alfie again and asked to meet him after work. Alfie had suggested a drink but that seemed too intimate. So it was coffee at one of the many cafés in the Lanes – the cosy normality of the surroundings contrasting with their topic of conversation. 'What do you suggest I do?' Sapphire asked after she'd filled him in on the situation.

'I wish I knew,' Alfie replied, looking concerned. 'There's no point in going to the police because he hasn't

230

done anything. I do know some stuff about him, but like I said before, I don't want to get involved.'

'You've got to tell me what you know!' Sapphire exclaimed. God, even just talking about Markov made her feel nervous and she looked anxiously through the the window at the pedestrians strolling by, fearing he might be out there.

'I don't think that's such a good idea,' Alfie replied. 'What you don't know can't worry you.'

'Tell me, Alfie,' Sapphire persisted. 'I really want to know.'

Alfie sighed and ran his hands through his blond hair. As he did so, Sapphire noticed he was wearing a platinum wedding band on his finger.

'Something you want to tell me, Alfie?' she asked, gesturing at the ring.

'Ah,' he looked embarrassed. 'Yes, Brooke and I got married last week.'

Sapphire raised her eyebrows in surprise.

'Yeah, I know what I said to you, Sapphire – about feeling I made a mistake and wishing I was back with you, but that's never going to happen is it? I think I've grown up these past months, finally faced up to my responsibilities. And whatever I feel about you, I have a son now and I want to do right by him. And,' he hesitated, 'I do love Brooke.'

'It's okay, Alfie, I wasn't exactly holding out for you,' Sapphire said drily. Then smiled at him. 'Really I'm happy for you.' And suddenly she realised that she was. Alfie had devastated her with his betrayal at the time, but she had moved on and he no longer had the power to hurt her.

'So now, tell me what you know about Markov.'

Alfie looked behind him, clearly even talking about Markov made him jumpy. 'All I know is that Markov is part of some Ukrainian gang involved in prostitution and drugs that wants to get a footing in legitimate businesses.

He's been trying to get in on our club but so far we've managed to head him off. He is bad fucking news. Unfortunately Ryan got involved with him when he was out in Ibiza – I don't know how exactly. I think Markov bought off some other gang who were dealing drugs in Ryan's club and causing trouble. And since then he's acted like Ryan owes him.'

'Well, why don't you go to the police?' Sapphire demanded. It seemed obvious to her. What was Alfie's problem?

'Because I've got a child and a wife,' Alfie let the statement hang in the air, while Sapphire stared at him in disbelief.

'Are you saying they would be in danger if you said anything?'

Alfie shrugged. 'I don't know, I just wouldn't want to risk it.'

Then he told her how he also knew Markov ran several escort agencies in London and was looking to open one in Brighton; he used girls from Eastern Europe who had come into the country illegally – frequently coercing them to work for him. He was also involved in drug dealing. But he wanted to be seen to be respectable – hence the London club, hence wanting a share of Alfie's club and his interest in Sapphire's business.

'He really is a nasty piece of work. I don't know why Ryan ever got hooked up with him, but I tell you he regrets it now and,' Alfie paused and looked awkward, 'he regrets how he treated you.'

Sapphire rolled her eyes, 'He can regret all he likes, I don't give a shit about Ryan after what he did.'

'Whatever – I know he's sorry. And all I can say about Markov is just keep your distance. Don't see him, don't take his calls, he'll get the message.'

But Alfie had underestimated Markov's interest in Sapphire. Two days later, on Valentine's Day, he sent her a huge bouquet of deep red roses. For a second Sapphire smiled when the delivery girl handed her the flowers – it was always nice to get something on Valentine's Day and not feel like a saddo single who no one wanted. But the smile vanished as she read the card: 'I'm still waiting for your call, Sapphire, M x'. Why wouldn't he give it a rest? Surely it was beyond obvious that she had no interest in him? Just how thick was his skin?

Sapphire was already feeling bad enough about Valentine's Day as it was, imagining how loved-up Sam and Jay were being. She threw the bouquet on the floor in disgust.

Then Jazz burst into the store with a grin that could have lit up the whole of Brighton Pier. She raced up to Sapphire and thrust out her hand.

'I'm engaged!' she said unnecessarily as the diamond ring told the whole story.

'Congratulations, Jazz!' Sapphire said as enthusiastically as she could; there was no way she wanted to rain on Jazz's parade. And she really was pleased for her friend. She knew that Jazz had been longing for this, practically since the moment she met Ben three years ago.

'It's brilliant, isn't it! Ben was going to propose tonight over dinner but he ended up coming over to mine first thing this morning and doing it then because he said he just couldn't wait any longer. So he actually proposed as I was eating my porridge in my pyjamas! I might have to get him to do it again when I'm all glammed up. I don't want to remember that the most romantic moment in my entire life took place when I was eating porridge! I mean, who am I? Goldilocks?' Jazz literally could not stand still for the excitement.

'Okay,' Sapphire said, 'tell me all about it – leave out no detail.'

'Are you sure?' Jazz asked. 'I know what you feel about marriage.'

'It's more what I felt about my own marriage,' Sapphire corrected. 'Really, I want to hear everything.'

Anything that kept her mind off Markov was welcome right now.

Jazz chatted away happily for the next ten minutes and when Christine turned up for work she retold the story. Then at lunch time Sam popped in. For one sickening moment when Sapphire saw her, she was convinced that Sam was going to reveal that Jay had asked her to marry him. Instead Sam had simply come to congratulate Jazz. She looked better than ever, glowing in fact. No wonder Jay had fallen for her, she was beautiful.

'Hey, Sapphire, it's great news about Jazz isn't it?' Sam exclaimed, looking awkward – and so she bloody well should. They had texted each other after the birthday party – Sam to say sorry, Sapphire to reply that she was cool, even though she wasn't. But texting was one thing and meeting face to face was another. Sapphire felt a fresh stab of pain, thinking of Sam with Jay. Okay, Sam didn't know that Sapphire had feelings for Jay, but couldn't she have fallen for someone else?

'It's brilliant,' she replied, slightly off. Then added, 'How's Jay?'

Part of her wanted to needle Sam, make her suffer. Sam instantly looked embarrassed, 'He's fine. Sapphire, I really am sorry that you had to find out like that.'

Oh God, she couldn't handle this right now. 'Yeah, well it wasn't ideal.' She paused and looked directly at Sam, who was mortified. 'Anyway, I'm going to open some champagne. This is supposed to be about Jazz. We should have a toast.'

Sapphire was glad to have the distraction as she popped open the bottle and poured everyone a glass, but she had never felt less like celebrating. Her mind was in overdrive wondering about Jay and Sam. No doubt they were going on a date tonight. Or would he cook for her and they'd spend the night at his flat, make love in his bed?

'So who are the flowers from, Sapphire?' Jazz asked, catching sight of the roses, which lay by the counter where Sapphire had abandoned them, not even bothering to put them into water. 'Is there someone you should tell us about?' She looked expectantly at her friend.

Sapphire pulled a face, 'They're from that Markov.'

'Oh yes,' Christine piped up, 'I think he really likes you, Sapphire.'

She said it as if Sapphire should be pleased. Just how bad a judge of character was her mum?

'Well, I don't like him, Mum, and if he comes round here again, I don't want you being nice to him or taking any messages. He is bad news and I want nothing to do with him.' Sapphire knew she sounded rattled, but couldn't help it.

'Tell him yourself,' Jazz murmured, 'here he is.'

Markov seemed to dominate the boutique when he pushed the door open and walked in, leaving his two bodyguards waiting outside. He was dressed in an expensive-looking suit and navy cashmere overcoat and almost looked like a respectable businessman, except for the dyed blond hair and the heavy gold chain he was wearing over his shirt.

'Good afternoon, ladies, I don't think I've ever seen so many good-looking girls in one room!' He smiled broadly at everyone, winking at Christine, who looked thrilled to be called a girl. What the fuck was he doing here? He walked over to Sapphire. 'Happy Valentine's Day, Sapphire, I hope you liked the flowers.' His lip curled slightly when he noticed them abandoned on the floor. 'Maybe you don't like roses? You must tell me your favourite flowers and I will arrange for those to be sent to you instead.'

'There's no need,' she managed to mutter, wanting to recoil from the overpowering scent of his aftershave as he walked over to her and kissed both her cheeks. His lips felt wet and cold against her skin and she had an overwhelming desire to wipe away the mark they left.

He smiled and said quietly, 'It seems that you are not going to call, so I have to come to you. I understand, Sapphire, you are a woman who likes to be wooed. I like that. I have had enough of silly tarts who throw themselves at me. I like that you make me work a little bit harder. Deferred gratification, always sweeter I think, yes?' He made her skin crawl.

He looked around the boutique with his cold grey eyes. 'And Christine,' he exclaimed, walking over to Sapphire's Mum and kissing her on both cheeks. 'You must be so proud of Sapphire,' he continued, putting his arm round Christine, as if he was an old friend.

'Oh I am! I just wish she wouldn't work so hard.'

'Well that is why I'm here, I agree with you. Sapphire needs to have some time off.' He reached into his coat pocket, and pulled out an envelope, 'So here I have two first-class tickets for Vegas. I would love you to come out as my guest, Sapphire.'

Sapphire stared back at him in astonishment. How deluded was he? Of course she wasn't going to Vegas with him.

'Wow!' Christine exclaimed, 'I've never flown first-class.'

'Well, next time, Christine, I'll take you,' Markov said smoothly, heading towards Sapphire. 'So tonight I have a table booked at Nobu. I can pick you up at six and we can talk about the trip.'

Sapphire stared at him blankly.

'I want to take you out for dinner, Sapphire.' He reached out and stroked her arm. 'You look as if you've

236

lost weight. I might have to revise the size of the clothes I send you.'

Sapphire felt sick. He must have been watching her all this time to find out about what she liked. Stalking her. A wave of revulsion and fear rolled through her.

'I'm afraid that's not possible,' Sapphire pulled her arm away from his touch. 'And please don't send me any more things.'

'Course you can go, Sapphire!' Christine butted in. 'I'll lock up tonight, I'm not meeting Jason until later.'

Sapphire flashed a furious look at her mum, before repeating, 'I'm sorry, I can't come.'

'But you heard your mother! She will look after the store for you! You shouldn't be always business Sapphire – even I know that.' He moved closer and lightly brushed a strand of hair from her face. 'Really, you should let someone look after you for a change. Let me look after you.'

Sapphire clenched her fists as she summoned all her courage and said, 'Please understand, Markov, that I am not interested in going out for dinner with you and that has nothing to do with my business. Nor do I want to go to Vegas with you.'

Markov smiled at her words but his eyes looked harder than ever. 'Very well, Sapphire, I will leave you alone now.' He turned and began walking out of the store. 'Lovely to see you again, Christine, enjoy your night with Jason.' Then at the door he paused and said to Sapphire, 'I'll be seeing you soon – even if you won't have dinner with me, I still have some business to discuss with you.'

As he shut the door behind him Sapphire wanted to scream in frustration. How much clearer did she have to be about her feelings? It must be his male pride that was making him so persistent. She got the feeling that it wasn't very often that he didn't get his own way. She glared at her mum who was now caught up with serving a customer, and then because she was still feeling so wound up she grabbed her bag and coat and called out, 'I'll be back in ten minutes.' She just had to clear her head.

But the walk wasn't exactly guaranteed to improve her spirits as every single shop window she passed was on full Valentine's Day alert – filled with love hearts and wall-to-wall pink decorations. She walked past Kurt Geiger, usually one of her favourite shops, but not even the array of gorgeous brightly coloured heels could raise a smile from her. She felt completely trapped. Trapped by her business, trapped by Markov's unwelcome attention and trapped in her love for Jay, which was never going to have a release. It seemed that in a matter of months her whole life was unravelling and she simply didn't know where to begin to make sense of it. She was so deep in thought as she headed towards the sea that she almost bumped into Jay as he came towards her.

'Hey, Sapphire!' he called.

She stopped. Great. She had rushed out of the store without even checking her appearance, she probably looked a right state.

'Oh hi,' she replied, surreptitiously smoothing down her hair, even as the wind whipped it out of shape.

'So, how are you?' he asked. And she noticed that he seemed just as put out about seeing her as she did about him. He wasn't at all his usual, easy-going self. He kept fiddling with the zip on his grey hoodie. He was probably on his way to meet Sam.

'I'm fine,' she replied, knowing perfectly well that she didn't sound it.

'I've just heard about Jazz's news, it's great isn't it?'

Sapphire had a flashback to the moment Jay had proposed to her. If only she could go back and change what she said. But no way could she let on that anything was wrong. 'It's brilliant for Jazz and Ben, really fantastic.' Now she worried that she sounded sarcastic.

Jay looked awkward. 'I meant to call you to say sorry for the other night.' He coughed and looked self-conscious, 'I shouldn't have said those things. I was totally out of order.'

Shouldn't have said them because they weren't true, or shouldn't have said them because they were too harsh? What did it matter? Jay was with Sam. End of.

'Don't worry about it, we all say things we regret. I do it all the time,' Sapphire replied. She held Jay's gaze for a second. 'I'm cool about it,' she lied.

'Really? That's a relief, I didn't like to think that I'd upset you.'

Sapphire managed to give a snort of laughter, but really she felt like bursting into tears – at this rate she'd better take up acting, as pretending to feel something she didn't seemed to be all she did. 'I'm not upset, I promise. Anyway, I've got to get back to the store. Busy day and all, there's bound to be loads of men popping in to buy last minute Valentine's presents and I want to guilt trip them into buying the most expensive items.'

Jay gave a brief smile. 'Good for you, Sapphire, always so focused.'

Sapphire forced another smile and then muttered, 'See you later.'

She felt if she stayed and talked to Jay as if they were nothing more than friends she would surely crumble. Just how much more could a girl take? she thought to herself as she practically ran back to the boutique.

She was in a foul mood for the rest of the day, snapping at her mum – maybe it hadn't been such a good idea to have her helping out – finding fault with the beauty rooms not being clean enough, shouting at Kiki when she knocked over her coffee on the cream rug.

'You should have gone out for dinner with that Markov – no woman wants to be on their own on Valentine's night,' Christine told her as Sapphire was cashing up at the end of the day.

That did it! Sapphire slammed her fist down on the desk. 'I can't stand the man! Why can't you get that into your head! He's vile!'

'He seemed okay,' Christine continued obliviously. 'Maybe you would have had a good time. You need to get out more and have fun. Take it from someone who knows.'

Sapphire glared at her mum – God, she really had no idea! Just because she was all loved-up with Jason. She was just about to go into some of the reasons why she most certainly did not want to go for dinner with Markov when her mobile rang. And suddenly Sapphire's Valentine's Day blues lifted as Emily, the producer from *Morning Edition*, the TV programme she had appeared on several months ago, asked if she would be interested in joining the show as one of the entertainment reporters for a month while the regular reporter recovered from an operation. They wanted her to specialise in reports on how to have fun in the credit crunch.

'Do you really think I could do it?' Sapphire responded, amazed that she'd been asked.

'Absolutely! You were a natural in front of the camera. We're only talking five-minute features. You just need to be ballsy and have plenty of opinions. I know you'll be great.'

Sapphire hesitated, 'I'm not sure – I do have my own business to run as well.'

'No reason why someone like you couldn't do both. I think you'd be a great addition to the team, and it's only for a month anyway, what do you say?'

Sapphire thought of how good it would be to try something different. Just lately she felt as if she'd only been going through the motions.

'Okay, then yes! I'd love to do it.'

And Emily filled her on all the details – she'd have a week to prepare and she would shadow the programme to understand how it worked and she'd be given some training in interviewing techniques.

'My God, you're actually smiling,' Christine exclaimed when Sapphire walked back into the boutique, 'I thought I was never going to see that again. So who is he then?'

Sapphire laughed, 'This is absolutely nothing to do with a man – it's all about me!'

Yeah, she thought, it was definitely time for her to become kick-ass again, she really was not cut out to be the heartbroken moping type.

Chapter 15

'Are you sure everything's okay? You know you can call me any time?'

Sapphire was speaking to her mum on the phone from the temporary London flat she was renting, overlooking the Thames.

'Yes, everything is fine – don't even give it a second thought. Just concentrate on the TV work. I'm so glad it's going well – everyone I talk to about it thinks you're brilliant!'

'Thanks, Mum,' Sapphire replied, grateful for Christine's enthusiasm. 'I'll call you tomorrow.'

For the week she trailed the programme, she had commuted to London each day, but just four days into the real thing she realised she would have to have a London base and it was too much to run a business and do her reporting job. It was time for the control freak to delegate, so her mum had taken over running the boutique, with Jazz's help.

Although it was scary doing something new, Sapphire was also getting a huge adrenalin kick from reporting. Emily had been right in her assessment: Sapphire was something of a natural in front of the camera. She felt she was herself as she chatted away to the interviewees and then bantered with the presenters in studio. Off air it was a different story – she was still consumed with longing for

Jay and really missed her friends. As always, her way of dealing with it was to keep busy. She worked out at the gym every day for an hour, and accepted every invitation that came her way, which was why tonight she was going to an NSPCC charity ball with Cal – a cause close to his heart as he was one of their ambassadors.

She considered herself in the mirror in the floor-length black dress – she'd had her hair put up in a sleek up-do and was wearing huge fake sapphire earrings, and no other accessories. It was quite a dramatic look but Sapphire thought it suited her, and black was just about the only colour she felt like wearing right now – even her nails were black, Chanel of course. Jazz had been outraged when she'd heard Sapphire was wearing black and had begged her to wear a bright colour, telling her black was such a safe option, it was plain boring, 'I just don't feel like it,' Sapphire had told her. And then asked the question she asked every time she spoke to her friend, 'How's Sam?'

Really it was code for finding out if she was still seeing Jay.

'She's fine, counting down the days to the marathon. You should call her.'

'I'll text her,' Sapphire replied, knowing that she'd find some excuse not to. I mean what was she supposed to say to her? How's it going with the love of my life?

Sapphire paced round the apartment, sipping a vodka and tonic and looking out at the river, while she waited for Cal to pick her up. The apartment was modern and situated next to the Oxo Tower on the South Bank. It was owned by one of the production team who was out of town and he had rented it to Sapphire at a reduced rate, otherwise she doubted she would have been able to afford it and its impressive views of the capital. From her living-room window she could see the Houses of Parliament and the London Eye to the left and the Tower

243

of London to the right. It gave her such a brilliant sense of excitement and possibilities being in the heart of London. And of course it was great being by the river – having lived by the sea all her life Sapphire always wanted to be near to water, it calmed her and stopped her feeling hemmed in.

The buzzer rang and she walked over to the entry phone to let Cal in. She opened the front door while she made a quick final check of her appearance in her bedroom. 'I'll be with you in a second,' she called out as she heard Cal walk into the apartment. She loaded her lipstick and eyeliner into her clutch bag and gave her hair a blast of spray. Then she froze in horror. It wasn't Cal she could see behind her, in the mirror, it was Markov. He strolled into her bedroom, hands in his jacket pocket and casually sat down on her bed, his eyes never leaving her.

'What are you doing here?' she demanded, struggling to contain her apprehension, horribly aware that Markov was between her and the door.

'I just thought I'd see how you were, Sapphire. You're looking very well. London life must suit you. I always thought that Brighton was too small a city for someone as ambitious as you. And,' he held up one hand and considered his manicured nails, the large diamond catching the light, 'I know Alina came to see you and no doubt spun you a story of lies about me. Now I understand why you wouldn't come to Vegas. But really, Sapphire, she was lying.'

Oh God! What had he done to Alina?

'I'm about to go out,' Sapphire replied, aware that her voice sounded tight with fear. 'You'll really have to go, I'm expecting my boyfriend any minute.'

She started moving towards the door. If she was quick maybe she could get to the front door before him. If only she wasn't wearing her bloody heels. Markov didn't move, but when she was almost at the bedroom door he

244

stood up and grabbed her arm and pulled her to him. Sapphire almost gagged as she caught a waft of his overpowering aftershave.

'Please don't tell lies, Sapphire. I really find that a most distasteful habit. Cal Bailey is not your boyfriend. You are simply friends. You do not have a boyfriend, Sapphire.' He was smiling but his grip on her arm was painful. Sapphire struggled to get away but he only gripped her harder. She could feel panic bubbling up inside her. She was only too aware of how vulnerable she was, but she tried to keep a lid on the fear. She had a feeling that Markov thrived on people's fear, especially that of women. On the dressing table her mobile beeped with a message.

'Okay, but he is due here now and Cal is never late.'

'That's true, he is always punctual, always – except when he discovers his beloved Bentley has been vandalised and he phones the police to report it. I expect that text message you just received was him, telling you he is going to be a little late.'

'I don't believe you,' Sapphire tried to sound defiant. She turned her head and looked at her phone where it lay on the dressing table.

Markov saw where she was looking, and hesitated for a moment before replying, 'Check if you like.'

He let her go and Sapphire hurried over to get her phone, feeling as if her insides had turned liquid with terror. Her arm tingled painfully from his tight grip. Oh God, had Markov set this up so that she would be alone with him? With trembling fingers she picked up the mobile and accessed the message. It was indeed Cal, letting her know that he was going to be half an hour late. Sapphire's eyes scanned the dressing table, looking for something that she could use against Markov – perfume, hairspray and then she realised she was holding it – her phone.

'You were right,' she said, summoning all her courage, and holding the mobile behind her back she turned towards Markov. 'I wonder how you knew? Are you psychic or did you have something to do with vandalising Cal's car?' She wanted to keep him talking as she speed dialled Cal's number.

Markov laughed, 'I do not concern myself with such trivial matters as that.' He stood up and held out his hand, 'Give me the phone please, Sapphire.'

Pick up, Cal! Sapphire willed her friend. 'No I won't! I want you to get out of my apartment now. If you don't, I will call the police.' She was shouting now, praying that Cal would answer his phone and hear her distress.

Markov strode over but before he could grab her she bolted into the ensuite bathroom and slammed the door shut. She quickly turned the lock as Markov threw his whole weight against it, causing the door to shake. In her urgency to escape she had dropped the mobile on the marble floor and it broke open, the battery skidding across the floor.

'Oh no,' she whimpered, scrabbling to put it together as Markov continued pummelling the door. 'Open the door, Sapphire!' he shouted.

'I'm calling the police,' she shouted back at him. She fitted the battery back in the phone and pressed the on switch but the screen remained blank. Oh God, oh God, oh God, think, think! she told herself.

'I want the police,' she said in a loud, clear voice, as if talking to an operator. 'I'm reporting an intruder at flat 20, Riverside, Gabriel's Walk, please come now. I'm locked in the bathroom and he's trying to get in. Yes, I'll keep holding,' Sapphire carried on pretending to have a conversation, praying that it would be enough to get rid of Markov.

'You're making a mistake, Sapphire, just open the door, I only want to talk to you.'

'Get out of here!' she screamed back. 'Please,' she appealed to the imaginary operator, 'send someone as soon as you can, I'm in danger!'

She flung open the bathroom cabinet and grabbed a pair of nail scissors, then clambered into the bath and opened the tiny bathroom window, 'Help!' she shrieked out. 'Help me!' She was eight stories up and she wasn't confident that anyone would hear her. She could see the people strolling by the Thames below, oblivious to her screams. Behind her she could hear Markov still trying to break down the door. She remembered reading that people rarely responded if they heard someone shouting 'Help', it was 'Fire!' that got them going. 'Fire!' she redoubled her shouts. But no one responded.

She had to do something! She couldn't just wait for Markov to break the door down. Frantically she looked round the room and her gaze fell on the matches in the bathroom cabinet. She could light one of the candles by the bath and hold it up to the smoke alarm. She climbed out of the bath, grabbed the matches, and with trembling fingers tried to strike a match, but her hands were shaking too much and it took five attempts before she could light the candle. She stood up and held it under the smoke alarm. Come on! She urged the alarm. Thankfully a few seconds later, the ear-piercing alarm went off. 'Thank God!' Sapphire thought with relief, but it was short-lived as at that moment Markov managed to smash open the door. He staggered in as the door gave way, clutching his shoulder, and rushed at Sapphire.

'Don't do this!' he yelled at her. 'I only want to talk to you.'

'Get away from me!' she screamed, cowering against the wall as Markov lunged for her. This was it, one part of her thought, it was all over, she was trapped, helpless to do anything. But suddenly her survival instinct kicked in, she swung out the hand holding the scissors straight at his face, slashing his skin and at the same time brought her knee sharply in contact with his groin. As Markov bent double, groaning in agony, she sprinted out of the bathroom, through the living room and out of the front door. She raced down the stairs to the landing below and started hammering on people's doors, shouting, 'Help, I'm being attacked.'

The first three doors she knocked at remained closed, and all the while she looked anxiously over her shoulder, fearing that Markov would have pursued her. Finally a twenty-something City boy in a suit opened the door. 'Please help me,' she gasped. 'A man broke into my apartment, he's still there, I have to phone the police.' The man looked in two minds about letting her in, 'Please, I'm not a crazy person, please let me in.'

The next few hours passed in a blur as the police turned up, closely followed by Cal, who had alerted them too after hearing Sapphire's anguished voice on the phone. When the police checked out the apartment Markov was long gone, just a splatter of bloodstains in the bathroom and the broken door testified he'd been there. Sapphire couldn't stop shaking as she went over what had happened with the detectives. They seemed sympathetic and put out an alert for Markov, telling her they would need her to come to the station and make a statement.

'I'll come with you,' Cal told her, holding her hand reassuringly.

'What about the ball?' Sapphire asked.

'Sapphire, I think I can miss one charity ball – you're more important.'

By the time Sapphire came to give her statement at Blackfriars police station, in the shabby interview room, sipping an overstrong cup of tea with sugar, she was calm; a slow burning anger was taking the place of fear. How dare that man terrorise her? She thought it was

248

obvious that the detectives would arrest and charge Markov but they didn't make any commitments. DI Moustache (she couldn't remember their names) said that they would have a have a strong word with Markov. While DI Mullet Hair (God, was he auditioning for an eighties cop series?) said that they would tell Markov not to go near her. It didn't sound as if they had taken the break-in at all seriously. In the reception she froze as standing at the desk, chatting to the duty sergeant, was Markov. Instinctively she clutched Cal. 'That's him!' she exclaimed.

At that moment Markov turned and looked at her. There was a narrow strip of surgical tape under his right eye. 'I came as soon as I could, I had to get this wound taken care of.' He turned back to the duty sergeant, 'I don't want to press charges, really I came to put the record straight. We just had a bit of a misunderstanding.'

By now the two detectives who had questioned Sapphire appeared.

'A bit of a misunderstanding!' Sapphire couldn't stop herself from shouting. 'You broke into my apartment and then attacked me.'

Markov smiled, 'Correction – you let me in to your apartment and you attacked me!' He gestured to the wound on his face. 'The nurse said if it had been just two centimetres higher, I might have lost my eye.'

'He's lying!' Sapphire exclaimed, 'He broke down the bathroom door to get at me, I swung the scissors at him in self-defence!'

'I broke down the bathroom door because I was worried that you were going to harm yourself. You've been very depressed lately, darling.' He looked at the two detectives, 'It's the credit crunch, it's taken its toll on her business.'

Markov sounded so reasonable, it was terrifying the spin he was putting on what had actually happened.

'That is not what happened!' she said urgently to the detectives. 'Please believe me!'

Without acknowledging her, they approached Markov. 'Can you come with us, Sir,' DI Moustache said. 'We'd just like to hear your version of what happened, for the record.'

'Of course,' Markov said easily, 'I'm always happy to help you boys in blue. But I don't want to waste your valuable time. It really was all just a misunderstanding.'

He began following the two detectives to the interview room and then turned and said, 'I'll see you soon, Sapphire, and no hard feelings.'

'Oh my God, Cal, do you think they'll believe him?' Sapphire asked as she and Cal walked out of the station.

Cal put his arm round her, 'Of course not, don't worry, it will be all right.'

Cal insisted on her coming back to stay at his apartment in Mayfair. Although Sapphire tried to make out that she'd be fine going back to her place, Cal wouldn't hear of it and it was with relief that she gave in. She really wasn't up to being alone.

Cal's apartment was as beautiful and stylish as its owner. It was comfortable and had a warm vibe, with bright colours, vintage Bond posters on the walls and practically everywhere you looked there were photographs of Honey and Angel. Sapphire paused in front of a large canvas print of the mother and daughter. Angel was so beautiful, and with her arms wrapped round her daughter, smiling away at the camera, Sapphire thought she had never looked so contented. She sighed with sadness, thinking about what Cal must feel having lost her.

Cal put on the fire and then brought over a blanket for Sapphire which he insisted on wrapping round her as she huddled on the sofa. 'Don't move, I'm going to get you a brandy,' he told her.

Sapphire didn't reply that she probably couldn't move even if she wanted to, the shock of what had happened had completely wiped her out. Every time she thought of being trapped with Markov, she was engulfed by a fresh wave of horror.

Cal came back with two large brandies and sat next to her. 'D'you want me to call your mum or Jazz? Let them know what happened?'

Sapphire shook her head, 'I don't want to worry them, I'll call them tomorrow. Look, Cal, you can go to bed now if you want, I know it's late and you've probably got an early start.'

'I'm staying up with you until you're tired enough to sleep – you've had a big shock, Sapphire. You don't need to pretend that everything's okay to me.'

'Thanks Cal, you're a real friend, I appreciate it.'

Just then Cal's phone rang it was DI Mullet wanting to let Sapphire know what had happened – Sapphire's mobile was still out of action so she had given the police Cal's number. Cal handed her the phone. She had hoped that Markov would be charged and arrested; instead the police said that they didn't have enough evidence to charge Markov with anything but they promised to keep a close eye on him and they had warned him not to go near Sapphire.

Sapphire ended the call in a state of shock. She quickly filled Cal in on what was said and then exclaimed, 'They just think it was a domestic, Cal, they're not going to do anything!'

Cal frowned, 'That's shit! But don't worry, I'm sure this Markov won't want anything to do with the police, he'll keep away from you. From what you've told me he's got too many things going on that he wouldn't want the police to know about.'

'D'you really think so?'

'Yeah, he's not stupid, is he? He'll keep away now.'

The two friends were silent for a few minutes, both sipping their brandies and staring into the fire. Then Cal spoke, 'So how's Jay?'

'How should I know!' Sapphire said defensively: 'He's going out with my best friend, end of.'

Cal frowned, 'It's not though, is it? You're in love with him. I think you realised it when you started going out with Ryan, but you didn't know how to tell Jay, did you?'

'No way!' Sapphire tried to bluster, stunned that Cal had been so spot on. She took a large slug of brandy, to avoid looking at Cal, nearly choked as the alcohol burned her throat and then decided to fess up. 'Yes, you're right,' she said quietly, 'but what difference does it make, Cal? He's with Sam now, I could never say anything to him and I would never want to hurt Sam.'

'I think you should tell him,' Cal replied. 'For all you know he has feelings for you and his relationship with Sam is a rebound thing.'

Sapphire shook her head. 'Jay's not like that. He wouldn't lead Sam on if he didn't really care about her.'

Cal shrugged. 'I told you he sounded worth holding on to.'

Sapphire hung her head, 'I know that now, Cal. I completely fucked up.'

'Hey, I didn't mean us to have this conversation so you could beat yourself up. I just wanted to let you know that you can tell me how you feel. God knows I've gone on long enough to you about Angel. If anyone knows about fucking up something good it's me.'

'Here's to us fuck-ups then,' Sapphire said ironically, clinking her glass against Cal's.

He shook his head. 'No, I'm not drinking to that because one day you'll be back with Jay I reckon.'

'And one day you'll be back with Angel,' Sapphire added. Cal frowned. 'Oh no Cal! You can't give me a happy ending and then not have one of your own,' Sapphire protested.

'I treated her so badly, she'll never have me back,' Cal said sadly. 'And somehow I've got to live with that.'

They stayed up for another couple of hours chatting and watching an episode of *The Hills*. By 2 a.m. Sapphire thought she might finally be able to sleep, but as soon as she was in bed and the light was off the nightmare images of Markov lunging towards her flashed up in her mind. And much as she tried to tell herself that it would be all right, that he wouldn't dare to come near her, she knew instinctively that a man like Markov did not give up easily . . .

She only managed to get a couple of hours' sleep in the end and stumbled into the kitchen the following morning feeling awful. 'God, I hope the make-up artist can do something with me, otherwise I'll break the camera,' she exclaimed and then stopped when she realised Cal had company. A beefy-looking ex-SAS-type man, with a flat nose and a buzz cut, sat drinking coffee at the kitchen table. He was dressed like a throwback to the sixties as a mod in a tightly fitting black suit and narrow black tie.

'Sapphire, meet Colin.'

'Hi,' Sapphire replied, feeling self-conscious about her dishevelled appearance.

'Morning,' Colin said cheerily.

'Colin is going to be looking after you for the next month or so.'

'What do you mean?' Sapphire asked.

'He's one of the guys I use for security sometimes and I want him to look after you. He'll take you to work and pick you up, stay at the apartment. Be your bodyguard, I suppose.'

This was totally unexpected, and control freak Sapphire wasn't at all sure that it was something she wanted. 'Can I have a private word with you Cal?' she asked, adding, 'no disrespect, Colin.'

'None taken.'

She marched into the living room, followed by Cal.

'I don't need a bodyguard!' she exclaimed as soon as he had shut the door. 'And no way can I afford one either!'

'You don't have to; Colin is on loan from me. Seriously, Sapphire, I want you to have him. It's not that I think Markov will come near you, but I just want to be sure and Colin will be there to make you feel safe. I know you didn't sleep last night, I heard you get up about five times. Do yourself a favour, have Colin look after you.'

'But Cal, it'll cost so much money!' Sapphire protested.

'Sapphire, you're one of my closest friends, I want you to be safe. Think of it as a favour for me, that way I won't be worrying about you. I'm going to LA at the end of the week and this would really put mind at ease. Please, Sapphire, let me do this for you. It's really no big deal.'

Sapphire bit her lip; she was so unused to accepting help from anybody and then she decided to break the habit of a lifetime, 'Thanks Cal, I really appreciate it.'

Cal grinned broadly, 'Come and have breakfast then and get to know Colin, he's a real diamond, even if he is stuck in a style rut.'

In the two weeks that followed, Sapphire was intensely grateful to have Colin. It meant that she could live her life without looking over her shoulder in fear all the time. In fact, she adapted incredibly quickly to having him around. He would drive her to work, then pick her up and take her shopping or to the gym. If she went out with friends from the production company, he would drop her off and then pick her up. He stayed in the apartment too, which she was hugely relieved about. 'What would you do if I got lucky one night?' she joked when he picked her up after one of her nights out.

'I'm very discreet,' he told her as he drove her home, 'but Cal tells me there's only one man you're interested in and he lives in Brighton.'

'What! You and Cal have been gossiping about me!' Sapphire exclaimed in mock outrage. 'I thought men never talked about emotional things.'

Colin replied, 'Not me and Cal. He was brilliant when me and the missus were going through a rough patch, really made a difference.'

Sapphire gave an ironic smile – Cal the marriage guidance counsellor, who had been unable to save his own marriage.

'So, have you spoken to this Jay bloke lately?' Colin continued.

Sapphire shook her head and said sadly, 'Colin there is no point. He's going out with one of my best friends and anyway I don't think he even likes me any more.'

'Nah, it's a rebound thing, I reckon. A man doesn't propose marriage to a woman and get over her that easily. But you'll have to make the moves, tell him how you feel. He'll have his pride.'

'Colin, I appreciate you and Cal's concern, but I have to face facts. Jay has been going out with Sam for three months now. I think it's serious.'

'Rebound,' Colin muttered under his breath as he pulled in to the underground car park.

'Anyway, you'll see them at the weekend as it's the marathon and they're coming round to the flat afterwards.'

Sapphire had hoped that she could get away with just watching the couple in the race and she had only agreed to do that as Jazz had begged her, guilt tripping her by saying how much it would mean to Sam and how important it was that she was doing the race for Cancer Research. It was all very well but Sapphire couldn't help feeling very differently about Sam and every time she thought of the couple together, she was almost physically sick with jealousy. But in spite of her feelings she had then found herself agreeing to invite Jay and Sam to her place for breakfast before the marathon and then to come back afterwards for a celebration meal and to stay the night. She had told Colin that she wouldn't need him at the weekend because she would be with her friends but he insisted that he should be with her. 'Just because Markov's done nothing, doesn't mean you should let your guard down. Not that I am saying he will try anything,' Colin added hastily. 'But I wouldn't be doing my job if I wasn't looking out for you. Anyway, I'm going to cook for you and your friends. Cal said you were a terrible cook and I love cooking.'

Sapphire was in fact dreading the weekend. Jazz was coming up on Saturday night but even with the support of her friend, Sapphire didn't know how she could face seeing Jay and Sam. The longing she felt for Jay hadn't diminished during the time she had been in London – on the contrary, it had grown more intense. She spent the week before obsessing over the meeting, and then for added torture she logged on to Sam's Facebook profile where she had put up photos of the couple in training.

'It is wicked to see you!' Jazz exclaimed when she arrived at the apartment on Saturday night.

'You too!' Sapphire replied, hugging her friend. She had missed her so much. Jazz had only been able to see her a couple of times in London as work was so hectic for both of them.

'And this is Colin,' she added as Colin popped his head round from the office, where he was holed up watching *The Sopranos*.

'Hi, don't worry I'll leave you girls to it, I know you've got lots of catching up to do, but just to let you know I've made a salade niçoise. It's in the fridge, and there's a fresh dressing for it in the blue jug.'

'Oh my God!' Jazz squealed as the girls went into the kitchen to grab a glass of wine. 'You've got a bodyguard slash personal chef – you're like a Hollywood star, I'm so jealous!'

Then she stopped herself, 'Sorry, I didn't mean that. I know why you've got Colin. '

Sapphire had told her friend the whole story but so far she hadn't told her mum; she figured she would when she moved back to Brighton – she wasn't up to dealing with her anxiety on top of her own. 'It's okay, Jazz, really I could do with laughing about the situation. And actually I'm really going to miss having Colin around.' She put on a posh voice. 'It's amazing how quickly one adapts to having staff.'

Both girls collapsed into giggles. 'Come on, let's have a drink!' Sapphire exclaimed, opening the fridge and taking out a bottle of cava.

'I thought you'd only be drinking Cristal, now you're on telly.' Jazz teased as they trooped back into the living room with drinks and snacks.

'Nah, cava is credit crunch champagne. But I've got some real stuff to celebrate Sam and Jay's marathon.' Even just mentioning the couple changed her mood dramatically, which Jazz was quick to pick up on.

'It's really good of you to invite them over, Sapphire. I know Sam really appreciates it. And I'm sure they won't be all loved-up in your face,' Jazz said.

'Oh, I know,' Sapphire replied, curling up on one of the huge plum velvet sofas. 'It's just seeing them together, it does my head in.'

Jazz sat down on the other sofa, 'Still feel the same about Jay then?' she asked sympathetically.

'Yes,' Sapphire groaned, 'I can't seem to get him out of my head and it's not like I haven't seen any fit-looking

257

men in London when I've been out – I've even been asked out by one or two, but I'm just not interested.'

'Perhaps you should go out with one, maybe you just need to have a distraction, there's nothing like a hottie to put a smile back on your face.'

Sapphire shook her head, 'I've thought of it, but then remember what happened with Gavin, and I don't want to end up in that situation again. I'd rather stay single and hope that I get over him one day.' She took a sip of cava, then added, 'And maybe he and Sam will split up. Colin thinks it might be a rebound relationship.'

Jazz winced, 'Sorry, babe, it doesn't seem like that to me, I wouldn't pin your hopes on it.'

'Okay, change of subject,' Sapphire declared, trying hard not to show how hurt she was by Jazz's last comment. 'Tell me how the wedding plans are going.'

Jazz and Ben were planning to get married at the beginning of September and it was going to be a full-on number. Jazz flicked back her blonde hair and looked uncertainly at Sapphire, 'Are you sure you want to hear about it?'

'Absolutely!' Sapphire said. 'I want an update on the dress, the bridesmaids' dresses, the menu and the cake!'

And fortunately for Sapphire, who just wanted the attention off herself, after only the smallest persuasion Jazz launched into a full and thorough debriefing of where the wedding arrangements currently were at – even whipping out her BlackBerry to show Sapphire pictures of potential dresses, cakes, and table displays. She seemed to be planning her wedding with the precision of a military campaign.

'If I ever got married again – which as we all know is never going to happen, but if I did – I would so want you to organise my wedding, you've thought of everything.'

'That's what Sam said,' Jazz said happily, then clapped a hand over her mouth, mortified by her comment. 'Not that she's getting married, Sapphire, I swear. I'm sorry, I didn't mean to say that.'

Sapphire sighed, 'It's okay, Jazz, you don't have to say sorry – they're a couple and I've just got to accept it.'

Words that were easier to say than mean. Sapphire couldn't help being sent on a downward spiral by Jazz's view that Jay and Sam were pretty rock solid and to make herself feel better she ended up hitting the wine. So instead of being bright-eyed and fresh when Jay and Sam arrived at the flat the next morning at quarter to seven, Sapphire was decidedly the worse for wear. She had just about managed to have a shower and get dressed and slap on some make-up, but she knew she looked like shit, in spite of Jazz telling her she didn't.

I look like a dog, she thought when Jay and Sam arrived, looking like models – Sam showing off a killer body in a fluorescent pink T-shirt and black running leggings, Jay gorgeous as ever in a white T-shirt and black shorts. It was slightly awkward between the three of them when they first met – Sapphire kissed and hugged Sam then didn't know whether she should do the same to Jay, then he came over and kissed her but it all felt forced. Sapphire took the opportunity to escape into the kitchen to make everyone a cup of tea.

'So how's it going with you, Sapphire?' Jay asked from the doorway, causing Sapphire to jump and spill the milk in her confusion at being alone with him. 'That Markov hasn't bothered you again has he?' Jay walked into the kitchen and leant against the table.

'No.' Sapphire could hardly bring herself to look at him. She was so aware of his beautiful body so close to her.

'Well, at least you've got Colin looking after you – he seems like a good bloke.' He paused, 'I was really sorry to hear about what happened, it must have been terrifying.'

Now Sapphire looked up at him; his brown eyes were warm with concern.

'I try not to think about it to be honest, but yeah, it's great having Colin.' At that moment the man himself walked in, 'And here he is, my hero.'

Colin laughed and walked over and put his arm round her, 'She's a trouper this one and the easiest-going person I've ever had to protect. I've just got to improve her cooking.'

At that the two men exchanged a meaningful look. 'Yeah I remember, it was atrocious,' Jay put in.

'It was not!' Sapphire exclaimed in outrage. 'My scrambled eggs were great.'

'But that was the sum total wasn't it?' Jay said cheekily, 'God, I remember that mushroom pasta dish you cooked, it was vile.'

'You ate it though!' Sapphire shot back.

'Babe, I was just being polite and it was the first thing you had ever cooked me. I didn't want to hurt your feelings.'

Both of them froze at Jay's subconscious 'babe' while Colin chatted on. 'Pasta, I mean who can mess up pasta? By the time I leave here I want you to be able to cook at least one signature dish. A sophisticated woman like you has to have more in her repertoire than scrambled eggs. What do you reckon, Jay, does that seem realistic?'

Jay struggled to collect himself. 'Um, yeah. I'd better see how Sam's doing.' And with that he made a rapid exit of the kitchen.

'I'll take the tea in,' Colin said cheerfully, giving Sapphire a wink as she too struggled to get herself together.

Jay called her 'babe' – did that mean he still had feelings for her, or was it just a slip of the tongue?

Jay and Sam quickly had their tea and then set off for the start of the race at Greenwich. Jazz and Sapphire were going to watch them from somewhere along the

Embankment and then they were all going to meet up in St James's Park.

'See, that went okay,' Jazz said once the couple had left.

'Yeah, it was fine.' Sapphire wanted to say it had been sheer bloody torture and to analyse Jay's babe comment. But she knew she couldn't, not with Jazz, it wouldn't be fair as her loyalties would be divided between her friends.

'By my reckoning they should be going past any time now,' Jazz said checking her watch, as she, Colin and Sapphire stood on the Embankment, near Blackfriars Bridge. They had managed to get themselves a prime position by the crash barrier to watch the runners go by. 'Sam's been running for nearly four hours.'

'God, I hope she can do it,' Sapphire replied, wanting her friend to do well. Much to her surprise she had been totally caught up in the atmosphere, cheering on runners, shouting out the names of ones who seemed to be flagging. It really was awesome seeing so many people – all ages, all sizes – putting their heart and soul into the race. So many people running for charity and some poignantly, like Sam, for close relatives who had died. There were people who were amazing natural runners, and people who were definitely not. She managed to put her encounter with Jay to the back of her mind for a while.

'You should do it,' Colin told her from his position at her side, from where he was seemingly drinking endless cups of tea from his thermos and sharing out snacks from his rucksack. Sapphire decided that Colin was definitely someone you would want with you were you ever to get lost in the middle of nowhere. 'You'd make a good runner and I think you'd enjoy it.'

Would she bollocks! Then Jazz squealed out that she could see Jay and Sam. Sapphire's throat suddenly felt dry. She just did not know if she could shout out for the couple. Being here was surely enough.

'Come on, Sam! Come on Jay!' Jazz shouted, more than making up for Sapphire's silence. She waved the banner which had 'Go Sam! Go Jay!' emblazoned across it in orange and pink neon felt pen. It had been made by Jazz, of course, who had matched her outfit to the sign in a pink hoodie, orange hairband and orange skinny jeans.

'You can do it!' Jazz screamed as the couple ran past them, turning to wave at their friends. Well, Jay waved, Sam looked absolutely shattered.

Then Sapphire managed to put her feelings to one side and shout out, 'Come on Sam! We love you!'

Sam managed to give her the thumbs up. Sapphire and Jazz watched and cheered the couple for as long as they could see them.

'Sam looked exhausted, didn't she?' Jazz said anxiously. 'I really hope she can make the finish, she'll be totally gutted if she can't.'

'She'll do it,' Sapphire replied. 'Look how determined she was to lose weight and she did it, and she's been training so hard for this and Jay will help her, you know he will.'

'He's a good lad that one,' Colin said wisely. Sapphire didn't need the reminder.

They hung around a little longer cheering on more runners and then decided to head off to St James's Park where they had arranged to meet up with Jay and Sam. It was slow going because of the crowds. They had just reached Trafalgar Square when Colin's mobile rang. 'My daughter's just had a baby girl!' he told them when he finished the call.

'Congratulations!' Sapphire exclaimed, hugging him, followed by Jazz.

'Yeah, my first grandchild. I'm so proud!' Colin said

with tears welling up in his eyes. 'I can't wait to see her tonight.'

'What do you mean tonight? You must go now!' Sapphire told him.

'I can't do that, I'm staying with you until I can arrange someone to take over.'

'Don't be ridiculous,' Sapphire said firmly, 'I'm perfectly safe with Jazz and just look at all the crowds, not to mention police.'

Colin hesitated, 'I really can't leave you Sapphire.'

'Colin, go and see your granddaughter! I am fine.'

Colin looked around them, as if weighing up the situation. 'Promise me you'll stay with Jazz all the time. I'll get one of my lads to come over to yours tonight. It's most likely to be Barry.' He leant towards Sapphire and whispered, 'The password will be "butterfly". And I'll text you his picture.'

The girls had to walk very slowly through the crowds after Colin left them. 'That's great news for Colin, isn't it?' Jazz chatted away happily.

'It's brilliant. I can't believe he was even thinking about not going till later.'

They stopped off at a café just off Trafalgar Square for a latte, speculating how much longer Sam and Jay would need to finish the race. They'd been standing for hours and it was with relief that the girls found a seat by the window.

'Shit!' Sapphire exclaimed, 'Colin was going to cook dinner for everyone.'

'No worries, I'll give you a hand – it's fish pie, isn't it?'

After making Jazz promise that she would help as Sapphire really wanted to give Jay and Sam something good to eat, the two girls sat in companionable silence. Jazz got out her mobile and texted Ben, while Sapphire looked through the window and enjoyed a bit of people watching. She admired a woman in a floral playsuit and platforms, very fashion fast forward she thought to herself, and smiled at a little girl who was licking an ice cream which was nearly as big as her head. Then everything felt as if it was in slow motion as she caught sight of a flash of dyed-blond hair. She did a double take. No way, surely it couldn't be. But to her horror it quite clearly was. Markov was standing on the opposite side of the road, looking right at her. Terror pulsed through her, this could not be a coincidence. How did he always know where she was? When Markov saw her looking he put his hand up to his lips and blew her a kiss. Sapphire reached over and clutched Jazz's arm. 'He's here,' she somehow managed to say, feeling weak with fear.

'What?' Jazz asked, glancing up from her phone. She followed Sapphire's appalled gaze, 'Oh my God, that's Markov!' Jazz clutched her banner as if it could be used as a weapon against him. Markov, seeing Jazz, waved at both the girls, entirely unconcerned.

Sapphire scrabbled for her phone and held it up, 'I'm calling the police!' she said loudly as if Markov could hear her through the glass. Markov simply shrugged and started walking away. Sapphire quickly took a picture of him while he was still in view, then he turned a corner and was lost to her.

'Go on, then,' Jazz urged her. 'Phone the police. He shouldn't be anywhere near you. He must have been following you.'

'I'll call them when we get home, there's nothing they can do now anyway, he's gone. They'd only want to take loads of statements down at the station and I want to go and meet Sam and Jay – I don't want their big moment ruined because of some fucking psycho.'

Jazz tried to persuade her to change her mind, but Sapphire was stubbornly insistent. She was deeply shaken by seeing Markov, but she would not, could not, allow him to ruin today. All the same she felt incredibly exposed as she and Jazz left the café and began walking towards St James's Park and she found herself scanning the people around her, fearing that one of them would be Markov and every time she saw a man with blond hair she experienced a jolt of fear.

St James's Park was absolutely crammed with people – runners being hugged by family and friends, and the drone of the person announcing through the loud-speaker the names of the runners crossing the finishing line and their times. Fortunately there was a system in place to help runners meet up with their friends and many of the trees had been hung with a large letter and designated as a meeting place. Sapphire and Jazz had arranged to meet Sam and Jay under the 'S' tree. It was now just over an hour since they had seen the couple and Sapphire hoped they would have completed the course – she knew Sam was aiming to make it in five hours.

'There they are!' Jazz squealed, waving her banner in excitement as they saw Jay and Sam, both wrapped in foil capes. Jazz charged ahead and hugged both of them.

'I did it!' Sam exclaimed, as Sapphire hugged her.

'That is so brilliant,' Sapphire told her. Caught up in the excitement, she hugged Jay, then pulled away, self-conscious at the feel of his body against hers. 'Well done, you're both stars.'

Jay smiled and gave her the thumbs up. 'You'll have to do it next year Sapphire,' he said, clearly expecting her to say that there was no way that she could.

'Actually, I just might. It was awesome watching the runners, really inspiring,' she replied.

Jay looked surprised.

'Hah, I bet you'll try and do it quicker than me,' Sam put in, not looking quite so pleased. 'You're always so competitive.' There was a slight edge to her voice.

'I'm not,' Sapphire protested. She couldn't help but feel offended. She hadn't found it easy watching the couple or being round them. She felt Sam should have been grateful she had come at all.

'Well, I'm definitely not doing it!' Jazz quickly put in, sensing the discord. 'I mean it's impossible to look stylish when you're running that distance, not that you didn't look great, Sam,' she added quickly.

Once they had walked slowly back to the apartment, Jazz reminded her that she had a call to make. 'Go on, Sapphire, you promised you'd phone the police once you were back.'

Jay and Sam had collapsed on the sofa and were drinking from bottles of water. But at Jazz's words they both looked over curiously at Sapphire. She shrugged, 'Okay, I'll do it.'

'What's going on, Sapphire?' Jay asked, sitting up on the sofa and looking concerned.

'I saw Markov when we were out. It could have been a coincidence but it did kind of freak me out.'

'No way was it a coincidence,' Jazz jumped in. 'He'd obviously been watching you and waited until Colin wasn't with us.'

'You must phone them right now,' Jay told her. 'I can't believe you didn't do it earlier. You shouldn't be so careless about your safety. I mean, Jesus Christ, Sapphire, the man attacked you!' He seemed really put out that Sapphire hadn't made the call.

'I think Sapphire wanted to wait until she'd congratulated you guys,' Jazz put in.

There was an awkward pause, where Jay seemed to regret being so outspoken.

'I'll make the call right now,' Sapphire said, walking out of the room for some privacy.

In her bedroom she took a deep breath and called the

266

number the detective had given her; he wasn't on duty so she left a message with one of his colleagues.

She also had a message from Colin letting her know that Barry would be arriving at ten. When she returned to the living room Jay was on his own, flicking through the TV channels. He switched it off when he saw her, 'Hey, did you call?'

She nodded as she sat down on the sofa opposite to him. 'They didn't seem bothered, maybe it was a coincidence.'

Jay shook his head, 'No way. He'd had someone following you. He deliberately let you see him, probably gave him a power kick, weird fucker that he is.'

'Yeah,' Sapphire replied. 'Anyway,' she said, getting up from the sofa, 'I'd better get on with dinner.'

'Oh my God, you're not going to cook are you?' Jay said cheekily, 'I haven't just nearly killed myself running the marathon to be finished off by your cooking.'

'Bastard,' she shot back, 'Jazz is going to help me.'

'She's no better! I tell you what, you and Jazz start chopping, then I'll take over when I've had a bath.'

'Sure,' Sapphire replied, as the image of Jay lying naked in her bath popped into her mind.

Jazz and Sapphire got on with the preparations, while Sam stretched out on the sofa and watched TV, too exhausted to do anything else. Jay emerged from the bathroom with only a white towel wrapped round him. He came into the kitchen to check on the preparations. He looked so delicious, so clean and so sexy, Sapphire could hardly take her eyes off him, and nearly sliced the end of her thumb off.

'Ouch!' she yelped as blood poured out of the gash and all over the onions, she'd just sliced.

Jay rolled his eyes. 'I knew I couldn't trust you.' And he took her over to the tap and ran cold water over the wound.

'Ow! Do you think I need stitches?' Sapphire wailed, hamming it up because she was so enjoying the feel of Jay's hand over hers and being so close to him.

'Stop being such a baby, and keep still,' Jay ordered.

'What's she done now?' Sam exclaimed from the doorway. She looked decidedly pissed off to see Jay touching Sapphire. He let go of Sapphire's hand.

'It's nothing,' Sapphire replied, 'I'll just get a plaster.'

'And I'll get dressed,' Jay muttered, walking swiftly out of the kitchen.

Sam walked over to the table, wincing as she lowered herself onto the chair. 'I'm shagged,' she said, half yawning as she did.

'Are you sure you wouldn't rather rest on the sofa?' Sapphire asked.

'No, I'm fine here,' she replied, a little abruptly. And Sapphire had the distinct impression that Sam wanted to keep an eye on her. To try and lighten the atmosphere, Sapphire got out the champagne and poured everyone a glass.

Then, when Jay returned after getting dressed, Sapphire left the kitchen, saying she had some research to do for the following day's show. She felt as if Sam would be happier if she wasn't there; it seemed a sad ending to the day, which should have been about celebrating her friend's success. In the end dinner was a subdued affair – both Jay and Sam seemed too exhausted to speak, and went off to bed shortly afterwards. Jazz left to get the train back to Brighton. Sapphire waited up to let her stand-in bodyguard in and then went to bed herself, though in spite of being exhausted, she barely slept. How could she, knowing that Jay was in the next room, lying in someone else's arms . . .

Chapter 16

The final two weeks in London passed without incident. Sapphire was pleased that her brief stint as a TV reporter had gone so well – in fact, the producer had said there was bound to be more work – but was also looking forward to going home to Brighton and taking over the running of her business again. She had found it hard delegating to her mum and Jazz. She desperately wanted to be back in control. She also wanted to see Jay again. He had seemed to be warmer towards her the last time they'd met, less critical and offhand, so maybe, just maybe, they could be friends. And even though it would be hard, at least she would still have him in her life. The fact was she was wretched when she didn't see him.

The police had been to see Markov who denied being anywhere near the marathon. One of his friends gave an alibi for him and the police thought it stood up. When they reported this back to Sapphire, she almost began to doubt that she had seen him, but then she remembered him blowing her a kiss. No, it had been him, there was no question. Colin was mortified that he hadn't been with Sapphire. He hardly let Sapphire out of his sight. Originally he had been planning to hand over her protection to one of his colleagues when she returned to Brighton, but with the Markov incident he was now adamant that he was going to come down with her and no amount of arguments from Sapphire that she'd be fine would persuade him otherwise.

She returned to Brighton late Friday night after going out for farewell drinks with the production team and was back in the boutique at eight the following morning, going through the accounts. Things clearly hadn't been great; her mum must have been keeping the full picture from her. The books were in a mess, and the figures didn't quite add up. She sighed; it was just as well she was back.

Jazz was the next to arrive, at half eight, bubbling over with excitement because it was her engagement party that night. 'So good to have you back, babe!' she exclaimed, handing Sapphire a latte and croissant.

'That's nice of you, Jazz.' Sapphire was starving.

'We're meeting at Star Bar at nine', Jazz called out as she dashed off upstairs.

Sapphire knew 'we' included Sam and Jay. She hadn't spoken to Sam since the marathon; they'd texted but both seemed to be avoiding an actual conversation. Sapphire had found it so hard seeing Sam with Jay. It had definitely affected her friendship. She was half dreading, half excited about seeing Jay again. She had thought about him a great deal since their last meeting, endlessly analysing what he'd said to her – the 'babe' had played over and over in her mind on a loop, the way he had looked at her, how it had felt when he held her hand. She was completely torn – wanting him to still find her attractive, not wanting to hurt her friend. She felt on edge for the rest of the day. God, it was doing her head in!

'Wow!' Colin exclaimed when he saw her dressed in her party outfit later that night. 'Lads of Brighton, beware! Heartbreaker on the loose.'

Sapphire rolled her eyes and took one last look in the mirror, was the outfit too much? To give herself confidence she had gone for it in a wickedly short pleated skirt, tight black polka dot sheer top and heels. Yes it was a full-on look but Sapphire felt as if she needed to reassert her confident side. She'd been so miserable these last months; she wanted to sparkle again. She was still nervous though as she walked into the Star Bar. Straightaway a group of lads recognised her from the TV and one of them asked if she would have her picture taken with him. Sapphire shook her head, she was so not into that kind of thing.

'Oh go on,' the lad insisted, 'it's my birthday.'

'Go on, Sapphire,' Colin reassured her, so reluctantly Sapphire posed and just hoped none of her friends had seen. But as she scanned the bar she saw they all had and were laughing. There was no sign of Jay, although she could see Sam. Maybe they'd had an argument? Stop it! Sapphire ordered herself, she must not think like this. She turned to Colin, needing reassurance. 'Will you come over with me?' she asked.

'No, I'm just going to get a ginger beer and sit at that table in the corner. Go on and enjoy yourself.'

Sapphire walked across to her friends. Jazz looked prettier than ever. She seemed so blissfully happy – all Sapphire's usual cynical thoughts about marriage no longer seemed to ring true and suddenly she realised that she envied Jazz her happiness, that committing to one person seemed an exciting thing to do, that it didn't seem like the end of something. It seemed like the beginning.

'So aren't you going to tell me not to go ahead and get married?' Jazz said defiantly as Sapphire sat down next to her at the table. 'That it won't last, that Ben will cheat on me?' She looked at Sapphire, daring her to puncture her happiness.

'I think it's brilliant you're getting married and as for Ben cheating – he never would.'

She sounded so serious that Jazz looked at her in surprise; she had clearly been expecting Sapphire to make one of her usual cynical comments.

Sam was looking at her with a similar expression. 'What's happened to you, babe?' Sam asked. 'Have you met someone in London since we last saw you?'

She shook her head, eager to get the spotlight off herself. 'Ben knows that I would pay him back big time if he cheated on my mate.' She glanced over at Ben who winked at her. At least the serious mood was broken.

'So are you going out on the pull tonight, Sapphire?' Ben teased her. 'Or are the Brighton lads not good enough for you now you're a celebrity?'

Sapphire smiled, 'I'm so not. I just want to dance all night with my girls.'

'Yeah, too right!' Sam exclaimed. 'It's been ages since we all went out clubbing.' She paused, and said quietly, 'It's really good to see you, Sapphire, I've missed you these last weeks.'

Sapphire was desperate to ask where Jay was, but just felt that she couldn't without giving away how much she wanted to see him.

'I've missed you too, it's just been so full on at work, I haven't really stopped. I'm sorry that I haven't been in touch as much as I should. And it was brilliant you ran the marathon, I'm so proud of you.'

'Thanks,' Sam smiled in appreciation. 'We're thinking of doing the New York one next year.'

'Good for you,' Sapphire managed to say. Obviously they hadn't argued, they were still the perfect couple. Sam, sensing that this was a subject she wasn't comfortable with, asked her how work was going.

Sapphire shrugged, 'The TV show went really well, but business is not quite so great as I've been discovering

272

today. But please, let's not talk about it. Tonight I just want to dance and drink.' At this she raised her glass. 'To Jazz and Ben!'

A couple of large vodkas got Sapphire through the first part of the night and she found that she could banter with her girlfriends and light-heartedly flirt with Ben's friends. But by the time they headed to Revolution, on one of the roads just off the seafront, she was feeling horribly apprehensive about seeing Jay again. A mixture of so many feelings were aroused in her – longing, pain, jealousy. It seemed too much to contain. Colin wanted to come into the club with her but Sapphire assured him that she'd be okay. 'I'm with my friends, Colin, there's no need for you to be here. The music will just give you a headache, go back to the apartment.'

'No way am I doing that!' Colin exclaimed. 'I'll be outside in the car if you need me.'

'We'll be with her all the time,' Jazz assured him. 'Ben and his mates will be looking out for her. And anyway,' she added cheekily, 'I don't think you'll get in in that outfit.'

Colin looked down at his shiny, grey mod suit that, like all his suits, was slightly too tight as he'd put on weight over the years but had not changed his style of dressing to accommodate the excess. 'What's the matter with it? It's vintage. I thought all you youngsters went mad for vintage?'

'Where do I start?' Jazz replied.

Colin shook his head in mock disgust, then pointed his finger at Sapphire. 'Right, madam, I want a phone call from you when you think you're about to leave and I'll come in and get you.'

Sapphire tried to protest that he really didn't have to, but Colin was having none of it.

*

Inside the club Sapphire found herself looking around for Jay, as did Sam, but he didn't seem to have arrived yet. 'Why's Jay late?' Sapphire asked, standing next to Sam and shouting to get herself heard over the house music pumping out. She could hardly bring herself to say Jay's name, convinced that her true feelings would register on her face.

'He had a business meeting in London with an investor. He's thinking of setting up his own personal training company – maybe in London, depending on the costs.'

'So does that mean he would move to London?' Sapphire asked, struggling to take in the idea of Jay leaving Brighton.

Sam looked slightly awkward, 'We both might, actually. I'm thinking of moving there with him.'

'Wow, that's quick!' Sapphire couldn't stop herself exclaiming.

Sam nodded, 'I know. But I love him and I just want to be with him.' She looked anxiously at Sapphire. 'I understand it must be weird because you went out with him but it was never serious for you was it?'

It took all Sapphire's strength to reply, 'No it wasn't, you know me.'

And then because she really didn't think she could bear to come out with any more lies, she made an excuse about helping Ben get the drinks in. She wove her way through the clubbers; any desire she had to dance the night away had left her.

She had no idea that things were so serious between Jay and Sam. She wanted so badly to believe that it was just a rebound thing for Jay; that he didn't really have strong feelings for Sam, but deep down she knew that couldn't be true. Jay was not the kind of man to mess around with someone's emotions. He was obviously in love with Sam. She had completely misread all the flirtatious signals that she thought had been reignited between them.

Ben had already ordered the drinks when Sapphire managed to get close to him. She tapped him on the arm and he grinned at her, 'I thought you'd be cutting up the dance floor, Sapphire.'

She shrugged. 'I think I need another drink first.' Or five, she thought miserably.

She helped Ben carry the drinks back to the chill-out area where the group had managed to grab a couple of sofas. Instantly her heart flipped when she saw that Jay had arrived. He was standing next to Sam with his arm round her. How was it possible, she wondered, that he looked better than ever? And how could she ever have thought that he was too boyish for her? He wasn't by any means boyish – he was a devastatingly handsome man. She made sure she was standing as far away from the couple as possible as she sipped her drink and chatted to Jazz. Only she couldn't resist looking over. Jay caught her eye and mouthed 'Hi', Sapphire simply nodded and turned back to her friends.

'Come on, Sapphire, you promised me you'd dance,' Jazz grabbed her hand and practically dragged her to the dance floor. Sapphire forced herself to look as if she was having a good time and after two songs she felt as if she was getting into it. At least with the music pumping out, so loud she could almost feel it vibrating through her body, she could forget about Jay and Sam. But try as she might to block them out of her mind they made it so hard for her when they came and danced next to her and Jazz. Then it was torture as Jay and Sam moved fluidly together, so close their bodies were almost touching. Sapphire felt her whole body tense and it was as though her limbs had been turned to lumps of concrete, except even that would probably have been able to move with more grace, she felt bitterly.

She lasted through Lady GaGa's 'Poker Face' – how ironic was that title – then shouted to Jazz that she was going to the bathroom. She looked at herself in the mirror, suddenly feeling self-conscious about the outfit. She had wanted to impress Jay but what was the point of that? Even if he still found her attractive, he was lost to her.

She felt completely despondent as she trailed out of the bathroom, moving out of the way of groups of giggling girls heading to the loos. She couldn't face joining her friends just yet, so she moved into the chill-out room, and leant against the wall trying to collect her thoughts and pull herself together. But she was thrown into further confusion by the arrival of Jay.

'Hey, why are you here on your own?' He had to stand close to her so she could hear him over the music.

'No reason, just needed five minutes by myself,' she replied.

Jay didn't catch what she said and bent closer so she could repeat herself. When she spoke to him they were so close that their faces brushed together – his skin smooth and clean-shaven. He asked her about moving back to Brighton, wanted to know where Colin was. She just couldn't bear to ask him where he'd been, didn't want to hear how he was moving in with Sam.

'How's the thumb?' he asked.

She stared at him blankly, then remembered. She held it up so he could see. He took her hand and examined her thumb close up, his hand warm on hers.

'Looks okay to me,' he declared. 'So how are you, Sapphire?' He was still holding her hand. She felt breathless and reckless with desire.

'I'm fine,' she lied. 'So what's this about you moving to London?'

He shrugged, but didn't let go of her hand. 'Nothing much for me in Brighton, might be good to have a change. I've got plans. I need to do something different with my life. I'm not going to be a personal trainer for ever. I want my own business.'

He was gazing directly at her, Sapphire gazed back and she knew her eyes told the truth about her feelings for him.

'I'll miss you,' she said quietly, so quietly that he had to bend his head closer still,

'What?'

'I said I'll miss you.' She paused, hardly daring to breathe, 'I miss you, Jay.'

'Yes,' he murmured. 'You too.' And he brought her hand up to his lips and lightly kissed it.

At the feel of his lips against her skin Sapphire felt something in her give way, she could not resist. She knew she should pull away, but she was powerless. And then she kissed him, kissed him with all the intensity and desire she had been feeling for so long, building inside her, a hard, longing, burning kiss that said take me, I'm yours. And he kissed her back with an intensity that matched hers. She found herself pinned against the wall as Jay pressed his body into hers, wove his hands through her hair. It was as if they were blind to everything else except their own reckless desire for each other.

Sapphire was the first to come to her senses. 'No,' she gasped. 'We can't do this. I can't do this to Sam.'

And before Jay could stop her she moved out of his embrace and pushed her way through the clubbers. She didn't know where she was going, she just had to get away from Jay. She found herself at one of the bars. She would have a drink, calm down and then return to the group. Her heart was racing wildly, she felt giddy, desperate, capable of anything. As she paid for her drink she was aware of the man next to her staring at her. She turned and found herself staring back into Ryan's green eyes.

'Sapphire, hi.' He sounded casual as if there should be absolutely no reason why Sapphire shouldn't welcome him with open arms.

'What are you doing here? Shouldn't you be at your own club?' Surely he didn't expect her to be nice to him?

'Just having a night out with some mates, why don't you join us?' Ryan seemed drunk, his green eyes slightly unfocused, but still raking over her, taking in the skimpy outfit.

She folded her arms and shook her head, 'No thanks.'

'We're in the VIP area upstairs if you change your mind. I'm with a couple who are getting married and the girl's thinking about having her hen weekend in Brighton. I could put in a good word for you. They're high rollers. And the new owner of this club's in, he might be worth meeting.'

Sapphire hesitated; she really didn't want to spend any time with Ryan. On the other hand it would be good to meet his friend and at the very least hand over her card and get her details. The books didn't look great. It was quite possible that she might have to reduce Kiki's hours, something which she didn't want to do. And at the very least, it would give her chance to get her head together after the encounter with Jay.

'Okay, I might join you in a while.'

But when she returned to her group she discovered Jay was back there as well, sitting on the sofa with Sam on his lap, as if the scene with Sapphire had been something she imagined. Why was he doing this to her? Was it some kind of revenge? Or did he still have feelings for her? He surely didn't by the look of him with Sam – the couple looked so loved-up that Sapphire couldn't bear to be near them. She quickly walked over to where Ben was chatting with his mates, and told him that she was going to the VIP area.

It was a tiny balcony up a flight of stairs and to call it a

VIP area was a bit of a joke. Ryan's party occupied the booth furthest from the stairs. Ryan was sitting next to a tarty blonde who looked completely caned, opposite two other men. He saw Sapphire and waved her over.

He made no attempt to introduce her to the two men he was with, who both seemed to be foreign. Sapphire did not like the way they all looked at her and then talked amongst themselves. She sat down opposite Ryan, while one of the men poured her a glass of champagne. Ryan introduced her to the drunk woman, 'Megan, this is Sapphire Jones, she could give you the best hen party ever.'

Ryan tried getting through to Megan who looked at him blearily through her false lashes.

'Here's my card,' Sapphire told her, sliding it across the table.

Megan picked it up and squinted at it. 'Pretty colour,' she said, then popped it into her bag.

Sapphire asked her all the usual questions about her wedding plans but the woman barely seemed able to follow her. She was wasted and the music was way too loud to make small talk over. It was pointless.

Sapphire turned to Ryan, 'I'm going to go back to my friends, thanks for the introduction.' She made to stand up, but Ryan grabbed her hand. 'At least finish your champagne. I haven't seen you for ages.'

He paused then leant closer across the table, 'And I wanted to say sorry, Sapphire. I feel so bad about what happened. I miss you.' He looked at her intently, none of the usual flirtatious cheekiness in his eyes.

'Look, Ryan, forget it, okay? We were never serious, don't sweat it.'

She just wanted to go now. She'd drunk too much and her head was beginning to hurt.

She picked up the glass of champagne and took another sip of it; it tasted strange, but she put that down to drinking it after vodka.

'So how have you been, Sapphire?' Ryan asked. 'I saw you on TV, I thought you were really good. A natural.'

'I'm fine, Ryan. But I must get back to Jazz – it's her engagement party and she'll wonder where I am.' She drained the glass of champagne.

'Well, well, Sapphire Jones sitting at my table. What a pleasant surprise. I thought I saw you on the dance floor earlier.'

Sapphire jerked her head round and found herself staring directly into Markov's cold shark eyes. And there was the smell of that revolting aftershave again.

Immediately she stood up and made to go, but Markov remained blocking her path. With a mounting feeling of panic she looked round for a way of escape.

'You shouldn't be anywhere near me,' she managed to blurt out.

'But you have come to me, this is my club – didn't Ryan tell you? I must say how lovely it is to see you.'

Markov reached across the table and filled Sapphire's glass of champagne before she had chance to stop him. Then he held up the now empty bottle and said to Ryan, 'Go and get some more champagne.' It wasn't a request, more of an order.

'Ryan, please, don't leave me with him,' Sapphire begged her ex. Ryan hesitated, clearly torn, then the man next to Sapphire said something in Ukrainian which decided him. 'Sapphire, I'll be back in a minute,' Ryan told her, 'just chill.' Why couldn't he grow some balls! she thought.

'You heard what your old friend said, Sapphire,' Markov told her, sitting down and pulling her down next to him, 'just chill.'

Sapphire was trapped between Markov and another man. 'Markov, I didn't realise that you would be here, now please, let me go, otherwise I'll have no choice but to call the police.' Despite her best intentions there was a quiver in her voice. She felt really weird and out of it.

Markov fired off something in Ukrainian and the other man gave a nasty laugh.

'So melodramatic, Sapphire. I just want to talk to you. Everyone else round here is drunk,' he gestured dismissively at his friends, saving a particular look of loathing for the drunk woman.

'So tell me, Sapphire, is it true that you're not interested in Ryan any more?' Markov said, inching closer to her, far too close for her liking. 'You know you're a very beautiful woman, and clever too, I like that.'

'I swear if you don't let me go, I'm going to scream, you'll only make things worse for yourself with the police.'

Markov reached out and ran his hand along her bare arm. Sapphire flinched at his touch as he leant closer still and said, 'A woman like you needs a real man to love her. You should be with someone like me, Sapphire. I thought that the moment I first saw you. I wish there hadn't been this misunderstanding between us, I really do. If I could turn back the clock, I would, believe me. But I can forgive you the incident with the scissors.' At this he reached up and stroked the small scar under his eye.

Sapphire was cornered, he was so close that she could see the black hairs in his nostrils, the tiny nick on his chin where he had cut himself shaving that morning, his freaky hairless arms, everything was magnified and intense. She had to get out of there. Where the hell was Ryan? She abruptly stood up and all at once felt so giddy she had to grab onto the table for support.

'Steady,' Markov said, reaching out and grabbing her arm and pulling her back down. Sapphire tried to push him away but the giddy feeling was overwhelming and suddenly it felt as if she was underwater, everything felt muffled and distant, she tried to speak but it was too much effort. Her eyes felt so heavy, she could hardly keep them open. 'I have to go,' she said, her words seeming to boom and echo round her head.

'We'll take you to my office,' Markov said. 'You don't seem very well, Sapphire. I'll look after you.'

He put his arm round her; Sapphire tried to push him away but found that she couldn't. Then Markov and another man were standing up and pulling Sapphire from her seat. Each had an arm round her and they practically dragged her along the corridor and into an office, with walls of blacked-out glass. Sapphire wanted to tell them to stop, let her go, but she couldn't do anything. She was completely powerless, she was drifting in and out of consciousness. Help me! she tried to shout, but no sound came out as her mouth uselessly opened. Then everything went dark.

She lost track of time. She opened her eyes, struggling to focus. She was lying on a grey suede sofa and couldn't move. She could hear men talking round her. She tried to get up. Markov loomed over her, pushing her back down.

'Get off me!' she tried to cry out.

Darkness again. Then shouting, she could hear Jay calling her name. But she couldn't open her eyes. She felt someone hold her hand, and then nothing.

'I'll sit with her, you two go and get a coffee.'

It was Jay speaking. She must be dreaming. She shifted in the bed, wanting to snuggle down in her duvet, she felt completely wiped out. But there was no duvet, she only had a sheet and blanket on her. It didn't feel like her bed and why could she smell that antiseptic hospital smell?

'Sapphire? Are you awake?'

With some difficulty she opened her eyes to see Jay sitting next to the bed and looking at her with concern.

'Why am I in hospital?' she asked in bewilderment,

282

struggling to sit up and wincing as she experienced a thumping pain in her head.

'Hey, take it easy,' Jay said. 'You really can't remember anything?'

Sapphire frowned. 'I remember meeting Jazz and everyone at the Star Bar and then going to the club and dancing a bit. Then I saw you and—' her cheeks flooded with colour at the memory of their kiss and it was with some difficulty that she continued. 'Then I saw Ryan, I think. But I can't remember anything after that. Why am I here, did I have an accident?' She rubbed her right wrist which felt sore.

'So you don't remember seeing Markov?' Jay asked gently.

'No!' At the mention of his name an icy feeling of dread unfurled in Sapphire. She thought of his predatory shark eyes. He was pure evil. Suddenly an image of Markov leaning over her flashed into her mind. She felt fear spike through her, why was last night a blank? She had no more than four drinks, no way was she that drunk. She looked at Jay, 'Why can't I remember? What happened?'

Jay reached out and took her hand. 'You're okay, nobody hurt you.'

The fear and panic increased. 'What do you mean? Please tell me, Jay.'

'We think Markov spiked your drink with something, possibly Rohypnol.'

Sapphire's eyes widened in shock. 'The date rape drug? Oh my God, Jay, what happened?' She suddenly found herself shaking as a feeling of horror and helplessness invaded her.

Jay held her hand more tightly. 'It's okay,' and he went on to tell her that after the drug had taken effect on Sapphire, Markov and one of his gang had dragged her into his office. Meanwhile, Ryan suspected what had

283

happened and came and found Jay and Ben and they'd got Colin. Ryan knew that Markov would have taken Sapphire to his office and they broke in and found her lying on the sofa. There was a scuffle and they managed to overpower Markov and get her away. Jay looked at Sapphire's stricken face and said, 'He hadn't touched you.'

At this Sapphire's face crumpled and she put her hands up to her face as tears streamed down her cheeks. 'He was going to, wasn't he?' she sobbed. 'Oh God, this is so horrible.'

'Don't think about it, Sapphire, you're safe now, that's what matters.'

Jay moved from the chair and sat on the side of the bed and put his arms round Sapphire. He held her so close to him that she could feel his heart beating. She buried her face in his shoulder and put her arms round him and held him tight.

'Dad, I want my dad,' she suddenly cried, feeling helpless and lost.

'Ssh,' Jay gently stroked her hair, 'you're safe, Sapphire, I promise.'

Sapphire didn't know how long they stayed holding each other, but eventually her sobs subsided. Even though she was distraught by what had happened, as Jay held her it felt as if she had come home, as if she was where she belonged. Sapphire held him tighter – she closed her eyes, it would be all right. Jay was here.

But suddenly the curtain around her cubicle was pulled open and Jay let go of her and moved away. Sam and Jazz were back. 'Sapphire!' Jazz exclaimed. 'Are you okay?' Both she and Sam looked anxiously at their friend.

Sapphire nodded, she just wanted to be left alone with Jay. Traumatised as she was, she had still detected the shadow flitting across Sam's face when she saw Jay holding her.

The girls were desperate to know what happened, both outraged that Sapphire had been drugged. Sapphire managed to tell them what she could remember. Jazz reached out and held her friend's hand but Sam hung back. 'What I don't understand, Sapphire, is why you went anywhere near Markov in the first place,' Sam said, when Sapphire had told them the little that she could remember.

Sapphire stared at her friend in disbelief. Sam sounded as if she thought Sapphire had recklessly put herself into danger.

'I had no idea he was there, Sam! Do you seriously think I would have gone anywhere near him?'

'Chill, Sam,' Jay interjected. 'Just let Sapphire be for now, she's had a big shock. She doesn't need you to have a go at her.'

'If Sapphire hadn't gone and talked to that lowlife Ryan none of this would have happened! I expect you were trying to network as usual,' Sam said bitterly.

There was shocked silence at Sam's outburst. Sapphire was certain she had only said it because she felt threatened by Jay's concern for her, but it hurt all the same. Sam seemed to regret her words too as she quickly said, 'I'm sorry, Sapphire, I didn't mean that, none of us got any sleep last night.'

'It's okay,' Sapphire told her, but it wasn't. She was deeply upset by Sam's accusation.

Jay and Sam left shortly after that. Jazz stayed while Colin turned up next, totally shell-shocked that Sapphire had been the victim of such an attack.

'But the police have said that Markov has disappeared. And I hit him as hard as I could, Sapphire. I reckon he'll leave the country. He won't want to be arrested. It'll be okay. Trust me.'

Sapphire's next visitor was her mum. 'Sapphire, I'm so sorry, I was over at Jason's last night and forgot my mobile, I've only just found out.'

285

Christine dissolved into tears at the sight of her daughter in the hospital bed.

'It's okay, Mum, I'm all right, nothing happened.' As usual Sapphire was the one reassuring her mum.

'It's not all right!' Christine exclaimed. 'When I think of what that bastard might have done to you! I had no idea how vile he was. Why didn't you tell me he'd been stalking you in London! He said he wanted to surprise you with a present, it sounded so romantic. I had no idea he would do something like this. He seemed so charming and so rich.'

Sapphire stared at her mum in disbelief. 'It sounds like you've been seeing quite a bit of Markov, what's going on?'

Christine looked awkward. 'He'd come into the boutique for a chat and to buy presents for his sister. He was always so polite and generous. But I never would have accepted the loan if I'd known what he'd done.'

Despite her banging headache Sapphire sat bolt upright. 'What loan?'

Christine bit her lip and looked anxious. 'No, I don't want to worry you now, you've been through enough. Just lie back down and get some rest.'

'What loan?' Sapphire repeated through gritted teeth.

Christine took a deep breath as if she was steeling herself for the confession, 'While you've been away in London, things really haven't been great with the business, but I didn't want to worry you. Markov offered to put some money in to the business and I accepted. I was trying to help you.'

'What?' Sapphire exploded. 'Why the hell didn't you tell me! He is the last person in the world I would ever accept money from. We've got to give it straight back to him.'

'We can't,' Christine said quietly. 'It's already gone – half to pay wages and suppliers and half –' she hesitated, 'to clear a debt I'd run up.'

'Oh my God, you've been gambling again! You used money from my business didn't you?' Sapphire exclaimed. 'How could you have been so selfish?'

'I wanted to go on holiday with Jason and I didn't have enough money and he's paying so much in maintenance to his ex-wife that he doesn't have any to spare and I thought I'd try and win some. It's been years since I went abroad.'

Sapphire slumped back, hardly able to take on board her mum's words.

'How much?' she demanded.

'Thirty grand,' Christine said quietly.

'That's it, then,' Sapphire whispered. 'My business is over, I'll have to sell it to pay Markov back.'

'You don't have to do that, surely?' Christine replied, shock etched on her face. 'He'll go to prison for what he did to you, you won't have to pay him back.'

Sapphire gave a mirthless laugh, 'Even if that happened, he's got a whole network of people working for him. Don't you get it, Mum? I'm ruined.'

Christine wanted her to come back home with her when the doctor came round to discharge Sapphire, but her mum was the last person she wanted to be around right now. She could barely look her in the eye, let alone stay in her house.

She took a taxi back to her apartment and spent ages in the shower as if the water could erase the memory of what had happened. Then she bundled up the clothes and shoes she'd worn the night before and threw them away, knowing that she couldn't face wearing them ever again. She paced round the apartment, realising she was going to have to sell it, though God knows how she'd be able to in the current climate – maybe she'd have to rent it and get somewhere cheaper. How could her mum have been so stupid?

She jumped when her doorbell rang. It was the police, wanting to take her to the station to make her statement. She had to go through the whole story of what happened with her and Markov yet again.

'And there was nothing going on between you and Markov?' the male detective asked.

'What do you mean?' Sapphire asked.

'Did you have a sexual relationship with him?' the female detective clarified.

Ugh, just the thought of it made Sapphire want to throw up. She shook her head, 'I couldn't stand the man. He made it clear that he was attracted to me, but I swear I never gave him any encouragement.'

'So why were you sitting at his table in the first place?' the male detective continued, sounding as if he didn't believe her.

'I was just saying hello to my ex-boyfriend who introduced me to a potential client. Look, I don't know why you're asking me all these questions! I'm not the one who did anything wrong!' Sapphire could feel herself getting more and more wound up.

'No one is suggesting you did anything wrong, we just need to establish the facts.' Female detective.

'And why aren't you arresting Markov?'

'We've got a warrant for his arrest but at the moment we can't track him down. It looks like he may have fled the country,' said the female detective. 'We want to talk to him about quite a few other things, he is very well known to us and the Met.'

'You really think he might have left the country?' Maybe he would go back to whichever hole he'd crawled out of and stay there for good.

'We'll know for sure in the next few hours. Now if you can just sign your statement you'll be free to go.'

Sapphire returned to her apartment, totally wiped out by

her experience; all she wanted to do was crawl into bed. She was just putting on her PJs when the doorbell went again. Wearily she went over to the monitor to see who it was. All her weariness vanished as she found herself looking at Jay.

'Hi,' she said, shyly.

'Hi, I've brought you supper,' he held up a carrier bag.

Sapphire buzzed him up then quickly raced to the bathroom. Shit! She exclaimed out loud, looking at her reflection in the mirror, she looked awful! She quickly brushed her hair, put on some mascara and blusher, then raced back into the living room to open the front door.

'Isn't Sam with you?' she asked, letting Jay in.

'Nope, I think she's seeing her mum or something.'

Jay sounded unusually vague – had he and Sam had a row? Sapphire wondered and tried not to hope that they had.

She followed Jay into the kitchen and watched him getting out containers of food. 'I'm never going to eat all that! I'll have an arse the size of a house if I do!' she exclaimed.

'It's for the next few days – I didn't think you'd feel like going shopping. I've made you some meals and so has Mum. There's macaroni cheese, lasagne, minestrone soup. What do you fancy?' Jay asked.

You, she thought. Instead she crossed her arms and mumbled. 'Minestrone sounds great.'

'Soup coming right up – why don't you go in the lounge and I'll bring it in.'

'Thanks,' Sapphire replied, though she would have preferred to stay with Jay.

She hadn't been on her own with him like this in a long time. 'Will you have some with me? I'd feel strange eating on my own.'

'Sure,' Jay replied, 'I can stay for a while. I figure you could probably do with the company.'

He's just being kind because he's a nice person, she told herself as she curled up on the sofa, but she couldn't stop the butterflies and the hope that it was something more than that. But if it was more than that Jay was keeping it well hidden. He brought the soup and French bread in, poured them each a glass of red wine and asked her if she wanted to watch a film.

'I don't think I want to watch anything right now.'

There was a pause, when Jay looked awkward. 'I'm sorry about what happened in the club, you know, between me and you. I think I was a bit drunk and when you kissed me I just got carried away.'

Sapphire wanted to say carried away like you did that night in the hotel? And that Jay should face facts, that they were both attracted to each other in a big way. But she just couldn't do that, couldn't put herself in such a vulnerable position.

'It's okay, I think I'd had a bit too much to drink as well.'

'So, we're cool?' Jay asked. Sapphire nodded, feeling less cool than she had ever felt in her life. 'Shall I put on some music?'

Sapphire nodded and then inwardly winced as Jay put on the first CD on the pile. It was Estelle which had been one of their favourite albums. She couldn't stop the memory flashing up in her mind of the last time they had listened to it – late one Friday night, lying on the sofa together, in each other's arms. She wondered if Jay remembered. She could hardly bring herself to look at him.

'Bad choice,' he said, suddenly putting down his plate, 'I'll put something else on.'

So he did remember.

'How are you feeling?' he asked, after changing the CD to Duffy.

'I still feel freaked out,' Sapphire replied, 'I'm trying not to think about it if you must know.'

Jay leant closer to her and said urgently, 'Don't bottle things up, Sapphire – you can tell me and your friends.'

'And that's not all,' Sapphire sighed and then went on to tell Jay about her mum accepting the thirty grand from Markov.

'Christ! Sapphire, I'm really sorry, is there anything I can do?'

'Thanks, Jay, but I think I'm going to have to sell the business, even if Markov is out of the country I can't be in debt to him. It feels like he thinks he can buy me.'

At this, Sapphire felt her eyes well up with tears. She felt she had lost everything – Jay, the business, her apartment – what did she have left?

Jay came and sat next to her and put his arm round her. 'Hey, it's not that bad, surely? Maybe the bank will loan you the money so that you can pay Markov back if and when you have to. You can't give up because of that bastard, that just isn't the Sapphire I know. You're strong, you can get through this. You inspired me, you know. I've just heard that I've got the loan to start up my personal training company.'

'How you? That sounds fantastic, Jay.' Sapphire had no idea Jay was so ambitious. Yet another reason to regret losing him. Jay was about to reply when his mobile rang.

'I'd better get that, it might be Sam,' he said, moving away from her and taking the call. 'Hey, babe,' he said, then moved towards the window with his back to Sapphire.

Sapphire wiped away her tears and tried not to look as if she was eavesdropping. Jay seemed to be reassuring Sam; she kept overhearing him say, 'It's okay.' After a few minutes he ended the call.

'I'm going to have to go, Sapphire. I'm sorry, I wanted to stay longer but I need to sort things out with Sam. You probably guessed we had a bit of a row.'

Jay looked strained and on edge, the old Sapphire would probably have quipped that was the thing about relationships – they were such a drag, but she didn't feel like that any more.

'Thanks for coming round, Jay,' she said warmly, 'I really appreciate it.'

'And you'll be okay? Why don't you get Jazz over?' Jay asked picking up his leather jacket and heading for the door.

She followed him over and for a second they stood looking at each other – Jay's gaze searching and serious.

'I'll be fine, thanks, Jay,' she answered, longing more than anything for him to stay.

'Okay, well I'll see you soon,' he replied, ducking his head down and lightly kissing her cheek.

Chapter 17

In the days after her attack Sapphire went into survival mode, put on a brave face and tried to carry on as if she didn't feel as if her life had fallen apart. The police were now certain that Markov had left the country and assured her that were he to try and return they would know about it. Colin insisted on staying with her for the next two weeks, and Sapphire was relieved. She tried to put her fears about Markov firmly to the back of her mind. But inside she felt devastated by both Markov's attack and the loss, she was certain, of her business. She used to be so in control.

She went to see her bank to try and secure a loan of thirty thousand but they simply weren't prepared to give it to her in the current economic climate, or even give her half that. It was terrible knowing she was being buoyed up by Markov's money. But good things happened too – her mum, horrified by what she had got her daughter into, agreed to contact Gamblers Anonymous and begin the long road of acknowledging that she had a problem. It would take time for Sapphire to trust her mum again but it was a start.

And Jay called her every day, often twice a day, to see how she was. He was just being a friend, a good friend, she tried to tell herself, trying to subdue the rush of longing that speaking to him or even seeing his name flash up on her phone evoked in her. Whatever Jay's motives, the calls were the highlight of Sapphire's day.

By the weekend she seemed to be turning a corner, and she had some very good news indeed. Cal had returned from LA and offered to lend her the thirty thousand. At first Sapphire turned down his offer, she was so fiercely independent, she wasn't sure if she could accept help from anyone, even if that person was a friend.

'And how did you even know about the situation?' Sapphire demanded, when the two met for an early evening drink. 'Did my mum tell you?' God! She was so interfering.

Cal shook his head.

'Was it Jazz or Sam?' Sapphire asked, wondering why her friends hadn't told her.

'It was Jay,' Cal said quietly. 'He didn't want you to know he'd asked. He called and told me what you'd been through. He sounded so worried about you.' Cal paused, 'I think he still has really strong feelings for you, Sapphire.'

Sapphire remained silent for a few minutes, reeling from what Cal had told her.

'He's still with Sam,' she said finally. 'He's just being a friend.'

Cal smiled, 'Oh no, Sapphire, he's way more than that. Just wait and see.'

After several vodkas and plenty of persuasion, Sapphire finally agreed to accept the loan on the condition that she paid interest on the money. It was only a nominal rate but it made her feel better.

Back at home she couldn't get Cal's words out of her head. Was he just saying those things because he was such a romantic himself and haunted by the loss of his great love? Or were they true? Later that night she found herself looking through her jewellery box for the engagement ring, holding it in her hand as if it were a lucky charm and could tell her the truth.

Sapphire didn't see Jay or Sam for the next couple of weeks. Jazz told her that Sam had a lot on her mind and she couldn't decide whether to make the move to London. She knew Jay was busy helping to arrange his mum and dad's twenty-fifth wedding anniversary party but they continued to talk on the phone. Jay told her about the plans for his personal training business, which matched personal trainers to clients outside of a gym. Jay had realised that in the current climate not everyone wanted to fork out a monthly subscription to a gym.

Sapphire got a real kick out of hearing how it was going and in return she confided in him about her own business. She suddenly realised that Jay had a very good head on his shoulders and that he was someone she could talk to about work. Neither of them ever mentioned Sam.

'So, you're definitely going to come to Mum and Dad's, aren't you?' Jay asked her during one of their late-night phone calls.

'Are you sure?' Sapphire asked dubiously, not at all sure that his parents would want her there, but at the same time longing to see Jay.

'Mum will bloody kill me if you don't come. She's always asking after you and you know she and your mum are thick as thieves now.'

It was warm for May, the air sweet with the promise of summer. Sapphire felt some of the tension of these past weeks leave her as she walked along the promenade, gazing at the beautiful sunset blazing across the sky. Cal's loan was such a relief. The last six months had been so fraught and now at last she felt there was some hope for her. The memory of Markov stalking her was beginning to recede, now it seemed like a bad dream. Sapphire was just relieved that he was out of the country. True, her love life was still a disaster area and she was no closer to getting over Jay, but at least they were friends now.

Vicky and Clayton were holding their twenty-fifth wedding anniversary at a restaurant on the seafront. They had hired the whole of the downstairs and the terrace. She could see the guests milling about outside, drinking champagne, the fairy lights strung round the terrace giving off a soft glow. A few weeks ago she would have been dreading being at the same event as Sam and Jay, now she was resigned.

Vicky was the first person she saw when she arrived – as usual she looked fab and considerably younger than her forty-six years, in a peach strapless dress.

'I love your dress!' Sapphire exclaimed.

'Isn't it great! It's a total rip-off of the Matthew Williamson one I saw Cheryl Cole wearing. I got it off ASOS. You look gorgeous too, love.'

Sapphire had gone for sexy sophistication in a flame red satin dress that made the most of her curves. 'Thanks,' Sapphire replied. 'I just can't believe that you guys have been married for twenty-five years, you don't look old enough.'

She took a glass of champagne one of the waiters offered her as Vicky exclaimed, 'I guess I'm just lucky and happy, plus I'm wearing *loads* of make-up! But promise you will tell me if I ever look mutton. Marissa and Estelle are way too self-obsessed to comment on their poor old mum, but I can trust your judgement.'

'Of course,' Sapphire reassured her, 'but I don't think you ever will.'

'She looks great doesn't she?' Jay appeared next to his mum and put his arm round her. Sapphire had thought that she was cool about seeing Jay but the sight of him close up blew that thought out of the water. He looked so handsome, so sexy in a white shirt and jeans.

Automatically she looked round for Sam. 'Where's Sam?' she asked.

Vicky glanced at Jay before saying that she was off to circulate.

Jay waited until his mum was out of earshot before replying, 'She's not here.'

Jay looked awkward as he went on, 'Actually we broke up two days ago.'

Sapphire was torn between feeling sorry for her friend, wondering why she hadn't said anything and, well, she couldn't stop herself – she felt secretly thrilled that they had broken up. She couldn't stop herself getting a rush of excitement. Jay was single. So was she. She studied Jay's expression, trying to work out his feelings. Was he hurt, upset, angry? She could read nothing. He seemed pretty matter of fact. 'I'm sorry,' she mumbled, knowing that she didn't sound it.

'Yep, she dumped me, told me she didn't feel as if we were going anywhere, said she wanted to be with someone who could really commit to her.' Jay took a long swig of beer from the bottle of Beck's.

'I had no idea,' Sapphire replied, still unsure why her friend hadn't called her. She felt sad to think of how distant they had become over the past months.

'I don't think she's told anyone. She's gone to stay with her brother in London, said she needed to get away from Brighton.'

'I must text her,' Sapphire said, automatically reaching inside her bag for her mobile.

Jay reached out and touched her arm, 'Don't right now.' He hesitated and looked less matter of fact. 'You were one of the reasons we split up; I don't think she'll be ready to hear from you just yet.'

Sapphire gazed back at Jay. What did that mean? She

was all set to ask him when Estelle and Marissa joined them, wildly giggly on one glass of champagne and wanting to fill Sapphire in on all the gossip about Estelle's new boyfriend. Meanwhile Jay's attention was claimed by some other guests. As she chatted away to the twins, her mind was in overdrive – why had she been one of the reasons Sam and Jay split? She was desperate to get some answers from him but then it was the meal and she was sitting on a different table to Jay. Since they broke up she had been ruthlessly strict with herself about not giving away her feelings, putting on her tough-girl act that everything was fine, but his words had unleashed all the pent-up desire and longing she felt for him and she could hardly keep her eyes off him during dinner. Once or twice he caught her eye and smiled but he didn't seem to share the same inability to tear his eyes away from her. Never had a meal gone by so incredibly slowly. Both Vicky and Clayton gave wonderfully touching speeches about each other and their marriage. 'We've had our ups and downs, it's true to say,' Vicky told the guests. 'Clayton's business went bust in the early years of our marriage, and I had a miscarriage before I went on to have the girls but Clayton has always been there for me. He's the love of my life, twenty-five years on, as much as he ever was.'

Sapphire was relieved to see that she wasn't the only guest surreptitiously wiping away a tear. It was just so emotionally charged! And hearing Vicky and Clayton's heartfelt comments about each other clarified something that had been in her mind since breaking up with Jay – she did want a committed relationship with someone. She no longer wanted to have flings with men that meant nothing. In twenty-five years' time she wanted to be able to stand up with her husband and talk proudly about their marriage. And she knew exactly who she wanted that man to be . . .

After the speeches the guests gathered on the terrace while the tables were cleared to make way for dancing. Now, Sapphire thought she would get chance to talk to Jay, but he was helping pour out glasses of champagne and handing them out to guests. It felt as if everything was conspiring to keep her away from him. Direct action was needed. Sapphire walked over to where he was and stood in front of him. Jay briefly looked up at her, before continuing his waiter duties. 'I have got to talk to you, Jay.'

'I've got to talk to you too, but as you can see, I'm busy.'

'I'll help,' Sapphire offered, glad of the distraction while she waited for Jay to be free and for the next ten minutes she circulated among the guests with trays of champagne, smiling and chatting away as if she didn't have a care in the world, while all the time all she could think about was Jay. Finally, when she returned to the bar area Jay looked at her and said, 'Now, but not here, let's walk.'

The pair quickly wove their way through the guests and onto the promenade. Sapphire waited until they were well away from the restaurant before blurting out, 'I can't wait any longer, you have to tell me why I was one of the reasons you split up with Sam.'

'Can't you guess?' Jay asked, putting his hand on hers to stop her walking on. They stood gazing at each other, and it seemed to Sapphire that nothing in her life had ever been as important as this moment. She wasn't sure if Jay expected an answer but he took a step nearer to her, reached out and gently traced his finger along her jaw, tilting her face up.

'I couldn't get you out of my head; I haven't been able to stop thinking about you.'

There he had said it. Fireworks of happiness exploded in Sapphire's mind as she murmured back, not wanting to break the spell, 'I haven't stopped thinking about you either.'

And then they were kissing, a passionate, desperate, 'I want you' kiss that sent pure lust pulsing through Sapphire.

Jay pulled away. 'Let's go back to yours,' his voice was husky with longing. He took her hand and they started running through the night, oblivious to everything but their overwhelming desire for each other.

Then it was everything that Sapphire had been longing for, burning for, as they shut the door behind them and fell on the sofa, not even making it to the bedroom. This was not the time for slow caresses and foreplay, this was raw intense passion. They were ripping off their clothes in their desire for each other, for a fuck that was urgent, desperate, perfect, right.

Afterwards they moved to the bedroom and lay in each other's arms, spent, sweaty, satisfied. Sapphire took a deep breath. Now it was time, time for her to tell Jay that she loved him; that she always had. She was about to speak when Jay said, 'That was just the best, Sapphire. This is all I want. Let's go back to the way we were, except this time we'll play by your rules: no-strings-attached fun, with no demands.' He stretched his arms over his head and smiled. 'Yeah, you were so right, who wants relationships? We can be friends that fuck. Perfect.'

And with that he closed his eyes, turned over and seemed to go to sleep.

Sapphire was too shocked to reply. For the first time in her life she was lost for words. She lay staring at the ceiling in utter disbelief. How was it possible that Jay felt like this? It was so bitterly ironic. She had turned Jay into the man she thought she wanted, only to discover that she wanted the man he had been . . .

Chapter 18

The weeks that followed were like some kind of sweet torture for Sapphire. Yes she was now back with Jay but only on his terms. He saw her only when he wanted to, never said he missed her when they met up, hardly ever called or texted her and seemed far more concerned with going out with his mates and setting up his personal training business. Though at least he appeared to have abandoned his plans to move to London. Sapphire hoped that had something to do with her, but really it was a fragile hope as she seemed to figure very low down on his list of priorities.

She realised that must have been exactly how she treated Jay when they were together the first time. It wasn't pleasant being made to feel so unimportant and it was very damaging to the self-esteem. God, she had no idea that she had been such a total bitch. Well, that was certainly coming back to haunt her, as however offhand she used to be with Jay, he seemed to take it a step further. He had been far nicer to her when they were simply supposed to be friends. Sapphire just didn't understand him – was it his way of punishing her for how she had treated him? Or did he genuinely want this kind of easy come easy go arrangement?

Jazz, ever the optimist, told her things were bound to change, that Jay was just learning to trust her again.

'Babe, he wanted to be with you, just give him time,' she told her on one of their nights out. They were waiting in the Star Bar for Sam to join them. It was the first time Sapphire had seen her friend since she had started dating Jay again and she was nervous. She really didn't want to hurt Sam. But it seemed Sam had well and truly moved on as she breezed into the bar with a very good-looking man on her arm.

'Sapphire, Jazz, this is Enzo. He's Italian,' she added slightly unnecessarily, as with his olive skin, jet black hair and chestnut brown eyes, he more than looked the part.

Enzo double-kissed both girls before insisting he buy a bottle of champagne to celebrate meeting Sam's friends. Jazz and Sapphire watched as he strode to the bar. 'Wow!' Jazz exclaimed, echoing Sapphire's sentiments exactly.

'He's well lush, isn't he? We've been going out for three weeks now and I have to tell you the sex is amazing. I always thought it was a myth what they said about Latin lovers, but it's not!' She looked at her friends – a slightly defiant expression on her face, which left Sapphire hoping that this wasn't a fling because she was so gutted about Jay.

'That's brilliant, Sam,' Sapphire said. 'So you're happy?'

'Yeah!' Sam exclaimed. 'Enzo's taking me to Milan next weekend, what's not to love! ' Then she paused, and said quietly, 'I know you think this is a rebound thing, but I really like him and he likes me. Being with Jay was great, but we wanted different things. He didn't want to commit, whereas it's only early days but Enzo is the opposite, I've already met his mum and dad.'

'I'm really glad,' Sapphire replied. 'So you and me are okay aren't we? God, we seem to have put each other through it.'

There was a pause before Sam replied, 'We're cool,

you'll always be my joint best friend with Jazz. And as you and Jay want the same thing, it's best that you are back together. And that way no one gets hurt do they?' Sam bit her lip and for a fleeting moment seemed upset. Maybe she hadn't found it that easy to get over Jay?

Sapphire didn't have the heart to disclose that actually she wanted very different things to Jay; fortunately Enzo appeared with the champagne and made a big show of pouring everyone a glass and giving a toast to his beautiful Sam.

Enzo was easy company and was clearly infatuated with Sam – he gazed at her adoringly and hung on her every word and if Sam did still have feelings for Jay, she was keeping them well hidden.

'So, where's Jay tonight?' Sapphire was jolted out of her reverie by Sam's question.

Sapphire had no idea, all she knew from the text Jay had sent earlier was that he was busy and that he'd call round later if he could.

'Seeing some of his friends from football,' Sapphire replied. Well, it might be true.

'And how's it going second time round?' Sam asked the one question that Sapphire simply couldn't answer truthfully.

'Good,' she replied. 'Yeah great, you're right, we do want the same thing.'

Sam managed a small smile, 'That's good – you've had such a shit time lately. I hope Jay's looking after you.'

Sapphire just nodded. It was a perfectly enjoyable evening with her friends, so why then, as Sapphire got a taxi back home, did she feel so empty? She texted Jay asking if he wanted to come over but he didn't reply – maybe he was asleep or maybe he was out and didn't hear his phone, or maybe, and this was the maybe she really didn't want to think about, maybe he couldn't be bothered, or worse still, he was with someone else. In

whatever they had going on between them – which
Sapphire knew she couldn't call a relationship – they had
not talked about fidelity, there had just been lots of
comments from Jay about how great it felt not being tied
down. She only hoped the not being tied down didn't
allude to having an open relationship.

In fact, she didn't see Jay for the rest of the week and he
didn't call until Friday. It had taken all Sapphire's willpower not to text him again. She felt powerless and
vulnerable, a toxic combination. When he finally called
he was offhand and casual. 'A group of us are going to
PURE tonight, d'you fancy coming?'
Sapphire had a full-on weekend with a hen party
booking and she knew she really should get an early
night, but she was so desperate to see Jay that she agreed.
Jay was all set to meet her in a bar with his friends – not
at all what Sapphire wanted. 'Can't you come round to
mine first, Jay?' she asked.
He laughed, 'Does my lady need servicing then? I
guess it has been a few days. Yeah sure, I'll be round
around nine.'
Sapphire did not appreciate Jay's laddish attitude at all.
There was way more than sex at stake here – above all,
Sapphire wanted to be with Jay, to spend time with him,
to talk to him, connect with him. Having a no-strings-
attached non-relationship with someone you were in love
with was proving much harder than she ever imagined.
In the event it was closer to eleven when Jay finally
turned up. 'God, we haven't got long for this booty call,'
he exclaimed, throwing his leather jacket on to the sofa as
he walked into the living room, 'D'you want to do it on
the sofa or the bed?' He hadn't even said hello. Sapphire,
who was inwardly seething at Jay's treatment of her,
decided it was about time her instinct for self-
preservation kicked in. She had spent the whole week

304

thinking of him, longing for him, and now he was treating her as if she was a bit of fluff. Half of her wanted to tell him to fuck off, the trouble was the other half wanted to fuck him too badly to ever see him walk out the door. She looked at him coolly. 'Get on the sofa,' she ordered, slipping off her briefs. He didn't need to be asked twice.

'That was amazing,' he panted, as Sapphire slid off his lap and got up from the sofa.

'Not bad,' she replied, heading for the bathroom, 'I'll expect more later.'

Jay just laughed, 'Oh you'll get it.'

Sapphire looked back at him; it was so hard pretending to be tough. 'Jay, are you sure you want to go out? We could just chill here?'

'It's Friday night, Sapphire! I've been looking forward to seeing my mates all week. But you don't have to come if you don't want to.'

'It's okay,' Sapphire lied. 'I'll come.'

In the bathroom Sapphire looked at herself in the mirror and couldn't stop her eyes welling up with tears. She just didn't know how much more of this she could take. She thought she wanted nothing more than to be with Jay, but if this was what being with him was like, she didn't know if she could take it.

Somehow she pulled herself together as she and Jay headed out to the club. 'So who's going to be there?' she asked, struggling to keep up with Jay in her heels as he strode along the promenade.

'Oh, you know, my mates from football and some of their girlfriends, and Luke and his boyfriend Simon.'

Great, her number-one fan, not.

'So what was Luke's reaction when you told him you were seeing me again?'

'He just said to watch myself, but I told him everything

305

was cool.' He paused to look at Sapphire. 'I told him I wasn't the same person I was when you and I started seeing each other.'

No, you're not, Sapphire thought sadly.

'But anyway, I handed my notice in at the gym and my new business is finally going ahead. So tonight's a bit of a celebration. I'm going to be a business person just like you. What do you reckon?' He said it so defiantly as if he was waiting for Sapphire to shoot him down.

'I think it's brilliant, Jay, and I'll do whatever I can to help you. That's one lesson I've definitely learnt: you do need other people. We should think about what I can do – I can certainly advertise in the boutique.'

'Would you?' Jay seemed surprised by her interest.

'Of course! I want you to do well, Jay, really.'

The old Jay would definitely have made her feel more included with his friends; the new Jay barely wasted time on introductions in the club before getting engrossed in conversation with one of his football friends. Sapphire's spirits plummeted as she took a sip of vodka and tonic and caught Luke looking at her. As usual his expression was less than friendly. She quickly looked away; everyone else seemed to be having a great time, everyone except her. She checked her watch, it was half midnight. God knows how long Jay would want to stay here.

'Hi, Sapphire, you look a bit lost.' Luke had sidled over to her. 'Shall I introduce you to some people? Jay seems tied up.' They both looked over to Jay who was laughing and joking with his mates and the extremely pretty blonde Sapphire had seen him with just after they broke up. Sapphire hoped the flash of jealousy she felt didn't show on her face.

'Sure,' she said casually.

'Here's Dean – he's into business, like you, so you'll have a lot in common I expect.'

306

Sapphire found herself shaking hands with Dean, who when he wasn't wheeling and dealing apparently had a very intimate relationship with fake tan. His teeth looked ridiculously white against his overly tanned face. He reminded her far too much of Ryan, with his cocky self-confidence and brash good looks, for her to enjoy his company. Straightaway he launched into a monologue about his business – he was a property developer and apparently had interests all over Europe; Sapphire stifled a yawn and tried to look as if she gave a damn. Then he wanted to know about her business.

By now the club was even more packed and Sapphire found herself pushed up against one of the pillars with Dean standing very close to her. In vain she peered over his shoulder for a glimpse of Jay, wanting him to come and rescue her, but he was nowhere to be seen. She gave the briefest account of what she did, Dean seeming to hang on her every word. She wasn't wild about the lecherous expression in his eyes; surely he didn't think she was available? He was getting closer to her as well which she didn't like, so close that she could see the beads of sweat on his forehead and smell the tobacco on his breath. She began to feel claustrophobic and slightly panicky.

'I've never met such a talented and beautiful business-woman before,' Dean said, reaching out and resting one of his arms beside Sapphire's head, making her feel even more hemmed in.

Sapphire forced a laugh. 'Thanks, but I'm going to get another drink, do you want one?'

'Not until you've given me your number. I have got to see you again, Sapphire.'

She shook her head, 'I'm sorry but I'm with Jay, I'm not into giving other men my number.' The sensation of panic increased.

'Yeah, but he won't mind will he? I thought you had

307

one of those open relationships. Have you seen him dancing with Carly?' He moved slightly to the side, giving Sapphire a view of the dance floor, where amongst all the clubbers she saw Jay dancing with the blonde. They seemed to have eyes for no one else. Sapphire looked away, as tears blurred her eyes.

'So, you see, you don't have to worry on that score. What about coming back to mine and we can get to know each other better?' And with that he slid his arms round Sapphire and homed in for a kiss.

Sapphire didn't move her head quickly enough as Dean planted his lips on hers and attempted to force his tongue into her mouth. What the fuck was he doing? She struggled to push him off her, but he was insistent, bearing down on her, pressing her against the pillar. She felt as if she couldn't breathe and suddenly she had a flashback to the night Markov had spiked her drink. Panic overwhelmed her, she struggled some more and when that still had no effect on Dean's ardour she poured her drink over his head. That did the trick.

'Fuck!' Dean exclaimed, wiping his eyes, while Sapphire took the opportunity to leg it away from him. She pushed her way through the clubbers, desperate to reach fresh air. She had almost reached the exit when she ran into Luke. 'Going so soon, Sapphire?' he said bitchily. 'I thought you and Dean were getting on so well. Shall I tell Jay you've gone?'

Sapphire was through with pretending to overlook Luke's snide glares and barbed comments. 'Fuck off, Luke, just fuck off! I don't know what sick little game you're playing but you can fuck off!' she yelled.

And without giving him a second glance she ran up the stairs and out into the night air. Since the incident with Markov she had avoided being on her own late at night and she felt a stab of fear as she burst out onto the promenade. There was a group of girls heading up to the taxi rank and she tagged along just behind them and got a taxi even though it was only a short distance home.

Back in her apartment she could not stop shaking, despite putting on a hoodie, wrapping herself in her duvet and drinking tea. She kept thinking back to the night Markov had spiked her drink. It seemed that she'd blocked out the full terror since then and now the incident with Dean had brought it rushing to the surface. She kept expecting Jay to call her or even to come round and see her but he didn't. She stayed curled up on her sofa until 6 a.m., too wired to sleep, before finally crawling into bed and falling into an exhausted sleep for two hours.

'You've got to tell him that you can't go on like this!' Jazz exclaimed the following day when Sapphire had managed to drag herself into work. 'He's treating you like shit! He's well out of order.' Jazz drummed her coral nails against the counter to emphasise her point.

Sapphire took another sip of coffee – she felt strung out from lack of sleep and was smarting from Jay's complete disregard for her. He had yet to call her.

'He's just treating me how I used to treat him,' she said quietly.

'Yeah, well you were never *that* bad to him,' Jazz said loyally.

'I flirted with Ryan, and kissed him and put Jay second in everything I did,' Sapphire replied sadly. 'I don't think Jay is ever going to let me in again. I did this to him.'

'Well I still think you need to tell him that he can't treat you like this. And,' Jazz hesitated, 'you need to tell him that you love him.'

'Oh God, I just can't!' Sapphire's entire being rebelled against making herself so vulnerable and open to rejection. 'I just can't,' she repeated.

'Jay told you that he loved you,' Jazz said stubbornly.

'And just look at how I reacted,' Sapphire replied.

'Well, something's got to give, because you can't go on like this, babe.'

Sapphire spent a miserable weekend, obsessing over what to do about Jay. She kept thinking that she should phone him, but every time she went to call up his number something stopped her. It wasn't until late Sunday night that Jay finally came round to her place.

'Sorry I didn't call earlier,' Jay said, walking into the apartment and flopping down on the sofa without even giving her a kiss. 'It's been such a mad weekend. I didn't go to bed until midday Saturday and then it was Carly birthday and a group of us went clubbing again. I didn't ask you as I knew you'd be working.'

Sapphire sat on the opposite end of the sofa to him, and hugged her knees to her chin. Just hearing Jay talk so casually about his life without her made her realise that Jazz was right: she could not go on like this.

'So you had a good time on Friday with Dean? Luke thought you two would get on.'

Sapphire shook her head. 'No, Jay, I did not have a good time. Why d'you think I left? I don't know what Luke's told you but whatever it was, it isn't true. I had a totally shit time.' She paused, 'But you seemed to have a good time with Carly. Does Luke approve of her? Is she not such a challenge to him?'

Jay looked put on the spot. 'Carly's just a friend, we have a laugh.'

God, was he seeing Carly? Sapphire couldn't take this. She had to tell him how she felt. It was killing her pretending to be casual.

'I can't see you any more like this,' she said quietly.

Immediately Jay got up from the sofa; he seemed angry. 'Fucking hell! I don't understand you! You're the

310

one who wanted things kept casual, no commitment.'

'No Jay, not any more.'

Jay glared back at her, as hurt and anger flashed across his face. 'Well, thanks a lot, Sapphire. Jesus Christ, what a fucking idiot I was to ever get involved with you! I might have known you'd end up screwing me over yet again.'

'Please, Jay, it's not like that, just let me explain,' Sapphire pleaded, stunned that her bid to reveal that she loved him had backfired like this. 'I need to tell you something.'

But Jay was heading for the door, where he paused and shook his head. 'No Sapphire I don't want to hear any more about how I'm too young for you, or how important your business is or whatever. This is it; I never want to see you again.'

And before Sapphire could say anything else he had opened the door and walked out, slamming it behind him.

'I love you, Jay,' Sapphire said to the empty room. Then she sank down on the sofa in despair. That was it then. Jay didn't want anything more to do with her? How was she ever going to tell him that she loved him now?

Chapter 19

A week went past. A week when Sapphire thought she was sleepwalking in misery. She could hardly keep it together. Jazz kept coming across her crying in her office. 'Please, Sapphire, you have got to tell Jay how you feel!' she urged her. 'I'm sure he wouldn't have walked out if you'd told him you loved him.'

'I wouldn't be so sure,' Sapphire said miserably, reaching for yet more tissues.

She felt she had cried more in this past week than she had in her entire life. She didn't want to do anything other than curl up and cry but Jazz was insisting they went out for a drink that night. Colin was down for the weekend seeing friends and Cal had agreed to come out as well. Finally Sapphire gave in. Maybe it would do her good to go out. Staying in only gave her even more time to brood about Jay.

Sapphire wandered into the Star Bar a little after seven that evening. Jazz, Ben, Cal and Colin were already sitting at a table. They looked vaguely guilty when Sapphire joined them, though quite why she couldn't fathom. Cal kept checking his watch as they all caught up.

'Have you got to be somewhere else?' Sapphire asked when he'd done it for the fifth time.

'Nope, I'm just expecting a friend,' Cal said casually, looking over to the door. 'Yep, here he is.'

Sapphire, expecting to see one of Cal's footballing friends, almost did a double take when she turned and saw Jay walking towards their table. When he caught sight of Sapphire he stopped and looked as if he was going to turn round and leave there and then. Cal quickly got up from his seat and walked over to him, putting his arm round him and steering him to where Sapphire was sitting.

'Hi,' Sapphire said uncertainly, while Jay looked pissed off.

He shot Cal a filthy look. 'What is this, mate? I didn't know Sapphire was going to be here.'

'And she didn't know you were going to be here,' Cal replied evenly. 'But me, Jazz and Colin reckoned it was about time that you two talked. I mean *really* talked. And listened to each other. So why don't you sit down and do just that?' And he practically pushed Jay down on the chair opposite Sapphire.

'What is there to say? She dumped me. End of.' Jay leant back and folded his arms. He looked furious at being forced into a corner.

Sapphire clenched her fists; part of her wanted to run a mile, part of her knew that this was probably her last chance to tell Jay what she really felt. 'I didn't dump you, Jay,' she said quietly. 'You didn't wait to hear what I had to say.'

'Great, so now I get to hear all over again all the reasons why we shouldn't be together.'

Cal stood up. 'Come on, guys, we're going to leave them to it now.' Jazz and Colin reluctantly stood up. 'So you two, sort it out,' Cal said as he grabbed his jacket and walked out of the bar.

'I feel like I'm suddenly in a scene from *EastEnders*,' Sapphire tried to joke, desperate to ease the tension.

'Let's just have a drink and then go,' Jay replied. 'We

313

can tell them we talked and get them off our backs.' He had such a hard, set expression on his face. Suddenly Sapphire didn't know how to reach him. She felt as if she was about to make a leap into the unknown and she knew she had to make it, whatever the consequences.

'No, Jay, please. I do need to talk to you. The reason why I told you I couldn't see you any more is because,' she paused, gathering all her strength; she had not said these words out loud to any man since Alfie, 'I love you.'

Jay stared at her, he seemed stunned by her declaration.

'I love you, Jay,' she said again, 'and I know you probably don't want to hear that, I know I probably killed the love you once had for me, but I can't help it and that's why I said I couldn't see you any more. I can't pretend that I want a casual relationship.' She looked expectantly at Jay, hardly daring to breathe. She had never felt so raw, so exposed, with all her barriers down, since her father died. 'And if that means I have to lose you, then I'd rather do that than live a lie.'

'You love me?' Jay asked in wonder. 'Did I really hear you say that?' He ran his hand over his head. 'I feel as if I must be dreaming.'

He made no move to get close to her. Sapphire bit her lip and hung her head, waiting to hear the inevitable words of rejection. But they didn't come.

'Tell me again,' Jay said quietly.' Sapphire looked back at him and saw he was gazing at her intently.

'I love you, Jay, is it so hard to believe that?'

Jay shook his head and reached out for her hand. 'Not so hard. I love you too, Sapphire,' he murmured, 'I always have. I'm so sorry for what I put you through these past weeks. Luke suggested I test you out and that's why he got Dean to hit on you.'

314

'What?' Sapphire exclaimed, pulling her hand away from him. 'He set me up!' In the midst of the emotional whirlwind which seemed to be tearing through her, she was suddenly angry.

'I regret it now but Luke thought it would be a good way of finding out if you'd changed. When you went off with Ryan, it did my head in. I was devastated.'

'But you were the one who left me!' Sapphire shot back.

'Only because you made it clear that you didn't want a committed relationship.'

Now the anger went, she knew exactly how Jay felt because that's what she'd been feeling recently. Jay stood up and came and sat next to her, putting his arms round her. 'I'm sorry if I hurt you.'

She slid her arms round him, 'I'm sorry for everything I did before.' For a while they held each other, oblivious to the other people in the bar, in their own world.

'I love you, Sapphire,' Jay repeated, 'I'm sorry.'

'No, I'm the one who's sorry, I spent all this time thinking that I was the one who knew what they wanted and instead I pushed away the one man I loved. Well, no more, Jay.' Suddenly Sapphire knew exactly what she had to do, it was so blindingly obvious to her. She reached for the necklace with the engagement ring on it and squeezed it tight to bring her luck.

'You once asked me a question, and I didn't give you the right answer. So now I have to ask you the question,' she paused to gaze into his deep brown eyes. She had to ask it, even if he rejected her, she had to know. 'Will you marry me, Jay?'

He gazed back in amazement. 'You really want this? But I thought you didn't believe in marriage?'

'I thought so too, but not any more.' She bit her lip and squeezed the ring even tighter, the diamonds cutting into her palm.

'Yes,' Jay replied, then exclaimed, 'Yes! I will marry you, Sapphire Jones!'

Sapphire held up the ring, 'So I can wear this officially now.'

Jay took the ring and removed it from the gold chain. 'Give me your hand,' he said and Sapphire held it out for Jay. He gently slid the ring on to her finger where it fitted perfectly. At that there was a loud cheer from the open window. The couple turned round to see Jazz, Colin and Cal giving them the thumbs up.

'Oh my God! I thought you'd gone. Were you listening?' Sapphire exclaimed, laughing at the sheer cheek of her friends.

'No! 'Colin replied, in mock outrage. 'We were just having a bit of fresh air. But now I've seen the ring, we're coming back in. Drinks are on me. I love a happy ending, especially when you two took so long to get there.'

'So you're really sure about this?' Jay said later as they lay in bed, tracing his finger round the engagement ring.

Sapphire snuggled into him. 'More sure than I've ever been about anything in my life. You're the best thing that's ever happened to me. I think I always knew it, but didn't want to admit it.'

'We don't have to get married, you know. I know how you feel about marriage. It's enough for us to be together.'

Sapphire shook her head. 'It's not enough for me. I want to get married and that's final.' She ran her hands over Jay's rock hard abs, 'And you know I always get my own way in the end.'